THE AMBER OWL

Also by Juliet Marillier

Sevenwaters
Daughter of the Forest
Son of the Shadows
Child of the Prophecy
Heir to Sevenwaters
Seer of Sevenwaters
Flame of Sevenwaters

Twixt Firelight and Water

Saga of the Light Isles
Wolfskin
Foxmask

Bridei Chronicles
The Dark Mirror
Blade of Fortriu
The Well of Shades

Shadowfell
Shadowfell
Raven Flight
The Caller

Wildwood
Wildwood Dancing
Cybele's Secret

Blackthorn & Grim
Dreamer's Pool
Tower of Thorns
Den of Wolves

Warrior Bards
The Harp of Kings
A Dance with Fate
A Song of Flight

Standalone Publications
Heart's Blood
Prickle Moon
Mother Thorn and Other Tales of Kindness and Courage
Beautiful

THE AMBER OWL

JULIET MARILLIER

First published in
the United Kingdom 2026 by Solaris
an imprint of Rebellion Publishing Ltd,
Riverside House, Osney Mead,
Oxford, OX2 0ES, UK

www.solarisbooks.com

First published in
Australia 2025 by New Dawn Publishing

ISBN: 978-1-83786-772-1

Copyright © 2025 Juliet Marillier

The right of the author to be identified as the author of this work has been asserted in accordance with the Copyright, Designs and Patents Act 1988.

All rights reserved. No part of this publication may be reproduced, stored in a retrieval system, or transmitted, in any form or by any means, electronic, mechanical, photocopying, recording or otherwise, without the prior permission of the copyright owners.

This book is a work of fiction. Names, characters, places and incidents are products of the author's imagination or are used fictitiously.

10 9 8 7 6 5 4 3 2 1

A CIP catalogue record for this book is available from the British Library.

Designed & typeset by Rebellion Publishing

Printed in the UK

To my family, with heartfelt thanks for your ongoing love and support.

1

STASYA

'I SAVED A life this morning,' she said.

'Really? Tell me!'

Lukas tilted his curly head back against the great sun-warmed rock and closed his eyes. This was their precious time. Here on the edge of Heartwood Forest, they could look down over the sloping field where Lukas often brought the goats in the late afternoon and share tales: the old ones about the forest, of which there were many, and new ones they invented as they went along. At some distance below them lay the settlement, whose sounds – someone chopping firewood, the creak of cart wheels, children shouting as they chased a ball – were muted. After her long day's work, in this place Stasya could breathe. The many voices of the great forest came to her, from the song of wind in the tall pines to the scuttle of tiny feet in the undergrowth. Flip had crept onto her lap and now lay curled up there, a small warm presence, dreaming. High above, birds exchanged calls. Not far off, a stream flowed over stones, making a rippling music.

'It was down near the burial ground, when I was on the way to Vidas's farm; I've been helping him with the sheep today. You know that paling fence, the one with the carving at the top? I saw a lot of magpies close by. They were acting oddly: coming in close, then edging away. And so quiet. Not a sound.' She couldn't tell the full truth, even to the trusted friend she'd known since they were children. Lukas knew she sometimes saved creatures in trouble. What he didn't know, what nobody but Flip knew, was that she could open her mind to theirs, understand their thoughts and share her own with them. If that gift ever became public knowledge, she wouldn't only be labelled strange, weird, a loner. They'd call her a witch, and she'd be lucky to escape with her life.

'I came up closer,' she went on, 'and I saw a magpie hanging from the fence. Its neck was wedged between two of the uprights and it was completely limp. I was sure it was dead. But the other birds were all looking at me, waiting for something. I came in close and put my hands around the hanging one, thinking I could at least give it a kind burial. And then...' Stasya paused, glancing at Lukas. He was tired from his long day on the family farm. But the look in his eyes told her he'd been captured by the tale. Even Flip was sitting up, ears pricked, wanting more.

'And then I felt it twitch. It was still alive. I eased it upward as gently as I could, talking to it all the time, hoping that might help.' She'd spoken to it, not only in words but also in mind-pictures. *There, brave one. You're safe now. And look, your friends are all waiting for you.* 'I thought it might be terribly injured or too weak to fly. But as soon as I opened my hands it was off into the trees, and the others went with it, bursting into song. It sounded like they were saying, *Free! You're free!*'

Lukas gave a sigh of content. 'A wonderful true story. You'll be a friend of magpies from now on. But maybe you already are.'

They sat in silence for a while, simply enjoying each

other's company. Stasya thought how lucky she was to have such a true friend. When she'd been sent to Heartwood to live with Grandmother, as a child, the other boys and girls had taunted her, calling her freak or cry-baby. From the first, Lukas had defended her, though he was only a little older. He'd understood that sometimes she couldn't find the words people wanted, and sometimes had so much in her mind that it was like a flood, drowning her so the only thing she could get out was a scream. He'd known there were times when she needed to be alone.

Like most people in the village, Lukas's family still thought her odd. They did talk to her sometimes. Had to, when they needed her to work for them. All the local farmers knew she had a knack for keeping animals calm. None of them questioned that, not to her face anyway, because it was so useful. But Lukas's parents did not want her as a friend. Not for themselves and especially not for their only son. That had never changed, even though Lukas and Stasya were no longer children, but man and woman.

'Your turn now,' she said. 'Unless you're too tired.'

Lukas sat up straighter, putting his arms around his knees. 'I'm never too tired for a story. This one is called... Cake Magic.'

He made Stasya laugh with a tale about three brothers on a quest to find treasure, and how two were tricked by a wily monster that stole the first brother's best shoes and the second brother's lucky hat. The third brother found the way to the monster's secret hoard by offering a share of the excellent plum cake he had baked and brought with him. Nobody had ever given the monster a gift before, and he was so delighted he handed the young man a bag of gold in exchange.

By the time the tale was done, the goats were gathering in the lowest corner of the field, by the gate. Time for the shelter of the barn and a warm bed for the night. They knew the dark was coming.

'I'd best be moving them on,' Lukas said, rising to his feet. He reached out a hand to help Stasya up.

'Thanks. See you tomorrow?'

'If I can.' There was a shadow over his features now. 'Father wants me for slaughtering in the morning. And there's other work later.'

No need to ask more. The goats weren't kept only for milk, but also for meat; slaughtering was just part of the job. And although Farmer Jurgis had other helpers, he knew his son was best at doing it: swift and sure, so the creatures didn't have time to be frightened. If they were spooked, Jurgis said, it spoiled the meat. Lukas did what he had to do. The farm would be his one day, and his father needed him. But he hated the killing. His goats were dear to him. They all had names of his choosing. Stasya saw the pain in his eyes and knew he would lie awake in the dark. Jurgis had asked her to help with that job once and she'd said no, even when he offered her a substantial payment in the household goods that sustained her and Flip. Lukas had been furious with his father.

'You do it as well as anyone could,' Stasya told him. Lukas gave a half-nod. He kept hold of her hand. After a little, she said, 'I'd best go now. Come up and see me tomorrow if you can. Later on. It might help.'

'I may not be fit for company.' He attempted a smile.

'If you can't sleep tonight, think of good tales, not sad ones.'

'I'll try.'

She watched him go, a fine man now, taller than his father. He shepherded the flock out of the field, made sure the gate was securely fastened, raised a hand to her in farewell as he headed down toward the farm. Stasya's home was the other way, further along the forest edge. She took a long, looping path, past the Ancestor. While Flip investigated something among the roots, Stasya paused, as always, to lay a hand on the great oak's trunk and thank the tree for watching over the valley and the settlement. The Ancestor spread her limbs wide, offering shade to all who passed. Her hollows and crevices had housed a myriad of small creatures over the years. In the shelter of her canopy, generations of birds had reared their young. Her acorns had nourished squirrels through the chill winter. Her fallen timbers had been carved into objects of beauty; they had warmed both hearths and hearts. The folk of the village gathered by the tree to celebrate betrothals and hand-fastings, to give thanks for babes safely born, to sing farewell to folk who had passed to the Afterlife. The Ancestor had guarded the people of Heartwood settlement since a time before memory.

Stasya murmured farewell, then gathered Flip up and walked home to the cottage that had been theirs since the bleak season when Grandmother had died, peacefully in her bed, when Stasya was eleven years old. The place suited her. It was far enough from the settlement to deter unwanted visitors but near enough so she could present herself quickly for work if someone needed her. Best of all, it was right on the forest edge. She could walk under the trees every day, drink in the sights and smells and feelings, let her mind fill with new stories and old. She could check that all was well, tend to creatures that needed her, and keep a watchful eye on all growing things, as Grandmother had for most of her lifetime. Sometimes Lukas came with her; more often Stasya went alone. If the tales and rumours didn't keep folk out of the forest, fear of wolves and bears did. People would venture in a certain distance to gather firewood, but once the task was done they'd be quickly out again. Back at the cottage she kindled a fire on her little hearth, heated water, cooked herself a meal of vegetable soup. The baker, Irina, had given her a small loaf in part payment for yesterday's work, and most of it was still left; it would go well with the soup. She'd be helping at the bakery again in the morning but she'd be free after that, unless some new need for her arose. 'We might go walking, Flip,' she said aloud. 'Up as far as Toad Rock, hmm?' She pictured the place in her mind. But Flip was gnawing on something she had brought in from outside and did not respond. The little dog preferred to catch her own food, which was fine with Stasya provided she dispatched her prey swiftly and not too close to the house.

After the meal they sat awhile by the hearth, and Stasya used mind-pictures to tell Flip her favourite bedtime story, which was the true tale of how she'd found the dog trapped in brambles deep in the forest and brought her home, years ago. Later still, after Stasya had taken off her work clothes – an old tunic and trousers that had belonged to Lukas – and put on her nightrobe, she and Flip lay in bed as the long twilight gave slow way to night. They fell asleep to the sighing of wind in the pines and the soft calls of owls.

That was the last good day.

2

STASYA

STASYA WOKE TO a rumbling noise, men shouting, horses neighing. Flip was off the bed in a flash, by the closed door, quivering with tension.

Wait.

Flip calmed at the familiar command; in some ways, she was quite like an ordinary dog. But Stasya knew something was wrong. Badly wrong.

She got out of bed and opened the shutters a crack. She was wary of uninvited guests, especially at this hour – the light told her it was not yet dawn. Nobody was outside her house, as far as she could tell. But the sound was everywhere. Something was happening down at the settlement. Trouble of some kind. The shouting went on and on. A family argument that had blown up into something worse, perhaps. But there were many voices in it, more all the time. When a dispute happened, the village elders would generally step in and make sure everyone calmed down and sorted out their problems without the need for blows. The high-up folk, the ones who made up the laws and rules of the Northlands and ensured ordinary people abided by them, were too far away to trouble themselves with a small, remote settlement like Heartwood. There was trade between Heartwood and the two nearest villages, goat meat for grain, cheeses for wool, oil for beeswax candles and so on. That went on smoothly, for the most part. Once or twice there had been a visit by a priest from the Church of the Godly. Grandmother had warned Stasya about such folk, and she'd made sure she stayed at home behind a closed door while he was in the settlement. But mostly Heartwood was left to look after itself.

The noise was getting louder. Someone was making a speech or shouting what might be a speech. She needed to know what was happening; she was supposed to go down to the bakery for work later. But the thought of being in a crowd, with people yelling, made her feel sick. 'We'll walk along to the lookout,' she said, picturing it in her thoughts. She had never been quite sure if Flip understood human speech as well as the silent language of the mind. 'Just far enough to see what's going on.' She performed a quick change – nightrobe off, tunic and trousers on, shawl over the top. She ran her fingers through her hair, pushing it back from her face. *Stay with me*, she told Flip, showing the dog what she meant. *Keep close and keep quiet*. She bent to give Flip a quick scratch behind the ears, both reassurance and sign of trust.

From the lookout there would be a partial view of the village square, the community's main gathering place. At this hour there were usually few folk about, though some would be starting the working day. Irina would have a fire lit in her big stove, readying it for the first batch of bread, and on the nearby farms people would be rising to tend to their animals. Poor Lukas. How he would hate his morning's work.

By the time Stasya reached the lookout, the rumbling sound had died down, but the voices were louder. Angry shouting, not just one man but many. Women's voices too. Then a roaring command, '*Silence!*' There were lights down there, uneven, flickering. Torches. As she came up to the vantage point, her heart thumped in shock. Flip moved closer, pressing against her leg. The sense Stasya got from her was, *Bad. Very bad. Go back. Hide.*

The square was full of people. Outsiders. Men on horseback, so many of them, wearing leather jerkins, knee boots, belts with weapons strung on them. Cloaks for travelling. Some wore leather helms. One carried a flag with a dragon on it. Further back along the road stood carts with teams of heavy horses still in harness. That explained the rumbling. Where had they come from, so early? Those horses were weary from a long journey. Stasya felt their exhaustion in every bone of her body.

The shouting man was standing on the steps outside the village hall. His call for silence hadn't calmed things much. Within the circle of armed riders – trapped there, almost – were local folk, gesturing, arguing, calling out. Stasya thought she saw Farmer Jurgis; he, too, was shouting. What was all this about? *Bad,* conveyed Flip again. *Not safe. Home now. Hide.*

Lukas was down there; he was with his father. And there was Irina at the door of the bakery with her son Tomas behind her. She had her arms out as if to shield him. Chill fingers gripped Stasya's heart. *I can't run away,* she told Flip. *I need to know what this is.*

No. No closer. Flip edged back, as if she might bolt for home on her own.

I'm working for Irina this morning. I'll have to go down there some time. Stasya showed Flip an image of herself in the bakery, kneading dough on the worktable.

I will go. The mind-picture showed a small bird flying down to the square, settling unobtrusively in the young linden tree beside the village hall. Flip did not wait for approval. The change was almost instant, dog to house sparrow. A quick ruffle of the wings, and she was away.

'Don't—' Stasya breathed, far too late. Not that it would have stopped Flip. She'd been her own mistress almost from the first, as soon as she'd recovered from whatever disaster had left her alone in the forest. Stasya bit her lip as she watched the tiny bird wing her way toward the square.

This did make sense. In that form, Flip could stay unnoticed down there, watch and listen, bring back news. She understood the danger that lay in her ability to change her shape. Though every instinct pulled her to follow, Stasya knew she must watch and wait.

There was constant motion in and around the square. Now the armed men were splitting the villagers up, herding them one way or another. Barked orders; furious protests. Blows. Who were these people and why would they do this? Where had they come from, to reach Heartwood so early?

Some of them were starting to unload the carts. Were those tools of some kind? The harnessed horses were restless, stamping, tossing their heads, unnerved by the press of folk. Their distress weighed on Stasya. She closed her eyes, but the feeling was still there: weariness, confusion, alarm, a deep need to return to a known place, a safe place. Just as well Flip had stopped her from rushing down there. At closer quarters she would have struggled to keep any shield over her mind. She might have felt compelled to act, to relieve that distress in some way, and that could have led to disaster. Best go home now before someone spotted her.

In the cottage, her mind whirring with unanswerable questions, she went through the motions of an ordinary start to the day. She kindled a very small fire. She heated water; washed and dried herself; brushed her hair and did her best to tie it back neatly. The amber owl watched her from the shelf where she'd placed it for safekeeping. Now she put the amulet back where it belonged, around her neck on its cord, under her tunic. Foolish, perhaps, to wear such a treasure every day, when she might be working with cattle or climbing ladders. But the owl was special; it belonged with her. They'd found the amber in the lake they'd named Clearwater, which was the furthest she and Lukas had ever ventured into Heartwood together. It had taken them a full day to get there and back, and Lukas's parents had asked some awkward questions afterwards. But it had been such an adventure. Lukas was clever with a knife, and he'd carved an owl from the amber and given it to her on the first day of spring. It was precious, perfect and full of magic. Stasya had known that from the first moment. In the privacy of her cottage, she could wear the little talisman openly. When she was among other folk, she made sure her clothing concealed it, if only to avoid the narrowed gaze of Lukas's mother, Rasma, in whose plans for her son's future Stasya most certainly played no part.

Stasya shivered. Rasma. Jurgis. Irina and Tomas. Lukas and his sisters. The old folk of the settlement. All of them down there in that great press of people and horses and carts. The anger, the violence, the arrival so early in the day. She could make no sense of it. And Flip still hadn't come back. Had she, too, been caught up in it all?

She made herself draw a deep, steadying breath. This was meant to be a bakery day. Irina would be expecting her. She should brew tea, have something to eat, get ready for work as she'd usually do on such a morning. But she had no appetite for food. And what if one of *them* spotted smoke rising from her chimney and came up the hill to investigate? Forget the tea. Let the fire die, cold as the morning was. She felt sick. Sick and scared. If Lukas had been with her, this would have been the moment to ask him for a story. There were plenty of tales for comfort. There was one for every occasion. More than one. But her mind was filled with a rising dread. She felt like a bird at the mercy of a capricious wind. *Go. Stay. Be brave. Be cautious. Pack a bag for the day's work. Climb back into bed, shut your eyes, wish it all away.*

She found herself pacing, four strides across the room, four back again, hugging her shawl around her. Every part of her was strung tight. Her jaw hurt from clenching her teeth so hard. Her eyes fell on the image hanging on the wall above the storage chest, its once jewel-bright colours now darkened with age and smoke, and she made herself be still; made herself gaze on the woman in the picture and breathe. The woman looked back. A thing of paint and canvas she might be, an artist's creation from long ago when Grandmother was young, but there was a life in her that had never died. Those eyes saw you; they saw deep within, and what they offered was reassurance. *Trust yourself. You will get through this.* Whether the painted woman was a saint or a deity of some ancient faith, Stasya had never been sure. The only name Grandmother had given her was the Mother. In the painting there was a stream running by her feet and a waterfall behind her, and there were creatures too, painted small: an eel, an otter, a long-legged wading bird, a dragonfly. The sky in the image had once been of the deepest blue, and the sun almost like gold. Whenever Grandmother had performed a ritual, she'd included words of respect to the Mother. If not a goddess, Stasya thought, the woman in the painting was certainly more than mortal; a kindly spirit of rivers and streams, perhaps. When she and Lukas had found Clearwater, Stasya had imagined her there, sitting on the bank in the quiet, with her bare feet in the water and her creatures around her.

Maybe she should try to conjure a vision, something that might make sense of what was happening beyond her safe walls. But no; for that she needed the fire, and she could not risk it. She would wait until the end of the day, when folk were abed. Then she would seek wisdom in the flames.

Stasya felt Flip coming before the little bird flew in. The two seldom shielded their minds from each other; they shared each other's pain and joy, good news and ill, provided the distance between them was not too far. She knew this news was bad, so bad that Flip could hardly hold it in her tiny, quivering body. She changed, bird to dog, and Stasya gathered her up, making soothing sounds. Flip leaned against her chest, her whole body trembling.

Stasya made herself wait as Flip calmed and her breathing slowed. She stroked the little dog's back. From down in the settlement came crashing sounds. They must still be unloading those carts. Where could so many horses be taken to rest?

There were times when Stasya wished Flip could talk in human words; times when images were not enough. But they had learned to understand each other well. Flip lifted her head; looked Stasya in the eye. A flow of pictures came: a big angry man with a dark beard, his riding clothes part-covered by a tunic with the image of a dragon on it. He shouted orders. When the villagers protested, the armed men moved in. Some bore long staves. People were struck down. Others struggled to help friends or family in the crush and were themselves felled. The chaos increased as some of the villagers tried to leave the square and were blocked by the men on horseback. It looked as if the newcomers were making the local men unload the carts. And on the first cart, when the covering of oiled cloth was stripped back, were great saws and axes and other tools. Farmer Jurgis was arguing with the big man. Two guards grabbed him and held him in place while the big man struck him across the face, hard. And Lukas – Lukas was about to leap to his father's defence, only Jurgis gave him a look that meant, *Don't do it, son*, and Lukas retreated, melting back into the crowd.

'But what does it mean? Why are they here?' Stasya could not show this as a picture; she set Flip down on the floor and gestured instead, arms out with palms up, brows lifted.

Bad. All bad. Go. Hide. Flip scurried across the room, leaped onto the bed and burrowed under the covers, vanishing from sight. There was a part of Stasya that longed to do just the same. But she couldn't. What use would hiding away be? At the very least, she should show up at the bakery as she'd promised. The work of the settlement still had to be done. Irina was expecting her.

She made mind-pictures for Flip: the little dog sleeping the day away under the blanket. Herself at the bakery mixing, kneading, shaping loaves, tending the fire in the big stove. Wiping down the worktable, sweeping the floor. Herself again, coming home as the light faded, and the two of them peaceful before their hearth fire in the quiet of evening.

Flip made a sound of disapproval. She did not so much as poke her nose out of the bedding.

Stasya checked her bag. She put on her boots. It had been chilly outside earlier; she took off the shawl and donned the padded jacket of felted wool that had been Grandmother's, a garment whose many shades of brown and green were in some way comforting. Wearing it reminded her of the wisdom Grandmother had shared with her: the lore of forests, the care of trees and plants and creatures, the deep understanding of ancient things. Since the very first day she'd come to live in this cottage, Stasya had been learning. It amazed her, still, to think that Heartwood was only one of several great forests within the Northlands. She had never travelled further than Vita's Hope, where the market was held. It could be that each forest had its own kind of trees, its own lakes and valleys and ancient stones, its own old tales. Maybe each had someone like Grandmother, who knew ways to help things grow and thrive. Now Grandmother was gone, and Heartwood only had Stasya. She had to find her own learning.

She pulled a woollen hat over her hair, and with a whispered goodbye, perhaps to Flip, perhaps to the painted woman, she slipped out the door.

In the square, everything was wrong. She could make no sense of it. The leather-clad men were directing things, or so it seemed. Stasya did her best to be unobtrusive – she was good at that; it helped her steer clear of awkward conversations – but it was hard with folk scurrying about everywhere. Local men were still unloading carts. Some were carrying tools and other bundles toward the covered storage area at the back of the village hall. Two of the outsiders were unharnessing the first team of draught horses; Stasya could feel the animals' relief, tinged with unease, for this was not their familiar place of rest. Across the square, two village women were supporting an injured man; she could not see who it was, but he could barely walk. One of the outsiders barked an order at them: 'Move on, you're in the way!' and one of the women – it was Marina, who kept chickens – turned her head and swore at him. The speaker strode forward as if he might strike her, but halted when the bell outside the village hall rang out. All heads turned toward it. Stasya seized the moment and sprinted for the bakery.

The door was shut. She pushed but it did not budge. It must be barred from inside. Rising panic – so many people, so much noise – threatened to drown her. She hammered on the door with a fist, and a voice came from inside. 'We're closed. Go away.' Tomas, sounding shaky and terrified.

'Tomas, it's me. Stasya. Let me in. Quick.' Silence.

'Tomas! Open up! Please!'

The door creaked open. A white-faced Tomas peered through, his eyes shadowed. He pulled the door just wide enough for Stasya to squeeze through, then slammed it shut. She dropped her bag and helped him push the bolt home.

'Where's Irina? Is she all right? Do you know what's happening, Tomas?' The bakery was warm. The fire was on in the big stove. From the scattering of flour and the mixing bowls on the table it was clear Irina had started the day's work before the outsiders put a violent stop to the pattern of life in Heartwood settlement. 'What do those people want?'

'They made Mother go to the hall. For a meeting, they said. They told all the elders to go there. Mother said I should stay in here. She said not to open the door for anyone.' Tomas was big for his age; he looked older than his eleven years. But right now he was a frightened child. 'He said... that man said... they came from the Ruler. They want to cut a path through the forest, all the way to the Hermit. Broad enough for carts. They're going to stay here until it's done. That's what he said. But they couldn't do that, could they? How could anyone do that?'

Stasya had no words. It couldn't be. It wasn't possible. It had been hard enough for her and Lukas to make a steep, winding progress on foot as far as Clearwater. There were no paths through Heartwood Forest save those of bear, deer and wolf. The trees grew close, and they were many. Higher up, the terrain was steep. The Hermit was far away. There was no telling how long such a journey would take, save that it would be many days. And that was before you considered the stories, in which not a single person had ever reached the Hermit and come safely home again. Could this man be intending... could he really mean...?

'Stasya? He couldn't do it, could he?'

She struggled for a calm tone. 'I don't think anyone could, Tomas. Why? Why would he want to do such a thing?'

'I heard him say something about treasure. Hidden treasure. You know, like in the old stories.'

Stasya made herself breathe. She swallowed the howl of rage that was building inside her. Counted to ten silently. There was a verse Grandmother had taught her, something that helped when her thoughts went crazy, but right now the words wouldn't come. Her mind was saying, *I should go there right now. To the meeting. Explain to them why they can't do this.* She opened her mouth to tell Tomas this, but left the words unsaid. His face showed her she couldn't leave him on his own, and she wouldn't take him out there. She cast her eye over the preparations on the table.

'The bread. They'll still need the bread. Will you help me?'

3

RIHARD

A TOWN MEETING. Or rather, a village meeting: this place was a straggling hamlet at best, remote, insignificant. These were simple folk, grubbing a living from the dirt, ignorant of the world outside their own little patch of ground. How hard should it be to gather their leaders and get the message through, with his men to keep order? But these people did not know their place. They were unruly, wild, deaf to authority. When Lady Elisabeta had laid out the mission for him, he had known there would be challenges. He had planned for that. What he had not expected was a pig-headed lack of cooperation on the very first day.

His men already had five or six of these wretched folk in custody, shackled to the back of a cart for want of better options. This had to be sorted out right now. He could not afford to fail.

'Let me make it clearer for you,' he said, speaking slowly. How many times would he need to explain the situation before the message got into their thick skulls? 'Perhaps you have not heard that Lady Elisabeta is Ruler now, taking the position after the death of her uncle, our beloved Lord Kasimir, may he rest in peace.' Had he been speaking in private, *beloved* was the last word he would have chosen. Never mind that. Kasimir was gone; a brighter future beckoned. 'It is your Ruler's command that a path be cut through Heartwood Forest. For too long, the treasure known to be hidden at the Hermit has lain untouched. A treasure that might change all our lives. Untold wealth. The key to a power and influence such as this land has never known.'

The folk who had entered the hall – the so-called elders of Heartwood, an unimpressive lot – were silent now. Their expressions were somewhat blank; their eyes lacked the fire he had hoped his words might kindle. *Make it personal.* He imagined one of the Ruler's advisers suggesting that. It was the sort of thing Aleksis would say. Nonsense, of course, but perhaps it might help him get through to these dull-witted folk. He cleared his throat; drew himself up tall. 'Success in this mission could transform your settlement completely.' He made himself look around the room, trying to meet every eye. God, the place was shabby; how could people live like this? Village hall? Rickety old shed, more like. 'It could bring untold wealth and prosperity to this district. Opportunities for trade. Work for everyone. The wherewithal to mend your houses, to increase your herds, to extend your pastures, to... to live a life of honour, of respect.'

Silence. He'd done it; he'd captured their attention at last. Then a voice rang out. 'At what cost?' The fellow was tallish, with a head of greying curls. His tone was defiant. Before Rihard could respond, other voices chimed in, each of them as angry as the first. Had none of them heard a word he'd said?

'You can't cut a path through Heartwood! It's dense forest; the trees are hundreds of years old. We have one of the most ancient oaks in the Northlands right here in the village.'

'What do you mean, to live a life of respect? We're fine just as we are.'

'How much respect did your men show when they struck out with their staves?' It was a woman speaking, her sleeves rolled up and an apron covering her gown, as if she had been midway through some task when the meeting was called. 'When they manhandled our folk and frightened our children? Where's the honour in that?'

Rihard drew a deep breath. 'You will address me as sir,' he said, loudly enough to silence the preposterous questions. 'Or Commander. I am here on orders from the Ruler. As for the forest, trees can be felled. Undergrowth can be scythed. I saw plenty of fit men out there, well able to help with the work.'

A babble of voices now; a dozen of them were trying to speak at once. He gestured to his men, who were stationed around the margins of the hall. As one, they took a step forward.

'Be silent!' he called. 'You're not here to raise objections, but to hear our plan and ensure your people are prepared for the work ahead.' He set it out for them: that all able-bodied men aged fifteen or over should immediately put aside their usual work so they could assist in the great enterprise, under the direction of himself or his deputies. That a camp would be set up to accommodate his men; that an enclosed building such as a barn should be provided as part of that camp. That appropriate stabling and fodder should be provided for the horses. That meals should be supplied for his men as required. It was only reasonable.

'What do you mean, set aside our usual work? Who's going to look after the stock, do the spring planting? What about lambing? And how are we supposed to feed so many folk? Where are the supplies?' It was the same troublesome fellow again, the one with the shock of curls.

'Your women can shoulder the work of the farms. The old folk and the youngsters can lend a hand. You may need to slaughter a few extra beasts to provide for us. A minor setback in view of the opportunities ahead.'

An old woman spoke, vinegar-sour. 'That talk of treasure hidden up at the Hermit, *sir.* It's all old tales, you know. Same as the stories about spirits and fairy folk and the like. Nobody's ever been up there. You can't reach the place unless you're a fox or a bird. Yet you talk as if there's gold lying about on the mountain, just waiting. Easy pickings.'

'Where's your proof?' someone else called out.

By all the powers, would this go on forever? Time to make the message plain. 'Enough of this! You will obey orders. You will provide the support I require. Any refusal to cooperate will be met with severe punishment, and that applies to *elders*,' he gave the word a particular emphasis, 'as much as to the more lowly folk of your settlement, such as those we already have in custody. Do I make myself clear?'

The voices had died down. He was getting through to them at last. 'And unless you're content to have the disobedient shackled to a cart day and night, you'll set about finding that empty barn I mentioned. And some workers to shape it into something more suitable. Understand?'

Again, no response. That fellow with the curls was looking anything but compliant. He'd need watching. 'You!' Rihard pointed. 'What is your name?'

'What does a name matter, if you plan to treat us as less than human?' That was it. Enough. Talk was useless; the situation required action.

A glance at his deputies and a jerk of the head were enough. 'Take that nameless man into custody.' Another jerk, in the direction of the apron-wearing woman. 'And her.' As his men moved to apprehend the two troublemakers, he addressed the remaining folk, who were restless, muttering objections, likely to get themselves hurt as they attempted to stop the arrests. Not that he'd care much, but there were some strong-looking individuals among them, useful for the job ahead. Better to keep them capable of work. 'This meeting is over,' he announced as the two were removed from the hall. 'Get out there, tell your people what's expected of them and what the consequences will be if they refuse to comply. And make it quick.'

'Sir?' A voice from the back of the hall, as the others made their exit.

'I said it's over! Are you deaf or half-witted, man?'

'Sir – Irina, the woman your men just took out – she's the village baker. All of us rely on her…'

Rihard gestured toward the door, and the fellow left without another word. What was wrong with these people? Couldn't their wives or mothers bake bread?

'Commander.' Leonas, one of his deputies, had come to stand by him.

'A pox take these people! They're deaf to reason!' He drew a deep breath; forced himself calm. 'Yes, what is it, Leonas?'

'The woman. Irina. I'm told she bakes for the whole settlement. Many loaves daily. She's all set up for it and she knows what she's doing. Would you consider releasing her? There's nowhere else in the village to bake on such a large scale. I can warn her of consequences if she doesn't keep her mouth shut.'

Leonas was not quite meeting his eye. But both his deputies were reliable; they wouldn't have gained promotion if there'd been any doubt of that.

'Very well. Tell them to release her, but make sure she knows the risk to her bakery – and to her family – if she doesn't keep her mouth shut. These folk must understand from the very first that we will not tolerate insubordination.'

'Yes, Commander.'

'We'll want double the usual number of loaves today. And tell her that's likely to increase.'

'Yes, Commander.'

One thing was plain, he thought as he followed his deputy out. Talk was a waste of time. Give these folk a chance to answer back and they'd keep it up until their last breath. What was needed was a display. Something bold and spectacular. Thanks to that farce of a meeting, he knew just what it would be.

4

STASYA

TWICE THE USUAL number of loaves. It meant the three of them were too busy to talk much. Because Tomas had been there when his mother came back from the meeting, ashen-faced, Stasya suspected Irina's account of it had been missing the more confrontational details. She'd told them what the Commander had said and that folk were angry. The three of them needed to stay in the bakery with the doors closed and bolted, she'd said. Which meant they were hot, sweaty and, now that a good part of the work was done, almost too tired to go on. But they had to, and not just until the end of the day. There'd be tomorrow and the next day and however long the outsiders needed feeding.

Another batch of loaves out of the oven, set to cool on the wire rack; a fresh batch into the heat. Stasya stretched, trying to ease her aching back. Tomas was sweeping again.

'I'll brew a pot of tea.' Irina sounded the way she looked: weary to the bone but determined to get the job finished. 'Sit down, the two of you. Take a break. You've done well.'

Stasya fetched out the cups. If she sat down, she thought she might never get up. Under the exhaustion that came from a long day's work, there was a crawling uneasiness deep inside her. What was happening beyond the bakery doors? Could it actually be true that they meant to cut down trees, to hack their way into the forest? Maybe it was all talk. Maybe she'd walk out that door and the nightmare would be over. Maybe the intruders had already seen how ridiculous the idea was and called a halt. But her gut told her no. Irina's face told her no. And she couldn't ask, not with Tomas listening. Anyone could see he was scared half out of his wits.

They sat, drinking their tea. Stasya tried to distract herself by guessing which herbs were in the blend. But she could not forget the sounds that had come, all day, through the small, high windows of the bakery. Cart wheels again. Hoofbeats. A lot of shouting, the words unclear. Heavy things being dragged about. As the day passed there'd been a few knocks on the door. Once it had been Rasma, desperate for help with Jurgis in custody and Lukas off helping to set up a camp for the outsiders. With neither man available to deal with slaughtering the goats, and the demand for meat likely to be high, could Stasya please come and help her with the job? Dread had overcome Stasya; she had slumped down onto a bench with her floury hands over her face. Through the bolted door, Irina had spoken kindly to Rasma, telling her Stasya was indispensable at the bakery and would be for some days. Marina came later, asking if Tomas could be spared to keep an eye on her young children while she killed and plucked some hens. Again, Irina said no through the closed door. Stasya heard the iron in the baker's voice, and the love and fear beneath it. This time she managed to keep a fragile control over herself, but she longed for the solitude of her cottage and Flip's company. Would the long day never end?

* * *

She walked home in twilight, her churning thoughts at war with her tired and aching body. She'd slipped out the back way. Pretending she was a creature evading wolves, using what she'd learned over season after season in the forest, she'd managed to get past the guards patrolling the settlement and to avoid the eyes of some local men who were carrying lengths of timber down toward Vidas's farm, knowing that if they saw her, they would likely ask her to help. Strong she might be, but after today's work she felt incapable of carrying more than the loaf Irina had insisted she take home despite the need to fulfil the double order. 'You can't work if you don't eat,' the baker had said. 'And you can come in a bit later tomorrow. You need sleep. I'll ask Agnese to help for a few hours.' Agnese was one of the village grandmothers. She was too old for the heavy work, but there were plenty of tasks she'd be able to handle.

Deep in Heartwood Forest the owls were waking. As she climbed the path toward home, Stasya wrapped her hand around her talisman, the tiny form warming against her palm. She wondered if Lukas was safely home; she wondered if his mother had managed the goat killing without help. Lukas had sisters. The eldest, Kristina, was only two years her brother's junior and capable at household tasks, but Stasya could not imagine her wielding the knife or holding a creature still and calm while her mother performed the grim job. Kristina's chief talent was fine embroidery. Her kerchiefs, shawls and skirts sold for good prices at the market in Vita's Hope. Being shut in the bakery all day had spared Stasya from the terrible tide of fear those goats must have endured; the distress of the draught horses inadequately cared for after a gruelling journey; the sorrows and hurts of a thousand small lives beyond the walls. She had wondered, often, why her gift did not work the same way with her fellow humans. *Their* thoughts and feelings she had to read from their eyes, their expressions, their movements and gestures as anyone else might. Perhaps that was just as well. Who would want to see into the mind of that shouting man, the one they called the Commander? Surely he was full of remembered hurts and imagined horrors, his goodness buried so deep in dark things that even the most magical of stories could not call it out.

Home at last. The moon was rising; its light allowed Stasya to open the door, find flint and tinder, take the knife from her belt and start a fire on the small hearth. She lit a candle, whose wavering light showed two bright eyes watching her from the bed.

'Have you been there all day, Flip?' She showed Flip a mind-picture, the little dog rolled in blankets, only her nose showing, as the sun moved across the sky. Showed, *I'm tired*, and, *I'm glad to see you.* She filled her kettle from the water bucket and hung it over the fledgling fire. Put on more wood as the flames grew stronger. Crouched down beside it and tried not to shed tears. *A long, long day.* All she wanted was to get warm and go to sleep, hoping for a night of no dreams.

Flip left the bed not with a leap, but with a flight. The small brown owl landed precisely on Stasya's shoulder. No need for a mind-picture here; the message was perfectly plain. *A ritual. Now is the time.* Owl form meant the seeking of visions, the search for answers that went beyond the everyday. *Too tired*, Stasya showed her. *Worn out. Sad. I'll do it tomorrow.* As she prepared for bed, she recognised the painful truth: after a day like this, she was afraid of what such a vision might show.

SHE WOKE WITH a start. Something bad. Something so terrible her heart clenched tight and her blood ran cold. 'Flip? Flip, where are you?' It was light outside; she had slept late.

The little dog emerged from deep under the blanket. Her eyes were wide open, her body tight with trouble. The sense Stasya got from her was, *Wrong. All wrong.*

It was cold in the cottage. Stasya threw on her shawl and went to open the shutters. The sounds were different this morning. No rolling of cart wheels. No neighing of troubled horses. But… something. The horror that had gripped her with her first waking breath grew deeper. A grinding metallic sound, not so very far away. Could they already… could it be…?

'I have to see,' she said aloud. 'I have to go, I have to…' She struggled into outdoor clothing, clumsy with distress. She shoved her feet into her boots. Why was it so hard to breathe? Why did it sound like she was sobbing? 'Let me be wrong,' she whispered. 'Please, please let me be wrong.' But the feeling inside never lied, and now it was a scream of cutting and hurting and death, of things gone so terribly awry that there might be no fixing them, not in a thousand years. Without a doubt, the sound she heard was made by a great saw.

Careful, warned Flip, showing an image of men moving between the settlement and the forest's edge, and someone with a staff in their hands stepping out to block Stasya's way along the path.

I have to see. I have to know. A physical pain in her belly now, sharp and insistent, making it hard to walk out the door, hard even to set one foot before the other. She was in no doubt of which way to go. Straight for the Ancestor. Flip had changed to sparrow form and kept pace with her, fluttering from one clump of bushes to the next.

Not too close, the bird warned. *Stay under cover. Don't let them see you*. They crept along, keeping low. The sawing sound intensified. It was joined by creaking, groaning and a shout. 'Watch out, it's coming down!' From the shadow of the trees, Stasya saw it, and she felt the mortal blow. The Ancestor fell. The sound of its landing was a doom, a curse, an ending to all good things. It took several smaller trees with it, and a scattering of debris flew in all directions. The men who had been wielding that great saw, four of them at each end, roped so they could work in tandem, now stood silent, shielding their heads from the shower of small branches, twigs and leaves. One of them was a tall young man with a crop of nut-brown curls.

Stasya's legs would not support her. She collapsed to the ground with her hands over her eyes. She heard the crash over and over again, felt the little lives lost, squirrels, martens, owls, beetles, chicks still in the egg, smashed, crushed, broken. The pain was a great wave that broke and broke inside her.

Home. Flip was on her shoulder, tiny beak tapping gently against her ear. *Home now, before they see you. There is nothing you can do*. A pause, then a new thought. *Later, when they are gone.* The picture showed Stasya alone by the fallen giant, gathering something in a basket. And Flip herself, perched atop the trunk, watching. *For a ritual.*

'I'm supposed to go to work.' There was something wrong with Stasya's voice; it hurt to get the words out. She showed Flip *bakery* and *Irina.*

Later. Home now. Get up. Walk. Suddenly Flip was a dog again; a bigger dog, tall enough for Stasya to lean on. *Come with me. I will help you*.

This was a loss too great for tears. A wound not to be endured. How could Heartwood go on without the Ancestor? How could *she* go on? It was as if some deep part of her had been ripped out and cast away, broken in pieces. Everyone in the village would feel this loss. Without the guardian tree, who would watch over their celebrations of new life, their farewells to loved ones departed? Nobody could remember a time when the Ancestor had not been there. Stasya staggered home, her mind in turmoil.

Inside the cottage, Flip was herself again, small enough to cuddle up close. They sank down on the floor by the hearth, sharing their warmth. The sounds from out there had faded, but men would still be busy doing what needed to be done. Stasya could not stop shivering; could not summon the will to add even a single piece of wood to the fire.

I should go down to the bakery. She did not think she could move. But Irina would be needing her. *All I want is to be with her, the Ancestor. To grieve beside her. And…*

Later. Flip showed, again, an image of Stasya by the fallen oak, basket over her arm, gathering something. In that scene the light was of late afternoon. *We need not pass that place on the way to the bakery. Up, now.*

If I meet that man, I will scream at him. I won't be able to stop myself. The scream was inside her now, building and building, waiting for its moment.

Then make sure you don't meet him. You know how to do that. A new image came: the two of them dodging behind a drystone wall, hiding behind a shed, creeping across open ground while guards patrolled not far away. *Bakery. Now.*

No need to tell Irina what had happened. Everyone in the settlement knew. Everyone had watched the men go up the hill with the great saw or heard the sound and rushed outside to see the gash on the hillside, the gap in the forest, the crushing blow this day had inflicted on Heartwood. Tomas muttered a greeting, then went on sweeping. Agnese was painting a goat's milk glaze on a tray of rolls; she gave Stasya a dour nod.

Irina did not put Stasya straight to work. 'I'm guessing you didn't have breakfast,' she said. 'There's tea brewed. Sit down, have a drink before you start. And some of that fruit loaf. Do it, Stasya. We have a whole day's work ahead. You need something in your stomach.'

Stasya managed the tea; the cup's warmth between her hands was welcome. She had no appetite for the bread. Nobody was saying much. Tomas was red-eyed. Irina looked worn out, even so early. Agnese kept her eyes on her work. Time passed; the rhythm of the working day, so well-practised that it flowed even on a morning such as this, did little to dull the pain. The scream waited in Stasya's body, a trembling mass of grief and fury, biding its time. She worked as hard as she could, hoping to hold it back long enough. She whispered Grandmother's verse to herself, the way she'd learned it, pausing at the end of each line, taking time to calm herself. *The oak's deep roots hold fast to the earth. I, too, will be strong. The graceful willow moves with the wind. I, too, will dance. The mighty ash towers to the heavens. I, too, will stretch high. The sun gleams on the still pool. I, too, will hold the light.*

Flip was a sparrow, perched in the tree outside. Stasya would have welcomed her company in the bakery, but Irina had made it plain long ago that dogs were not permitted to enter – and as far as the folk of the settlement knew, that was all Flip was. Her thoughts came to Stasya once or twice as the day advanced, showing her the men returning from their work of destruction, with Lukas among them. In the bakery, they did not speak about what had happened, but it was a silent presence in the room, weighing them down.

Irina sent Stasya home early again, despite the late start, and she did not protest. At the cottage she gathered what she needed – basket, small sharp knife, soft woollen scarf – and waited while Flip flew ahead to perform the necessary check. It did not take long; the sparrow returned with the message, *Nobody there. We can go.*

She had witnessed the fall of the giant. She had seen the devastation. But that was nothing like walking close. She touched the Ancestor's rough bark, moving along the trunk, setting her feet down with care lest she trample some small creature that had, against the odds, survived the violent destruction of its home. Stasya did not weep. This was beyond tears. Heartsick, she searched until the fading light made it impossible. Gathered small corpses and laid them in a sheltered place, on soft moss shielded by bushes. Whispered words of love and farewell over each dead creature, each little vanished life. There were cracked shells with their half-formed chicks within. Some eggs were smashed entirely, the contents spilled to lose themselves in the debris or be devoured by passing weasel or marten. The warm scarf would not be needed; there was no survivor to care for, to nurture back from the brink of death. Or… perhaps there was. As she considered what to take away in her basket, she felt a faint cry, a thread-thin plea for help. She followed its pull along the great fallen trunk, stepping over broken branches, ducking under those still holding to the oak.

It was a vole, moving weakly against the tangle of growth that had netted it close to the ground, right by the tree. It was bare inches from being crushed by that great fall. *Wait,* Stasya conveyed. *Only wait*. The vole quivered in its prison, terrified by her approach. Too distressed, too close to the end to know its call for help had been answered. Stasya imagined a small hollow in the roots of a tree like this – shelter from cold and rain, protection from enemies, a safe place. As she sent those good thoughts to its panicked mind, she disentangled the small one, cupping it in her hands. One close look told her this would not be a miracle recovery like that of the magpie. The damage was too great. To set the small one free would be to prolong its agony; to take it home would have the same result, for these were injuries no human hand could mend. The creature was too weak to scream, but the message that reached her from the tiny form was of pain beyond endurance. She felt it in her own body, sharp knives piercing everywhere, as if she were being pulled apart. And she heard the silent plea, *Make it stop.*

Stasya thought of rest, imagining a green place of flowing water and tall trees; she pictured the Mother seated there, surrounded by her creatures, smiling to greet the newcomer.

Farm work had given Stasya strong, sure hands. 'Rest well, little friend,' she whispered as she broke the tiny neck. She closed her eyes, feeling the pain ebb from her own body as life fled from the creature. She allowed herself tears. This never got easier, even though it was the right choice, the only choice. It was a burden to be carried; a weight that never quite left her. After a time of silence, she carried the small one into the forest. Safe shelter, even in death; would not any creature want that? There would be no safe shelter so close to the fallen tree. If that man, the Commander, had told the truth about his mad plan, this was only the start. It was the first step in what was meant to be a path through Heartwood Forest. They would not leave the great oak lying here; it could no longer be a refuge.

In the half-light, she could not venture as far as she would have wished. With the tiny corpse cradled in her hands, she halted by a younger oak, perhaps grown from a seed of the Ancestor. Grandmother had said, 'The forest is forever. It is our work, our duty, to make sure that stays true.' At the time, young Stasya had not quite understood what that meant. It was plain to her now. She whispered, 'Stay strong. Keep growing. The bad times will pass. In time, you will give shelter to the small ones of the forest.' She laid the vole down nearby, in a place where roots and rocks and natural hollows provided hiding places for the small. It was the best she could manage. Taking a life hurt her heart, even when done in love. She was human, like the Commander. Like those men from the settlement who had carried out his foul orders. *I can't make it right*, she thought. *How can I ever make it right?*

Flip was by her side again, in dog form. *Dark soon. Home now. Soon.* Back by the Ancestor, she added an oak leaf to the basket, an owl feather, a strange little stone with a hole in it, a scrap of broken eggshell. *Yes, home now.*

She wondered, approaching the cottage, if she had the strength to perform a ritual. But once inside, she closed the shutters and built up the fire so it would last long enough. She took off her jacket, draped the shawl around her shoulders, lit the oil lamp and made sure it was safely shielded. Eased the owl talisman out from its hiding place under her tunic and set it on the shelf beside the Mother, where it could overlook things. Flip was up on the bed. Stasya settled on the floor by the fire, cross-legged. She laid out feather, stone, leaf and eggshell on the hearth before her. She did not see Flip change, but felt the small weight of the owl as it settled on her shoulder.

Grandmother had taught her the way of conjuring visions by flame or by water. First, simply breathing, slow, slower. Then, spirits to be recognised, words to be spoken, not always the same, but with the same intent: to honour the natural world and to seek wisdom for the path ahead. Later, when her mind was clear enough, the question. *What will come from this ill? Show me a path to rightness, to healing. How can I walk forward in courage and wisdom?*

She gazed at the flickering flames, the glowing embers, the rising smoke. For a long time, nothing. Then… then a nightmare landscape of fallen trees, earth slipping from barren hillsides, choked waterways. Men moved there like ants, cutting, slashing, sawing at what little remnant of vegetation remained. The sky was ominous, with heavy cloud presaging a storm. No birds flew over this desolate place; no creatures could be seen there. Even as Stasya struggled to understand this, the image changed, and she saw the Heartwood settlement, and beyond it that same treeless wasteland. In the village there was a great fire. Folk were screaming, and the Commander was shouting orders. Then an image of carts being loaded – could this mean the intruders would soon leave? – and a different man in charge, younger, wearing the dragon emblem on his clothing as the Commander did. Folk being herded onto the carts. Someone with a shawl over her head and shoulders, glancing back for a last look at the ruin of all she held dear. Blanched face. Shadowed eyes. That haunted woman was herself.

Stasya felt the sudden dig of claws on her shoulder and sucked in a sharp breath. The flames wavered, and the vision was gone. But wait – had there been something else, right at the end, just a moment, a glimpse? A face, not hers but that of an old woman, and hands reaching out toward her? Her grandmother, in the Afterlife? Or had she only imagined that? A knock on the door. Stasya froze. It was dark out there. This could not be good. She sat motionless, scarcely breathing, willing the intruder to decide the cottage was empty and go away.

'Stasya? It's me, Lukas.' He sounded unsteady, hesitant. Lukas did not come to visit her after dark. He was seldom in her house; they usually met at the grazing field or in the forest. No point in sparking gossip, however foolish that gossip might be. But today was different. After today, nothing would be the same. She got up and let him in.

Lukas did not sit down, even when she motioned to the bench seat. He stood awkwardly, shifting from one foot to the other, his whole body restless. He had a livid bruise on his cheek. The look in his eyes chilled Stasya. She thought of him helping to wield that instrument of destruction and did not know what to say.

'You need to go, Stasya. You need to pack up and leave Heartwood first thing in the morning.' And when she did not reply, he said, 'That man is pure evil. He'll destroy us all. You're not safe here.'

'Leave? Where would I go?'

'Anywhere is better than here.' Lukas sank onto the bench, as if his legs could no longer support him. 'Into the forest at first, then over to Sweetwater or Vita's Hope.'

She had been to Vita's Hope once or twice, helping Vidas take sheep to the market. It was a long way from the forest. A place too full of people and noise, though she'd liked it when a band played and folk in bright clothing danced in the square. She imagined herself going to a stranger's door unannounced and trying to explain. Unthinkable. Besides… 'I need to be here,' she said, seeing how her friend was hugging his arms around his chest, as if something hurt. 'I can't just go. I need to…' She couldn't put it into words. Irina needed her help; so would many others, if the women really were supposed to obey the Commander's orders and shoulder the men's work as well as their own. Besides… 'Is nobody going to stand up to them? Are we all going to do as he tells us, even when it's so wrong? I can't run away, Lukas. This is Heartwood. I'm part of it.' She could not speak the words; could not accuse him. But the judgement must have been in her eyes.

'They threatened my sisters,' Lukas said, in a whisper that held sorrow, regret and shame all together. 'I had no choice. They still have Father in custody.'

Silence between them. Stasya added wood to the fire, fetched water, put the pot on to boil. Irina had insisted she take the fruit loaf home; now she sliced some onto a platter, set it on the table, brewed tea. Lukas sat with his head in his hands.

'I'll be careful,' she said when all was ready. 'I'll stay out of trouble. But I'm not running away. I can't leave Heartwood now.'

'I want you to be safe. You're all by yourself up here, just you and Flip. They're ruthless, Stasya. Whatever that man orders them to do, they do. Not one of them would dare speak against him. And if any of our folk question things, they get a beating.'

'Drink. Eat. I bet you've had nothing at all today.'

'I don't deserve your kindness, Stasya. And I shouldn't stay; folk will talk.'

'Eat, Lukas.' Who cared what people thought about Lukas visiting her on his own after dark? What did that matter when such evil had descended on Heartwood? 'You need to stay strong. We all do.' But for what? Her vision had suggested there was no remedy for what the Commander's men had started. No way to stop it. No chance to save the forest. 'There must be a way out of this.'

Lukas drank his tea. Managed one slice of bread. Got to his feet. 'I have to go. Stasya, promise me you'll have a bag packed. Promise me you'll leave if things get worse. You could survive in the forest. Take some supplies, forage as you go.'

'Lukas.'

He halted on his way to the door. 'What?'

'Did they beat you? Are you injured?'

He turned. His mouth twisted in a strange sort of smile. 'I'm a farm boy. I can stand up to rough treatment. Don't worry about me, Stasya. Look after yourself. Please take care.'

She stepped forward, wrapped her arms around him, rested her head against his shoulder. When he made a small sound, she pulled back. 'Oh, did I hurt you?'

His arms came around her, strong and gentle, drawing her close. 'I have a bruise or two, nothing much. You could never hurt me.' His hand came up to stroke her hair. 'I must go. Think about what I've said. Please.' His lips touched her brow.

'Be careful on the way home,' she said as he stepped out into the dark. 'I don't suppose I'll see you tomorrow.'

Lukas shook his head in reply. Stasya thought she caught the glint of tears in his eyes. 'Sleep well, Stasya.' And he was gone.

5

STASYA

A SHADOW HAD fallen over the Heartwood settlement. Strong women were pale and drawn. Young women looked old beyond their years. The oldest folk cooked, cleaned, tended to infants and vegetable gardens so their daughters and granddaughters could keep farm, workshop or smithy running. Women shod horses, ground wheat into flour and killed stock for meat – tasks which, in ordinary times, would either be performed by the men of the settlement or at least shared by them. And all the time there was the knowledge of what those men were suffering. On the hillside above the settlement there was stark evidence of the vile, backbreaking work they were doing.

Some returned home at night fit only to collapse into exhausted sleep. Some paced, muttering words of rage and despair. Some could not find a kind word for wife or children. Some woke at night, weeping or shouting. Many bore bruises. Some did not come home.

A place had been established, high-fenced and heavily guarded, where those who had defied their captors, shown disrespect, refused to work or challenged their orders were placed. Some were there only a day or so, emerging white-faced and silent. Some, like Farmer Jurgis, had been confined there for many days. Rasma had approached the guard at the entry, and with her clenched fists hidden in her apron pockets asked with careful courtesy when her husband might be released. The man replied that it was for the Commander to say. Anyone who continually spoke up against the authorities and stirred others to dissent could expect a long stay in the lockup. Rasma wanted to punch the fellow in the face. But she held back. With three girls at home, the eldest of whom had already attracted unwanted attention from some of the Commander's men, and the work to be done without her husband or her son, she could not afford to get into trouble.

Stasya heard this story from Irina. Of Lukas, she saw almost nothing. She glimpsed him occasionally when a working party headed up to the forest edge in the morning, implements of destruction in hand, or returned, shoulders bowed and eyes on the ground, at the end of the long working day; that was all. Once or twice, when she was free in the late afternoon, she went to sit in their favourite spot overlooking the grazing field. Perilous, perhaps; if one of *them* happened to see her apparently doing nothing, she might be punished for idleness. But she needed those precious moments of peace. To remember good times, and try to believe they would return. To hope that her friend would survive this ordeal and not be too much changed by it. Now nobody was bringing the goats here for their time of sweet grass and sunshine. And the herd was dwindling. The demand for meat was high with so many men in the settlement, and she'd heard that even the milk goats might be under threat. It seemed these people didn't know much about farming.

There came a day when, by some quirk of fate, Irina didn't need her and nobody else had asked her to work. Someone would probably want her later. But she would not wait to find out. It was barely light, and all was quiet save for the voices of birds in their dawn conversation. *Awake!* they called. *Yes, yes! The sun!*

Stasya had been longing for such a day. She packed a small bag with some provisions, thinking how lucky she was to have bread. How long before Irina ran out of flour? How long before someone had to take a cart over to Vita's Hope and trade some goods for what was needed? What would happen when there was nothing left to trade?

A walk? Flip had been eyeing the preparations from her spot on the bed. *Toad Rock?* The image the little dog shared with Stasya was unmistakable: the two of them atop the outcrop, looking out over Heartwood Forest. The view from that place gave joy to the heart. Getting there was more of a climb than a walk. The paths were a haul and a scramble, more suited to wild creatures than men and women. But she and Flip had done it many times before, often with Lukas. It was too long since they'd been into the forest. Stasya felt a weariness in her bones that went far beyond the aftermath of hard labour. This would lift her fading spirits. And Flip would love it. *Yes, that's where we'll go. Ready?*

Flip responded by leaping off the bed and scampering to the door, where she stood waiting. She might have been any ordinary dog eager for an outing.

Shimmering birches fringed the Heartwood settlement, with here and there a stately oak. Beyond this the great forest was mostly pine and larch. Juniper clung hard on the steeper ground, finding a purchase between rocks, seeking the sunlight of more open places. Moss and lichen crept over the great stones and formed delicate carpets near the small waterways that threaded the forest. Ferns and grasses grew in abundance.

The day brightened. The air warmed, though under the taller pines it was shadowy. As Stasya climbed, many voices came to her. Frogs were busily announcing their presence to prospective mates. Birds exchanged calls high above. And there were the voices in her mind: not cries for help, but the thoughts of a wolf on the hunt, senses attuned to every smell, every small sound; a marten scaling a pine, confident on sharp claws; a hedgehog nosing out delicious beetles part-hidden under a decaying log. The forest was a place of wonders, great and small. Sorrow and death, too. A wolf or a marten did not eat without first killing. Even the hedgehog crunched the life from its wriggling prey. As with Lukas and the goats. A cycle. That did not make it easier to kill, even in mercy. It did not lessen the terror of a creature facing death. Stasya knew that feeling well; had shared it often. She wondered what she would do if that creature was a human being dying in agony, desperate for the end to come. Would she find the courage to wield the knife? Would it feel the same, when she lacked the ability to share her thoughts with her own kind? Perhaps she would not even find the right words to say.

They stayed awhile on Toad Rock, enjoying the food and the sunshine, gazing out over the folds and rises of Heartwood with its many shades of green. If there were unwelcome sounds, the shouts and axe blows and sawing that meant the men were back at work, they did not reach Stasya here. She practised the breathing Grandmother had taught her as a child, whispering her way through the old verse, line by line. In her mind, she thanked Grandmother for her wisdom and kindness, and for teaching her the art of storytelling and the lore of the forest. Might Grandmother still be watching over her in some form? A spirit? Maybe a bird? *If you're there,* she thought, *please share some wisdom with me now. What can I do? How can I save Heartwood? Or was the vision true? Will the forest fall, and will these cruel people win?*

She closed her eyes for a while; opened her mind to answers. But there was nothing.

Flip nosed her arm; made a little sound.

'Mmm, we should go back.' Stasya rose to her feet; slung the bag over her shoulder. 'I hate being helpless, Flip. I wish I could make that man see sense.'

***

SHE HEARD THE knocking before her cottage came in sight. Sharp, insistent. And a man's voice. 'Are you there? Open up! You're needed!'

That sounded like Kiril, Vidas's farmhand. She'd heard he was one of the few men spared from the Commander's control, perhaps because he walked with a limp. Not that it slowed him down much.

'Coming!' Stasya called back. The feeling of wellbeing was already fading. After the freedom of the forest, she had no wish to go and help on the farm. At least, in the bakery, she could be behind closed doors and with folk she trusted. In the open, the Commander's men were everywhere, and they didn't need much of an excuse to strike a person or drag them away to the lockup. That filled Stasya with horror. She'd seen how that place could turn a man into a walking ghost.

Kiril looked upset. And she was starting to feel it, in her spirit, in her bones: an animal in utter panic, at its wits' end, driven mad by pain. Now she could hear something too, faintly. Was that a horse screaming? 'What's happened, Kiril?' She opened the door, let Flip inside, set down her bag.

'There's a lot more men down in the settlement. Horses and carts, same as before. Came in not long ago. Men-at-arms, like the others. Some folk from Sweetwater too, brought here to work, I think. But... there's a cart horse, one of theirs, a big strong fellow, and he's gone crazy. Still in harness, with the cart half in the ditch, and there's a man trapped underneath. Nobody can get close.'

Stasya was glancing around while he spoke, wondering what might be useful to take. A sharp knife, yes. No time to make up a calming herbal mix. That could come after she freed the horse. 'Where is this? On the farm?'

'On the road. Blocking the way, near Vidas's main gate.'

That was close to where the Commander's men were lodged – they'd taken over Vidas's barn. There'd be people everywhere, an army of onlookers. The thought made her heart shrink. But that horse needed her. He was calling her. 'Ready,' she said. 'Flip, stay.'

As they headed along the forest edge, then down the track, Kiril glanced at her, frowning. 'Might not be safe. Not even for you. Never seen a horse in such a state.'

'What set him off? Is he injured?' The closer they came, the louder the screams, and the stronger the silent message beneath. *Stop! It hurts!*

'Don't know. The fellow that was driving the cart, he was talking about putting an arrow in the creature before he kills someone. Be a shame. Fine horse. Besides, if he collapses, the man who's underneath could be crushed.'

Every instinct told Stasya to run, run like the wind before someone made a stupid decision and a life was lost for nothing. But if the Commander's men were down there and she came sprinting onto the scene, they might decide to turn that arrow in her direction. Besides, Kiril couldn't run.

'Go on ahead if you want,' he said, as if reading her mind.

'Best if I go with you.' She took a breath. 'You could help me, Kiril. If you will. Once I've got him calm, someone may need to cut whatever part of the harness he's caught by. And keep folk away while we walk him to safety. I know you're good with the horses.'

He was silent for a while. Then he said, 'If I can. And Lukas could help.'

'Lukas is there?' Stasya's heart lifted. 'I thought he was up the hill, with the…' She couldn't make herself say it.

'Think they were called back down. When these other folk came in.'

The horse's screams were piercing now; Stasya felt them right through her body. Her head was full of a stabbing pain. It was hard to keep walking. She doubted the creature would pick up her thoughts when it was in such a state of distress, but she tried anyway. *I'm coming. Stay strong, beautiful one. I will help you.* And did not share what was foremost in her mind: *I only hope I can.*

6

LUKAS

As Stasya stepped closer, there was a buzz from the crowd. He could hear it even with the noise the animal was making. Part of him wished they hadn't called her in. This would be hard for her, with so many folk watching, including the so-called Commander, who stood unmoving with his feet planted apart and arms folded, looking as if he expected her efforts to be a complete failure. Lukas longed to wipe the smug expression off that man's face. As for the arrival of all these new men, the carts, the horses, what on earth did that mean? Weren't there enough of them here already, crammed into the makeshift living quarters, eating their way through stores that should have supplied the village for months ahead, making each day a grinding misery for men, women and children alike? The horse's frenzied kicking had damaged the cart it had been drawing; splintered timber added another peril. The Commander wasn't giving any orders, but another man was: one of the newcomers, with the emblem of a dragon on his tunic. At a nod from this man, two of the guards gestured to the crowd to move further back and to keep quiet. Lukas and his fellow workers had been called down from the forest when the new convoy came in, to help unload things. But this cart had come to grief before they could even start. The trapped man was ghastly pale, struggling to breathe; his position was such that nobody could get close. There would be no freeing him until the horse was out of the traces and off the scene.

Stasya hardly seemed aware of what was around her. She was standing very still, as if gathering herself. She was getting ready to do what she did when someone in the village needed to move a bull with a bad temper, or help a cow or ewe with a difficult delivery, or tend to a dog with an injured foot. The way she could calm a disturbed creature went far beyond the skill of an ordinary farmer. He'd watched her a few times, and it had looked like she'd moved into a place where there was only her and the animal. In this case, the massive, agitated horse. Now, as Stasya moved closer little by little, the horse began to quiet. The screams grew less; the thrashing slowed.

The cart was half off the road and the horse had twisted in its harness so it was facing almost backward. The sharp ends of the broken timber were dangerously close. The animal was struggling for balance on uneven ground; slip any further and it might break a leg or crash right into the ditch. That man's life hung by a thread. In the crowd, a woman was sobbing. 'Hush,' someone said. That man; the one wearing the dragon.

Stasya edged forward, her eyes always on the horse, until she was close enough to touch. The noise had stopped, but the animal's laboured breathing showed it was in trouble. Its mouth was open, frothing. Stasya reached up to lay her hand on its neck, as gentle as a mother soothing a child. Lukas wanted to move in, to help her, but if she wanted help she would say so. She knew what she was doing.

Now she was simply standing there, both hands touching the horse's face. The animal shuddered, then heaved a great sigh. Stasya looked at Kiril then; he'd been the one sent to fetch her, and he'd been waiting close by. With a quick movement of her head, she showed him she needed him nearer. Lukas wasn't sure if she knew he was there, until she turned to look straight at him and mouthed, 'Come in on that side.'

Kiril had a knife in his hand. Lukas drew out his own knife, and they both moved in from behind the cart. While Stasya held the horse's attention, the two of them cut away the tangled harness strap by strap, until the animal was all but freed.

'Wait,' Stasya said, keeping her voice soft and calm; she spoke only for her helpers. 'I need some more time.' The silence drew out as they stood there still as statues. Someone in the crowd called out, 'Get on with it!' and was quickly hushed by his neighbours. More time passed. Lukas could hear the Commander muttering under his breath.

A great shudder ran through the horse's body, breaking the stillness. In a flash something flew out of the animal's nostril and away, buzzing. A wasp. The horse whinnied, tossing his head. Stasya stroked his neck, and he quieted again. How had she known the insect was there? By her own magic, Lukas thought. She always knew.

'We should be able to move him now,' Stasya said. 'Kiril, come in slowly and take hold of the halter. Lukas, once he has a good hold, you cut that last strap. Someone be ready to move in quickly and support the cart before he does that. Farmer Vidas, please make sure the gate is open and keep people out of the way. We'll move this handsome fellow up to your stable and you can do something to ease the swelling. I think he's all right to walk.' As Kiril moved cautiously up to the horse's head, she coaxed the animal onto level ground and Lukas cut the final strap. Vidas motioned folk out of the way, checked the gate, waited in position as the two men guided the horse forward. Stasya led them, walking backwards, holding the animal's gaze. His gait was unsteady, as if he still felt pain, but he did not resist his keepers. From behind them, Lukas could hear activity. Folk moving in to support the broken cart, to get the injured man out and onto a stretcher of some kind.

'Wait!' The voice was the Commander's. Lukas had good cause to know what could happen if a person did not obey such an order. But Stasya kept moving; her gaze did not falter. He and Kiril and the horse followed as if nobody had spoken.

'I said wait!'

How long before some of the many armed men close by came after them, clapped them all in the lockup, ruined this remarkable rescue? Did that man not understand that at least two lives had just been saved, thanks to Stasya?

Another man's voice came now, quiet, authoritative. 'The Commander asks you to disperse. We don't need a crowd here. Make sure the injured man gets the attention he needs. Pavel, find some men to see to this cart, will you? Get it off the road, have someone check whether repairs are possible. The horse is no longer a threat.'

They'd paused at the farm gate. Stasya was speaking to Farmer Vidas, who was waiting to take the horse up to his stable.

'You! Girl!' It was the Commander again, now striding toward them. Two of his guards followed in his wake. 'Come here!'

Stasya was pale as chalk and unsteady on her feet. Anyone could have seen that she was exhausted. What she needed after that effort was to sit down in the quiet somewhere, have a drink of water, be given time and space to recover. But these brutes were blind to her needs. One of them seized her arm, and she made a little sound, wincing as if it hurt. How dare they lay hands on her when she'd done exactly what she'd been asked to do?

The second guard grabbed Stasya's other arm, and she cried out in pain.

'Let her go! You're hurting her!' Lukas lunged forward, thinking to topple at least one of the pair, but the long day's hard labour, on top of the beatings he'd received any time he spoke out against the new rules, had weakened him. A fist caught him on the jaw, and a moment later he was on the ground. Booted feet all around. More guards. Now they were dragging him away.

'What are you doing? Where are you taking him?' Stasya's voice, shouting. Scared, angry. And he couldn't do a thing to help her. There was dirt in his eyes, dust in his mouth. Everything hurt.

A different voice spoke. That other man's, cool and controlled. 'By your leave, Commander, we should perhaps retreat to a more private place to question this young woman. Are your headquarters nearby? Matiss, we might need your help.'

The dragging stopped. His captors hauled him upright but did not release their grip. Through slitted eyes Lukas saw a very large man approach. One of the newcomers? The fellow went straight to Stasya and spoke to her quietly. Her captors had backed off, but whatever he was saying kept Stasya standing by him. Vidas was leading the horse away; the animal, at least, would be safe. Kiril went with them.

There was something wrong with Lukas's eyes. Everything was blurry, and his head felt odd. He saw Stasya grab the amber owl, which was hanging against her chest in full view after the rough treatment. She stuffed it back under her clothing. A moment later, the blurring turned to shadows and then to utter dark.

7

STASYA

THE BIG MAN stood beside her, a solid presence, not touching. She wanted to run, to dash for home. But that would spell disaster. So, she waited, her belly churning. The Commander was angry. Maybe it was because that other man, the one with a dragon on his tunic, seemed to have taken control. There was a look about that man's sharp features, an intensity in his gaze, that made Stasya think of a hawk, winging after its prey with deadly purpose. That look said he would let nothing and no one get in his way.

'Get that cart off the road!' the Commander snarled at his men. 'Leonas, Erik, establish some order here. Clear the area of idle onlookers. Find quarters for the new men and get the other carts unloaded. Quick as you can; there's been enough time wasted already.' He motioned to Hawk Man, pointing toward a makeshift encampment that had been built next to Vidas's old barn. 'This way.' And to the big man, 'Bring her.' It was hard to stand straight. Even harder to put one foot in front of the other. They guided her into the shadowy interior of the barn, which was now, she dimly realised, living quarters for the Commander's men. Although the place was almost empty, she felt trapped, like a bird in a too-small cage.

One of the guards stayed by the barn doors. The other one, the big man, ushered her into a walled-off area at the far end. A small table; three stools. A shelf, and on it a jug and cups. A pallet with a neatly folded blanket. Her head was spinning and her chest hurt. The horse's distress had sent her heart into a wild gallop. Calming the animal had drained away her strength. But far harder had been reaching for the tiny mind of the wasp. Nothing there but a wild struggle to escape and the desperate need to keep on stabbing and piercing until the terror was gone. Somehow, she had managed to reach it, to convey, *You can move. Turn with care; slowly, slowly. Good. See, light! Air! Creep along to the light. Go free!* All the while keeping her gaze on the horse, gentling it as well as she could, splitting her thoughts to help them both at once. Now here she was, and the pain was slowly ebbing, but if they did not let her sit down soon she might collapse on the floor. What did they want? Why was she in here? No, she would not think of fleeing up to the forest edge, of holding Flip close, of letting her tears flow in the safety of her own place. She would not risk Flip. The little dog could become a bird, a butterfly, a beetle, and make her way out of the cottage whenever she chose. A locked door would not keep her in. And if she knew Stasya was in danger, she would come.

'Sit here.' Hawk Man was motioning to a stool. 'Matiss, wait just outside this door, will you? Don't let anyone in.'

Stasya collapsed onto the stool. The big fellow went back out. Now it was only her, the Commander, and this other man who'd been giving orders not long ago, as if he was senior to the Commander. He didn't seem old enough for that. What was he, a scholar? A priest?

'Account for yourself, girl!' The Commander did not sit down, but stood with hands on hips, glaring down at her.

Stasya stared back at him. Account for what? What was she

supposed to say? Words came into her mind and as quickly departed. She said nothing.

'Speak up! What were you doing out there?'

Stasya heard something, not far off; was that a man groaning in pain? Other men were jeering and laughing, as if enjoying good entertainment. Was that…? She found words. 'What have you done with Lukas? Where is he?' Her voice came out weak and wobbly.

'I'm asking the questions! Account for yourself!' The Commander thumped a fist on the table, making it rock.

Stasya wrapped her arms around herself. Out there, the groans continued. And the thud of blows landing. Blows hard enough to be heard even in here. That must be the place she'd heard about, where people who argued or wouldn't work or otherwise annoyed the Commander were locked up and punished. The place that sent them back out – those who managed to get out – as mere shadows of themselves. Why would she answer questions, even if she understood them? Why would she do anything for this vile person? She bowed her head and tried to put both Flip and Lukas out of her mind.

'Some water.' Hawk Man filled a cup and set it before her. 'You'll be somewhat shaken by your experience, I'm sure. What is your name?'

A sound from the Commander, as if he wanted to interrupt. A sound quickly cut off. Stasya lifted her head, took the cup, drank thirstily. Looked at Hawk Man. 'What is yours?'

'You can't—' the Commander began.

'I am Aleksis, son of Feliks. I am senior adviser to the Ruler, Lady Elisabeta. My convoy has brought reinforcements and supplies as requested. I'm also charged with reporting back to the Ruler. And you are…?'

'Stasya.' She counted her breaths, in, out, in, out.

For a long while, he simply looked at her, features impassive. He could have been thinking anything at all. 'I gather you were called in because you have a particular skill with troublesome animals. Useful in a community such as this, I imagine. Unusual situation just now. Explain to us how you calmed the horse. How did you know what the problem was?'

She did not answer.

'Sorcery. Witchcraft.' The Commander's tone was flat. 'She won't talk because she knows what the truth will mean for her. Am I right? Am I right, girl?'

Too loud. Too close. Too angry. Like the wasp, this man was buzzing, he was stinging with his words, all the time fighting, as if… as if he felt scared? Trapped? How could that be, when he wielded such power? She shook her head, not looking at him.

'Commander.' Hawk Man – Aleksis – again, holding his voice quiet. Not that she was fooled by that. The two of them wanted something from her, and she didn't trust either of them. Hadn't this man said he was the Ruler's senior adviser? 'This needs more time,' he said now. 'If I may—'

'There is no time!' For a heavily built man, the Commander moved quickly. Before Stasya could react, he was behind her, dragging off her hat, lifting up her hair, seizing the cord around her neck and bodily ripping the amber owl away. She cried out in pain. Aleksis was on his feet. The Commander was already back on his side of the table, holding the talisman up to catch the light, with a look on his face like that of a cat with a fat mouse ready for the eating. 'Now tell me you don't use witchcraft,' he said. 'Explain this!' And to Aleksis, 'Small, but a very pure specimen. Indeed, finer than any I have seen before, even in the halls of highborn folk.'

'Show me.' Aleksis took the owl between thumb and forefinger; moved closer to the lamp to examine it. 'Mmm,' he said after a while. Which might have meant anything.

Stasya wanted to leap up, to deliver a few blows of her own, to seize back her treasure and bolt into the depths of the forest, where nobody could find her. She should have taken Lukas's advice and left while she could. Now she was weak. Weaker without her talisman. Weaker because her dear friend was a prisoner and they were hurting him. Weaker because she did not know how to tell the lies that might get her released.

'Would you be more ready to answer questions if there were another woman here?'

She stared at Aleksis. The answer was yes, of course, depending on the woman. Irina, yes. Agnese, yes. Marina, possibly. But she shook her head no. To bring any of the village women into this was to put them in danger. The Commander was like dry kindling, all too ready to burst into flaming anger. And Hawk Man was a person of authority, close to the Ruler herself. He was just as responsible for all this as if he'd done it with his own hands. He might have better manners, but he was cut from the same cloth as the Commander.

Aleksis was studying her as if she were some sort of strange creature or plant he'd discovered and found puzzling. She met his gaze with one of her own. She wasn't feeling brave, but she could pretend. She could be a person in a story, on a quest, the sort who could stand up in the face of danger and know all the right things to say and do.

'This is a pleasing trinket,' Aleksis said. 'The Commander is right, the amber is exceptionally pure. Without flaw. Did you carve this yourself?'

'A friend made it.'

'Ah. I think I can guess who that friend might be.' The Commander's tone was hideous, full of suggestion. It made her skin crawl. 'The lad you asked about, Lukas, was it? A very special friend, mm-hm?'

'Your men hit him and dragged him away. That was his reward for helping rescue your horse. I know they're hurting him in there.' Stasya got to her feet, pointed in the direction of the vile sounds. 'He's done nothing wrong. Nothing!' Oh, gods, she didn't have the strength to stand; her knees gave way, and she sank back to the stool. Pretending to be brave was all very well, but how was she going to get home if she couldn't walk?

The Commander opened his mouth to say something, but Aleksis got in first. 'Just one more question, Stasya. Where did your friend Lukas obtain the amber to make this?'

She shrank from answering. This was deeply private. It was between her and Lukas. Nobody else was part of this story, except Flip, of course. But... if she refused to answer, they would try to get the truth from Lukas, and they would not offer *him* a cup of water and someone to keep him company. She'd have to tell. She had no idea what words they wanted, what a court adviser would expect from her. But one thing she did know: how to tell a story.

'Once upon a time,' she began, and the Commander scowled, on the verge of shouting again. Stasya straightened her back and lifted her chin. 'Once upon a time, two friends were walking in the great forest. Where were they going? Nowhere in particular. They loved to walk and climb and sit a while, listening to the sounds around them: the chirping of birds, the sighing of wind in the pines, the splash of a waterfall. It was a fine day, and they went further than they'd ever gone before, on pathways both crooked and straight, both steep and gentle, finding new wonders at every turn. Above the canopy, the sun moved across the sky, until it was nearly time to turn for home or they would not be back by nightfall.' She stopped for a mouthful of water.

'What nonsense is this?' muttered the Commander. 'We have no time for this!'

At least he wasn't shouting. And Aleksis had gone very still, his gaze intent on Stasya. He, at least, knew how to listen.

'*Just a bit further,* said the girl. *I want to see what's up there, where the sun strikes down between the trees.*

'They went up, and there they found a lake. The beauty of it took their breath away, for the water was clear and pure, and here the pines stood back, making way for softer trees. The lake seemed to hold a gleaming light, and by its edge was a flat strand. Here the two friends took off their boots and cooled their weary feet in the water, then walked along together in perfect silence.' Stasya looked the Commander in the eye, then turned her gaze on Hawk Man. 'And that was when they saw it, on the margin where water met earth. A lump the size of a small child's fist. They might have thought it an ordinary stone, save that its colour was a dull gold. As the boy bent to pick it up in careful hands, the girl heard the pines singing, and the song they sang was of a lost brother, gone long ago but never forgotten. *Amber*, said the boy. *It must have been washed down the stream*. The girl said, *A gift*. The pines sang, *Remember, remember.* And they did remember.

'The boy was good with a knife. When they were back home, he carved the amber to make a little glowing owl, which he gave to the girl on the first day of spring. She wore it around her neck to remind her of the long, slow passage of time, and the joy of friendship, and the sorrow of losing a loved one. While she wore it, she felt the deep, beating heart of the forest as if it were part of herself. And that is the end of the tale.'

For a little, once she was done, Stasya did feel brave. The sounds from beyond the wall had died down. Perhaps they would let Lukas go, and she could help him get home safely, if she could find the strength. She *would* find the strength.

The Commander was drumming his fingers on the table, frowning as if puzzled. 'This lake, this place you speak of,' he said. 'Less than a day's walk from here, yes? And you know the way?'

A silence. There were no safe words. 'Answer me, girl!'

'You killed the Ancestor. Why would I answer you?'

'What? What nonsense is this?' The Commander turned to Aleksis. 'The girl's a half-wit, a mad dreamer. She needs the truth beaten out of her.' *I will not be afraid*, Stasya told herself. *I will write my own story.* If ever there was a time to use the other side of her gift, it was surely now. But she would not. Escape that way and innocent creatures might die, while she would surely be pursued, found and punished as a witch.

Outside the room a sudden shout went up, many voices together. 'Sir!' someone yelled. 'Commander!'

The Commander heaved a sigh of exasperation. 'Deal with her,' he said to Aleksis, and strode from the room.

Stasya met the considering gaze of Hawk Man. She held her silence. In his quiet way, Aleksis was more frightening than the Commander. That calm regard suggested layer on layer of secrets.

'Matiss!' he called, startling her. The big man appeared in the doorway. 'Find out where she lives and get her home without any fuss.'

A trick, surely. Why would he do this? And what about... 'First give back my owl,' she said.

Aleksis's mouth quirked. Not a smile, exactly. She doubted such a man was capable of smiling. 'You have a choice, Stasya. Either the owl remains in our custody or you do. That way we can be sure you won't bolt. The episode with the horse tells me you're more useful out working in the community than shut up in here. On the other hand, it's evident that you have more to tell us. Go free now but stay within the village. Be careful with your actions and with your words. Make sure you're available to talk to us when the time comes. Matiss, get her out discreetly. Quick as you can.'

Before she had time to be surprised, the big man was ushering her out, and she found she could walk, though quick was hardly the word for it. Matiss gestured silence and Stasya complied. *Discreetly*, she guessed, meant, *with as few witnesses as possible*. She couldn't ask what they intended. Wouldn't ask. Wouldn't beg for her precious owl. Wouldn't plead for the release of Lukas, or of his father, or of any of those poor souls shut in that place. The story hadn't helped. Getting angry hadn't helped. Her ritual had provided no insights. All she knew was that she could not stand by and watch them destroy the forest.

As she walked home with the big quiet guard by her side,

Stasya made herself think of the day's gifts rather than the losses. A horse saved; a wasp saved; a disaster averted. A man saved from what might have been a painful and terrifying death. And now, a gift of time, though how long it would be before the Commander or Hawk Man called her back for questioning there was no telling, and she would not ask her companion, whose silence was itself a kind of gift. If Aleksis was like a hawk, Matiss put her in mind of a big faithful dog, someone's guardian and companion. Which was foolish. He, too, worked for the Commander. He shared the blame for the blight that had fallen on Heartwood. Without a doubt, he was one of *them*.

They reached her cottage, with its cloak of mosses and trailing creepers, its water trough, its neat wood pile. Inside, Flip was barking; she had heard their footsteps.

'I'll bid you farewell, then,' Matiss said. 'Might be wise to stay home for the rest of the day. Out of sight, as far as you can. And get some rest; you look worn out. Must take a toll, what you did.'

'Mmm.' The man was talking to her almost the way Irina might; as if he was her friend. All part of the strange game Aleksis was playing, a game whose rules were a mystery to her. 'I will.'

After a little, he said, 'Live on your own, do you? But for the dog?'

She didn't want to answer that. 'I don't have visitors here. I don't want them. Folk come to tell me if they want me to work, that's all. And yes, I have a dog. I'd best go to her now.' It was impossible to ask what she wanted to ask – if he could make sure the Commander did not learn where she lived.

'Lonely sort of life,' Matiss observed.

'It suits me.'

'I'll be off, then.'

He was heading away when she spoke again. 'Thank you for walking me home.' Because his act of kindness – the escort, the welcome quiet – deserved kind words in return, no matter whom he worked for. Matiss turned his head, gave her a smile and a nod, then went on his way.

8

LUKAS

THEY KEPT HIM in for seven days, then sent him back to the work party; back to the sawing and hacking and destruction. His body felt like an old man's, aching all over from the rough treatment. In the lockup, beatings were part of daily life. Speak out and you'd be punished. Break some rule you didn't understand, and you could expect a fist to the jaw, a kick from a booted foot, a pail of slops in the face. He'd raised a protest about his father, quietly at first, hard though it was not to shout and curse and return blow for blow. But the guards ignored him. His fellow prisoners had given up. They huddled in the makeshift shelter, not speaking, and devoured whatever scraps came their way. The place stank; the only latrine was a bucket in a corner, and it wasn't emptied often. And yet, when Lukas was finally beckoned out to freedom, there was a part of him that didn't want to leave. These wretched captives were part of his community. They had wives, children, elderly parents. This place was sucking out their souls. Could despair alone kill a man? How long did it take for hope to die?

He hadn't even seen his father, who was being kept in a separate area. It made no difference that Farmer Jurgis was a respected village elder and that his farm was helping feed them all. These people respected nobody. They didn't even respect themselves. Orders were snapped out and they obeyed out of fear, a fear they in their turn used against their prisoners. It had seemed, though, that sometimes their obedience was being shaken. Lukas had heard the guards talking among themselves in lowered voices. Their conditions were harsh. They faced dire punishments for insubordination, just as their captives did. For some, it seemed the impossibility of the task ahead was starting to sink in.

So, he was out at last, and able to return home after each long day's work to see his mother and sisters, who were coping as well as they could. Stasya was free, but all he saw of her was an occasional glimpse as she slipped like a shadow away from the bakery and up the hill at the end of the working day. Best that they stayed out of each other's way. Safest that the Commander and that other fellow made as little connection between the two of them as possible. Stasya had drawn their attention that day with the horse – what a remarkable save it had been, even by her standards – but they hadn't detained her, and that had to be a good sign. He missed her badly. With Stasya, he could be truly honest. He could confide his deepest secrets in her. She would listen, and sometimes she would tell a story that helped him make sense of things. Without her, his troubles built up inside him. The weight of them was harder to bear with each passing day. His father was still a prisoner. His mother and sisters were burdened with more work than anyone could reasonably handle. How long before the Commander or that sharp-featured man, who seemed to have high authority, called a halt to the whole wretched thing? And even if that happened soon, could Heartwood ever be the same again?

* * *

He woke at night, suddenly. Someone had cried out. His mother. A smell of smoke. A commotion outside. Lukas threw on some clothing and shoved his feet into his boots, ignoring the pain that was always with him now. His mother and Kristina were at the front door, looking out. The younger ones had not risen.

'A fire? Where?'

'Over there.' Kristina pointed. Even as she spoke, the flames flared up, lighting the night with a shower of sparks. It was taking hold fast; through the roaring sound of it came shouts and screams. 'Looks like it's on Vidas's land.'

His mother made a sound fit to break Lukas's heart. She didn't need words. The encampment with its lockup was next to Vidas's old barn. And Jurgis was prisoner there. Rasma snatched up a shawl as if about to rush out.

'I'll go, Mother. You stay here and keep the little ones safe.'

She pulled against his restraining hold, deaf to reason. He had to go right now; the flames were leaping higher.

'Buckets,' said Kristina. 'The well. The stream. Mother, stay here with the girls. You'll be needed to help if anyone's injured. I'll go with Lukas.' She snatched up the bucket from the corner and headed out.

'Stay calm, Mother. I'll find him.' Lukas could feel the wild beating of his heart; it was anything but calm. But his mind was curiously clear, as if sheer terror had made choices plain. Save whomever he could. Save Father.

They ran together, brother and sister, until they were close enough to see the flames devouring what was left of Vidas's barn and ripping through the makeshift structure that housed both prisoners and their keepers. The night was all roaring, crackling, shouting. Sparks danced in the air. People were running about everywhere, a madness silhouetted against the red-gold light. Lukas had grabbed a bucket on the way; Kristina now had one in each hand. By the stream, people were dipping their own buckets and bowls, and others were carrying them up toward the fire. It looked like a losing battle. Their efforts might slow the burning, but it was surely too fierce to be put out that way. Kristina joined the group by the water, passing her spare bucket to another girl, wading in to help. Lukas thrust his bucket into someone's hands and ran on toward the barn. Some of the men in there had been too weak to stand, let alone sprint to safety.

The heat was scorching. To go any closer was unthinkable. But he had to. Maybe the fire had not reached the area at the back. Maybe...

'Here!' Someone shoved an old sack into his hands. Others held sacks too, and were beating at the flames, trying to smother them. Vidas and Kiril were working alongside some of the guards. Even young Tomas was doing his share. And there... there was a big man, skirting the others and heading toward the rear of the barn. Timbers cracked; within the burning building, objects crashed down from above. Surely the roof must soon give way.

Sack in hand, Lukas ran after the big man. Some folk at least had escaped. Over by the fence, well clear of the fire, a group sat huddled, while someone crouched beside them, offering water. He did not see Jurgis among them.

A door. Not yet afire. The big man broke it down with a powerful kick and headed inside. Lukas followed. Gods, it was hot! The air was thick with smoke; it was hard to see, hard to draw breath. He battled forward, following the other man, who was shouting, 'Anyone there?' Lukas lost sight of him in the haze. Called out in his turn, 'Father? Where are you? Anyone?' He was choking over the words; not far off there was a thump as something fell.

Just as the big man reappeared, heading back out with a limp form in his arms, there came a weak cry. 'Lukas! Over here!' *Father.* Still alive.

As he made his way through the smoke, near-blind and wheezing like an ancient, something flashed above him and a fresh shower of sparks descended. Lukas batted them away. On, on. He had made a promise. Hands out in front of him, he moved forward. 'Where are you? Call out!' But Jurgis did not answer. From the doorway, someone shouted, 'Get out of there, quick! It's all going up!'

Three steps. Three more. And there was Jurgis, slumped in a corner, his wrists and ankles hobbled. Lukas sucked in a breath. Gods, his chest hurt! Why did it hurt so much? His knife… where was his knife? *Father… Promise… Out, quick.* He crouched by Jurgis. No breath to spare for words. His father held out his bound hands and Lukas severed the ties. Now the ankles. The smoke was thicker; he cut by feel alone, praying that he would get it right. And Jurgis was free. But he did not rise.

'Father, quick! We have to get out right now!'

No response. Lukas took hold of his father, trying to haul him to his feet. Jurgis was a dead weight.

'Can't… stand. Go, son. Save… yourself.'

Something smashed down behind Lukas. He did not turn to look. 'Here. Help me a bit.' He'd lifted enough goats and other creatures over the years to have the knack of this. 'Arm up around my shoulders, that's it. This might hurt.' A haul, a twist, then the backbreaking rise to his feet. Wobbling. Staggering, his father's weight across his shoulders. Finding balance as flame sheeted across the room and the heat was an oven, a bonfire, a funeral pyre. 'Good. Now we get out of here.'

9

STASYA

A NIGHTMARE. IF only she'd got up sooner, if only she'd known… Flip had woken her with a not-so-gentle peck to the ear. Stasya had smelled smoke, looked out and seen the flames, then dressed in a rush, making it clear Flip must stay home for her own safety. She'd run all the way down to the settlement, until the heat was in her face and the screams and wails were crowding her thoughts and she knew she was too late to stop this, too late to do anything but help deal with whatever came next. Up by the barn, nobody was saying much, apart from things like *drink this*, or *show me your arm*, or *this might hurt, try to keep still*. She should have known… But she *had* known. The vision had shown her this, the eerie light, the veiling smoke, the folk in pain, the conflagration. She should have done something. She should have told someone. But how could she have done that without the community turning on her? Good people did not perform rituals. So most folk believed. Decent people did not conjure visions. To do so, and to have the vision come true, was to work dark magic. Perhaps to be held responsible for whatever unfolded, as if the seer brought the vision to reality. People knew she'd learned the art of storytelling from her grandmother. But the skill of scrying had been taught in secret. Grandmother had made sure Stasya understood the perils of making this skill public knowledge.

Local folk and the Commander's men were working side by side, almost indistinguishable in the strange light. Fire had devoured the barn. Whether there had still been prisoners in there, she did not know. She joined the workers in their grim tasks, not speaking to anyone unless she must. Nodded in response to the question, *Can you help me with this?* Shared the weight of an unconscious man with one of the guards, all the way to the hall, where they passed their burden over to the village women who were dealing with the injured. Helped another man to walk the distance, his arm around her shoulders as he hobbled along beside her. He could hardly bear to put his right foot on the ground. He'd fallen, he told her, while running up to the fire with buckets of water. He kept on talking, blaming himself for spilling the water and for not taking care and now for wasting folk's time with what might only be a sprain, until Stasya lost her hard-won composure and told him to save his breath. She'd seen Aleksis giving orders – where was the Commander? – and men carrying away bodies, not to the hall, but to some other place. Bodies disfigured by burning. Bodies whose identities she could not even begin to guess at. She hadn't seen Jurgis anywhere. She hadn't seen Lukas. Another trip. Another man to help down to the hall, one of the locals this time. Oskar was around her own age; he was one of Kristina's many admirers. Not burned but struggling to breathe and so weak he could barely stay on his feet. He needed someone on either side or to be carried. But although he was of fairly slight build, she was growing tired. Could she perhaps put him over her shoulders? No, not sensible while he could hardly draw breath. She glanced around, wishing Lukas was there. 'Need help?' It was the big man, Matiss, walking to her out of the smoke like some warrior from an old tale. Though this warrior was exhausted. And sad. It was written all over his face.

Stasya nodded. On a night like this, differences must be set aside. 'He's having trouble breathing. Caught in the smoke too long, I think. Could you help carry him?'

'I'll take him.' Matiss scooped Oskar up without apparent effort, cradling him across his body as a person might hold a child.

'Thank you. I'll…' She looked around. Someone else was sure to need her help.

'Walk with me. The survivors are all out now. And I want to talk to you.'

So she did, helping to steady Oskar when they went over rough ground. Matiss said nothing until they were well clear of the barn.

'Your friend, the goatherd. He got out alive, but he's hurt. I thought you'd best know that before you see him down there.'

Stasya froze for a moment. 'Lukas? But he was free, I heard they'd let him go—'

'We'd best keep walking.'

'Tell me!' She went on, keeping pace with him, though part of her wanted to run, to be there right now, to see for herself.

'Your Lukas was a hero. He came to help fight the fire, and he went into the barn to rescue his father. Everyone else had given up by then. The place was full of smoke and starting to collapse. He got his father out. Both of them were burned, and the older man has… other injuries.' She made some sort of sound, and Matiss went on, 'I'm sorry, Stasya. We have one fellow with some healing skills, and he will do all he can to help.'

'Burned,' she echoed in a voice like a crow's. 'How badly?'

Matiss stopped briefly to adjust Oskar's weight in his arms, then moved on. 'We'll check down at the hall. After he carried his father out of the fire, Lukas collapsed.' Another silence. 'They were lucky to get out alive, Stasya.'

For a moment she was speechless. Feelings flooded through her, warring with one another. Rage rose to the top. 'Where was the Commander when this happened? This is on his head! And on yours! Why did you come here? Your kind knows nothing but destruction and ruin!'

This time, the silence drew out so long she thought he was not going to answer. Then he said, 'Rihard – the Commander – was otherwise occupied, or so I'm told. Had he been sleeping in his usual quarters, he might have perished in the fire, as others did.'

Words rushed to her mouth, bitter as bile. *I wish he had perished. He deserves to die for what he has done.* She made herself swallow them.

'As for myself,' Matiss said, 'I answer to Master Aleksis and, through him, to the Ruler. I caution you against making such comments where others can hear them.' He was overtaken by a sudden fit of coughing and needed to put Oskar down. Stasya moved to support the injured man, who stood shakily, his hand on her shoulder. Watching Matiss as he bent over, trying to clear his lungs, she knew this was no ordinary cough.

'Smoke,' she said. 'You were in there too.'

The spasm passed. Matiss wiped a hand across his mouth. 'I got a couple of men out, yes. Saw your friend heading in, tried to warn him, but he was set on saving his father. Brave lad.'

They got Oskar to the hall. Hawk Man was there, apparently in charge. Stasya felt relief that the Commander was still nowhere to be seen. Women were busy with blankets, water skins, rolls of cloth for bandages. The benches where folk would sit for a meeting had been moved to the sides, and the space was full of pallets. Almost all were occupied. There was a smell: blood, dirt, sweat, smoke. A couple of women were moving among the injured, speaking quietly to those who could hear, listening to those who could respond, checking on those who lay limp and silent. And one of the Commander's men was kneeling by a pallet at the far end, with Kristina beside him. A glance told Stasya the person lying there was not Lukas, but his father. What to do… where to go…

'You could help.' Matiss still stood beside her, though he had passed Oskar over to another man who was steering him to an empty pallet. How many of these folk would die right here, lacking the expertise of a physician?

'Me?' Yes, she could carry heavy things, run with messages, fetch water from the well. But she was no healer.

'You tell a good story. In times of trouble, that helps. When a man's in pain. When he's scared. When he has to wait, not knowing what's coming.'

He was right, of course. But how did he know she told stories? Oh. He'd been outside the door when she'd told the tale of the amber owl, thinking only the Commander and Hawk Man could hear. 'Matiss?'

'Yes?'

'Could you find out where they've put Lukas?'

The big man nodded and left her. Stasya forced down the urge to rush off in search of Lukas herself, to find answers when there were no answers. Rasma was not here with her husband. Perhaps Lukas was back home, under her care. Or maybe she was out searching for her son. Stasya moved between the pallets; stopped beside a man who was reaching blindly upward. Not a villager; one of *them*. Right now, that didn't make any difference.

She crouched down beside him; took his hand in hers. 'It will be all right,' she murmured, hoping it wasn't a lie. 'You're safe here. Just wait a bit.'

'I'm scared.' Like a child, but with a rasp in his voice; this was surely another affected by the smoke. 'My chest hurts.'

She glanced over to the spot where Aleksis was now conferring with some village elders, Vidas among them. Outside, someone was wailing. *Shut it out*, she told herself. *You can't do everything.* But perhaps there was one thing that might ease this man's suffering, at least a little. 'Can you sit up, if I help you? You might be able to breathe more easily. Good, well done.'

He gripped her hand more tightly, as if afraid she might leave him.

She settled by him, helping him stay upright.

'Do you know the tale of the brave soldier and the giant frog?'

His lips twitched; perhaps that was a smile. 'Once upon a time…'

She moved from one man to another, keeping her voice soft, pushing down the need to run, to scream, to curl up with her hands over her ears and wish it all away. She told tale after tale; held the hands of the fearful, the suffering, the dying. It was hard to shut out the sounds of pain and distress. She tried not to look beyond the man she was comforting; tried not to see the moment when a blanket was drawn over a limp body, covering even the face. Time stretched out, impossible to measure. Women came in and out, some helping to tend to the injured, some bringing supplies, some seeking out a husband, a father, a brother, a son. Men came in and out, some to speak to Hawk Man or one of the guards, some to collect one of those covered forms and carry it out of the hall. The man she'd seen earlier tending to Jurgis must be the healer Matiss had mentioned; he went around to everyone in turn, examining injuries, speaking to the women in attendance, conferring with Aleksis.

Stasya finished a tale. This man had burns to his feet; he would not be marching with his fellow guards again. Agnese came and applied poultices, wrapping the wounds in linen, speaking kind words as she did so. She acknowledged Stasya with a nod.

Matiss had been gone a while. There was a knot of dread in Stasya's stomach. Perhaps the big man had been caught up in other things and had not had time to look for Lukas. But her mind showed her other pictures, dark ones. Kristina was still in the hall, sitting beside Jurgis. She'd applied some kind of salve to her father's wounds, then bandaged them. She must know something. Would Lukas's sister be so calm if she, too, did not know where he was? She should go and ask. But Kristina wouldn't want to be bothered by her. When had the folk of Heartwood ever really wanted her, unless there was hard work to be done? Stasya thought of Flip, all alone in the cottage. There was a powerful longing in her to feel the familiar weight of the little dog on her knee, to be warmed and comforted by her touch. *Shut it down, Stasya*, she ordered herself. To bring Flip to her at such a time was to put her friend at risk. Never mind that Flip, in bird form, could have gone searching more or less unobserved. Never mind that Flip might have found Lukas swiftly. She would wait. Or... she would make herself go and speak to Kristina. Now.

She got to her feet, cramped from so long sitting on the floor. Made her way carefully between the pallets, heading for the spot where Jurgis lay. Wondered if, the moment she said Lukas's name aloud, she would dissolve into tears in front of all these people. But before she could reach Kristina, there was Matiss. He went first to Aleksis. The two conferred briefly, then Matiss turned toward Stasya. What message her face held, she could not imagine, but he moved to one side of the hall and beckoned her over. People were watching. Agnese. Kristina. Others. Disapproval was written all over them. What did they imagine, that she had made friends with the enemy? That she was trading secrets? If Matiss shouted at her and marched her away, would they think, *Good riddance?*

He spoke quietly, his words only for her ears. 'Some of the injured were taken to a smaller barn, further to the south. Your friend is among them. Aleksis is sending our healer there now.'

'Can I go and see him?' The words were out before she could stop them. 'How bad are his burns?'

'I don't have that information yet. The Commander has claimed that place as his temporary headquarters.' Matiss's voice was barely a murmur. 'You should go home.'

She felt as if she were being pulled in all directions at once, though she stood perfectly still. *Breathe, Stasya.* 'You need to tell his sister,' she made herself say. She indicated Kristina, who was still looking her way.

'Aleksis will speak to her. Stasya, I strongly advise you to go home now. I'll find someone to escort you—'

A scream from just outside, a jarring, tearing sound. The door slammed open and in strode the Commander, with a woman following, her mouth open wide, her hands clinging to his tunic so she was half-dragged after him. Her face was a mask, a thing from an old tale of grief and fury made real. Her shrieking made Stasya's heart clench tight in terror. It was Irina; Irina of the orderly bakery, the calm manner, the steady, quiet work. What could have done this? Only one thing, Stasya thought. Only one terrible, unthinkable thing.

Irina held on until two guards peeled her off the Commander and restrained her. Still the words flooded out. 'You killed my son! You killed my Tomas! Not even twelve years old, a child! You are a menace, a vile curse! Torturer! Murderer! You have ripped out our hearts!'

The Commander struck her in the jaw with his clenched fist. Pinioned as she was by her two captors, she could not avoid the blow. Stasya started forward; Matiss laid a restraining hand on her arm.

Irina sucked in a laboured breath; squared her shoulders. 'I will not be silenced!' She spoke through sobs, but still she met the Commander in the eye. 'I speak for all the women of Heartwood! You have brought nothing but evil to this place! If your mother could see you now, she would regret the day she gave you birth!'

He struck her again, harder this time, and she sagged between the two guards.

'Commander.' It was Aleksis's voice, perfectly calm. 'I'll deal with this.' He moved toward the group with steady purpose.

'I knew that woman was a troublemaker. Take her away.

Put her under guard. Leave her to consider her actions overnight.' The Commander spoke as if he had not heard Aleksis. As his guards took Irina out, he dusted off his tunic as if to remove any trace of her and folded his arms. He cast his gaze around the hall. Matiss stepped in front of Stasya as if to shield her. But she didn't want his protection. She didn't want to hide away. It was time to be seen; time to be heard. Never mind that more guards were coming into the hall, perhaps drawn by Irina's screams, perhaps following the Commander's lead. She stepped away from Matiss and met the Commander's eye across the rows of pallets. Let him listen. Let him hear.

'That woman, as you call her, is a respected elder of this village! You and your men have been fed all this time because she's worked herself to exhaustion baking for you. Is what she said true? Has Tomas been killed?' The Commander opened his mouth to respond, but Aleksis was quicker. 'Sadly, that is true. There was a young boy among the dead; killed by a fall of burning timber. A freak accident, which we very much regret. I believe this was the baker's son.'

Tears stung Stasya's eyes. That sweet boy. A good son, full of such promise. This was too big, too sad, too terrible to speak of in anything but a story. 'Once upon a time,' she said, somehow finding a voice that would reach every ear in the hall, 'a monster came to a peaceful settlement. What little the folk owned, the monster broke or spoiled or burned. Even the trees were cut down. Nobody knew why he was doing it. Nobody wanted him there. But they could not drive him away, not even when their sons and brothers and fathers were maimed or killed by the terrible work he forced them to do.'

'What is this nonsense?' roared the Commander. He seemed about to charge straight at Stasya, even if it meant striding across the rows of pallets with their sad occupants, but Aleksis put a hand on his arm, and a guard did the same on his other side. Stasya went on.

'The local folk could not fight him. He had lackeys at his bidding who would frighten and beat and starve those who spoke out against him. So, the villagers tried being kind. They baked him delicious bread. They slaughtered their goats and sheep so he and his men could eat roast meat, even though that meant lean years ahead for the farmers. They built a place for the monster and his lackeys to sleep in and be sheltered from the rain. They did the work of destruction that he ordered, and every night they came home weary and hurt and despairing. Some died in accidents. Some died by fire. Even children died. What did the monster want? A treasure. A treasure that was so far away, so hard to reach, that more and more folk would fall in the monster's pursuit of it. This treasure was known of from ancient tales. Who knew whether it really existed? The tales told of spirits that haunted the forest, their cries enough to freeze a man's blood in his veins. They spoke of uncanny folk living high in the hills, folk who could make trees walk and cause rivers to rise and fall at will. And everyone knew the forest was full of hungry wolves and bears. The monster must surely be out of his wits to think of going into its heart, even if such a journey were possible. Everyone in the village would be dead and their lovely home a wasteland before a way to that treasure could be found. What were the people to do? Who could help them?'

The hall had fallen eerily quiet. Matiss had not moved from his position beside her, though she sensed the tension in him; he was ready to act at an instant's notice. From across the sea of pallets, the Commander glared at her, red-faced. The silence drew out, until he said, 'Well? How does the tale end?'

Stasya held his gaze. If only she could see into his mind, the way she'd be able to do if he were one of those wolves or bears, or a dog, or a bird. If only she could understand *why*. 'Only you can make the ending, sir.' She kept her voice calm, though the drumbeat of her heart was strong and fierce. 'It is your story, and it is not yet finished.'

The Commander drew a shuddering breath. She expected him to shout again, but he simply turned to Aleksis and said, 'You told me you'd deal with it. So deal with it. Get her out of here, lock her up where she can't cause any more trouble. The girl's out of her wits. Needs to be put away for life, if you ask me.'

By her father's pallet, Kristina rose gracefully to her feet. 'She speaks for all of us,' she said. And if her voice was shaky, her gaze was not. 'She speaks the truth.'

Grey-haired Agnese stepped forward from the bench where she'd been cutting cloth for bandages. 'She speaks the truth.' Then, one by one, every woman in the room stood and faced the Commander, echoing those words. The hush that followed was profound.

The Commander broke the silence. 'Take her away!' he rapped out, glaring at Aleksis. 'You see what she's doing, stirring folk up with her stupid stories! Get her out of here!'

Stasya brushed away sudden tears. When Matiss took her arm to guide her to the door, she did not resist. She was suddenly too tired to argue, too tired to attempt an escape, even when they were out in the open. She stood waiting while some kind of silent communication happened between Matiss, Aleksis and the young fair-haired guard who had helped hold the Commander back when he seemed about to charge at her. That man was familiar. She thought he'd been there when she calmed the horse. Another of Aleksis's men.

They took her only as far as the bakery. The door was not barred. Inside, the place was still warm from the day's work. There was no sign of Irina.

'You'll stay here for tonight,' Aleksis said. 'I'll put guards on both the doors. I want your promise that you won't try to escape. If you won't give that, we'll have to restrain you in some way.'

Stasya nodded. She stood still while Matiss lit lamps. The other guard walked around as if checking for hidden assailants. She wanted to see Lukas. She wanted to know if Irina was all right. She needed Flip. But there was no point in asking. Perhaps, if she did what they wanted now, they'd let her go home when the sun rose.

'Your little dog,' said Matiss. 'All right on her own up there?'

Would he go and fetch Flip for her if she asked him? Maybe yes. But she didn't want anyone inside her cottage. 'She'll be all right until morning.'

The men exchanged another look. She could not read it. She was so tired that things were starting to blur before her eyes.

'Get some rest,' Aleksis said. 'You'll be safe here. Matiss, Pavel, stay alert.' And with that, he was gone. Matiss stationed himself by the main door of the bakery, first bolting it from the inside. The other guard, Pavel, took up a post by the back door. It seemed neither planned to sleep.

'Don't you need rest too?'

'We're trained to cope without. Not forever. But for long enough. Go on, do what you need to do. Wash, sleep. We won't disturb you.'

The habits of the bakery died hard, despite everything. A bucket of water stood ready near the stove. Stasya washed her hands and splashed her face. Thinking of Irina, thinking of poor Tomas, she built up the remnant of the fire, boiled a kettle, brewed tea. Tea was good when you were tired out and your thoughts were full of darkness. More from habit than anything, she got out three cups and filled each. 'There's tea, if you want,' she said, taking her own cup with her as she retreated to Irina's sleeping quarters, which were screened from the working area by a curtain. A proper all-over wash and some fresh clothes would have been welcome, but the pump was outside, and she wasn't going to ask for permission. As for relieving herself, there was a pot in the corner for the purpose. She would empty it in the morning.

Small sounds came to her as she lay on Irina's shelf-bed, feeling the ache of utter exhaustion in her body. The clink of cups. Matiss's deep voice and Pavel's lighter one in muted conversation. Well, they'd locked the place up. They hardly needed to stand at the doors all night. Though there was a monster out there; it wasn't only in the story. Tomas was dead. She couldn't get her mind around that. Then there was Lukas, who might be all right and might not. Jurgis, a respected leader in the village, unable to stir or speak a single word, it seemed, even with the Commander a few paces away roaring his anger. And Kristina, the village beauty with her delicate embroidered creations, standing up like that, speaking out when she knew what the cost might be. Agnese, a quiet grandmother. The other women. They had all supported her. But for nothing. The Commander was deaf to their voices. Deaf to reason.

I'll be home in the morning, she thought. *Home with Flip.* She imagined walking into the forest with the little dog by her side, moving on soft feet under the towering trees, hearing nothing but the song of the wind and the whisper of the grasses. No Commander. No guards. No people at all. Just herself, and Flip, and Heartwood.

10

STASYA

For a few hours she slept like the dead. Voices woke her. She sat up, still groggy. The high windows of the bakery showed faint light; dawn must be near. Matiss was talking to someone, beyond the dividing curtain. The other voice was not Pavel's. Was that Aleksis? What was he doing here so early? Half-awake, she struggled to catch their words. Something about moving quickly. Something about a cart. Horses. Names of places. Some she knew: Sweetwater, Vita's Hope. Some she had never heard of.

Could it be that the Commander had given up his ridiculous mission and was withdrawing his forces from Heartwood? Had the destructive fire finally convinced him the cost of his venture was just too high? Or was that too much to hope for? As the vile memories of yesterday returned to her, Stasya got out of bed. She wished she had not slept in her clothes, though what alternative was there under the circumstances? All too aware that she was grubby, dishevelled and still half-asleep, she drew aside the curtain and stepped out into the bakery.

The three men standing in conference by the table fell instantly silent. Matiss, Pavel, Aleksis. Each wore the same expression as they turned to look at her. Alert. On edge.

'What?' She glanced from one to another. 'What's happened now?' She held back the words, *When can I go home?*

'We're leaving.' Aleksis's tone was calm, steady. But Stasya felt the restlessness in the group, a need to be moving.

'All of you?' The Commander was giving up? Oh, how she longed for this to be true.

'A smaller group only. I will lead it; some of my men will accompany me. We'll convey the more seriously hurt to one of the larger settlements, where they can receive better care. Some will travel on to Dragon's Keep with us.'

'Dragon's Keep?'

'The Ruler's residence,' said Matiss. 'You'll be going there. And we must leave soon.'

Stasya was without words. This was a joke, surely. Why would she go anywhere? She wasn't injured or in need of care. And what about…? A sound came to her ears. A little dog barking. She must be just outside the door. Oh, gods. 'We live here. Flip and me. This is our home. Our forest. I can't go—'

'There's no time for this.' There was a harder edge to Aleksis's voice now. 'You will come with us. Willingly, I hope. I don't want to have to restrain you. Come freely, and you can make yourself useful on the way. As for why, the Ruler wants to speak to you.' And when she simply stared at him disbelieving, he added, 'Lady Elisabeta has requested your presence at court. It's my job to get you there safely. Now gather whatever you need and be quick about it.'

Gather what you need. But her things were all up at the cottage. Her clothes, her hair comb, the precious objects she had used for that last ritual. The painting of the Mother. She made herself breathe; swallowed the scream of protest that was building inside her. 'I ran down here to help. When I saw the fire. I brought nothing but the clothes I'm wearing.' *Don't make me come with you, don't, don't. Don't make me leave the forest.*

'The baker will also be travelling with us,' Matiss said. 'She will not come back here beforehand. Take what you need from her things; you might gather some necessities for her also. Hurry, please.' He turned to the other men. 'Go ahead, I'll meet you down at the gate.'

As soon as the door was opened, Flip came barrelling in, ending the charge with a wild leap into Stasya's arms. 'I can't— I don't—' Stasya stumbled over her words, clutching the little dog to her chest. 'What—?'

'Go on, Pavel,' Matiss said. 'I'll bring Stasya.' And when Pavel had followed Aleksis out, shutting the door behind him, the big man said, 'Your friend Lukas will be with us. His burns need expert attention. He might welcome your support on the journey.' And when Stasya gave no answer but an indrawn breath, he added, 'You need to come. You spoke out earlier; drew the Commander's attention, and not in a good way. Now, can I help you gather what you need? By the time we walk to the gate, they'll be ready to leave.'

Dimly, Stasya remembered that the Commander had now established his headquarters further away; perhaps they were leaving early to avoid some sort of scene. But a whole group of riders? Horses and carts? Those would be hard to overlook unless a man was sunk very deep in sleep. Lukas. They were taking Lukas.

'Stasya. We must go.'

She set Flip down. Found a bag, stuffed some items in. Irina's comb. Some clean rags, kept for dealing with the monthly bleeding. Hers was due soon; she could only hope she would not have to deal with it until after they reached this place. She chose sparingly from Irina's clothing. For herself, a nightrobe, a shawl, a gown that would be too short and uncomfortably tight, but that hardly mattered. If they'd let her go home first, she could have packed her spare tunic and trousers, twins to the ones she was wearing. But they were out of reach, and she would not fit into Tomas's things, even if she could have made herself take them. For Irina, she snatched up some items the baker wore often. And one precious item: Irina's wedding ring, which she did not wear while baking; it was on its shelf beside the bed. A narrow silver band, memory of a husband who had perished from a winter ague when Tomas was only an infant. If Stasya had still had her owl, she could have strung the ring on the same cord for safekeeping. Oh, the amber owl… What would the Commander do with it? The thought of it in his hands horrified her. But she could not ask about it; these men were in a rush and would not listen. She slipped Irina's ring into her tunic pocket, willing it to stay there. A knife would have been useful; her own had been left in the cottage when she rushed out to the fire. But she could not take one from Irina's kitchen supplies without Matiss noticing, and she was sure he wouldn't let her keep it.

Flip had jumped up on the shelf-bed and was watching solemnly. There was no time to exchange any messages with the little dog. It might have been better if Flip had arrived in bird form, but it was too late for that now. The men had seen a dog, and that meant no more changing while she travelled with them. Heartwood… they were leaving Heartwood… That knowledge was a cold stone inside Stasya, weighing her down, chilling her spirit. There was no escaping this. Not with Lukas in these people's grasp. The talk of better care might be all lies. Was it really likely there would be skilled healers in those other settlements? She'd been to Sweetwater. It was bigger than Heartwood village, yes, but in other respects much the same. Not grand. Not wealthy. Did they plan to leave Lukas and Irina there?

They left the bakery. In the pre-dawn light, the settlement was eerily quiet, though now Stasya could hear sounds of activity from the direction of Vidas's front gate. Matiss carried the bag; Stasya carried Flip. It felt like a walk to the scaffold. Like the end of all good things. Like a terrible dream, one that grew still more troubling when she saw two carts waiting, each with a pair of horses harnessed up – there was a tall and handsome creature she recognised – and a small contingent of mounted guards close by, Pavel among them. Aleksis stood by the carts. In the early light, he looked especially grim. That should not surprise her; there were injured men in the cart nearest to her, men who wore bandages around their heads, makeshift splints on their limbs; men who lay still, men who sat upright on the straw, backs against the cart's wooden sides. No sign of the person who had been tending to the injured last night. Who would look after them on the journey?

Matiss gave her a gentle push toward the second cart, which was also cushioned with straw. A man sat ready to drive. And there in the back… that figure lying in the straw, his head pillowed by a bag, was Lukas. He was a wan shadow of her hardy, smiling friend. His eyes were on her; his lips formed her name. Beside him in the cart was Irina. She sat slumped over, head bowed, fingers toying with a wisp of straw. A sad ghost. Her wrists were joined by a length of knotted cord, as if, unrestrained, she might leap out of the cart or try to attack someone. Her russet hair, usually pinned up in a tidy roll, lay in a tangle across her shoulders. Did these men not understand that she had just lost her only child? Stasya hugged Flip closer for a moment, then lifted the dog into the cart. Matiss threw the bag in and helped Stasya up. As the sun crept up over the horizon and the convoy got under way, she settled next to Irina, murmuring a greeting to which the other woman made no response at all. Flip curled up beside Lukas as if to keep him warm.

Stasya told herself she would not look back. She told herself she would not shed tears, even though her heart was breaking. But as dawn came nearer and the morning birds of Heartwood lifted their voices in celebration of the light, she gazed on the passing forest, knowing this was goodbye, perhaps for ever.

It had happened so fast. She hadn't said farewell. She hadn't gone to the fallen Ancestor and spoken the right words. Maybe there were none. Could any words be deep enough for the hurt her own kind had inflicted on this ancient place? For the losses suffered by those that made it their home? Every living thing, from the great bear to the tiniest dragonfly, from the tall pine to the creeping moss, would suffer for no better reason than the greed of humankind. Every creature would, in time, feel as she did now: ripped from her home, set adrift on a journey she did not understand. Powerless to stop this. Breaking the solemn promise she had given when Grandmother was on her deathbed.

She needed to scream. The words of grief and fury were clamouring to be set free. But she could not let them out, not with Lukas lying limp and defeated beside her, and Irina sunk deep in her own sorrow. Not with the injured guards in the other cart, perhaps in pain. It would only get worse with the jolting. She wished she could help them. But how?

The wheels rolled on; the horses' hooves thudded on the pathway.

The noise almost drowned Lukas's voice. 'Stasya? Tell us a story.'

11

ALEKSIS

HOW LONG WOULD it take for Rihard to realise he'd been told only part of the truth? How long before the man understood that asking Aleksis to deal with things meant a loss of the control that mattered so badly to him? The journey was long, and it would be slow with carts. They'd need overnight stops along the way to sleep, to rest the horses, to pick up fresh supplies. If they forced the pace, the injured would suffer for it. Would Rihard send men after them? Might the Commander jump on a horse and pursue them in person? Unlikely. Rihard had lost at least eight of his guards in the fire. Several of the village men who'd been working alongside them had been killed. Many of the survivors were weakened. They'd be unable to go on with the backbreaking work of tree felling and hauling. Rihard had been too angry with the chaotic situation, too distraught at the unravelling of his plans to think the thing through.

On the night of the fire, the Commander had been staying at the home of a certain accommodating woman who lived some distance from the main settlement. He'd learned late about the unfolding disaster and seemed all too ready to step back from both the flood of injured people and the voices of angry ones. After that scene in the village hall Rihard had given his deputies some vague orders then retreated, perhaps back to the woman in question. He'd known Aleksis was planning a return to Dragon's Keep at some point. But he would not be happy when he woke to realise the convoy had already departed. He would be furious when he found Stasya gone as well, even though he'd seemed to understand why Lady Elisabeta would be interested in the girl. With luck, Rihard would simply wait for further communications, pushing neither his own men nor the local folk to keep working on the impossible task. In the aftermath of the fire, those capable of labour should be helping the farmer rebuild his barn. They should be assisting with care of the injured, not only men and women, but also farm stock. Rihard's deputies were capable men. If the fellow would leave the practical decisions to them, something might yet be salvaged from the sorry situation. But Aleksis wouldn't be standing around in the vain hope Rihard would see sense. Stasya had spoken out boldly. It was clear she'd had no idea what a risk she was taking. There must be no repetition of that.

They left two injured men at Sweetwater, where there were local women with healing skills. They travelled on to the larger settlement of Vita's Hope. No physician there either, but Aleksis and Matiss went to talk to the town elders, while the rest of them, under Pavel's direction, made camp for the night. It turned out an old man who lived in the settlement had once been infirmarian in a religious order. Why he'd left the order, nobody said. Thrown out? Lost his faith? That didn't matter. They called him in to take a look at the injured men, and Aleksis was impressed by his practical manner. The fellow knew how to treat burns and the aftermath of breathing in smoke. It was agreed that three of the remaining injured would stay in Vita's Hope, which meant the only invalids still with the convoy were Aleksis's own men. And the goatherd. The old man, still known as Father Mikelis, had recommended that Lukas also remain there, travel by cart being ill-advised for a man in his condition. The elders would have been happy to take him along with the others. But Lukas refused to stay behind unless Stasya, too, was staying. And Lady Elisabeta had demanded to see Stasya in person.

The injured were taken away under the supervision of Father Mikelis. Stabling was found for the horses. The remaining members of the convoy settled in their camp, gathering by a small, well-contained fire to eat a hearty meal provided by the local people. At a certain point, Stasya drew Aleksis aside, where others could not overhear.

'What happens to Irina?' she asked straight out, not bothering with *Master Aleksis* or other niceties. 'You see how she is. Not burned or otherwise injured, but… not herself. Could she stay in these people's care? She's… she's broken.'

It was true; the woman was a shell of her former self. She did not speak; she did not want to eat or drink; she had no will for anything. He thought only Stasya's care was keeping the baker alive. The suggestion made perfect sense. But…

'It would be irresponsible of me to take you on this journey without another woman to accompany you.' It sounded rather pompous; he saw that reflected on Stasya's face. But it was true. A young woman alone, travelling with so many men… it was wrong. And they were friends, weren't they, she and Irina? 'She can be cared for at Dragon's Keep. Well cared for. There is a court physician.'

Stasya's lips tightened. She made to say something, then stopped herself.

'Speak up. Say what you want to say.'

'Irina is weighed down with grief. She's lost the last family she had in the world. Father Mikelis and the folk of this settlement would surely be a better choice than a court physician.'

'Perhaps. Or she might bolt for home, despite her fragile state, thinking this place close enough. I cannot take that risk.'

Stasya looked at him. The light from the bonfire showed her features in gold and shadow, almost like a painting. An odd creature. He never knew what she would say next. She'd told stories on the way, many stories, to take the minds of her friends off their hardship. The noise from hooves and cart wheels had made it difficult to hear, but he'd noticed how the men tried to ride closer to that cart so they could listen.

'Oh, you care about her now?' Her tone was unusually hard. 'A show of compassion. A pity that did not happen earlier, before you worked her to exhaustion. Before the fire. Before she lost her only son.'

Briefly, Aleksis was lost for words. He could have pointed out that it was not he who had forced Irina to bake for Rihard's men. He had not caused the fire. He had not suggested her son join the fight to extinguish it; had he known about that, he would have tried to keep the boy away. He could have reminded Stasya that it was Rihard who had set the whole chain of disasters in action. He could… but no. Rihard had acted under the Ruler's orders. Lady Elisabeta was responsible, though she could hardly have foreseen such a disastrous result. And he was Lady Elisabeta's adviser. Her trusted senior adviser. They'd started out well, he and she, when Elisabeta was new to her position of authority and finding her feet. He could not say the same for more recent times. 'The baker will accompany us to Dragon's Keep,' he said. 'If you're worried about her on the journey, or about the goatherd, please draw your concerns to Matiss's attention.'

Stasya turned her back and walked away without a word. Shoulders squared, head held high. He watched as she returned to Irina's side, in the warmth of the fire but not too close; as she coaxed Irina to sip water, to nibble on a piece of bread; as she talked, made gestures. She was telling another story, he knew it. But over the sounds of the encampment, he could hear nothing.

12

STASYA

VITA'S HOPE HAD meant noise, people, questions. But at least those folk had understood. They'd gone out of their way to help. Everyone knew what the Commander had done in Heartwood, though the arrival of Aleksis's party was the first they'd heard of the fire, and the first they'd seen of its terrible human cost. Father Mikelis had seemed a good soul, capable and skilled. She'd wished Lukas would stay there to be looked after properly. As for Irina, nobody really knew how to help her. Stasya kept trying without much success. Stories calmed Irina, but there was no real sign that she understood them. Flip squeezed up close, licking her hands or face. Sometimes Irina stroked the dog, but her gaze was fixed on something beyond the camp, or the cart, or the changing land they passed through. Beyond this day, this place.

The road took them on. There were forested areas: lovely, green, full of life. Birds flew overhead, calling. But it was not Heartwood. It was not home. There were broad lakes, shining in the spring sun: sky captured in water, sheer magic. Fields with cattle, sheep, sometimes goats. Miles and miles of road.

Other stops, other settlements, larger even than Vita's Hope. Sometimes they were halted before they could ride in. Men in uniforms threw questions at Aleksis: his purpose, his destination, the strange cargo of damaged people in his carts. He didn't offer much in the way of explanations, simply identified himself as the Ruler's adviser and showed them some sort of token he wore around his neck. The men waved the convoy onward. That brought back a memory: the Commander ripping off her amber owl as if it were his to take. He'd never given it back. Did he not understand that had been like tearing away part of her very self, something that made her whole and strong and hopeful? And there'd been all those questions. She wished now that she hadn't told him and Aleksis the story. How could men like that understand? Now, every mile of the journey took her further from Heartwood, further from her home and haven, and further from the amber owl. Perhaps it had been burned in the fire. Wouldn't it have been in the Commander's quarters? If only she could perform a ritual. Questions were building up inside her, more each day. Questions she couldn't ask Aleksis, or even Matiss.

She learned a little from listening to the guards talk when they were camped for the night. Dragon's Keep was the Ruler's home and headquarters. Not a house, a fortress. Many folk lived there, not only the Ruler and her household, but guards and serving people too. There were stables; kennels for dogs; space for farm animals. Someone spoke of prisoners, but when they realised she could hear them they started talking about something else. Dragon's Keep had a wall around it, and a settlement beyond the wall, and the whole thing was on the shore of a lake called Brightwater. That settlement would surely be bigger than any of those they had passed through so far. Dragon's Keep would be full of people, full of voices and noises and activity. The idea of being stuck there turned her stomach. She wanted to be a hedgehog, able to roll into a ball and show only spikes to the world. Or a fish, to dive into that lake and swim away, her ears open only to the swish and splash and bubble of water. Or a bird, a magpie perhaps, flying in and out at will. Content within its own small tribe, unconcerned with the ways of humankind. Except, of course, for those rare and precious times when the two could help one another. When some kind of magic happened and they understood one another. The memory of that moment was still strong in her mind, when she'd lifted the bird free from the palings and felt it move in her hands. Knowing it lived. *Fly free*, she thought. *Live your life, friend. May Heartwood stand strong and stay safe for you, and for your brothers and sisters.* But as the cart wheels rumbled and squeaked, and as the passengers were jolted up and down, and as the long days passed, Heartwood was moving further and further away.

Her moon-bleeding started when they were still on the road. Awkward, even though she had those strips of linen in her pack. Aleksis did stop the convoy from time to time during each day's journey, not only to rest the horses but so folk could relieve themselves under trees or behind bushes or stone walls, or openly in the case of some of the men. At those times, Irina would get out of the cart, and the two of them would find a private spot together, not too far off. There would always be a guard keeping an eye on their general location without actually looking at them. Should either of them have attempted an escape, they would soon have been halted. As things stood, Irina did not have the will to run, and Aleksis must know Stasya would not try; she would not leave either of her friends behind.

So, blood on her clothing, and several more days of bleeding to come. Somehow, she had to deal with it. They seldom stopped long enough to wash anything, though they'd spent two nights in Vita's Hope and managed to get some items clean and dry. She'd have to talk to someone, ask for privacy, ask for an extra stop, maybe. She wasn't going to strip off any clothing while riding in the cart, in full view. Matiss was probably the best choice. And the right time was now, with the convoy halted and the horses unharnessed and led to a nearby pond to drink. She helped Irina down off the cart and rummaged in her bag for what she needed. Where was Matiss? Ah, over there near an old stone building that might once have been a pigsty. It looked as if he was on his own.

Stasya whispered to Irina. 'Wait here for me. I have to talk to Matiss.' She remembered how Irina had helped her when she had her first bleeding at twelve years old. By then, Grandmother was gone, and although Stasya had understood what the blood meant, she'd struggled to cope with the mess and the awkwardness and the sore belly that came with it. Irina had explained everything calmly; helped her have a warm bath; provided a supply of the linen bindings and pads, and made sure she knew to use them. Stasya wondered, now, if Irina had longed for a daughter of her own.

'Matiss? May I speak to you privately?'

She explained as best she could, using plain words rather than referring to *women's troubles* as she'd heard some folk do. It felt strange to be telling him something she would have hesitated to tell Lukas.

'We should be there the day after tomorrow, or the next day,' Matiss said, as if such requests were not at all out of the ordinary. 'I'll make sure you aren't disturbed unduly. We can give you some linen bandages, if those will suit the purpose.' He scrutinised her, as if to judge whether she might suddenly faint or be sick. 'You look a bit pale,' he observed. 'More stops tomorrow, and for longer. There's a place we know, not so very far off. A farmhouse. You should be able to wash out a few things and dry them by the fire. And take a bath if you want.' A pause. 'I'm sorry. Awkward timing for you.'

'Please make sure nobody watches us when we're… attending to matters. We won't bolt. I can promise you that.' She glanced back. Irina was still waiting by the cart, with Flip in close attendance. Pavel, whose golden hair made him easy to recognise even at a distance, was helping Lukas down. The men had been good with Lukas, taking it in turns to make sure he relieved himself, stretched, walked a little. Pavel in particular had taken time to talk with him. For that she was grateful. Maybe, just maybe, when they reached Dragon's Keep with its court physician, Lukas could be made well again. Along with the burns, he bore many bruises, and that was not to mention the dimming of his brightness and the loss of his hope. His old self was all but gone. The Commander had much to answer for. 'And thank you,' she made herself say. In another world, in another life, this man might have been a friend.

'I'll need to mention it to Aleksis,' Matiss said. 'Not the men; they'll be glad of a slower pace, as will the horses, and never mind the reason for it.'

There was a stream not far off, and plenty of cover. Matiss himself kept watch while the two women performed their basic ablutions. Flip disappeared into the bushes; with luck, she would catch herself a meal of some kind. For a little, Irina watched as Stasya struggled with the linen strips. Then, abruptly, her trancelike state broke.

'Not like that, Stasya – here, let me help.' The baker's fingers shook a little as she folded and twisted and knotted the cloth, then helped Stasya make the necessary adjustments to her clothing. Today she was wearing the borrowed, too-small gown. There was a bloodstain on the skirt. Irina ripped off a short length of linen, dipped it into the stream, and sponged the stain hard until the mark was all but invisible. Now her hands were steady. 'There,' she said. 'Not perfect, but it'll do. If anyone asks, tell them you slipped in the mud.'

Stasya had tears in her eyes. She had thought her friend lost forever in the shadow of her grief. 'Thank you, Irina. Matiss said they might stop for a while at a farm, so we can get things washed and dried.'

Irina looked her up and down. 'Your hair could do with a good wash,' she said. 'And isn't that gown one of mine?'

Stasya didn't want to think of that rushed departure, the hasty stuffing of items in her bag, the leaving of Heartwood without any sort of farewell. She didn't want to think of Tomas, let alone speak of him before Irina was ready. 'I didn't get the chance to go home that night,' she said. 'They told me to borrow what I needed and take some things for you. Oh.' How could she have forgotten something so important, so vital? Something as precious to Irina as the amber owl was to her, if not for the same reason.

'Oh, what?'

'I have something else of yours. In my bag… let me find it for you.' She knew exactly where it was: right at the bottom, wrapped in a beautiful silk scarf she'd seen Irina wearing on special occasions, a splendour of swirling blue and green and violet that made the baker look like a lovely flower. 'I should have given you this earlier. Here.' She put the ring in Irina's hand.

Irina slipped the ring on her finger. Closed her eyes. Stood there perfectly still for a few moments, then put her face in her hands and burst into tears. Her body was wracked with sobbing, as if the sorrow held back for the weary days of the journey had now, at last, been set free. Stasya put her arms around her friend; Irina wept against her shoulder. At a slight distance she could see the tall form of Matiss, standing under a tree, unmoving. She had never considered that the Ruler's men must have homes, families, lives beyond the cruel work they did. Now, the thought came to her that Matiss might have a wife, daughters, sisters. 'It's all right, it's all right, cry all you want,' she murmured, knowing it wasn't all right, not for Irina, not for herself, not for the folk of Heartwood or for the forest. Who could mend the wrongs that had led to this? Who could change the greed and cruelty, the disregard for what was right and good? And yet, in the middle of it all, there was one man who practised kindness.

'You're a true friend, Stasya,' Irina said between sobs. She scrubbed her cheeks and pushed her hair back from her face in an effort at control. 'Henrik – my husband – had this made especially for me.' She touched the ring; took a steadying breath. 'Do you think... do you think they are together now, somewhere, my son and his father? A comfort to each other in the next world? If I could believe that, if I could... It might not feel so wrong to go on...'

Flip chose that moment to emerge from the bushes, licking her lips. Clearly her mission had been accomplished.

'I do believe it,' Stasya said. 'None of us can know what form that world takes. But I believe they are watching over you, Irina. Guardian spirits, who might be anything. A bird in flight. A ripple on the water. New leaves opening on a tree. A smile of welcome. They are always with you, if you know how to look.' She had often felt this about Grandmother, whose wisdom had still seemed close even after she was laid in her grave. 'We'd best go back, if you're ready.'

As they walked back, she wondered if Aleksis had a family. She could not imagine it, though he must have had parents, as she had. Perhaps, like her, he had no memory of them. Were they watching over him now, as Irina's lost ones surely were over her? And if so, what would they think of their son? He was the Ruler's personal adviser, young as he was. That might be seen as some kind of achievement, at least in the world of courts and armies. But in the end, hadn't he been in charge of the whole sorry situation at Heartwood? That would make the shades of his family turn away from him. Surely, such a man would always walk alone.

SHE HAD IMAGINED that the whole convoy would camp at the farm Matiss had mentioned. But it wasn't like that. They stopped in early afternoon, by a stream, and the men dismounted, tethered their horses and began to set up camp. The man who was driving their cart got down, and so did

Stasya, ready to help her friends. But Aleksis was suddenly beside her. 'I'll take you on to the farmhouse,' he said in a voice held deliberately low. 'The three of you. It's not far. Get back up.' Too surprised to respond, she did as she was told. Aleksis climbed onto the carter's seat, flicked the reins, and drove the two horses quickly back to the road. For someone whose work involved a lot of talking and giving orders, he seemed surprisingly expert.

True, it wasn't far; not as the crow flew. But the way was neither straight nor simple. Aleksis drove the cart around many turns, onto more than one branching way, and Stasya began to wonder if it was all some kind of trick, and he was taking them, not to a comfortable farmhouse, but to some other, darker place. Flip seemed unperturbed, though she sent Stasya some mind-pictures that worried her. It was clear she wanted to be a bird, to fly ahead through this wooded area and investigate. Stasya responded with a picture of her own: Flip the dog securely in the cart, exercising patience. The last thing she needed right now was for Aleksis to see Flip change.

The farm gates were closed. Stasya got down and went to open them without being asked, and Aleksis drove the horses through. She was still fastening the loop of rope that held the gate secure when a large dog came hurtling down the track toward her, barking an ear-splitting challenge. Flip jumped onto the seat beside Aleksis, hackles up. Aleksis was saying something, but the farm dog's voice drowned out his words. Stasya turned to face the hound. She opened her mind to its thoughts, which were full of the duty to guard, to protect. It was doing its job, and doing it well. She raised her hands, palms forward: a slow gesture of peace. Sent an image of herself and the big dog together, sitting on a mat before a hearth fire, her hands stroking its shaggy pelt. Pictured it laying its head on her knee, licking her fingers, sighing and falling asleep. *I will not hurt you. You are a good dog.* She did not look the creature straight in the eye. Neither did she turn away. The dog quieted but held its ground.

Aleksis got down from his seat. Flip jumped down too, running up to the farm dog without hesitation, though it was many times her size. 'Good boy, Rusty,' Aleksis said. 'Remember me?'

It seemed Rusty did. Perhaps it was the combination of Stasya's mind-pictures, and Flip's confident trust, and the dawning recognition that there was someone here whom the dog had met before, but Rusty stood calm and quiet while Aleksis walked forward and offered his hand to be sniffed. Flip, meanwhile, had been distracted by some interesting smell in the long grass nearby. And now, coming down the track from the farmhouse was a sturdily built woman clad in a homespun gown with a bright red apron over the top. Her greying hair was pulled back in a scarf both practical and decorative; its vivid stripes of red, yellow and blue suggested an exotic bird. 'Aleks!' she exclaimed, beaming. 'This is a surprise.' Her gaze moved from Aleksis to Stasya to the waiting horses and the cart with its two occupants. 'You'd better come on up. Is the gate secure?'

Stasya nodded. Aleks. These must be folk who knew him well. Family, perhaps? That seemed unlikely. Did a son of farmers get to become the Ruler's senior adviser? Maybe, here, she would find answers. Maybe what she discovered would help her when she had to face the Ruler in person. That prospect terrified her. How would she know what to say or how to say it? What if she said the things she really felt, the way she had when the Commander confronted her in the village hall? What if her words dried up altogether?

The woman was called Laima. Stasya liked that; it was the name of a forest spirit in an old story. Her husband was Ivo. Aleksis gave them the briefest of explanations – they were heading for Dragon's Keep, they all needed rest and an opportunity to wash themselves and get some clothing clean and dry – and both Laima and Ivo accepted it without further questions, other than to ask for the names of their unexpected visitors. Laima took Stasya and Irina into a kitchen area and sat them down beside a big warm stove, then bustled off and was heard giving someone directions about hot water, cloths, salves. Ivo and Aleksis guided Lukas away to some other part of the farmhouse; Stasya had to trust that he was in good hands. It was, at least, better than the constant jolting of the cart. She felt as if she had bruises on bruises. How much worse must it be for Lukas, injured before they even began this journey?

It was so wonderful to be warm. It felt blissful to be out of the cart and off the road. But Stasya knew she must not drop her guard, tempting as it was; she could not waste time simply enjoying the comfort of this place. A bath, yes. That was entirely necessary, and after two younger women, perhaps Laima's daughters, carried in a tub and filled it with deliciously warm water, she did allow herself to stay in a little longer than was strictly required to get clean. Irina had her turn. Laima returned with garments which, if not a perfect fit, were perfectly adequate for both women to wear, and she provided Stasya with further materials to deal with the bleeding and a bag to keep them in. They brushed and braided each other's hair. One of the young women brought hot tea and pastries on a tray, then the two of them left. Perhaps they were farm workers, not daughters. Stasya did not ask.

'And you'll want these things washed and dried, mmm?' Laima asked as they ate and drank. The dirty clothes lay in a heap in the corner. Stasya could hear no sound from elsewhere in the house; where had they taken Lukas?

'I'll do that,' she said. 'As soon as I've finished my tea. You just need to show me where. The sooner I can get them hung up, the sooner they'll be dry. There's a good breeze today.'

Laima gave her an assessing look, then nodded. 'If you're happy to do the job, I'll show you where everything is. But you must be tired. Rest first if you like; there's a room where you can both lie down for a while.' She glanced at Flip, who was cleaning up stray crumbs of pastry from the tiled floor. 'And your little friend, of course.'

'Irina might like a rest.'

'No, I'll help you with the laundry. You don't need to do everything. But I wouldn't say no to a sleep after that, unless there's some other way I can be helpful. It would be bliss to lie down somewhere comfortable.' In the end, all three women dealt with the dirty clothes, soaking, scrubbing, rinsing, wringing and hanging the garments from a line strung between two trees, where they would catch both the breeze and the spring sunshine. Then Irina retreated to rest, and Stasya, looking out over green fields dotted with grazing sheep, and copses of birch and elder, and a narrow winding pathway that ran beside the stream, knew there was one thing she really needed to do. 'I'd like to take Flip for a walk, if that's all right. I won't disturb the stock. I grew up in a farming settlement.' Why was it that with some people, like Laima who was a virtual stranger, it was quite easy to talk and with others almost impossible? 'Go ahead, Stasya. Keep to the pathways and make sure your dog doesn't go near the bull; he's rather edgy at present.'

'Laima? You saw Lukas, who came in with us. He badly needs his injuries tended to. Burns and other things. I've been doing my best, but it's not enough. Where did they…?'

Laima put a reassuring hand on Stasya's shoulder. 'Ivo's good at these things. You can trust him. He can mend animals when they're hurt, and he can do the same for his own kind. No magical cures, sadly; just good common sense and years of practice.'

'Thank you.' She wanted to ask how they knew Aleksis; what the link was. But that would be one question too many. 'I'll be back in time to help with anything else that needs doing.' A treacherous part of her wished they could stay here for longer than one night. The place felt like a safe harbour, a refuge from the storm. But she had to go on. Even supposing she could escape from the convoy, there could be no returning to Heartwood, not while the Commander's forces were there. And these people, good souls as they seemed to be, were not offering her a home, a place in their household, work for her hands, even though she could be genuinely useful on a farm such as this. She didn't belong among folk. She never had. She'd always be the odd one out. 'Keep moving,' she muttered to herself as Flip ran ahead along the pathway. 'Keep on going, even if you're scared and mixed-up and nothing makes much sense.'

A walk. The simplest of things, and yet it could lift the heart so. This was no great forest. There were no rocky outcrops to climb, no streams to leap over or wade through, no trees the equal of the Ancestor. But it was beautiful. So many small and wondrous things: sun on the pale trunks of the birches; the rustle of the breeze in their silvery leaves; a warble of birdsong from above, a greeting that had her smiling and waving a hand toward the singer. Flip was here, there, everywhere, intoxicated by a multitude of new scents. That was no surprise after the long days in the confinement of the cart. She tried to convey to the little dog that it was still best she not change her form. Aleksis must not know. Nobody must know. But perhaps, now, just for a little…

The response was quick. Flip dived into some bushes, and a very small bird, a tawny-feathered brambling, flew out almost immediately. Stasya showed Flip an image of herself calling and the bird flying straight to her, a dog again the moment she landed at Stasya's feet. 'Make sure you don't forget,' Stasya murmured.

The bull was by the gate of his field, separated from his cows and looking far from pleased with the situation. The brambling flew to him without hesitation, alighting on his back. Stasya sucked in a breath, wondering if Flip had interpreted the warning as applying to her dog form only. As it was, the bull did not seem especially disturbed by her presence, only twitching his ears a little, and that made Stasya bolder. She was under the trees, at some distance from the creature, and had intended to back away and seek another path. Instead, she opened her mind, not only to the bird that was Flip, but also to the powerful animal she had chosen as a temporary perch. *You are such a handsome boy. Strong and fine. Soon they will let you go to your wives. Wait only a little.* The bull raised his head and let out a bellow. Not anger. Not distress. Pure pride. And longing, a deep and powerful physical longing that was uncomfortable to share. Stasya closed her eyes, making herself breathe slowly, then gave the bull a nod of recognition and went on her way. A moment later the brambling alighted on her shoulder, its weight so slight she hardly felt it. They moved through the birch grove, and there, under a patch of open sky, was a perfectly round pool, bordered by pale stones. The brambling flew down to the water's edge. By the time she landed, she had become a small owl.

'Mmm. You and I have the same idea,' murmured Stasya. For a ritual did not need fire; it could be performed in many different ways, and this pool was surely a place of wonder. There was time. Aleksis was occupied at the farm and Irina was resting. Laima knew where she was. Lukas was not yet capable of such a walk. Time to risk it, even if there were no insights to be had. Even if what she saw was as alarming as that vision of fire and death, a horror that had later become truth.

First she must gather some items to assist her. She must find tokens for the four elements, and somehow show what wisdom she was seeking. No amber owl this time. That most powerful and beloved of symbols might never return to her. But there was the real owl, big-eyed, feathered in patterns of fawn and brown, her small form neat and complete. As Stasya regarded her, Flip plucked out a single breast feather and held it in her beak, fixing her eyes on her companion. 'Thank you,' Stasya said with a grave nod.

One element they had in abundance. And among the stones by the pond, there was one with a shallow indentation at the top. She scooped up water in cupped hands and poured it into the hollow, making a tiny version of the pond. 'Thank you.' Air. Water.

Now Earth. She took off her shoes and stockings and moved barefoot back toward the trees, stepping with care lest she crush some beetle or hopper or many-legged wriggling creature. She took a small handful of soil, a fallen leaf, and a birch catkin, whose seeds might perhaps be planted later. 'Thank you.'

She would not make fire. How else to honour its blessing? Without the recognition of all four elements, the ritual would be incomplete and there might be no insights. Stasya arranged her items the way Grandmother had shown her. Water in the west; earth in the north; air in the east, where Flip stood by her feather gift as grave and still as an owl of stone or wood. Stasya paced a small circle around the offerings, and for each she spoke words of greeting and welcome, acknowledging the elements' blessings. As she came to the south, whose quarter bore no symbol, the clouds parted and a ray of sunshine struck down between the birches, casting a warm blessing on the ritual and its participants. Acceptance. Acknowledgement. Stasya bowed her head. 'Thank you.'

Then a time of slow breathing, of opening the mind to visions. And when she was ready, the request. 'I am troubled by this journey. I fear what lies ahead for me and my friends, and for my beloved forest of Heartwood. And for all forests, for all the years ahead. I am only one person. How can I be strong enough? How can I stand up for what I know to be right?'

She waited, listening to the music of grove and pond. Birds chirping; the gurgling call of a frog; the whisper of leaves. The air was sweet with the scent of flowering chamomile, and the sunshine hinted at the summer to come. Where would she be then? *Focus, Stasya. Make your mind still.*

A ripple on the pond's shining surface. Then, shockingly, the image as before: the fire, the screams, the smoke. She forced herself to hold still, to keep her eyes open. It was blessedly shorter than last time. Images of Heartwood in the aftermath. Nothing of herself, or Irina, or Lukas. Nothing of Matiss or Aleksis or Pavel, or any of the men who had left Heartwood with them. Briefly, there was Jurgis, looking old and weak, being tended to by his wife and daughter. At home; that was something. The Commander, up by the forest, shouting. A crew of men hacking at trees, men who looked hollowed out, as if haunted by demons. A team of exhausted horses harnessed to a huge log, dragging it down the hill. Stasya felt their weariness in every part of her body. This was beyond tears. It was beyond belief. And yet, she knew it for truth.

A shadow seemed to come over the image, as if dark clouds had filled the sky above Heartwood, though here by the pond the spring sun still painted the birches in white and silver. Then, in the water, Stasya saw the woman from her earlier vision, a crone whose face was clearer now. Not her grandmother. A stranger with calm features and clear grey eyes and long hair the colour of thistledown. She held out her hands in welcome, then beckoned to Stasya, *Come, come!* Behind her was a steep rock face and what looked like a cave entry. And another figure, a tall person in a hooded cape, standing so still they might have been part of the rocks. The figure turned, but before she could see their face the vision faded and was gone.

She sat awhile, breathing slowly. There must be some meaning in this, some answer. Maybe it was only, *Keep on going*. Maybe whatever was to be done, she must do alone, since the vision had contained nothing of her friends or of the men who had taken her away from Heartwood. Perhaps her journey did not end with Dragon's Keep or the Ruler, Lady Elisabeta. Wherever that place of the cave was, she knew in her bones that it was far from any human settlement.

Flip was a dog again, pushing her head into Stasya's side, prodding her to get up and go. She was right; stay too long away and Aleksis might come looking for her, thinking she was trying to escape his custody. She walked back slowly, taking time to remember some of the stories about Heartwood and, in particular, the huge rock formation of the Hermit. Somewhere in that lore were the secrets that fuelled the Commander's quest to make a path there, even if it meant the ruination of the great forest. Among the tales of fey folk and evil spirits, of treasure and adventure, love and loss, lay the key to a mystery. Perhaps the amber owl, her own lost treasure, was itself a key.

Not long now before they reached Dragon's Keep and people started asking her questions again. Questions she did not want to answer.

13

ALEKSIS

THERE WERE PROTOCOLS to be observed when meeting with the Ruler, even for her senior adviser. He waited for Elisabeta's serving woman, Paula, to tap on the door to the council chamber then, after a carefully judged pause, open it a crack. 'Master Aleksis to see you, my lady.'

'Enter, Master Aleksis.' The Ruler sounded, if anything, rather weary. Aleksis came in, closing the door behind him. He'd bathed and changed into appropriate clothing for court, formal garments in cream and dark blue in place of his travel-stained riding clothes, soft leather shoes instead of riding boots. 'My lady.' He gave the formal bow appropriate to such occasions.

Lady Elisabeta was not seated in her comfortable chair by the fire. Instead, she was at the head of the long table that could, if required, accommodate twenty or more. She offered a stiff nod of recognition. 'Master Aleksis. Time for a talk, I think. It's been some while since your most recent message from Heartwood reached me. I replied promptly, requesting that you return as soon as possible with this young woman you mentioned. I had expected you at court much earlier.'

'It is a long way, my lady, and as we had injured men with us, we had to bring carts. That mode of travel is notoriously slow.'

'Injured men, yes. I observed them coming in. And not only the girl, but another woman and a… goatherd? I'm told you've requested the services of the court physician, not only for our own wounded, but also for this person.' Her brows went up.

'The circumstances were such that I could not send a full report from Heartwood, my lady. You'll have gathered that Commander Rihard's mission went badly awry.' Aleksis refrained from reminding her that his own advice, some while ago, had been never to put Rihard in charge of a mission again. 'Such a report could only be delivered by myself, in person. In a nutshell, my lady, a great deal of damage has been done to the village of Heartwood, its inhabitants and the forested area close by. As for the mission itself, I'd have thought anyone could see the terrain makes it impossible for a path such as Rihard described to be created. Many men would be lost in the attempt, for no gain at all.'

Lady Elisabeta's expression gave nothing away. 'Sit down, Master Aleksis,' she said with cool clarity. 'Some mead?' On a smaller table, close to that cushioned chair, there stood a flask and two cups.

'Thank you, no.' He seated himself on a bench, facing her. 'If you want further details, my lady, I can provide them. You mentioned an interest in Stasya some time ago, after I first reported back from Heartwood with certain observations. After I sent that message, the situation deteriorated quickly. Rihard continued to work the local folk too hard; his response to any sign of insubordination was to mete out severe punishment. Stasya's ability intrigued him; her habit of speaking out angered him. I believed her to be at risk and decided to bring her here. But it would have been inappropriate for a young woman to travel so far in company with a convoy of men. She needed another woman for support. Irina was the village baker; Stasya worked for her.'

An icy pause. 'And the goatherd?'

'A friend of Stasya's. A fire in the village claimed the lives of many. The goatherd was badly injured and needs expert medical attention. Stasya would not have come without him.'

'Ah.' There was a note of interest in the Ruler's voice at last. 'More than a friend, perhaps?'

'That, I can't tell you. A close friend, at least.'

'That might provide a useful bargaining tool, should the girl be disinclined to share her secrets,' the Ruler said, rising and moving over to the hearth. With her back to Aleksis, she added, 'I wish to speak to this young woman as soon as possible, Aleksis. I know you've had a long ride. In recognition of that, we'll wait until tomorrow.'

Tomorrow. Aleksis bit back the words that sprang to his lips. It had perhaps been a mistake to sit as he had, his back perfectly straight, his hands relaxed, as if he had not just spent most of the day on horseback. A royal adviser learns how to create the right impression. In this case, competence. Restraint. 'I believe she does have useful information for us,' he said. 'My advice is that you allow her significant time to rest and recover before she's asked to speak.'

Elisabeta turned a certain look on him. At such moments, one became acutely aware that she was a person of great power. 'Significant time. What does that mean, precisely?'

'A few days, at least. The opportunity to be out of doors, as that seems to lift Stasya's spirits. If you want her to answer questions, it's worth remembering that.'

'This is making no sense to me, Master Aleksis. I have never known you to waste my time before. You are a person of authority. She is some village girl, now, it seems, entirely dependent on our goodwill. You have questions; she has answers. Why would she not speak up?'

There was plenty he could say. But he had something more effective in hand. 'It's worth going about this with care, my lady. Let me show you something.'

He rose and went to stand by her, unfastening the soft kidskin pouch on his belt. He loosened the drawstring and fished out its contents, placing the amber owl carefully on the small table, where the firelight caught its glow. 'I think you understood the reference in my message, though I did not specifically mention amber. Rihard took this from Stasya by force; she believes it to still be in his custody.'

Lady Elisabeta took the owl up, turning it one way then the other. 'This is exceptionally fine. How could a farm girl come by such a treasure? Surely she has stolen this?'

'From what I have observed, stealing is not in her nature, my lady. She chose not to answer a straight question as to its origin, but instead told a story. Stasya seems more comfortable talking that way. In her story, a young man and a young woman found amber washed up by a forest stream. The young man carved this token as a gift for the young woman. She did not specify where that was, but it was well known in the village that she and the goatherd, Lukas, frequently went walking in Heartwood Forest, venturing further than other folk dared. It's said there are many such tales about the place, some of them very old.'

Elisabeta simply looked at him.

'As I said earlier,' he went on, 'we'd be well advised to proceed with care, my lady. Much hangs on Stasya's response to your questions. We're not long arrived here. Wait a few days and you will get better answers.'

The Ruler heaved a sigh as she set the amber owl down again. 'You know what's at stake here, Aleksis. I must have plans in place before the next Grand Council. That may seem far away, but the days pass quickly, and I must strengthen my position. Lord Kasimir was well-regarded by the leaders of our neighbouring states; I don't need to tell you that. I, on the other hand, am seen by some as a raw newcomer, almost an interloper, and there are certain parties who will not hesitate to take advantage if I show any sign of weakness. A large deposit of such a valuable trading commodity would help set us up as a credible ally. You know, and I know, that the amber in this trinket is of extremely high value. If we find the source, we might form alliances with more distant trading partners. Shore up our borders. This girl is here at court; she and her friend are well accommodated in the servants' quarters. Warm, fed, comfortable. It's evident that she knows pathways through the forest and how to use them. And something more. I heard that she has an unusual gift with animals. It's not hard to see how useful that might be on such a journey. She may be able to guide a party all the way to the Hermit. It's in her best interest to tell us the full truth. Without delay.'

'With respect, my lady, if you want the full truth, you should wait longer. Three days, at least. I think it highly likely that too much pressure will send Stasya into complete silence.'

'Two days. I won't argue the point any further. Arrange what you want for these folk in the meantime, but they're to be watched by a guard day and night, all three of them, and they don't leave the servants' quarters. You may go, Master Aleksis. Speak to the girl. Make sure she understands what is required.'

Aleksis rose to his feet. 'Yes, my lady. And...' He glanced at the amber owl. 'By your leave, I'll put that safely in storage.'

'Make sure it's locked up securely. We'll need it.'

'My lady.' He executed the required bow, returned the owl to its pouch and walked out, closing the door behind him.

14

STASYA

DRAGON'S KEEP WAS full of activity, full of noise, full of rules she didn't understand or couldn't see the point of. There always seemed to be a guard around, watching her, but she saw none of the familiar faces. No Matiss, no Pavel, not one of those who had accompanied them on the journey. Aleksis had been there earlier, talking to a woman called Biruta, who was in charge of the serving people. So many of them – what did they all do? Flip was scared at first, shivering, wanting to be carried, which was understandable considering the crowd of folk. She might easily have been trampled.

They took Lukas away. When she tried to protest, nobody would listen. Later, Biruta explained that men and women had separate areas within the servants' quarters and mingled only at meal times or if their duty required it. There were some married couples among them; those folk slept elsewhere, in their own quarters. When Stasya asked about Lukas, whether he would get proper treatment for his burns, whether he would have somewhere quiet to sleep, Biruta enquired whether she was related to Lukas – his sister, his betrothed? And when

Stasya said no, the housekeeper responded with, 'Then it's none of your business.'

The place was a maze of hallways and storage areas and chambers used for various purposes, most of which were a mystery to her. The stone walls were pierced, here and there, by narrow windows which let in both sunlight and cold drafts; these provided Stasya with glimpses of the world outside. On the second day, standing close to one of these windows, she smelled rain. She was tempted to let Flip fly out in bird form, if only to bring back the reassurance that trees and grasses and wild things were still within reach beyond the fortress walls. But she could not risk that, even though Flip herself was restless, eager to be out of doors. How long would they be shut up in this place? How long could they survive it?

Dragon's Keep had extensive, busy kitchens. Even in the servants' quarters the meals were substantial. Stasya fed Flip from her own platter and nobody objected. There was an outdoor privy with a small paved area beside it, set too low to allow any view over the wall. Biruta had made it clear that Stasya must take Flip out there several times a day to relieve herself. Even that small respite from the confines of the house was welcome. It was hardly a place to linger, but at least a person could see the sky.

Irina was too quiet. At Laima and Ivo's farm she had seemed to be emerging from the first shock of her terrible loss. Here, with endless time to think and remember, she was again shut in, not wanting to move, not wanting to talk, barely able to listen even to words of kindness. It did not help either her or Stasya that the female servants slept in one long, gloomy chamber on pallets set so close a person could stretch out and touch the hand of their neighbour, should they ever wish to do so. The space to store personal items was minimal. It was just as well, Stasya thought grimly, that they'd come with so little. At night, Irina pulled her blanket over her head and lay as if dead. But Stasya knew she did not sleep. Whenever she herself woke, which was often, she heard Irina's soft sobbing in the dark.

For two days and two nights they were left more or less alone, save for the near-constant presence of folk about their own business and the ever-watchful woman on guard. Whether she was present solely to stop the two of them from attempting an escape, or whether her role was to raise the alarm if there was some threat to the household, Stasya did not know and did not ask, having learned quickly that folk here viewed her as if she were some unusual specimen suddenly thrust into their midst, or a wild creature that might bite if spoken to the wrong way. It made her wonder what Aleksis had said to Biruta or to the Ruler. Much of the time, the other women went about their day's work as if Stasya were invisible. That should have made her happy. Hadn't she always preferred her own company? Instead, she felt trapped. Uneasy. There was a constant churning in her belly. If only she knew what would come next. If only someone would tell her how Lukas was, and where he was. If only they would realise that seeing her from time to time might help him. She couldn't heal his injuries; that was for more skilled folk to do. But her stories could take his mind off the pain, ease the sadness of being away from home and family, help him to stay strong. He had not deserved any of this.

On the third day, Aleksis came to find her. She was in the paved area outside the privy, gazing up at the sky while Flip nosed around, investigating this and that. Stasya heard a small sound and turned to see him in the doorway, tidy in his court clothes with his hair pulled back from his face and tied with a cord.

'Stasya. When I asked them to allow you some time out of doors, this was not what I had in mind.'

What question to ask first? They were bubbling to the surface, all of them together: Lukas, Irina, the Ruler, the future – no, she must make herself wait, she must be calm. She drew a deep breath.

'We'll go indoors, shall we?' he suggested. 'Or find a more pleasant spot to talk?'

Stasya felt her mouth curl. More grimace than smile. 'This is the only outside place where I'm allowed to go.'

'Come.' He reached out a hand. 'There's a garden not so far off. As my guest, you may certainly go there in my company.'

A garden. Was this some kind of trick? Stasya did not move, but Flip ran to Aleksis and put her paws up on his leg, seeking attention. He did not spare the dog so much as a glance. *The hawk,* Stasya thought. *Fixed on his purpose, as always.*

'I must take you to see the Ruler soon,' he said. 'It's best that you and I have a talk first, and this is not the place for that. Come, please.'

She did not take his hand but followed him as he led the way back indoors. The guard who had been just inside, watching her, was now nowhere to be seen. Aleksis took her along a series of passageways, out of the servants' quarters and into spring sunshine. She drew in a long breath, hardly believing what she saw. Flip hurtled away across a green lawn, around which grew well-tended fruit trees: peach, plum, others of a kind she had not seen before. There were wooden benches here and there, and large pots holding bushy herbs. The air was full of their sweet scents. At the far end of the garden a man was digging, perhaps preparing for a new planting. Despite everything, Stasya felt a smile spread across her face.

'It's quiet here,' Aleksis said. 'We won't be interrupted. Sit down awhile. You'll have questions, I'm sure. Ask them and I will try to answer.' She saw, then, that the gardener was not the only other person there.

By the door through which they had entered the garden, Pavel now stood keeping watch. This time, she suspected, it was not to prevent her from bolting, but to make sure nobody came in unless Aleksis wanted them there.

She sat. Flip was well occupied; investigating every corner would take her some time. 'I haven't been told anything about Lukas. I wanted to see him, perhaps to help, but the housekeeper said no. Is he all right? Are they looking after him?'

Aleksis stretched out his legs; he, too, seemed to be enjoying the sun. 'I've seen your friend. He asked about you. I am no expert, but I am confident he is being well looked after. They have him walking about a little, building his strength.'

'Has the physician looked at his burns?'

'I believe the physician was called away elsewhere on the day we arrived here. Certainly the dressings have been changed, and they give him draughts for the pain.' A pause. 'At this point, that is all I can tell you.'

'May I see him? I thought… I thought I might tell him stories.'

'That would require the Ruler's approval. Lukas is in the men's quarters, in an area reserved for folk who are unwell.' Aleksis gazed off across the lawn. Flip had found the gardener, who had set aside his spade and crouched down to pat the little dog. 'You'll have learned by now that this household has certain rules, including those that set out who may go where and speak with whom. Tedious at times but required to maintain order in an establishment so large.' Another lengthy pause. 'About the stories, I agree entirely. On the journey here, they gave the men heart. But this would not be my decision.'

'You're saying I should ask the Ruler?'

Aleksis's mouth curved in a smile, but there was nothing happy about it. 'When a person has an audience with the Ruler, it's the Ruler who asks the questions. I will try to raise the subject.'

A shiver ran through Stasya. The old fears were creeping back in, here in this place of green growth and sunshine, a place such as she would not have dreamed existed within the high walls of Dragon's Keep. 'And Irina? She needs help too. I do try, but she cries at night, and during the day she just sits staring at nothing. It's hard to get her to eat. At that farm, where we stopped on the way, she seemed quite a lot better, but now… If I could bring her out here into the sun, perhaps—'

Aleksis raised a hand, and she fell silent. 'I need to explain something to you before we see the Ruler.'

What was it with him? One moment he seemed almost friendly; the next he was like a stranger, carefully distant. If this was some sort of game, it would help if she understood the rules. But then, Dragon's Keep was a place of rules, and she had never much cared for those, even back at Heartwood. Birds and animals, plants and stones and water had their own way of being, with no need to set down the rules; they simply *were*. 'Say it, then.' Maybe that sounded rude, but never mind. Plain speaking was good. Perhaps he thought she was lacking in some way, a half-wit. She'd heard one or two of the women whisper names like that, looking at her sideways as they passed.

'We're going to speak with Lady Elisabeta as soon as we're called.' Aleksis had dropped his voice to a murmur, though the gardener was still too far away to hear. Pavel had not moved from his post near the doorway. 'There are accepted ways of doing these things, and I advise you to comply with them, no matter how you feel. The Ruler is exactly that: the head of this household and the head of the Northlands. Nobody stands above her.' He glanced over toward Pavel, then turned back to Stasya, his expression as grave as if he were about to announce a death. 'She knows about your amber owl; she has seen it.'

Stasya could not keep quiet. 'Seen it? So it's here? You brought it here? I thought—'

'It is here, and safely locked away. Lady Elisabeta will ask you about it: where you found it, whether there is more amber in that place, where that amber might have originated. She will ask you about the trips you and Lukas made into the forest, and how you traversed terrain other folk think impassable. She wants a way to the Hermit.'

'I know that.' Bitterness rose in Stasya. 'Didn't she send

the Commander to find a way, even if it meant the deaths of ancient trees and creatures, and the ruin of the Heartwood settlement? Why would I tell her anything?'

Aleksis did not answer this question. He waited, not meeting her eye now, then said, 'Something further. Word came to her, not from me, of what you did with the panicking horse. Some of my men spoke to folk from Heartwood. I gather there are rumours about your ability to do something similar with wild creatures. I don't know how much truth there is in those tales; perhaps they belong with the stories of ghosts and uncanny folk that you sometimes tell. Lady Elisabeta asked me about the episode with the horse, and I am almost certain she will want your account of it as well.'

'Why would she do that? I am good at keeping animals calm, I help farmers quite often. But that has nothing to do with finding amber or making a way through the forest.'

'It could do.'

Stasya felt a cold trickle down her spine. If anything was certain, it was that she would answer no questions about this particular matter.

'I strongly advise you to answer calmly, tell the truth, and remain as courteous as you can be. Speak only when spoken to. Keep your answers brief and to the point. I will be present all the time; you won't be left alone with Lady Elisabeta.'

A slight sound from the entry; when she looked over, another man stood in front of Pavel. A tall man in a guard's uniform, but all in black. Something in his expression chilled Stasya to the bone. He lifted a hand, and with the merest twitch of his long fingers indicated to Aleksis that they should come. It was time.

Stasya found words. 'I thought… for a bit I really thought… that she would be kind, that it would be all right. When they gave us a bed and food and didn't lock us up, I thought… But it's not all right, is it? You say, *tell the truth*. But how can I tell the truth and be courteous? The truth is, her mission is destroying all I care about.' Her voice rose. 'The truth is, folk have died and been hurt, and folk are going on suffering! The truth is, the forest is still being cut down! The Commander is still doing his vile work in Heartwood!'

'Stasya.' They were both standing now, and Aleksis put his hands on her shoulders. The touch startled her and she flinched away. 'Stop,' he said, and although he spoke in a murmur, something in his tone caught her attention. His eyes went to the man in black, then back to her. 'Breathe. You must heed my warning. Answer only the questions she asks; do not stray to other matters. Keep your answers simple. Be polite. Stay calm. I will help where I can. But I, too, have rules to follow. Now we must go.'

15

STASYA

THE CHAMBER WAS large, grand, shadowy. A long table dominated the space and the ceiling was high. Stasya glanced up, wondering if bats or owls ever made their way in; there were many good roosting places. Aleksis had made her leave Flip outside with Pavel, and she had not argued the point. He'd said *stay calm*. Arguing with any instruction he gave her did not seem wise. Perhaps the Ruler didn't like dogs in her audience chamber, or whatever this echoing place was. The black-clad guard had followed them in and now stood by the door, silent and watchful. It was easy to imagine him as a creature of dark intent masquerading as a man. Even with her back to him, she could feel his gaze.

At one end of the chamber there was a hearth, and on it burned a cheerful fire. Set close to this was an elaborately carved chair with red cushions embroidered in gold thread, and beside it stood a woman who could only be Lady Elisabeta. She was not dressed in fine silks or festooned with jewels, nor did she wear her hair in an elaborate style, as Stasya had imagined fine ladies might do. But her authority could be seen in every inch of her, from the upright carriage to the tilt of her chin, from the elegant plain lines of her dark plum-coloured gown to the sleek tidiness of her wheaten-fair hair, braided up on top of her head with never a wisp astray. A small table by her side held a neat pile of documents; perhaps she had been studying them. She must be able to read. In Heartwood that skill was limited to the numbers and signs used by folk to aid in buying and selling stock or produce. There was a scribe in Vita's Hope who wrote letters for a small fee on the rare occasions that this was needed, but nobody closer to home could do so. This was another world.

Apart from the grand chair, the only seating nearby was a bench of fine oak wood. She and Aleksis stopped beside it, a good six paces from the Ruler. Lady Elisabeta neither smiled nor gestured in welcome. Instead she scrutinised Stasya from head to toe. Perhaps she should have gone back to the servants' quarters and changed into one of the gowns Laima had given her.

Aleksis bowed briefly. 'My lady, this is Stasya from the Heartwood settlement,' he said.

Was she meant to curtsy? She copied Aleksis's bow, feeling her face flush with the awkwardness of it. Why couldn't these folk just say: *Come in, sit down, how about a cup of tea before we get started?* Why couldn't they meet out of doors instead of using this forbidding chamber? It was such a lovely day out there, and if they wanted privacy there was no shortage of guards to keep folk away.

'So I see.' The Ruler's tone revealed nothing at all. 'Be seated.'

Aleksis motioned toward the bench; they both sat down. Although they were an arm's length apart, she could feel the tension in his body, and it surprised her. Wasn't this his home ground? Or was he just waiting for her to make some blunder, as she surely would?

'I will be blunt with you, Stasya. As Ruler, I deal with

matters of great importance to the Northlands. I make decisions that will shape the future for generations of people. Now, I have some simple questions to put to you, and you are to answer honestly.' Lady Elisabeta fixed Stasya with her gaze; the scrutiny made her belly churn. Should she say something? Aleksis had said, *Answer only the questions she asks*. And she had not asked a question yet.

'I'll proceed, then,' said the Ruler. Her tone was just a little chillier; Stasya wished she had Flip with her now. 'I have seen your trinket. The quality is good. Surprisingly good. Tell me where you found the raw material for it.'

Stasya glanced at Aleksis, confused. 'You mean the amber owl? I told that story in Heartwood. To the Commander, when he took my owl from me. Aleksis was there.'

'That's *Master* Aleksis to you,' Lady Elisabeta said. 'Show some respect. I was not present to hear this story from your own lips. I want it now.'

Stasya knew, somehow, that the tale of a nameless boy and girl on a walk through the great forest was not what this woman wanted. But it felt wrong to share such a precious memory without wrapping it in the protection of a story. 'My friend and I found the amber beside a small lake in the forest, my lady. A place we call Clearwater.' The words were good enough, she thought. A pity she couldn't keep her voice steady. 'We brought it back and my friend carved the owl. He's good with a knife.'

Another cold silence as the Ruler stared at her. 'And?' she said.

'That is all, my lady.'

Lady Elisabeta sighed. 'I see I must guide you through this step by step, girl. The friend you speak of – that is the goatherd, the young man who travelled here with you?'

'Lukas. Yes.' *The friend you will not let me see, even though he's hurt and sad. Even though I could help him. Even though what happened to him was done under your orders*. It was hard to hold back the words.

'Have you and your friend found amber in that place before? Or elsewhere in Heartwood Forest?'

That one was easy. 'No, my lady.' The scraps they sometimes discovered beside forest ponds, the ones that had caught up fragments of earth or stone or dead leaves before they hardened, were not what this woman meant by amber. It was not truly a lie.

'How did you reach the lake you speak of, when I'm told none of the local folk venture far into this forest? Is there a track nobody else knows of?'

'There are no tracks, my lady. Only those of bear and badger, wolf and hedgehog. A mission to take a party of men through the forest with carts and horses was…' She sensed a warning from Aleksis, though he did not so much as twitch an eyelid. 'It was always unlikely to succeed, for that reason. The terrain is steep in places; it's almost like climbing a cliff. The trees are tall and they grow close. It can feel like night underneath, even when the sun is up.'

Another piercing stare from Lady Elisabeta. 'While your demeanour is somewhat unusual, young woman, I can see clearly that you are neither badger nor bear, wolf nor hedgehog. How did you and your friend reach this lake?'

'Climbing. Walking. Staying watchful, looking for signs that animals had passed a certain way. It took a while to get there.'

'How long?'

'A day, there and back. A very long day.' The memory of it was still clear: setting out just after dawn, the hard climb, the twisting, tricky paths through the forest, the wondrous discovery of Clearwater. Finding the amber. Lukas's laugh of sheer delight. A meal shared on the rocks by the water's edge. A long way back; reaching her cottage at dusk and bidding him farewell. It had not been until the next day that she'd learned how displeased his parents were about his lengthy absence in her company.

Lady Elisabeta seemed to consider this for a while. 'A day

only,' she murmured eventually. 'Not so very far. Perhaps there are other lakes and waterways where amber might be found.'

As this was not a question, Stasya remained silent.

'Yes?' The Ruler's tone was sharp.

'Heartwood Forest spreads over many hills and valleys, my lady. I know there are other streams; one of them runs down into our settlement and provides our water. About amber, I don't know. We did not search for it; we just found it.' *As if it had been waiting for us,* she thought but did not say.

'Other folk in your village must know of this discovery of yours. Have others not attempted to find more? Amber of such quality could be sold for a high price, even in its natural state.'

Stasya struggled to put together a courteous answer. 'The forest is a dangerous place. It's not only the animals that live there and the difficult terrain. There are many tales of danger higher up, old stories of malign spirits and other guardians.'

'Guardians? What do you mean?'

'The stories, some of them, tell of uncanny beings. Different tales say different things about them. Nobody really knows. Nobody has travelled far enough to see them. If they are there.' But she had seen something. Something she had not told Lukas in case it worried him. Under the trees, up by Clearwater, there had been signs. White stones set in a pattern. Knotted grasses. A posy of tiny wildflowers laid by the water's edge. Whether those signs had been for her, there was no knowing. Seeing them, she had thought of Mother in the painting, the benign presence she had imagined sitting by that same lake, communing with her creatures.

'Foolish nonsense. Tales for children, to scare them out of wandering. Or tales told by old folk half out of their wits. I wonder that anyone gives them credence.'

There seemed no point at all in explaining that since people had told the same tales, or variations of them, since the time of the oldest ancestors, there must surely be some wisdom in them. In a place like Heartwood, where the forest wrapped itself around the settlement and was part of everyone's life, it would be foolish indeed to disregard those tales. Somewhere, deep down, they must hold truth. 'In the old stories,' Stasya said, 'never once does a person reach the Hermit and come safely home again. They vanish, or they're found dead, or they go out of their wits.' She did not mention the tales in which a person came home to find that a hundred years had passed and their loved ones were all gone.

'Are there other ways into the forest?' the lady asked. Had she not heard what Stasya had said? 'Ways that you and your friend have taken, starting from your village? Hard paths, easy paths, any path a strong man could walk or climb or thread a way through? I cannot believe this is the only one. As you said, it is a very large area.'

'Why do you want to know that?' Oh. She'd broken the rule, she could see it on the Ruler's face and in Aleksis's slight movement. *Answer only the questions she asks.* Which meant, *She asks the questions, you don't*. But she would not apologise.

'My reasons are none of your concern, girl. Are there other ways?'

'Lukas and I have gone no further than Clearwater.' She had trodden many paths, some with Lukas, some alone save for Flip. But she had always turned back in time to be home by nightfall. 'As I told you, the people of Heartwood do not venture far into the forest.' Her heart began to race. Her hands clenched themselves into fists. She made herself breathe in a pattern, in, two, three, four, and pause; out, two, three, four. Let this be over soon.

'But you walk in the forest often, do you not? I believe you have something of an affinity with creatures, perhaps even wild creatures.'

Stasya could not help glancing at Aleksis. He looked down at his linked hands, avoiding her eye.

'I... yes, I live quite near the forest's edge. I do... I do sometimes feed the birds or set food out for small wild things.'

That was no lie. It was the merest sliver of the truth, but she would not tell more.

'You seem reluctant to speak of this. Master Aleksis, remind this young woman what happened on the day you reached Heartwood. The horse.'

Aleksis looked up. 'Soon after we reached the village, and before we unloaded the carts, there was a mishap with a distressed horse, still in harness. It all happened very quickly. The cart was half off the track and a man was trapped underneath. The horse would not let anyone near. Stasya gentled the animal, showing no fear as she came close enough to touch. It turned out that a wasp had flown up the horse's nostril and was trapped there. Stasya kept the creature calm and after a time the wasp flew free. Under her direction, others helped the horse to safety and the trapped man was rescued.' A pause. 'I learned later that the local folk know Stasya to be a person with exceptional skill in such situations. They say she can calm the most agitated of animals, where even a farmer of many years' experience cannot.'

There was a longer silence then. *Let this be over soon*, Stasya thought. Aleksis had said the Ruler already knew about the horse. Why make him tell the story again? Could she actually think Stasya would have forgotten such a thing? Reaching the wasp, feeling its panic, helping it to freedom had been a challenge, yes; but also full of wonder.

Lady Elisabeta toyed with the papers on her little table. She turned one of her rings around and around on her finger. 'Such a skill,' she mused, not looking at either of the others, 'might be useful, might it not, if one were passing across territory inhabited by wild animals such as bears and wolves? A person with this skill would be invaluable to a group wishing to do so. On the other hand, folk might look at the demonstration of such an unusual ability and label it dark magic.' Suddenly her gaze was back on Stasya. 'Or even witchcraft.'

The woman was using threats now. A pox on this! The most frightening thing about what she'd just said was how close it came to the truth. How did the Ruler know this about her? What exactly had Aleksis told her? Stasya cleared her throat. 'There is no magic in what I do. It is… just a matter of staying calm, and trusting the animal, and taking time.' What could she say about wild animals? She lacked the ability to lie. But she would not tell Lady Elisabeta about the time when she helped a wolf with a thorn in its foot, or the time when she tended to an owl with a broken claw. Or the bear. She could not mention the bear. She would not even tell the tale of the magpie hanging from the fence. 'As for helping people to go through the forest, I would not do that if their venture would lead to its destruction. If their presence there was a threat to the trees or to the animals and birds, I would refuse to guide them. The Commander came to Heartwood under your orders, my lady. He laid waste to the forest edge; he cast a shadow on the settlement and its people, he destroyed lives and livelihoods—'

'Stasya.'

Aleksis's quiet voice, his hand on her arm. She was standing. She'd been almost shouting. She'd forgotten herself. But she would not say sorry. She glared across the chamber at the Ruler. 'I could never help anyone who had any part in that,' she said.

'How very unfortunate,' said Lady Elisabeta. 'Just how much help you might have to offer is still unclear to me. I should perhaps remind you that you and your companions have been escorted all the way here; you have been provided with excellent accommodation in Dragon's Keep, and your young man is receiving attention for his injuries. I have even tolerated the presence of your dog. You complain about what has occurred in your home settlement; you are all too ready to blame others for that, while it seems to me the failure of the local folk to cooperate most definitely contributed to the situation. Coming here has served you well. You need not fend for yourself any longer; this household is supplying all your needs and those of your friends. For now. And all I ask in return is civil answers to my questions.'

Imagine if this woman knew the true extent of her gift. Imagine if she applied the same thinking to that. Stasya wished she had not lost her temper, but she could not regret her words of truth. What had happened in Heartwood was an abomination. She would never, ever be a willing part of any expedition the Ruler or her underlings wanted. They had no respect for the ancient forest. They had no understanding of its importance. It was time to stop talking, lest she say something in anger that would later prove perilous. 'I can't answer any more questions.'

'I doubt you realise the implications of such a statement. You are obviously capable of speaking. Perhaps you do not mean *I can't*, but rather *I won't*?'

Stasya held her silence. It was Aleksis who spoke, rising to his feet. 'By your leave, my lady. Stasya is still weary from the long journey and the events that preceded it. She is not used to the customs and formalities of court, nor to living amongst so many folk. As I said earlier, this needs more time—'

The Ruler fixed him with a gaze as cold and sharp as an icicle. 'I reiterate, there is no time. I need answers. The girl will speak. Ah, not today perhaps'—she raised her hand as Aleksis made to interrupt—'but very soon indeed. This cannot wait.'

'I will speak with Stasya further,' he said.

'As it happens, you will not.' There was an odd look in Lady Elisabeta's eye, as if she were readying herself for a challenge. 'A message came in earlier from Bishop Petras. Some kind of unrest has broken out at Raven's Watch, and he has requested your assistance. He does not want armed men, only expert advice. I cannot trust anyone else to deal with it. You'll need to ride out today, as soon as you can be ready. Take Matiss with you, and another guard for security.'

Aleksis simply stared at her. It seemed some conversation was happening between them in complete silence. Then he gave a curt bow. 'My lady.'

'Stanislav!' The Ruler looked at the black-clad man. 'Have the other guard escort the girl back to her quarters.' And to Stasya, 'Young woman, apply your mind to your situation. Next time I speak to you, I expect common sense. You will be ready with answers.'

By answers, the Ruler meant *answers that suit me*. She was playing a cruel game, and Stasya would take no more part in it. 'My lady,' she forced herself to say. Her bow was less than courteous.

With Stanislav by her side, ushering her out, there was no chance to speak to Aleksis again and he left without so much as a glance. Pavel walked her back to the servants' quarters, choosing a route that did not take them through the garden. He was about to leave her when Stasya halted him. 'Thank you for looking after Flip. Pavel – how long would it take to ride to Raven's Watch?'

'Ah. You heard about that? With good horses, a day there, a day back at least. And however long it takes to deal with the matter, of course. They won't get there by nightfall, so they'll likely be gone for several days even if all goes well.'

'Oh.' As she watched him walk away, Stasya's mind filled with questions of her own. Was the Ruler sending Aleksis off on this mission so she could interrogate Stasya in his absence? Surely not; whether or not she talked further could hardly be of so much importance in this world of power and strategy. Besides, wasn't Aleksis the Ruler's trusted personal adviser? Maybe the two of them were playing a game, and she would be thrown from one to the other like a child's ball until she gave in. But what would be the point of telling them anything more? Yes, she could lead folk along paths they would not find for themselves. She could use her gift to help people stay safe. But she would never help them get to the Hermit, even supposing she could actually reach that far-off, mysterious place. Such a quest could mean nothing good for the forest or for its inhabitants. She would not break her solemn vow to keep Heartwood safe. *Forever and always, Stasya,* Grandmother had said. *Through the generations.*

It was odd. At times, Aleksis had seemed almost friendly, though not like Matiss. At the farm, she had felt safe with Matiss. But Aleksis had some understanding of her; it showed in the way he spoke of her to others. He knew she was worried about Lukas and about Irina. And those good, honest people at the farm had treated him like an old friend. That should mean something. On the other hand, Aleksis had reached a high position in the Ruler's court when he was still young. Perhaps he was the real master of this game. Stasya shivered. She might not trust the man, but she wished he wasn't leaving and taking Matiss with him. She must keep her head down, obey rules, do her best to be invisible. With luck, the Ruler would soon lose interest in her. And then... she did not really know what might come next. Make a plan? She had no idea where to start.

'You could escape,' she whispered to Flip, showing her a mind-picture: the dog becoming a bird and flying out from one of those narrow windows into a blue sky. 'You can if you want. I won't stop you. You could fly all the way to Heartwood.' Home. Her longing for it was an ache deep inside her. But the Commander and his men were still in the settlement; who knew what would have become of it, and of the forest nearby, since Aleksis had uprooted her and brought her to Dragon's Keep? 'If I could be a bird, I would go.' She showed Flip the image: a brambling flying over the forest, and with it a skylark singing a joyful song. Flip responded with her own version of this picture: the brambling soaring gracefully, the lark flapping about as if unsure what its wings were for. The message was clear: *You wouldn't know how to be a bird*. Stasya smiled at the joke. But her heart was far from glad. Lukas. That was the first step. She must find Lukas.

16

LUKAS

He was a sad shadow of his old self, hardly able to hold a cup steady in his hand. Stasya was somewhere out there, in this grand house full of strangers, and he couldn't do a thing to help her. Twice a day his keepers would get him out of bed and let him shuffle down the hallway and back. Not on his own; the journey to court, on top of what had happened at Heartwood, meant his legs could barely hold him, and he needed to lean on one of the men to walk even that small distance. There'd been talk of a physician earlier on, but no such person had appeared, and Lukas had not asked. He had a pallet, he had a roof over his head, he got two meals a day. Mostly those meals were a kind of gruel, which compared poorly with the fare back home on the farm, but at least it was keeping him alive.

He didn't ask to see Stasya. If she'd been allowed to visit him, she'd have done so; that was the way things were with the two of them. He missed her. He missed the stories that gave him heart in sad times and made him laugh at the end of a difficult day and helped make sense of things. He worried about her. She would hate being shut up in this place with no sight of the open sky. But the men who took turns tending to him were lowly members of the Ruler's household, servants who cleaned out privies and scrubbed floors and scoured cooking pans; they would know nothing of where she was or what had become of her. Perhaps she'd been housed somewhere better, in a place where she could go outside when she chose. Perhaps Irina was coming out of her shell now and the two of them were making friends within the household. A man could hope.

He'd become used to the pattern of days here, the visits of his keepers, the changing of dressings, the grey meals, the awkward exercise. The long, lonely nights and the troubling dreams, in which his family still suffered under the Commander's cruel control. Then, one night, everything changed. He was woken abruptly by someone ripping off his blanket and hauling him out of bed, someone with an iron grip and a harsh voice.

'Move, fellow!'

There were two of them, guards, men he did not recognise.

'What—'

'Shut your mouth and walk.'

'But where—' It was cold. He was in a borrowed nightshirt, a garment almost falling apart with age, and his feet were bare. His head was fuzzy with sleep. A dream. A bad dream.

'Ruler's orders.' They were more or less dragging him along the hallway now, one on either side. This was real. Lamps burned here and there; he could hear faint sounds of the household stirring. It must be nearly morning. 'You're being moved.'

Lukas did not ask where. He needed all the strength he could find to keep walking, not to sag between the guards like a sack of flour. Stasya would say, *Hold on to hope*. She would tell a story about… about someone who seemed powerless and ended up being a hero. He gritted his teeth, thought of warriors, quests and dragons, and forced himself on. Perhaps they would let him see her now. Perhaps this was the first step toward going home, standing up to the Commander, saving his family. Perhaps...

It felt like a long way. There were stone steps. His knees ached and his breath was short. For a bit they were outside. He judged it to be close to daybreak, but the sky was heavy with cloud. Briefly, he breathed fresh air; the cold hurt his chest. Then inside again, a different building with more guards, and sounds of... of... Sounds he did not want to identify, for they reminded him of the bad time in Heartwood, and the wretched place where the Commander had kept his prisoners.

His guards came to a halt. Lukas made himself stand upright, despite the pain. *I was strong before. I will be strong again.* In stories, sometimes the weak became heroes. Another guard opened a door for them. 'Down the end,' he said. As they went through, the disturbing noises grew and grew and became the voices of men. Men taunting him. Men rattling things against iron bars and shouting mad nonsense. Men weeping, screaming, shouting to be let out, please, please, their wives and children needed them. Worst, as he looked into the cage-like spaces on either side of the walkway, were the men hunched down in corners, their arms wrapped around themselves, saying nothing at all.

Down the end was an empty cell, barely big enough to contain one man. His captors pushed him in, threw his blanket after him, clanged the door shut and bolted it.

'Sweet dreams, fellow,' said one, and they were gone.

'Welcome to hell,' a voice called from the cell opposite. 'What did *you* do?'

17

ALEKSIS

THE RIDE TO Raven's Watch had never seemed so slow. It was just as well he had the others with him, or he would have been tempted to push his horse too hard, just to get the thing over and done with. He'd managed to speak with Pavel before they left, asking him to keep an eye on the situation with Stasya, but Pavel did not hold much authority at Dragon's Keep. It would have been better to leave Matiss at court. But the Ruler had made it clear Matiss was to go with him, and right now it was especially important not to anger the Ruler. As a second guard he'd taken Karolis, who had some knowledge of the warrior monks, having once briefly considered joining their order, a fact that was not known to Bishop Petras and would not be shared with him. And Karolis had a particular advantage: exceptional skills in hand-to-hand combat. When visiting the headquarters of the Church of the Godly, it was wise to take companions who were good fighters.

Since they were on the Ruler's business, the way could be eased by the showing of credentials. Aleksis had his silver pendant engraved with the Dragon of the Northlands, marking him out as a member of Lady Elisabeta's inner circle. All three men wore over-tunics with the same dragon embroidered on the breast. The robe Aleksis wore for official court duties was in his pack, carefully folded. Matiss and Karolis bore arms openly, as befitted their role as his protectors. Aleksis kept his own weapons concealed.

They spent the first night at an inn where Aleksis was known; the horses were ready for a rub-down, a good feed and a rest in well-kept stables. The next day's ride took them along a river valley and across a lake on a sturdily built ferry that could accommodate horses and other livestock. After recent rain the day was fine and the air fresh and sweet. Aleksis found himself thinking how much Stasya would enjoy the beauty of the shining water, with blue sky and scudding clouds reflected there, and the majesty of the wooded hills in the distance. Birds were flying above the boat, perhaps looking for fish, and for a brief time he felt peace in his heart. That feeling dissipated when Raven's Watch came into view on the far shore. He could never associate that place with peace, not since his earliest encounters with Bishop Petras and his warrior monks.

Lord Kasimir had been a peacemaker. Under his rule, the Northlands had not been involved in any major conflict, whether internally between landowners or town leaders or on a grander scale, with the rulers of neighbouring territories. As for disputes based on faith, belief or superstition, Kasimir had balanced taking a firm hand with a readiness to negotiate, to discuss, and to find solutions that kept everyone relatively calm, if not always delighted. The Northlands had prospered during those years. His death had been a great loss; that he had left only a single heir had been worse than unfortunate. Elisabeta had never lived at Dragon's Keep prior to becoming Ruler. It had been suggested, once it became clear that she would be her uncle's sole heir, that she might spend time at court in preparation. There was talk of an appropriate marriage for her, the thinking being to form an alliance with a neighbouring territory. But her visits to court had been brief and infrequent. She'd had a tutor at home and had perhaps believed that education was sufficient. As for a marriage, neither she nor her family had expressed any interest in that idea.

After Kasimir's passing, it had fallen to Aleksis not only to advise the new Ruler, but to remedy any potentially disastrous gaps in her preparation for the role. At first, they'd done well together; Elisabeta had been eager to learn and unafraid of hard work. She'd seemed keen to do the job well. But as time passed it was as if something were distracting her, making her swift to anger and often impatient. She was apt to dismiss his suggestions if they did not suit her, and some of her decisions had been troubling. Dragon's Keep itself had changed under her leadership. She dealt severely with those who angered her, was quick to order punishment for even minor offences against the law and allowed certain individuals among the guards remarkable authority when it came to dealing with offenders. He wondered sometimes whether she lacked understanding of what her decisions might mean for the lives of such folk, or whether she simply wished such unsavoury matters to be dealt with out of her sight. He feared she might take the same approach to her dealings with the highborn and powerful, such as Bishop Petras and the leaders of their neighbouring territories. Aleksis was senior adviser, yes. But as Ruler, Elisabeta would always have the final word. His unease had grown with every passing day.

As they crossed the lake and Raven's Watch came closer, Aleksis found himself glad that Lady Elisabeta and Bishop Petras did not meet in person more often. The Church of the Godly frowned upon the idea of women in positions of authority; a woman as Ruler would be viewed as a disaster, almost an abomination. But the laws of the Northlands must be respected, in public at least, so Petras had attended the ceremony at which the new Ruler was confirmed in her role. He'd been accompanied by a sizeable complement of warrior monks, clad in full uniform and armed to the teeth. Their presence had been something of a challenge for the Ruler's own guards, and indeed for the whole household at Dragon's Keep. Petras had congratulated Lady Elisabeta as all the other distinguished guests had done, not once saying what was in more than one mind on that momentous occasion: *If only…* But there had been something in the Bishop's manner, a certain note in his voice, that had set Aleksis's nerves jangling with unease. Matiss had felt the same thing. The man and his all-too-expert fighting squad would need to be watched. Aleksis himself was not a man of faith. Under Kasimir, many different spiritual paths had existed side by side in the Northlands, with disagreements sometimes played out in heated debate, but never developing into conflict. Bishop Petras was different. He had ambitions. The Church of the Godly had not originated in the Northlands, but in a nation of seafarers far to the south. Warrior monks, with their leaders, had brought the faith first to the Southlands, establishing the new beliefs and practices by force where they deemed it necessary. They had obtained land, and the towers and forts they had built were testament to the support provided by the nobly born and the wealthy. They had recruited new members with promises of a life of action and excitement as a warrior of the faith. Young men had flocked to join, dazzled by the fine uniforms and the demonstrations of martial skill.

Inevitably, the new faith had come next to the Northlands, where Kasimir, then a young Ruler, had already put in place various controls on all formally recognised religions. That had proved to be one of his wisest acts, and the leaders of neighbouring territories had congratulated him – in Petras's absence – for far-thinking.

'Nearly there,' observed Matiss, coming up to the rail beside Aleksis to gaze ahead toward the fortress that housed Petras's establishment. 'I can think of places I'd sooner visit.'

'Mmm.' Aleksis regarded the somewhat forbidding form of

Raven's Watch, a high-walled establishment built of dark stone. It housed a place of worship and a training ground for warriors, as well as stables, kennels and accommodation for a significant number of men. Bishop Petras had his own private quarters within. There was a settlement of sorts outside the fortress wall; Aleksis had wondered whether, in time of siege, the bishop would allow those who lived there, including women and children, entry into the fortress, which was otherwise exclusively a domain of men. The deity followed by the Church of the Godly was known as the One and Only God. His rules could not be described as egalitarian. And they were strict. 'Let's hope we can get this business done quickly, whatever it is. There was scant detail in the message I was shown. I'm not sure why Petras asked for me; he hasn't always welcomed my advice in the past.'

Matiss lowered his voice, though the nearest crew member was not close enough to hear. 'He knows you have the Ruler's trust. They're closer to the border here; could be some kind of pressure from Vidrik of the Birchlands, or even from our neighbour in the east. On the other hand, he may have done this purely to distract her, set her off balance before the council. You might be given some kind of vague, unsettling news.'

'Who knows? Keep your ears open. There'll be training of one kind or another; it never stops here. You and Karolis can show interest, get involved maybe. That's the way to pick up what's on folk's minds.'

Matiss grimaced. 'Get involved? Get ourselves killed, you mean, or at the very least sent home with broken limbs or dented skulls. Aren't we here to keep you safe?'

'Broken limbs? You?' said Aleksis with a grin. 'Never. And if I were a wagering man, I'd put silver on Karolis to beat any of theirs.'

'With the ride home still ahead, I intend to keep out of trouble. But I'll be cheering from the sidelines and talking to whoever wants to engage. Ah. Looks like we're about to disembark, and I see there's a welcoming party.'

The monks were in full ceremonial dress. The outfit managed to suggest both a military uniform and a habit suited to members of a monastic order. The cloth was dyed an eye-catching kingfisher blue. There were touches of gold thread here and there, and a broad leather belt for weaponry. Over all, each man wore a hooded cape. Each carried over his shoulder an unsheathed sword. It may have been a welcoming party, but the monks' faces all wore the same expression: sombre, verging on hostile. Their height, too, was startlingly uniform; perhaps that was a requirement in such a group. The aim, Aleksis thought, was less greeting than intimidation.

One man stepped out in front and performed a well-practised manoeuvre with his sword, whirling it around expertly, then lowering its point to the ground and placing both hands on the hilt. As a gesture of welcome it was somewhat startling.

Aleksis made sure he spoke first. 'I bring the respectful greetings of Lady Elisabeta, Ruler of the Northlands, to His Excellency Bishop Petras. I believe His Excellency is expecting us. I am Aleksis son of Feliks, senior adviser to the Ruler. With me come these two court guards as escort.' He indicated his pendant of office, which hung outside his tunic. 'We would be grateful if our horses could be given a place in your fine stables; they are weary from the journey.' He was tempted to add, *Nice day, isn't it?* but kept the thought to himself.

'Master Aleksis.' The guard, whom Aleksis recognised from an earlier visit, favoured him with a nod. That was good; one never knew, in this place, whether one might need to whip out a weapon instead of a greeting. 'Follow me.'

'MASTER ALEKSIS, WELCOME.' Bishop Petras's tone was courteous, but his curious, pale eyes were cold and his face its customary expressionless mask.

'Thank you, Excellency. I bring the Ruler's respectful greetings, and I hope you are in good health.'

They'd been conveyed by one of the brethren to a reception chamber, where the bishop appeared to be in the middle of a solitary meal; a half-consumed platter of roast beef and vegetables was on the table, and a flask of what looked like mead stood nearby.

'Brother Paavo, Master Aleksis will dine here with me. Show his men to the guest quarters.'

Without so much as a *Yes, Excellency*, the monk who had accompanied them ushered Matiss and Karolis back out and closed the door. Aleksis found himself glad that he still had his concealed weapons, though it would have been good to wash, change and rest before embarking on what might be an awkward discussion. 'May I sit down?' he asked.

'Of course, Master Aleksis. Food and drink will be brought for you. And your men will dine with the brethren downstairs.' Petras paused, scrutinising his guest. 'You needed protection on the journey, of course. Those two look well up to the job. But you won't want them dogging your footsteps during your stay with us. This place is full of trained fighters and, of course, we are under the protection of the One and Only God. Your men, I am sure, would welcome the opportunity to join the brethren in worship and in their practice of combat skills. The daily drills are quite something to watch.'

It was hard to find an acceptable answer to this. It would be a waste of energy to debate it. He did not let the bishop see how uneasy he was. Any fool could tell there were some tightly strung individuals among the monks, men who would snap at the least hint of insult or slight, men with the skill to bring a weapon almost instantly to hand and use it to lethal effect, but without the judgement to know when it was appropriate to do so. He'd prepared both his men for this. All the same, he would prefer that they be close at hand, for both their safety and his own. 'Thank you, Excellency. I am eager to learn why you requested my presence here. Perhaps after our meal…?'

At this point a polite knock at the door announced two monks bearing platters of food, knives and spoons, another flask and a cup, all of which they set out on the table before leaving without a word.

'Eat, drink,' Petras said, with what might have been a smile. 'Serious discussion can wait until tomorrow. You've had a long ride. You'll welcome a hot bath, I'm sure, and a comfortable bed, as will your men. Enjoy your meal, Master Aleksis, and perhaps some of this excellent pear wine, which is brewed on our own premises?'

The man was hardly going to poison him. 'Thank you, Excellency. I see the wisdom in not tackling whatever the issue is today. But I am rather limited in the time I can stay here; my presence is required back at court within a few days.' This must not be allowed to drag out. And he'd better find some way to keep either Matiss or Karolis close whenever possible.

He helped himself to food and, at Petras's gesture, poured his own wine, then topped up the bishop's drink. 'Your good health,' he said, raising his cup.

'And yours, Master Aleksis. Are both your men strong fighters?'

That was unexpected. 'They are trained court guards. Well-trained.'

'We must set up some bouts for them, give them a chance to show their skills. The brethren would enjoy that. We don't have a lot of visitors here.'

Aleksis said nothing. He'd talk to the others later, warn them that the man was full of tricks. He concentrated on eating. The beef was exceptionally good, though it was impossible to relax and enjoy it. And equally hard to make light conversation with Petras when all his instincts were urging him to get the business out of the way as quickly as he could. 'You seem a little tense, Master Aleksis,' the Bishop observed. 'Something on your mind?'

'I'm weary from the long ride. Nothing a good night's sleep won't fix.'

'I'll have one of the brethren show you around in the morning. I know this is not your first visit to Raven's Watch, but we've done considerable building work since you last honoured us with your presence.'

Aleksis was certain he heard a note of ridicule in the bishop's voice. He maintained a politely interested expression.

'An extension to the chapel, with new windows. And we've added an area for mounted combat. Our library, too, has been improved. You'll hardly recognise it.'

'Indeed?' There were questions he could have asked, related to how they funded this work and why any of it was really necessary. 'It sounds as if you have been very busy, Excellency. About tomorrow. Might you and I have a discussion after this tour, concerning the pressing matter you mentioned in your message to the Ruler? I see no reason to delay further. Unless you are waiting for others to be in attendance.'

Petras swallowed a mouthful of wine. 'Others? Oh, no. This is a matter to be discussed strictly in private, Master Aleksis, between you and me. Behind closed doors, with two of my men on guard. I may be otherwise occupied tomorrow afternoon. Perhaps the following day?'

Aleksis suppressed a sigh of frustration. 'Might you give me a general idea of what it relates to? I was under the impression that the matter was of extreme urgency.'

'Best that we leave it until you are fully recovered from your journey. For now, enjoy the meal, make use of our bathing facilities and allow yourself a good night's sleep. Tomorrow is another day, Master Aleksis. You are not under the Ruler's thumb here at Raven's Watch.'

'Got an invitation to a bout already,' Karolis announced, as the three of them settled in the capacious guest quarters some time later. They'd been given two adjoining chambers, one with benches, a table and a hearth complete with firewood, the other with comfortable beds. 'Day after tomorrow, against Brother Kalju, who's more Matiss's size than mine. Unarmed combat, which is something of a relief. Weapons can turn things rather bloody unless someone's applying strict rules of engagement.'

'You've agreed to it?'

'It seemed the appropriate response. The brethren might have taken offence if I'd refused.'

'What about you, Matiss? No invitations as yet? I would prefer not to have to ride home with either of you at less than full strength.'

'No bouts for me. There is a tug-of-war at some point, I think tomorrow, and I'll be on one of the teams for that. I'll do my best not to strain anything. We should aim to keep one or the other of us close to you at all times, Aleks. We're here to protect you. But that's going to be a challenge, and it doesn't help that folk keep telling us it's unnecessary.'

Aleksis felt his mouth twist in a grimace. 'Because the place is teeming with trained fighters, and the One and Only God is watching over us all? Funny, that. I don't trust either of those parties to keep me safe even for a moment. Not that I would express such a view outside the four walls of these remarkably accommodating quarters. The place is so well set out I keep wondering if it's a trap.'

Matiss laughed. 'We already checked for hidden entries and exits, concealed passageways, trapdoors and the like. Found nothing. I'm inclined to think the man really does want to talk to you, if only so you'll take word back to the Ruler that his establishment is more comfortable than Dragon's Keep. With better food.'

'He's delaying, and I don't know why. Not a hint yet of what it's all about. I don't want to be here too long; you know the reasons for that. Petras implied that our discussion may not even be tomorrow. Guided tour in the morning, and he's busy with other things in the afternoon. A game in which only His

Excellency knows the rules.' Aleksis realised both men were regarding him with amused expressions. 'What?'

'That game, my friend,' said Karolis, smiling, 'is the kind at which you are an absolute master. Though you have let us in on some of the rules, it's true, and just as well. You don't want to find yourself alone with this, Aleks.'

'It's a risk I'm prepared to take, if it comes to that.' Aleksis lowered his voice to a murmur. 'Best not talk about it here, even if you have checked the place for secret listening spots. But keep your ears open for any kind of talk that might be relevant. Gather what information you can without arousing suspicion. We want to know whether Petras has travelled to talk to other leaders recently, and whether his attitude to the new Ruler has changed in any way. Continuing to show tolerance because he has no choice? More hostile than before? We know his capability in the event of any kind of armed conflict breaking out. This is his main establishment, but there are several others across the Northlands, each with its contingent of warriors. If it came to a confrontation, which way would he go?'

Karolis spoke in an undertone. 'His own, would be my guess.'

A knock rendered them all instantly silent. Matiss opened the door to admit a small procession of monks carrying a bathtub, ewers of hot and cold water, and such useful items as soap, brushes and cloths for drying. When the bath had been set before the hearth and filled, Aleksis thanked the brother who seemed to be in charge.

'When you are finished bathing, Master Aleksis,' the monk said, 'please ask one of your men to step out into the hallway and signal to the brother on night watch. He'll be at the top of the stairs and will arrange for these things to be collected.' A pause. 'Of course, we also have a communal bath house, next to our own quarters. Your men would be welcome to use that whenever they wish.' There was an unspoken message behind the polite words. Whether it was *This has all been rather a nuisance* or *Guards don't get the same privileges as royal advisers* was unclear.

Once the door was closed, Matiss said, 'I suppose communal bathing would be a good way to pick up useful gossip. Do monks gossip?'

'When I last spent time in an establishment like this,' said Karolis, 'the communal facilities had only cold water. The fellows would conduct a drill or a mock battle or a series of exercises, then plunge in. Except, of course, in the depth of winter, when the water iced right up. There was some spiritual worth attached to that bracing experience. Today I'll gladly share the royal adviser's bath water. You go first, Aleks. Just don't stay in until it goes cold.'

18

ALEKSIS

THE CHAPEL WAS indeed beautiful, the roof arching high, the windows admitting light through intricate patterns in coloured glass. Aleksis could not see where the original parts of the building ended and the new parts began. Surely such work must have been carried out by the most expert craftsmen, perhaps brought in from beyond the borders of the Northlands. The bishop's coffers must be vast indeed. Whether this was the best use for those funds was questionable, lovely as the result was.

He'd managed to conceal his reluctance to attend a religious service. He knew how Petras worked. If he'd decided for reasons of his own that their discussion must wait, a demand for an earlier meeting would only irritate the man. Aleksis could have approached one of the more helpful monks and made a polite request. Instead, he decided to let the day flow as it might rather than cause a stir. Tomorrow would be a different matter. If Petras did not take steps to discuss whatever the mysterious concern was, he would apply some pressure, reminding the bishop that they needed to return promptly to

Dragon's Keep. He feared Elisabeta would subject Stasya to further interrogation, this time without his own moderating presence. Bullying would either send Stasya into a shut-down silence or, worse, cause her to shout defiant words as she had to Rihard that night in Heartwood. There was only one step from that to Elisabeta calling in certain individuals who would obey even the most unsavoury of orders. She'd done so a number of times before, generally when Aleksis was absent from court. The results were always unpleasant and sometimes dire, though the Ruler herself seemed to turn a blind eye to that, and none of the other advisers was prepared to speak out, since that would be to risk her disapproval and perhaps lose a well-paid position. As for Aleksis himself, he could tell Elisabeta was becoming tired of what she saw as his interference, and that made him fear not only for folk like Stasya who got in her way, but for the very future of the Northlands. He needed to be back at court.

The service was impressive. These brethren loved spectacle. The monks sang a wordless hymn to their god, the melody rising and falling in evocative peaks and troughs, while a long procession of senior brethren made its way toward the place where a statue of the One and Only God stood gazing out across the gathered men. No sign of Petras. And no folk from the community present; this was for the monks only. And, it seemed, for official guests, though the three of them had been seated on a bench at the rear of the chapel, not among the brethren. The carven God, his wooden form painted in the same bright hues as the garments worn by the faithful, looked down on them not with the benign expression of a deity who loves and cares for his flock but with a face that seemed to Aleksis somewhat detached. It was as if this god's mind was on other things entirely, such as the nice cup of pear wine he would enjoy when the service was finally over. Indeed, if the One and Only God resembled anyone at all, it was Bishop Petras himself, and Aleksis wondered if the sculptor had done that on purpose.

There were prayers and more prayers. Some, it seemed, required the faithful to lie flat on the floor, face down, while murmuring – or muttering – the words. Aleksis and his companions exchanged a glance the first time all those in front of them dropped abruptly from kneeling to lying prone. None of the three followed suit. Later, the brethren rose to kneel again, and one monk with an exceptionally fine singing voice rendered a chant that was a genuine pleasure to hear. Aleksis detected a second voice: that of Karolis, who was humming along very quietly. Then came a hush of expectation, and certain men rose from the ranks to walk with heads bowed to the feet of the statue.

Aleksis started in surprise when a bell rang out just behind him; he forced himself not to look over his shoulder. Once the men reached the carven God, the bell was quiet, save for a single ringing tone which seemed to signal that one man should fall to his knees. It was hard to see clearly; Aleksis suppressed the urge to stand up for a better view.

An older monk, perhaps senior in the Order, rose to his feet, about ten paces from the kneeling man. 'How have you offended, Brother?' he enquired in somewhat accusatory tones.

'I have offended the One and Only God by conversing with a woman, Father.'

A sound somewhere between a gasp and a murmur rose from the congregation; when the senior monk turned to look at them, silence fell. 'How could such a thing come to pass, Brother? Any novice of this order learns from the earliest days that discourse with females is strictly forbidden, save under exceptional circumstances. Were the circumstances exceptional? You speak at the very feet of our God. Tell nothing but the truth.'

'I was in the settlement, Father, collecting a load of firewood with the cart. A child ran across the road ahead of me; I only just managed to halt the horse in time. The child was frightened, screaming. The mother was distraught. I got down from the cart, offered her my apologies, made sure she and the boy were unharmed before I moved on. We exchanged no more than a few words.' A pause. 'It would have been discourteous simply to drive on without some acknowledgement, Father.'

The silence that followed was ominous. Matiss twisted his hands together, plainly disturbed; Aleksis imagined how Stasya would act if she were witness to this. He thought of her storming forward to deliver a fiery speech about compassion and common sense. Or to tell a story that made the same point.

'How long have you graced us with your presence at Raven's Watch, Brother?'

'Two years, Father.' The voice was unsteady now.

'Two years. And you think to instruct me in the interpretation of the God's law? You will remain in the chapel overnight, under watch. You will remain kneeling during that time. No falling asleep; if you do, another night will be added to your penalty. Do you understand?'

'Yes, Father.'

'Do not transgress again, or you'll face a far more severe punishment. Next!'

The bell rang again. Another man fell to his knees, told of how he had been exhausted and hungry after a long day's battle drills and had eaten not only his own ration of soup and bread, but also that of a fellow Brother. This meal had been left unattended on a bench and he had thought nobody wanted it. The penalty: three days without food.

And so it continued, until all of the offenders were accounted for. Each summoned by the doleful bell; each confessing with eyes downcast to breaching some rule; each given a penalty that seemed quite out of proportion with the offence. The whole thing was deeply disturbing. As the three of them left the chapel, Matiss's hands were clenched into fists. Aleksis struggled to maintain the impassive face of a royal adviser. Karolis seemed the least troubled. Perhaps he had known what to expect.

'PICKED UP SOME information earlier,' Matiss said as another evening came. He was reclining in the bath, to the extent that was possible for a man of his height. They'd given him first turn this time, in view of his contribution to the winning tug-of-war team. There'd been ten men on each end of the very sturdy rope; Matiss had been what was known as the anchor man for his team, the one at the far end, and in the absence of the bishop, who had not made an appearance all day, the brethren had been almost as noisy in their appreciation as any crowd of well-muscled locals celebrating a victory at a village fair. 'Might be useful, might not.'

'Tell me.' They were keeping their voices down, even in the privacy of their quarters.

'The bishop's often away for a night, a couple of nights. Takes the same monk as escort every time. Nobody knows where they go.'

'I could speculate,' Karolis murmured. 'But in view of the penalty for associating with a female, even for the most innocent of interchanges, I doubt I'm right.'

'Family?' Matiss rose from the tub, creating a minor flood on the slate floor tiles, and accepted the towel that Aleksis held out.

'Parents deceased,' Aleksis said. 'No siblings that I know of. They used to live in the south, near Oak Valley.'

Matiss raised his brows but said nothing.

'I wouldn't trouble yourself, Matiss. He's unlikely to be going so far, even supposing he still has connections in the area. Perhaps, after we get back to court, it may be worth investigation. Anything else?'

'Only that some of the monks aren't so bad,' Karolis said. 'Get them away from the rules and restrictions for a bit and they can be quite friendly. Though that might only mean they're trying to worm out our secrets, I suppose. One or two of the younger ones clearly have doubts about what they've signed up to here, but once they're in, it's pretty much impossible to get out. And they do enjoy the combat practice, the drills and so on. Might be different when it's real, and you're watching your comrades hurt or dying. Not to speak of killing people yourself. Perhaps that's one reason the rules are so strict here.'

'No hints of when some kind of real combat might last have happened?' Aleksis asked.

'A carefully guarded secret, as you'd expect. I did visit the stables to check on our horses. Amazing place, grand in scale. Had a chat to one of the workers about the best way to get horses ready for an extended trip. He spoke about the roads to the north, up as far as the border. I didn't ask too many questions, just let him talk. I believe the Order has a fairly new house there.'

'Established before the current Ruler's time, but newish, yes,' Aleksis said. 'Karolis, feel free to get in the bath. The sooner we all wash off the grime of the day, the sooner we can sleep. In the morning, if I don't get called to speak to Petras, I'll request a meeting. Maybe I'll suggest firmly but politely that if he doesn't talk to me I'll consider heading home anyway. I'd like to leave by midday if the ferryman can accommodate that. Another night at the inn, then straight to Dragon's Keep.'

'You're really worried.' Karolis had stripped off and was in the bath.

Soap suds almost concealed the bright auburn of his hair and beard. 'Close your eyes,' said Matiss, dipping a large cup in the water, then pouring the contents over his comrade's head. 'And one more. Aleks? What do you think she's going to do in your absence?'

'Perhaps nothing. But I have a bad feeling. Why send us here with such urgency if the matter in question doesn't require a meeting even on our second day? I think we've been got out of the way for some reason. I hope I'm wrong.'

THEY PACKED THE next morning as if for departure. Matiss went down to the jetty to speak to the ferryman and ensure that, if they needed it, he would take them and their horses across the lake some time close to midday. As Karolis was preparing for his bout with the monastery's unarmed combat champion, Brother Paavo came to fetch Aleksis. The bishop was ready for a meeting.

In the reception chamber where they had met before, Petras was enjoying a flask of wine.

'Master Aleksis, will you join me?' He waved a hand toward the second cup on the tray.

'Thank you, no. I'm pleased to have the opportunity to talk with you at last. I understand the matter is of some urgency?'

'Perhaps, perhaps. It is hard to tell. Word has reached my ears that there may be a challenge to the Ruler's authority at the next Grand Council.'

'A challenge. From what quarter?'

'The north. Vidrik of the Birchlands. Odd, you might say, that such a man would act thus toward a neighbour. But…' Petras paused for effect; it was as if he were telling a story, and Aleksis wondered how much of this was in fact truth, and how much the prelude to some different and more genuine matter. Along with most of his people Vidrik adhered to a very old faith based on gods and goddesses of earth and sky, fire and water. The people of the Birchlands were peaceable. Their festivals of faith were joyful events with music and dancing. For such a leader to threaten the authority and security of the Northlands would be odd indeed.

'But?' prompted Aleksis, thinking fast. He should not dismiss this out of hand. If such a threat were real, it would surely not emanate from Vidrik, but from another source entirely. One that was not difficult to guess. Aleksis waited for the answer he was almost sure would come.

'You look surprised, Master Aleksis. You can imagine, I think, that the impetus for such a challenge comes from beyond Vidrik's borders. A power far larger and stronger than that of the Birchlands is behind this.'

'You speak of the Grasslands?'

'I do. You are aware that our Order maintains a number of houses spread across both the Northlands and Southlands, some almost as substantial as Raven's Watch. We continue to build; the numbers of our faithful constantly increase. It has long been of concern to me that we have not established a footing in the Birchlands, thanks to the superstitious nonsense Vidrik encourages among his people.' Petras's voice dropped to a murmur, though it was surely not possible for the guards outside the door to hear their conversation. 'You may be aware that our most northerly establishment lies on the bank of the river Dekla, which marks the border between the Northlands and the Birchlands. Vidrik did not welcome our building activities there; a substantial settlement lies on his side of the river, directly opposite the site of our house. But he could take no action. The land on which we built was the Ruler's to bestow. What better place for the Church of the Godly to fly its banner than there, overlooking that realm of primitive earth-worshippers? So our men built, and settled, and spread the word of the One and Only God.'

Aleksis waited. There must be a *but* coming.

'The Dekla provides fine fishing; the catch helps sustain the residents of our house there, and also Vidrik's people who live on the other shore. Both our brethren and those village folk take small boats out in season, and there is also some fishing from the banks here and there. The One and Only God ensures his faithful of sustenance.'

The river also sustains those who do not believe in this

deity, Aleksis thought. This leader of men believed only what it suited him to believe. Where was the bishop going with this?

'Among our brethren in that house are some adventurous souls. When conditions are favourable, they take a larger craft some distance downriver. Once or twice they have put in at landing places on the other side and engaged with local folk; the bounties of the Dekla do encourage settlement close by the water. Indeed, we have at least one Birchlands man among our brethren, which has proved useful. He can guide us in understanding their speech. The tongue, you understand, is not the same as ours. Though not so very different.'

Aleksis restrained himself from tapping a foot in frustration. 'Engaged with local folk,' he echoed. 'Engaged in what way?'

'Talked. Discussed matters. Our men spoke of the faith and the opportunities it offers. There were some disagreements. Occasionally it came to blows. Nothing worthwhile is won without a fight.'

Ah. Now, at last, the man was getting to the point. 'What were your men hoping to win, Excellency? Hearts? New recruits? A better share of the fishing? Or perhaps a new place to build?' Aleksis managed to keep his tone to one of polite interest.

'We are constantly in search of fresh opportunities, Master Aleksis.' Petras cleared his throat. 'I had word that our brethren, in their travels down the Dekla, had experienced some odd occurrences. Interference with their nets; folk observing them from concealed positions on the banks – my brethren are skilled in detecting such activity – and one attempt to halt their progress when they came close to a certain fortified settlement on the Birchlands' side. Also whispers from some of the local people, suggesting spies from the Grasslands may already have a presence in that region. I'm aware that the Ruler can be somewhat… determined in her course forward. I have often wondered how you manage to do your job, Master Aleksis, when the lady has a tendency to make her choices without heeding the wise advice folk of greater experience can offer. Should those rumours be true, she cannot afford to ignore them. You and I know, Master Aleksis, how perilous an armed advance from that quarter would be, so close to our own border. And we know Vidrik is neither equipped nor inclined to stand against such an advance.'

'I see.' Aleksis's mind was working quickly. Important not to say the wrong thing here, or he would antagonise the bishop. If true, this was indeed a matter that should be drawn to Elisabeta's attention. But he suspected the account was exaggerated, at the very least. What did Petras really want from him? 'Have you raised this with Vidrik or his advisers?'

'Hah!' The sound was contemptuous. 'I'd only be given a lecture on interfering in other folk's business, I fear. Vidrik is the kind of leader who sees everyone as a friend. That is, until the moment they hold a knife to his throat. He's gullible. Naive. He might at the most suggest I withdraw the presence of the Church of the Godly from his borders. Or attempt to extract a promise that I and my brethren will not seek to convert the people of the Birchlands to the faith. While he sits, all unawares, in the shadow of an enemy with the power to destroy not only his land, but ours as well.'

An unhelpful response flashed through Aleksis's mind. *If your faith is so powerful, why not take your mission into the Grasslands instead? Should you turn those folk to your ways, the One and Only God would surely be impressed*. 'I see,' he said. 'What precisely is it you want from me, Excellency, other than advice on the matter?'

The bishop steepled his fingers, turning his gaze directly on Aleksis. One day someone would make a stone statue of the man and it would look just like this. 'Explain the situation to the Ruler as soon as you get back to court. The information my men pick up when they are in the Birchlands cannot be sent to Lady Elisabeta in writing. Pass on to her what I have told you, and demand that she raises this at the Grand Council as a matter of urgency. A decision must be reached there, in Vidrik's presence and before witnesses. We must prepare ourselves to stand together against the Grasslands, should the worst come about. We cannot have any dissent among the Council members.'

For a few moments, Aleksis could not wrestle his response into an acceptable form. Then, 'My role is adviser to the Ruler,' he said, governing his tone. 'An adviser offers advice. He does not make demands. Certainly, I will apprise Lady Elisabeta of your concerns and the basis for them, and will pass on your suggestion that this be discussed at the Council. Of course, as a Council member you would be free to raise the issue yourself. It might be wise to let Lord Vidrik know well in advance that this is what you plan. A message to him could be carefully worded so as not to reveal sensitive information, Excellency. I'm sure you are expert at such things.'

Something that might have been a smile passed fleetingly over the stony face. 'I want the Ruler to raise it. By calling you here now and informing you of the matter in full, I am allowing her plenty of time to think it through and offer a well-prepared plan at the Council. The threat is real, Master Aleksis. Make sure Lady Elisabeta understands that. She should be aware of our Order's capacity to support – or to lead – her forces in any action. Or indeed, to act alone should no such cooperation be forthcoming. That, of course, is highly confidential. For the Ruler's ears only.' The bishop rose from his seat while Aleksis was still trying to take this in. 'Now, if you have no further questions, I have other business to attend to.'

Aleksis, too, had risen; one did not remain seated when the bishop was standing. He had questions aplenty, but it would be wiser not to ask them. 'Thank you, Excellency. And as it seems our business is concluded, my men and I will head back toward Dragon's Keep today; I believe the ferryman is able to accommodate us. Thank you for your hospitality.'

'Safe journey, Master Aleksis.'

It was as Aleksis stepped out of the chamber that the hallway's narrow windows shone momentarily gold, and a few moments later came the rumble of thunder. A spring storm, come from nowhere. By the time he reached the guest quarters he could hear the heavy drumming of rain on the roof. Take the horses on the ferry in this? Hardly. Unless the storm passed quickly the paths would be a muddy nightmare and the river crossings too dangerous to attempt. They might not even get away tomorrow. Curse it!

No point in heading for the training ground. He prowled the room, his mind whirling with unsettling thoughts. Stasya. Lukas, Irina. The Ruler so caught up in her desire for amber that she seemed quite heedless of the damage she was causing along the way. Where had that come from? What had changed in Elisabeta, that so often now she seemed wilfully deaf to reason? He made himself sit down. With his head in his hands, he tried to summon his father's voice, a voice of kindness and common sense. *Keep the balance, Aleks. Keep the balance.*

19

STASYA

STASYA HAD BEEN mopping floors, scrubbing greasy pots, and generally making herself useful in the servants' quarters. Keeping busy helped the time pass more quickly. With luck the Ruler would not ask to see her again until Aleksis and the others were back. Aleksis had a way of calming folk down, giving them enough time to speak, explaining quietly instead of shouting the same thing over and over. Maybe all senior advisers were like that. It might be part of their training. Or maybe she'd misjudged him earlier on, just a bit.

Irina was on her feet at last, ghost-pale but moving about. Stasya noticed her watching intently as Biruta prepared bread dough with the help of several strong-looking girls. Perhaps Biruta and the others did not know Irina had baked bread for a whole village. Maybe she should mention it now.

Before she had decided whether that was a good idea or not, she found herself back in Elisabeta's council chamber, with the Ruler asking the same questions, just with different words. There was no point in listening. Instead Stasya told herself a tale in her head, about a loaf of bread that came to life and started giving all the other foods in the kitchen crazy orders. She imagined Lukas listening; pictured his sweet smile. When the Ruler struck her on the cheek, she was shocked back to awareness.

'Speak! Answer me!' Elisabeta's voice was iron-hard.

Stasya could find no answer. She had not heard the question, and even if she had, what could she say? How long had she been standing here, off in a dream? Too long, it seemed, for the Ruler was pale with fury, her hands clenched into white-knuckled fists. 'You will not return to the servants' quarters,' she said. 'More appropriate arrangements have been made. The guard will escort you. Think over your situation with great care, young woman. Your lack of cooperation puts more than one person at risk. Go now.'

Stasya did not even attempt a bow. This woman might be Ruler of the Northlands, but she was nothing more than a bully. A person like that should not be in a position of power. She was tempted to say so, but imagined Aleksis watching and held her silence.

The guard led her outside, not into the garden but to a place that smelled of pigs, though she could not see any sign of them. The building they entered was barn-like, made from wood, and constructed hard up against the high outer wall of Dragon's Keep. Oddly, its doors were reinforced with iron. Now she could hear the animals grunting, and their uneasy thoughts flooded her mind. *Where did my sister go? I heard screaming. They took my babies. They hurt me! I'm hungry.* And other voices. Rats, somewhere close by. An owl, perched in the rafters, dozing. If she was being put in here, she'd have to ask them to bring Flip, who'd been left with Irina. But not now.

The guard was explaining something. With an effort, Stasya shut out those other voices, the ones that came to her in silence. 'Sorry, what did you say?'

'Wait in here for a bit, they're bringing the other one.'

'The other one?'

'The other woman, your friend that came in with you.'

Before she could say a word, the man strode off, closing the outer door behind him. She heard the bolt slam shut; these folk must prize their pigs highly. Curse it, what was this? What was the point of it?

At least she was on her own for a bit. She might as well have a good look around the place. Pigs would likely make better companions than some of the human folk of Dragon's Keep. The barn might even offer opportunities for escape. The man had said, *You'll be in there*, and pointed to a closed-off area at the back. There was a door, bolted like the other one. She approached on cautious feet; perhaps the boar was in there, though more likely not. She would have felt his presence.

With her hand on the bolt, she opened her mind to whatever might lie beyond that barrier. *I am a friend. I won't hurt you.* She waited; the only response was a stirring among the rats, who might have many hideaways in such a place. Stasya drew a steadying breath and slid the bolt open.

It was dark in there. Apart from the door, the only opening was a single high window opening back into the main area of the barn, too small to admit anything bigger than a bat or sparrow. This was probably a storage area, though it was empty now save for a few wisps of straw on the earthen floor and a bucket in the corner. Was this really where she was supposed to stay? And Irina too? There was nothing here. And it was cold. Even if they brought her belongings and Irina's, even if they brought bedding, this would be... She imagined it with the door closed. At night, with no light at all. They couldn't do this. They couldn't! But of course they could. The Ruler of the Northlands could do whatever she wanted.

Stasya's heart was thudding; dark images swirled in her mind. Irina cooped up in here, just when she was starting to come out from the shadows. Stasya herself shut in, helpless to do a thing. Or a terrible choice: Stasya agreeing to what the

Ruler wanted, because if she didn't, bad things would start happening to the people she cared about. Lady Elisabeta had hinted at that. *Your lack of cooperation puts more than one person at risk.* Irina. Lukas. Flip. Oh gods!

There might still be time to get out, to take action, to find Lukas, to… Every instinct called her to move, to find a way even if it meant trying to break down a barred door. But no. That was foolish. And there was a more pressing need, one she could deal with if she was quick. She went back out into the barn. Stood perfectly still, struggling to steady her breathing. In, two, three, four; pause; out, two, three, four; pause. And again. Her mind reached for Flip; found her on the pallet in the women's quarters, half-asleep. *Flip. Move. Now.* She showed an image of the dog transforming into a tiny wren, flying out from whatever window she could find. It was hard to show the way to the barn clearly; the walk here had been confusing. Instead, she showed pigs, thinking the smell would guide Flip. She showed an iron-barred door, herself within the barn, the roosting owl, the rats hiding away. *Come here, quickly. Don't let anyone see you. Stay as a bird.* She willed the guard not to return and interrupt her until this was safely done. *Watch out for the owl*, she added belatedly. It might be daytime, but who knew whether a hungry owl might still wake and see the visiting wren as a surprise meal?

She paced, waiting. What if they went in to take Irina before Flip had left the sleeping quarters? What if someone saw her change? What if… *Stop it*, she ordered herself. This might not be as bad as it seemed. When Aleksis got back, surely he would… what? The Ruler was the Ruler. She gave the orders; he only advised. Yes, he'd made meeting Lady Elisabeta less of an ordeal for her, just as he'd made the ride to Dragon's Keep easier for Irina and Lukas. But hadn't he been carrying out the Ruler's orders at every point? He'd brought Stasya here so the Ruler could dig out her secrets and use them to reach the Hermit for her own selfish purposes. All that talk about making life better for her people was nonsense. What about the folk of Heartwood, whose lives she had ruined? The Ruler must consider them simple folk, too ignorant and lowly to matter.

Stasya pictured Irina lifting a tray of perfect rolls from the oven, the firelight illuminating her features. Lukas, his hands strong but gentle as he freed a goat that had become entangled in some bushes. Vidas grooming a horse in his stable yard, sharing a joke with Kiril; the two of them in gales of laughter. Kristina bending her head over her needlework, and a delicate border of wildflowers unfolding on the linen as she stitched. Farmer Jurgis addressing a village meeting, his voice strong and sure, his smile drawing in every person there. Simple folk, yes. Fine, good-hearted souls.

A high twittering from above startled her. Flip flew in. The owl stirred, then slept again, and the tiny bird came down to alight on Stasya's shoulder. Good; at least she was safe. For now. Stasya showed her what had happened. Warned her that the guard would be back. Took her into the storage room and showed images of the three of them, Stasya, Flip and Irina, shut in there. For that, surely, was what these people intended. Even if Aleksis came back soon, and even if he tried to persuade the Ruler to let them return to the servants' quarters, Lady Elisabeta would only say yes if Stasya agreed to her plan. She would sooner die.

For a moment Flip was a dog again, rubbing against her legs, whining to be picked up. 'No,' Stasya whispered. 'Bird!' But she gathered the dog up anyway, holding her against her chest, dropping a kiss on her head, touching her soft ears. *Bird. Now.* And Flip obeyed, flying up to perch high, but not too close to the owl. And just in time, for there were footsteps outside, and men's voices, then a scraping sound as the bolt was drawn on the barn door. They were here.

* * *

The cold penetrated every corner; by night it was enough to freeze a person to the bones. Stasya and Irina had one blanket between them, and a threadbare old thing it was. Stasya was close to breaking her own rules and asking Flip to change. On such a night, a warm dog would have been worth her weight in gold. But Irina did not know Flip was anything other than an ordinary dog, and Stasya would not risk revealing the secret even to her. Besides, who knew when a guard might suddenly come into the barn and see a dog where there had been none? Stasya wondered if anyone out there had noticed Flip was missing, or if anyone cared in the least that she and Irina were suddenly gone from the servants' quarters. Maybe this kind of thing happened all the time at Dragon's Keep.

It was too cold for sleep; the best way to get through the chill night would be by moving about and passing the time with conversation. Or stories. Since the two of them had been shut in here, Irina had huddled on the sparse straw, hugging the blanket around her and saying only the occasional word or two. 'Here,' when she'd offered Stasya a share of the blanket. That was earlier, when there had been enough light for them to see each other. 'Sorry,' when she stumbled over Stasya after visiting the privy bucket. Now, in the darkness, the sounds of pigs still came to them faintly. They were next door, Stasya guessed, in a separate enclosure to one side of the building. They were restless, scared, deeply unhappy. She should reach out to them, offer comfort of some kind. It was hard to know what to say, what mind-pictures to show. Perhaps they were awaiting slaughter. What story could a person tell that would be of any help? But she had to try. It was not only the wretched pigs who needed her, but also the woman shivering beside her.

'You keep the blanket,' she said. 'I'm going to move around and try to get warm.' The storage room was six paces long, four wide. As she walked to and fro, hands out in front to guide her, a story came to mind, sudden and startling. Should she tell it? Might it only make Irina sadder? Could the same story lift the hearts of both pigs and human women? Perhaps. It was worth trying. She'd tell it in words for Irina, and at the same time make mind-pictures for the pigs, and hope it helped both.

'Once, in the time of our grandmothers, and in a place not so very far away, there lived a mother who was strong and brave. She was not afraid of anything. Neither a noisy farmer, nor a heavy draught horse, nor the wild north wind could frighten her; neither the deep pond nor the dark storm clouds nor the demands of her children disturbed her. She was the strongest mother in all the valley.' A trace of moonlight showed itself beyond the small window, but within the chamber the darkness remained. Stasya sensed that Irina was watching her, but there was no reading her expression. High above them, Flip was following the story too; Stasya felt her thoughts: *Yes! Go on! And make this a happy ending!* But the true story did not have a happy ending. Tomas could not be brought back from the dead. The young of the pigs had been taken away to an uncertain future. The sows were unlikely to escape a life in which such losses must be endured over and over, the only alternative being the swift knife and the stew pot. *More*, Flip urged, jolting her back to the tale.

'Life was happy, peaceful, busy. Until disaster struck the valley, and folk died.' For the pigs, she showed a farmer herding them roughly into confinement, separating half-grown piglets from their mothers. 'The mother had been a leader. She had helped feed the folk of the valley and had been a good friend to all. She was kind and thoughtful, and the son she raised had grown up to be a quiet, good young man, helpful and courteous. But a terrible thing happened, and the good son left that place forever, on a journey to another world.' In the mind-picture, a sow watched as her piglets were loaded onto a cart and driven away, the young squealing in distress, the sow calling, calling as their voices faded away and the cart vanished down the road. From the pigsty nearby there was no sound at all. But Stasya knew the pigs were awake and aware.

'The mother wanted to go with her son, to follow him. But on that road, there was no following. So, she sought the wisdom of the great goddess of creatures, herself sometimes called the Mother, who had the power to grant visions of past, present or future; of this world and the Afterworld, and sometimes even the Otherworld. *Please show me my son,* the mother begged. *Show me where he is; show me he is well and happy.*

'In her mind the mother travelled then, a long, long way over stony ground, uphill and downhill. She walked in the rain, she walked in the freezing cold, she kept to the path through tempest and drought, one foot before the other. For even in visions, finding answers is not easy. At last, she came to a place like no other she had seen in her life, a place where warm light fell on fields of wildflowers, and strange birds flew overhead, singing in sweet voices. The mother knew without asking that she could go no further. To enter that place was to leave this world forever, and although she longed to take that one step forward, something held her back. She stood at the edge and called her lost one's name, raising a hand in greeting, for although she could see no sign of him, she knew he was there. She sang a little tune she had sung when he was a baby, a song about rabbits in their burrows and birds in their nests that used to lull him to sleep. And when she was halfway through, another voice joined in: that of the lost son. With tears rolling down her cheeks, the mother sang with him, the whole song twice through, and by the end she could see him across the field, with animals around him – pigs, goats, sheep, a flock of chickens, and never a squabble among them – and a beaming smile on his face as he waved back to her. Not only that, but there was a man with him, a familiar, beloved man who now put his arm around his son's shoulders. A man who would forever be five-and-twenty years old, and a boy who would be always eleven. There by his side was a faithful old dog whom she remembered well, a true companion.

'Oh, how she longed to run to them! But it was not her time. Her son was with his father; they were happy. The creatures were peaceful and content in that place beyond the world she knew. This was what she had asked to see. She waved again, and smiled through her tears, and then they were gone. She was alone by her hearth fire, in whose flames she had seen the goddess. The sorrow would never quite leave her, but she could make her peace with it. She could live her life.' In the mind-pictures, Stasya showed the sows their lost ones in a broad green field with a mud wallow, a shelter, ample fresh water. She could not offer them a better life, but at least their minds might be set at ease for a little. They might dream kinder dreams.

For some time after she finished, there was utter silence. Then Stasya felt Irina's arms around her, and Irina's head against her shoulder, and heard, through the sobs, Irina's soft words, 'Thank you, Stasya. Thank you.'

20

STASYA

'WE SPOKE BEFORE of amber. And of old tales. Are there any such tales that touch on its curative power?'

Today the Ruler was speaking softly and wearing a kinder expression. Stasya wanted nothing more than to edge closer to the hearth fire; she was filthy, exhausted and shivering after a night in that place. And Irina was still locked up there. No word of Lukas. No sign of Aleksis yet. Best attempt some kind of answer.

'There are some that I know of, my lady.'

'Oh, you're talking today?' Lady Elisabeta's brows rose in mock surprise. 'Tell me one of these tales.'

'May I sit down, my lady?' Her back ached; it was a struggle to stay upright. *I will be strong. I must be.* Irina. Lukas. Flip. She had to find a way out for all of them.

'Sit, sit.' The Ruler waved a hand toward the bench.

Stasya sat. Her body was full of pain. How many such nights could she and Irina endure? Had the Ruler really put them in that place deliberately, or was that the act of some wayward guard? She wanted to ask. But because of the smile and the softer manner, she would tell a story instead.

'Once, long ago,' she began, her voice less than steady, 'a race of uncanny folk lived in the depths of Heartwood Forest. They were tall and beautiful, fleet of foot and expert in magic, and the local people called them the Forest Folk. The race had been unseen by the human inhabitants of that place for longer than the oldest grandmothers could remember. But sometimes there were signs that the Forest Folk might have travelled a certain path, or bathed in a certain lake, or paused to admire a lovely shimmering birch or to wonder at a tall larch whose head seemed to touch the sky itself.'

The Ruler was listening, even without Aleksis there to keep things calm. She poured a cup of mead and passed it across to Stasya. One sip was enough. It was balm to her dry throat, but too strong to tolerate on an empty stomach. Fresh water would have been more welcome. Stasya nodded thanks.

'People wondered why the Forest Folk chose not to show themselves. If they had the gift of magic, they surely could not be afraid of humankind, for magic gave power. It gave strength. Or so people believed, though none of them had ever seen anything magical themselves, or if they had, they had not recognised it for what it was. For them, magic was frightening, a thing to be spoken of only in undertones, or whispered behind the shield of a hand. In particular, a person did not mention it before priests or other church leaders, as that might bring down the most severe of consequences.'

A fleeting smile crossed the Ruler's stern features. 'Go on,' she said.

'There was a boy in the village who was known as Amber. Perhaps that was his true name. Or perhaps it was a name folk had given him because he wore an amber token around his neck, strung on a cord. It was only a small thing, a scrap, smoothed by water into a shape something like a fish. Other children teased Amber, suggesting his real parents must have been Forest Folk, though everyone knew his mother was an ordinary village wife and his father a travelling merchant who had stayed with her awhile then moved on. As for the little token, Amber had worn it since he was a baby. The odd thing was that he never got sick. Other children caught coughs and colds in winter; they had upset stomachs in the season of fresh fruit, summer agues, sore ears, skin rashes. Not Amber. Not ever.'

Lady Elisabeta was listening intently. Something about this had caught her interest. 'Go on,' she said when Stasya paused to cough.

'Might I have some water, please? There was none left for us in the – the place where they put us.'

'Paula!'

The sharp call made Stasya flinch. The maidservant came in, the Ruler rapped out an order, and a flask and cup were fetched and placed on the bench, within reach.

'Thank you,' Stasya said, then drank thirstily. The maid gave her an odd look, then bobbed a curtsy to Lady Elisabeta and went out.

The story. Stasya drank again, then set the cup down. 'When Amber's mother fell deathly ill, the village was full of whispers. Nobody had ever asked the boy to share his necklace; it had felt wrong to suggest this when the thing had perhaps been a gift from his long-absent father, or even – if by some chance the rumours were true – from a fey father the lad had never met. Over the years, the folk of the village, folk of all ages, had endured their illnesses. Some had recovered; some had perished; some had survived in a weakened state.

'But when it was the boy's mother who lay in the grip of some unknown malady, would it not be right, folk murmured, for Amber to take the token from his own neck, strung on the cord that had been lengthened as the child grew, and place it around his mother's? Did he not want to save her life? Nobody was quite prepared to ask Amber directly; all feared the consequences of speaking out. If only they could ask the Forest Folk, who knew and understood such things, or so the old tales suggested. But those folk of ancient story did not show themselves.

'Amber was by now eight years old and devoted to his mother. He heard the whispers. He knew what people thought he should do. But he was scared. What if he saved his mother's life only to die himself without the protection of the necklace? But… that was selfish, wasn't it? There was nobody he could ask. His grandmother was there, tending to his mother, but he had always been a little afraid of her, with her moody silences and sudden outbursts of anger. She had more than once referred to him as *spawn of the devil*. He did not know what that meant, only that it sounded bad. So, Amber crept around the cottage like a mouse and watched his mother grow sicker each day. He was desperate to help, but what if he gave her the necklace and everything went wrong? What if his fey father, if there really was such a person, appeared on the doorstep and dragged him off to the strange home of the Forest Folk? What if a devil came?

'While Amber was still trying to pluck up his courage, Grandmother, too, fell sick. There was nobody to help; either folk were sick themselves or they were busy tending to others, and the boy was left to cope on his own. He did the best he could, but it was too much for him to manage. The food ran out; the woodpile was down to splinters and scraps. He could not leave the house to seek help. What could he do?

'Grandmother was not as weak as Mother, and one morning when Amber was trying to sponge her face with a wet cloth, her bony hand reached up, seized his beloved token and ripped the thing right off his neck. He cried out; it hurt a lot. But he did not snatch it back, indeed could not, for Grandmother's fist was tight around it and her rheumy eyes had a look in them that said, *Don't meddle with me or you'll be sorry*. She did not order Amber to take the token to his mother, to see if it would make her well again. No; Grandmother was keeping the thing for herself.'

Stasya paused for another drink of water. The Ruler seemed spell-bound by this story; she was waiting eagerly for more, sitting bolt upright on the very edge of her chair. Why had this one caught her interest? Did she believe that if amber had the power to cure the sick it would win her better trading profits? Best be careful with the ending.

'The boy Amber could do nothing but go on chopping wood for the fire, fetching water, trying his best to keep the two women clean and warm. One thing did change for the better. The day after Grandmother stole his necklace, he opened the door to find a covered dish on the step. Someone had left food: a tasty porridge, enough for all three of them, with some left over. Beside it, a little jug of fresh milk. Amber did not question who might have left it there. Instead, he wept a few tears of gratitude and brought the wondrous gift inside. He coaxed the women to try the food while it was still warm. Grandmother was well enough to feed herself with a spoon if he held the bowl for her. Mother, he had to feed like a small child, mouthful by mouthful, and she only took a little. But when she was done, she reached out her hand and touched his cheek, and murmured something that might have been, *Good boy*.

'So it went on: Amber as housekeeper and nursemaid, the two women bedridden, and supplies that arrived each morning before sunrise. There was food to sustain the three of them, and also wood for the fire, neatly chopped and added to the woodpile, though they heard no sound of an axe. Perhaps neighbours were doing this, though they never had before. Or maybe someone else was helping, someone who did not belong to the village or to the human realm at all. Amber did not care; the only thing that mattered was getting his mother well again. And his grandmother, of course.

'The illness passed; the village lost five good souls that winter. But Amber's mother was not among them. She rallied and grew strong again, sustained by the mysterious meals and by her son's love and dedication. Grandmother was not so fortunate, though she, too, had eaten the food and received the loving care. She passed away in her bed, with the amber fish still clutched in her hands. Before she called for the village undertaker, Amber's mother sat him down for a serious talk. She had removed the token from the old woman's body and returned it to her son, reminding him to wear it hidden beneath his clothing. She thanked him for his love and care. And she said they should never, ever tell anyone about those meals or the firewood or any part the amber might have played in events. *But,* said Amber, *it was Grandmother who had my amber fish, not you. She wouldn't give it back to me. Yet she died and you got better. Does that mean there's no magic?*

'Mother put an arm around his shoulders. *Maybe the magic is love,* she said. *Or maybe the magic only works if it's used in the right spirit. Care for others, compassion, kindness. You are made of those, my boy.* And she added, *Don't forget what I said. The food, the firewood, they were special gifts to us. If magic played any part in them, it was used to help a good boy look after those he cared about. And maybe the magic was not from the amber fish, but only the action of a kind neighbour. We'll never know. And we'll never tell.* The next day they buried Grandmother with prayers and songs. And if they spoke of the secret again, it was only between the two of them.'

The ending could have gone several different ways, for the tale owed as much to Stasya's imagination as to her knowledge of the old stories, and each telling was different, depending on the situation and the audience. Now, it was greeted with silence. The Ruler was looking at her, but her expression gave nothing at all away. Would she say thank you for the first time ever? Would she once again pepper Stasya with angry questions? Would she shout and slap her in the face? This story, too, this one happening right now, might have many possible endings.

'I see,' the Ruler said eventually. 'Now let us be clear about this. You, too, possess an amber token, like the boy in the tale, though yours is in the shape of a bird. Tell me this: have you worn that piece of amber since you were very young? Have you enjoyed the same excellent health as that child did?' There was something new in her eyes, something that alerted Stasya to danger, fuzzy as her head was feeling. She must focus. She must answer with care.

'Lukas and I were old enough to make that climb through the forest safely. We were not children. This is the third spring since we found Clearwater.' She could not help adding, 'And I don't have the amber owl, not any longer. It was taken from me. I understand it is locked away somewhere here at court.'

The Ruler's lips tightened. 'And your health? Did wearing amber make any difference?'

'That old tale is… only a tale, my lady. I can't afford to get sick; folk rely on me.' *And there's nobody to look after me.* She would not say that, true as it was. 'I've had the same coughs and colds other folk had in our village, both before and after I wore the amber owl, but mostly I'm in good health.' How long that would last if she and Irina were kept cooped up in the storage room without even fresh water to drink was another matter. She imagined Aleksis sitting beside her, whispering, *Don't lose your temper. Answer only the questions she asks.* But there was more to be said. 'Some folk do believe amber can ward off sickness. But it might only work if used in the right spirit. Or it might depend on how the person got the amber or where it came from. Many folk dismiss the idea as fanciful.'

'But you do not?'

'All old tales have some truth in them. That doesn't mean every single part of them is true. That story tells us about kindness, about acting unselfishly. That boy must have grown up to be a fine man.' As poor Tomas would have done, if the fire had not cut his life so short.

Lady Elisabeta moved then, taking two steps toward the fire, warming her hands, briefly facing away. Stasya drank the last of her water. She tried to straighten her shoulders. Her scalp felt itchy. Chances were she'd picked up lice. Dark thoughts crept into her mind: how she could bargain with this woman, one secret for a hot bath, one for a set of clean clothing, one for a meal for herself and Irina. An offer to lead the Ruler's men to the Hermit in exchange for freedom for herself and Flip, Irina and Lukas. She would tell a story about that feeling some time; about how easy it would be to give in when you were tired and sore and cold and hungry. But she wouldn't give in. She couldn't. The survival of the forest was at stake. And something more, something she could not quite name, but she only had to remember the women of the Heartwood settlement speaking out that night after the fire, raising their voices to challenge the Commander, to know how important it was.

'I'll ask this only once.' The Ruler turned toward Stasya. Her tone was weighty now. 'And before you answer, understand that your safety and that of your companions is not guaranteed indefinitely. Will you use your knowledge and skills to guide a smaller party through the forest for me? To seek out this place known as the Hermit, and discover whether there is indeed a deposit of amber there? No cutting down of trees. No laying waste to the land. Just a journey of discovery, for a good cause. Will you do that?'

Stasya rose to her feet. That was a mistake; she felt dizzy, as if she might faint. She set her cup on the bench. Took a deep breath. 'That's the same question as before, just in different words. I don't believe we could do what you suggest without causing harm. What the Commander did at Heartwood was monstrous. And he was under your leadership. I can't have anything to do with this, not even with a smaller group of people. The idea goes against everything I believe in!' *Stay calm*, came the voice of the absent Aleksis. *Breathe. Speak quietly.* 'The forest is precious. It is… eternal. Whatever may or may not lie at the Hermit, we have no claim on it. Its secrets belong to those who live there. Trees. Creatures. Maybe the Forest Folk.'

The Ruler opened her mouth to speak, then closed it again. For just a moment Stasya thought perhaps she had actually listened and would reconsider her plan. But no. Lady Elisabeta shook her head in a way that suggested, *What is the point of talking to you?* Then she called, 'Guard!' and in a moment there was a guard in the chamber, awaiting orders.

'Take her out to the garden and make sure she stays there until I send word.' She turned to Stasya. 'What unfolds from here is your doing, girl. Keep that in mind.' A long pause, then she said, 'We will speak again. Tomorrow, I think.'

In the garden, she could breathe, even with a guard watching her every move. This time it was a broad, bearded man whose belt held more knives, surely, than even a court guard could possibly need at one time. Perhaps he collected them. Perhaps, when he finished his working day, this was a man who would go to the inn with his friends and enjoy telling stories over a mug of ale. Perhaps he had a wife and children at home. Did the guards have any home beyond Dragon's Keep? And if not, did they long to get away from this place, or were they actually content to work under Lady Elisabeta's rule?

Whoever was supposed to bring word was taking their time. The guard stood close by, rocking to and fro in his big boots.

'May I sit down on the bench?' Stasya asked.

The guard gave a grunt that seemed to mean yes, so she sat. There was a bird in the garden, darting about after insects. A finch. But not Flip. Perhaps that was for the best. Oh, the sunshine was good; she had been so cold. What was the Ruler thinking, to leave her and Irina without food, water or the means to clean their bodies and their clothing? Surely she could not intend to keep them in that place for long. Best not dwell on that now. Best enjoy whatever time she had here in the sun, among the flowers. That gardener was working again, quite close this time. Emptying a sack of compost onto a bed prepared for planting and digging it in. She wished she could go and talk to him, speak of something clean and healthy and good. Growing vegetables. Picking fruit. Watching the seasons pass. Maybe she would talk to the guard, instead of imagining his story.

'What is your name?' she asked. 'Mine is Stasya.'

He looked taken aback, as if he had not expected her to speak. 'My name is Marek.' A pause. 'You must be cold.'

'It's sunny here. Warmer. But yes, I am cold. They...' Perhaps she was not supposed to say anything about what had happened. Perhaps she was not even meant to talk to this man.

'Here, put this around your shoulders.' He took off his short cape and passed it over to her.

The warmth brought tears to her eyes. 'Thank you,' she said. 'It feels... very good.'

'I'll have to take it back later. The uniform needs to be correct.' And after a moment, 'Sorry.'

'It's welcome for now.'

They waited, Marek standing alert, Stasya on the bench. She willed clouds not to cover the sun, not yet. After a while she asked, 'May I walk down the garden and back? I promise not to bolt. There's nowhere to go anyway.'

'I'll walk with you. That way neither of us breaks any rules.' Marek gave her a smile; she found herself smiling back. What a difference a simple act of kindness could make. And how sad that the Ruler of the Northlands, the most powerful person in the whole country, did not understand that. Sad and terrible. Something inside that woman was chewing her up, twisting her thoughts.

They walked to the spot where the gardener was working. The man straightened, leaned on his spade, gave Marek a nod.

'You wouldn't have an old sack or two to spare, would you?' the guard asked. 'The young lady's been getting cold, and I can't leave my cape with her for long.'

Stasya gazed at a frame supporting a fine crop of runner beans and another with ripening peas. In the bed below them sprouted the feathery green tops of carrots; some had been pulled already and lay sun-bright in a basket. 'Your beans look so healthy,' she said, imagining the taste and feel in her mouth. 'The whole garden is lovely.'

In response the gardener stepped out onto the soil and plucked a bean pod, splitting it open with a fingernail. 'Here. Try them. They're good.'

Good? It was the best thing she'd ever tasted. He gave her a pod of peas to try, explaining what went into his compost heap and why it worked so well. As she listened, Stasya savoured each bite, aware of how strange it was to be here, surrounded by green growing things, with the sun shining and two strangers being kind and courteous, while there was Irina, and Lukas, and the Ruler's threats, and the fact that she was half-dressed in filthy clothing and no doubt smelled like a midden. Yet Marek had let her wear his cape, and this man was offering the food he'd grown with his own hands, and neither seemed to be judging her. If only she could ask for their help. But they lived and worked at Dragon's Keep. Everyone here answered to the Ruler. 'These are so delicious,' she said. 'Thank you!'

'No little dog today?' asked the gardener.

How to answer that simple yet dangerous question? She had no gift for lies. 'Not today. She did like it here. Lots of interesting smells.'

'Ah, well. Another time. Wait here a bit, will you?' He went off toward a shed further down the garden and returned with two sacks over his arm. They were clean and uncrumpled – surely new. 'Will these do?'

'Excellent,' said Marek. 'Pity we can't offer you a tunic or a proper blanket, but these might help keep you warm after sundown.'

'And this,' said the gardener, handing her a small bag. She did not need to look inside to know it held beans and peas, enough for two women to enjoy a small meal. 'You'd best get on; someone over there is looking for you.'

For a moment, before she turned around, Stasya hoped it might be Matiss. Or Aleksis. Or Pavel, who had looked after Flip for her. But it was not. It was the black-clad man again. Stanislav.

The gardener was suddenly attentive to his work, wielding his spade busily with his back to all of them. Marek swore under his breath.

'What is it?' Stasya whispered.

'Bad news,' he murmured. 'Do exactly as you're told. Don't try to argue. Wish I could help you, but…'

'You've helped already.' She put the sacks over her arm, clutched the little bag, and followed him forward.

Stanislav was not inclined to talk. There was something forbidding about his presence. In a story, Stasya thought, this man would be a mysterious and powerful figure, someone who could be good or evil, and nobody ever knew which choice he would make. She looked for a moment into the darkest eyes she had ever seen. He might be Death. For Death could be both cruel and merciful.

'Come,' he said, and led her away from the garden, the green growth, the sunshine, and back to the barn. He made no comment about the things she was carrying, the sacks for warmth, the bag of vegetables. *Let him not try to take these gifts of kindness*, she thought.

There was, as it turned out, one more gift. Stanislav waited until they had crossed the main part of the barn and were at the bolted door of the storage room. Stasya was forcing herself not to look up. She could feel Flip's presence on the rafters and could not risk drawing attention to her. Stanislav pulled the bolt open, then took something from a hidden pocket.

'For you,' he said. His voice was like the tolling of a deep, soft bell. 'With the Ruler's compliments.' He put a small package in her hand, something wrapped in cloth. Before she could react, he had pushed her into the storage room and shut the door behind her. The bolt slid across with a grinding sound.

'Irina?' Stasya looked one way, the other way, wondering if her friend was huddled in a corner. She looked again. There was enough light from the high window to make the truth plain: Irina was not here. A reprieve? Had they seen sense and let her return to the servants' quarters?

The package Stanislav had given her felt damp and slightly sticky. She dropped the other things she was carrying and unwrapped the cloth, wondering if it contained some kind of food. At first she could not tell what the contents were. And then… and then the light caught a glint there, and her heart jolted. *It's not real, it can't be real,* she told herself. *It's just a bad dream, it's…* But it was no dream. There in her hands, laid out on the bloodstained cloth, was a severed finger. A human finger. On it, still clinging, was Irina's silver ring.

21

ALEKSIS

THE RAIN SET in with a vengeance, punctuated by rolling thunder and sharp bright shocks of lightning. Water cascaded from rooftops; it pooled in the courtyard; it rendered stone steps perilous and made the lighting of lamps imperative, even by day. The wind got up, gusting in, driving the birds away and whipping the lake into whitecaps.

Perhaps it was just as well, Aleksis told himself. Karolis had won the fight against his much heavier opponent but had strained his right calf in doing so. He could hardly have been expected to undertake the long ride without another night's rest beforehand. Riding on rain-soaked tracks would be bad enough. The last thing they wanted was to be stranded somewhere along the way, unable to go on. So, another day, another night, and he must hope the storm would be over soon. Anxiety gnawed at him. The Ruler was unpredictable. Growing increasingly wayward in her decisions, apt to resort to unpalatable measures if folk did not do as she wished. If this continued, she might be incapable of presiding over the Grand Council when the time came. Which made his own mission especially pressing.

He considered what might have developed at Dragon's Keep in his absence. None of the other advisers would be prepared to intervene in the matter of Stasya and her companions, or the outcome of Rihard's disastrous actions at Heartwood. Not one of them was prepared to challenge Elisabeta. His imagination supplied various scenarios, each of them more troubling than the last. Was he getting this out of proportion? Was he losing his grasp?

'Aleks?'

He started. He'd been so deep in thought, he'd almost forgotten that Matiss was with him in the guest quarters. Karolis was resting in the adjoining chamber after Brother Evald, the infirmarian, had rubbed salve into his leg and supplied a draught to help dull the pain.

'You were miles away. Troubled?'

'You could say that.' Aleksis kept his voice down. Even here, in private quarters with the door closed, one had to be careful what was said aloud. 'What if this weather keeps up for days? What if Karolis isn't ready to undertake the ride tomorrow, or the next day?'

'One step at a time,' Matiss said. 'And remember, you can't save the world, only do your best. Karolis is tough. He can do it. And…' He paused.

'And what? I'm a fool to let this bother me?'

'You? A fool? Nothing could be further from the truth, my friend. But it's not like you to let something disturb you this way. Chances are we'll arrive back at court and all will be well. And if not, you'll deal with it as capably as you always do. *We'll* deal with it.'

'I wish I had your confidence.' Aleksis peered out the window again. 'And the ability to conjure fair weather.'

Matiss put a hand on his friend's shoulder. 'A little more silver in the hand of a certain ferryman might make a difference. I'll have a talk to him, see if he's prepared to go in the rain, provided it's not too heavy.'

Aleksis managed a smile. 'Do it without any fuss. Best if our eagerness to depart doesn't arouse suspicions.'

'The man in question knows me. I made a point of having a chat about boats and sailing. Complimented him on his fine control of the vessel, which was no lie.'

'What would I do without you?'

'You'd cope. You always do.'

Maybe this is the one time I don't. 'It feels precarious,' Aleksis murmured. 'One false step…'

'Your planning is faultless. You know that, Aleks. We move on. What other choice is there?' Matiss, too, kept his voice down.

'None, my friend. Absolutely none. But…'

'But it depends on her? And you hold back?'

'I wish this had not unfolded as it did. But it is what it is, and we'll deal with it as best we can.'

Matiss grinned. 'Ah. You're saying *we* now. That gives me some heart.'

'You're all heart, my friend.' Aleksis moved to the window. 'Is it wishful thinking on my part, or is the rain starting to ease?' Perhaps, after all, they might be back at Dragon's Keep by tomorrow night.

22

STASYA

HER ANGER CAME out in a great scream, a flood of hot fury. There were people out there, she could hear them moving about in the courtyard, she could hear the pigs grunting. 'Let me out!' she yelled. 'I want to see the Ruler! Let me out now!' At least, that was what she tried to shout, but there was too much in her head, and she was sobbing, and the words that tumbled out might have sounded like nonsense. There was no response. The door remained shut. She shouted until she was hoarse. Beat on the door until her hands were red raw. Wept until there were no more tears in her. How dared they do this? How dared they hurt poor Irina, who had lost her only son and her home and her work, who had seen her whole world turned upside down? How dared they take a finger from a woman whose hands created the very sustenance folk depended on? Irina's baking had not only filled folk's bellies, it had been a daily reminder of home and community and harvest, of what nature gave them, of... How could anyone do something so foul?

In the end she slumped to the floor, exhausted. Nobody was coming. Nobody cared. Where had they taken Irina? Why had they done this, why, why, why?

She knew the answer, of course. To make Stasya talk. To make her do what the Ruler wanted. It was an evil thing, a terrible thing. It sent shivers through her whole body, a shaking she could not control, even with the two sacks wrapped around her shoulders. They felt damp; where had that come from? In the dim light from the little high window, she examined the rough fabric and felt her stomach heave with nausea. Blood. It was on her clothing as well. Now, when she looked, she saw a big dark stain on the floor, with wisps of sticky straw here and there. What had happened here was surely more than the severing of a finger. What had they done?

A rustling beside her, and there was Flip, a dog now, pressing against her, gazing up with sad eyes. She gathered the little creature to her chest; the warmth was a comfort. Flip might have witnessed everything. But… was it fair to ask her for the story? To make her relive it? Was it so important to know?

I have to. I owe it to Irina. Stasya shared a mind-picture with Flip: Irina in the shadows of the storage chamber. Irina with the ring on her hand. Someone at the door, sliding the bolt open. *What happened?* She stroked Flip's ears gently, though her hands were trembling. *It was terrible, I know. But please show me if you can. We must help her.*

Flip's reluctance was in every inch of her small body. Her mind-pictures reached Stasya in brief flashes, as if they were too dreadful to hold for more than the space of a breath. 'Good girl,' Stasya whispered. 'Brave girl.' She had expected to see scenes of torture, and she did. One man held Irina, splaying her hand against the wood of the door. A second man, one she recognised, cut off her finger with such speed and precision that she guessed he did this kind of thing often. A tall, silent man. Stanislav. Stasya choked back bile. No attempt to stem the flow of blood. Nothing. They were going to leave her bleeding and go… but no. In the image, something created a distraction above the men. Both looked up, their attention caught. In that moment, quick as a darting swallow, Irina seized the knife one-handed from Stanislav and plunged it into her own heart.

Beyond words. Beyond thought. Stasya held Flip tight as sounds washed over her: a bird crying outside as it flew past, the shout of one man to another as they rolled something across the courtyard, water trickling down a wall. Out there, it had started to rain. In here, rats scuttled within the walls. Irina was gone. She was dead. Perhaps that was what she had wanted all along, once she had lost Tomas. But no, surely not; on those better days, at Laima and Ivo's farm, she had spoken of going back to Heartwood when it was safe, to find out where her son was buried, to lay flowers, to say prayers. This… this was impossible. Intolerable. She had to do something. She had to confront the Ruler, make her understand. She had to get out of here, now, right now. She *would* get out, and if they tried to shove her back in, she would fight with every weapon she had. Which meant… which meant using her gift the other way. The perilous way. 'Rats,' she said aloud to Flip. 'They could help.' Rats couldn't break through stone. But the door that separated the storage room from the main part of the barn was of wood, and not as sturdy as it might be. She couldn't slide the bolt open from inside, but…

Stasya closed her eyes and tried to breathe steadily. She reached out to the rats, opening her mind to them. One in particular seemed to be a leader, alert, sharp, aware of her, so she shared the image with him first: many rats gathering at the base of the door, gnawing, gnawing. Making a hole that grew and grew and eventually was big enough for a young woman with broad shoulders to squeeze through. She'd deal with the outer door once she got there. She sent the rat leader an image of herself saying thank you when it was done. It would have been good to be able to promise cheese or carrots or… Ah. She did have something to give them. She shared a picture of fresh beans and peas, hoping rats actually enjoyed those things as much as she did. Then she sat quiet, waiting, and while she did, Flip sent a mind-picture in which she transformed into a very large dog indeed, then rammed the door with her head and somehow broke it down. 'No,' Stasya said aloud. 'Do that and everyone will call me a witch.'

The wait felt endless but was perhaps not so long. The rats crept out from their secret tunnels, more and more joining the army that gnawed on the wood. Stasya could not stop wondering if she could have saved Irina. Would the Ruler have spared her friend if Stasya had agreed to her demands? The cruel death of one innocent against the breaking of her solemn vow to defend the forest… they could not be weighed up against each other. Both were wrong, so terribly wrong, and the Ruler couldn't see it. She was surrounded by people who did her bidding without question. That sort of power was bad for a person. It made them believe nothing was as important as getting their own way.

The hole in the door was growing. She could have lain down on the floor and stuck an arm through, maybe both arms, but not yet her head and shoulders. 'Head Rat,' she said, making the images as she spoke, 'make it big enough for me to scramble through. Not to get stuck, that would be bad. Please tell your tribe they are doing a fine job.' Flip was following their every move, her body as tense as a hunting wolf's, and their nervous glances, the twitch of their ears, told Stasya they knew it. 'The dog will not hurt you.' An image of Flip curled in a ball, sleeping. She sent that one to Flip as well as the rats, in case she needed a reminder. She'd need Flip in bird form, safe out of doors, before she tried to leave the storage chamber. It didn't matter if the rats saw the dog change, but humankind was different. Once she was out, she'd be tempted to hide or try to run. She could feel the urge now, all through her body. But as far as she knew, Lukas was still somewhere at

Dragon's Keep. She could not leave him to his fate, whatever that might be. Besides, there was no convenient way out, no secret passage or tunnel she knew of, no carts being drawn up somewhere so she could sneak a ride and creep out once they were free of the place. Dragon's Keep was a nightmare. Yet, oddly, there was still some kindness here; some folk who would speak to her as if she were a real person, some who would offer gifts: the vegetables which had proven so useful, a smile, a friendly word or two.

A plan. She needed a plan. The hole was nearly big enough now, if she wriggled through on her belly like a snake. Then the outer door. There might be tools in the barn that she could use to break through. Then… she'd need to be brave. Hold her head high. Speak to the first person who saw her, tell the truth, ask to talk to Lady Elisabeta straight away, not wait until tomorrow. Tell Irina's story. Make the Ruler understand.

She had never wished so hard to have Flip's shape-changing gift. Oh, to grow wings, to be a bird and fly out that window and away. Or to become a beetle and crawl out between the stones, entirely unobserved. To confront the Ruler in the form of a great bear or a fierce wolf or a sharp-taloned bird of prey. But she could not, and she would not use Flip in that way, to guard her or intimidate folk. She had lost one friend; she would not risk another. 'Don't forget,' she said now, showing the little dog what she wanted. 'Stay in bird form, wait for me, and if I don't come back, fly home to Heartwood and be safe, sweet one. Please do as I ask.' Flip made a gruff noise that might have meant yes or no. The rats, startled, turned their heads to look, then as one scampered away from the hole they had chewed out. With so many, the task had not taken as long as Stasya had feared it might. Time to go. Time to get out of this place. She spread the sacks on the floor, away from the blood, and emptied the bag of peas and beans onto them. The rats moved in; she hoped all of them would get a share.

Squeezing out of the storage area was not hard; the rats had done a good job. Once in the main part of the barn, Stasya swallowed her tears and looked for a way out. The main door looked too sturdy to yield to kicks, and she'd seen those iron reinforcements on the outside. But there was a window in that wall, a window she judged big enough to climb through. It was high up, but not as high as the tiny one in the storage area. And there were jutting timbers here and there that would serve as footholds. Stasya was used to climbing trees to pick fruit or rescue wayward cats. She had fixed holes in folk's roofs. Getting up there would be easy enough. Getting down on the other side might be more of a challenge. Never mind that. She must escape. She must go now. She would find the Ruler on this day of blood and death, and she would make her understand what she had done.

She climbed. She was barefoot, and there were splinters. Still, she hauled herself up and up again until she could see through the opening. The angle was awkward. The courtyard below looked empty, but she could not see every corner. Still, no choice but to go through and down. She lowered herself, fingers gripping the windowsill, feet seeking any purchase they could find. It wasn't so very far down. She could do it… she could…

She froze, unable to move. She was breathless after even that short climb, and her head felt dizzy. *Do it, Stasya,* she commanded herself. *Think of Irina. Think of Tomas. Think of Lukas. Think of Heartwood*. Her hands hurt. Her back hurt. She wanted to scream. *Do it.* An awkward, twisting stretch. Toes wedged into a tiny crack, arm reaching for a drainage pipe that might, just might, support her long enough. Nearly there…

'You! Girl! What do you think you're doing?'

She fell. Someone caught her, setting her on the ground, holding on to her arms. For one wonderful moment she thought it was Matiss. But no; it was another of the royal guards, another unknown face, another body so strong that there would be no point at all in trying to fight.

'How in the name of the gods did she get out?' Another guard, and another after him, striding across the courtyard. While the first one held on to her the others slid open the bolt on the barn door and vanished inside.

'What in all hells is this?'

'Rats! Gods! A cursed army of them! Here, give me that shovel!' Squealing, crashing. A flood of pain into Stasya's mind, a crushing, snapping, brutal onslaught. There was no way to close herself off from it. The rats were under attack. They were dying in agony because of her. Because of what she had asked them to do.

And then came the barking. A small dog shouting defiance against two armed men.

Bird! Be a bird! 'Don't hurt her!' Stasya screamed.

The space of a breath. A shout of shocked disbelief from the men. And a tiny bird flew out through the open door of the barn and away.

'Did you see that? It changed!'

'Sorcery! Witchcraft!'

Another silence. The hands of Stasya's captor dug into her arms. The others emerged from the barn, faces pale with shock.

'This is your doing.' And when Stasya said nothing, 'You worked some sort of spell, didn't you? First with those rats and then with the dog? Answer me!'

She drew a ragged breath. 'I want to speak to the Ruler. Take me to her. I will account for myself there.' Another breath, more of a gasp despite her efforts at control. 'Now! Take me to her now!'

They stared at her, not seeming to understand. Then one of them said, 'Oh, you'll see the Ruler all right, no doubt of it once she hears of *this*. But folk of your kind don't name the time and place for such a meeting. You'll see the Ruler at a time of *her* choice.' He glanced at the others. 'She can't go back in there. Where do we put her?'

'Find Stanislav. Ask him.'

A silence. Glances passed between them; it seemed none of them was keen to volunteer for that duty. Maybe even Stanislav's fellow guards were scared of him.

'There's that lockup on its own. Been empty a while. You know the one I mean, down near the stables? No getting out of there. All stone. You'd need a dragon to break you out of that place.' A pause. 'I still can't believe it. But I saw it with my own eyes. Rats. An army of rats. And the dog…'

'Yes, well, keep it to yourself until the Ruler's been told. Don't want word spread around the whole place. Now come on, you. Only place for you is shut away where you can't work any more of your sorcerous tricks.'

'What about the dog?' asked one of the others, his voice not quite steady. 'If it can turn into a bird, what's to stop it turning into a… a bear or something?'

'Not without *her*. Anyway, it's gone. If it's stupid enough to come back here, it'll get what's coming to it. Like those flea-ridden rats. Good riddance.'

She could have argued. She could have struggled, but with three of them to one of her, that would have been pointless. At least, as things were, she knew they would report this to Lady Elisabeta. Flip had turned the botched escape into a disaster; why had she not changed to bird form as soon as Stasya was out? Now the Ruler was going to ask her about the other side of her gift, the side she had kept secret even from Lukas. Lady Elisabeta was going to demand that Stasya use that ability to help her get to the Hermit. To call on the help of wolves or bears or elk. After what had been done to the rats, it didn't bear thinking about. So, no screaming and fighting, no demands, she would just keep walking along and do what these guards told her to do. Then she would wait until the Ruler called her, which would surely be soon. She would wait in this lockup, and while she was there, she would plan what to say and how to keep calm while she was saying it. *Be safe, Flip,* she thought as they marched her on, one on either side and the third following. *Stay away for now. Wait until I call for you. Please wait. It may be a long while.*

Time passed, and nobody came. The floor was hard and cold under her aching body. It was like trying to sleep on ice. Not that sleep was possible. Any time she managed to nod off, she was soon woken by a nightmare of bone and blood, blows and vile words. Irina's dead eyes staring up at nothing. Flip captured and hurt. Lukas all alone, cold, hungry, desperate. And what came before: the fire, folk screaming, folk burning. The fall of the Ancestor, a great doom on Heartwood.

This time they'd put her in a tighter space. Stone floor, stone walls. No window, only some tiny holes high up that allowed her to tell night from day but would hardly admit a moth. There was a hatch in the barred door, far too small to offer any chance of escape. Once or twice, since they threw her in here, someone had opened that hatch and looked in, then shut it again without a word. What were they checking? Whether she was alive or dead? Did they care? Perhaps they thought she, too, had the ability to change into a bird. Once, she thought the eyes that looked in were those of Stanislav.

She'd tried her best to work out where the place was, but when they'd brought her here, she'd been hurt, scared and angry all at once, and her feelings had crowded out clear thinking. The cell was reached by a passageway, she recalled, and one of the doors they'd passed had been a half door. She had smelled horses. Near the stables, then. But where were they in relation to the servants' quarters or that garden or the Ruler's council chamber? She had no idea, and without Flip to spy for her, there was no way to find out.

The last time someone had opened that hatch it had been dark out there, save for the flicker of a candle. It was night. Why hadn't the Ruler summoned her? It made no sense. If Lady Elisabeta was so desperate to learn her secrets, why had Stasya been left in here even after those guards reported what had happened with the rats and with Flip? They must have told her what they'd seen. Why leave it so long?

Her mind was turning in circles. Her belly hurt. They'd given her a bucket for a privy; that was all. No blanket, and she was still in her filthy clothes. When you were in such a state, it was hard to be brave. Hard to make a plan. Hard to summon up the will. *For Irina*, she told herself. *For Tomas. For every soul who died in Heartwood. For them, I must be strong.*

The hatch creaked open again. At first she did not look up, fearing to meet the eyes of Lady Elisabeta's torturer once again. Then came a murmur in the half-dark. The clink of a cup.

'Stasya?'

She recognised the voice and was on her feet in a moment, despite the aches and pains in her body. 'Pavel?'

'Ssh!'

She moved closer, right up to the hatch. She could see him dimly; the candlelight caught the gleam of his fair hair.

'Take this.' Pavel passed through a cup of water, a hunk of bread. 'Don't tell anyone I was here. Hide the cup.'

'The others,' she whispered. 'Are they back yet?'

He shook his head. 'Here,' he said, and squeezed a tightly folded bundle through the opening. The hatch closed without a sound. She did not hear him walking away, but she knew he was gone.

Unfolded, the last gift proved to be a rough blanket, perhaps used in the stables, for it had a smell of horse dung and hay. Would Pavel be in trouble when the other guards noticed it in the cell? Would they interrogate her about who had brought it, and perhaps start cutting off her fingers? And where could she hide a cup in this place of hard stone? Never mind that. She would eat, she would drink, but not too much – she must save some for morning. She would wrap the blanket around her and be warm, or at least not quite so cold. She dared not try to sleep, not now she knew what horrors sleep would bring. She would get as comfortable as she could, and she would tell herself a story. A story of hope and courage. A story of friendship. A story of nature's magic, and how it could heal wounds that went deeper than the body. And in time the sun would rise again and it would be morning. A new day.

'Once upon a time…'

'AH.' LADY ELISABETA looked Stasya up and down, wrinkling her nose at the smell her captive had brought into the council chamber. 'You're here, then.'

It was not a question; no need to find an answer. Silence was safer anyway; she was a hair's-breadth from screeching like a madwoman, weakened though she was. Anger seethed in her at the sight of the Ruler standing there in another of her jewel-coloured gowns, with her glossy hair all plaited up and her warm fire burning on the hearth behind her. What would a person like her know of hunger or cold or fear? What would she know about friendship, kindness, the bonds of family and community? Stasya stood and waited, clutching the horse blanket around her shoulders. Her feet felt cold on the tiled floor of the council chamber, and they hurt; it had been too dark in that place to get all the splinters out. Now it was day, and she felt dizzy and weak and sad. She'd asked for this meeting, but now she wondered if she might collapse before she got a word out.

'Changed your mind? Decided to see sense at last?'

Words came. 'You mean, after your men tortured an innocent woman, a good woman who was a wife, a mother and a friend, who worked hard to help provide for every person in Heartwood? After they killed her? Why would that change my mind?' And after a moment's silence, 'My lady?'

The Ruler's lips thinned. Her eyes narrowed. 'It is my understanding that the woman took her own life and chose to do so in a spectacular and somewhat untidy manner. Be careful what accusations you make, young woman. That was no doing of mine.'

This was a twisted and perilous path, not to be taken at a run. Stasya knew the truth about Irina only because Flip had shown her those terrible mind-pictures. And she must keep Flip out of this at all costs. 'I was presented with a… a finger, my lady. Irina's finger, with her silver ring. And one of the guards told me she was dead. There was… there was blood, a lot of blood…' *Stand up straight. Hold back those tears.*

'As I said. If a guest in my household decides to take matters into her own hands, I can hardly be blamed for the consequences.'

'She did not cut off her own finger, my lady. Irina was a baker by trade; she worked with her hands. The ring was a token given by her late husband, whom she loved. Why would she do such a thing?'

Elisabeta smiled thinly. 'Why indeed? It is possible that injury occurred while my guards were moving her to a new location; perhaps she attempted to resist. These things happen. They happen in particular when people choose to be stubborn. When they refuse to cooperate.'

Would she be next to lose a finger? Perhaps all of them? She looked down at the floor, where the tiles seemed to be moving strangely. Why was it so hard to speak?

The silence drew out, until the Ruler spoke again. 'I'm told some remarkable things occurred yesterday, concerning your escape from a locked chamber and… your dog. Where is your dog?' Elisabeta glanced around as if expecting Flip to dart out from under the table or appear from a corner.

'I don't know, my lady.' True enough. 'I haven't seen her

since your men moved me to that place near the stables.' *Stay away, Flip, wherever you are. Say safe.*

'Mm-hm.' The Ruler put her head on one side, as if in question or disbelief. 'I'm told my men saw her transform into a bird. An unbelievable thing, yet it happened. My guards are not prone to fits of wild imagination. Did you do this? Did you use some kind of magic? Answer truthfully.'

'I can't change a dog into a bird. I have no magical powers. I'm an ordinary farm girl.' Stasya drew a breath, then added, 'Perhaps your men were mistaken. Maybe Flip bolted out of the barn so quickly that it looked as if she were flying.'

'I do not think they were mistaken. And what about the rats? A tribe of rats that ate a hole in the wall to let you out. Don't tell me *that* was not of your doing. It was an odd event, an unnatural thing, akin to the workings of witchcraft. And you understand what the penalties can be for that, yes?'

Stasya imagined herself burning, drowning, being slowly tortured to death. 'I'm only trying to do what's right,' she said. Why was it so hard to get the words out? Her head was reeling. 'It's not magic. It's not sorcery.' She wanted to say, *Set us free, let us go, and we will never trouble you again.* But that was a promise she would never make, no matter what it cost her.

A long silence, then, while the Ruler gazed at her, and Stasya thought of all the things she had been so desperate to say. It was pointless to try, and not only because she felt as if she might collapse any moment. The look in the Ruler's eyes told her the woman would do anything to achieve her end, whatever the cost.

'You still won't agree to it, will you?' The Ruler spoke as if she had looked into Stasya's mind. 'You won't lead my party to this place, the Hermit? I don't need to ask; I see it on your face. Even after the death of your friend, which might have been avoided had you seen sense. Even after that. It would be easy for you, Stasya. You know the forest. You know ways to pass through it without cutting down trees, without disturbing those things that seem so important to you. What if you guided a group that way? Not a war party, merely a group of travellers interested in what they might find there. You might use your… unusual ability… to keep that party safe from wild animals as they passed through the forest. They, in their turn, might protect you from folk who would not hesitate to harm a young woman if the opportunity arose. We would keep you safe; we would provide food and shelter. And when it was done, you would be free to return home. Does that not seem a reasonable request?'

Reasonable. From the person who had sent the Commander to Heartwood? Who had not hesitated to condemn poor Irina to torture? Who had caused her death as surely as if she herself had used the knife? The words burst out, a torrent of them, unstoppable. Her voice rang from the high ceiling of the council chamber; her fists banged the table; her whole body was alight with fury. With the words came gasping breaths and sobs and a wildness that made her tear at her own hair and stamp on the hard floor, heedless of her aching feet. It built and built until she could not see the Ruler, could not hear her voice, did not know anything but the terrible injustice of it, the hurt, the cruelty, the destruction. In her mind, over and over, the Ancestor toppled and fell, and creatures fell with it, dead, maimed, hurting, terrified. And over and over Tomas burned in the fire, and Irina lay lifeless in her blood, and good folk toiled and suffered.

The Ruler was talking again, but Stasya was on the floor, screaming, and she could make no sense of the words. *Whipping… fifty lashes… two chances… see sense…* Dimly, through the anguish, she was aware of being taken away. Carried, eventually, while she moaned and wept and struggled. The light changed and changed again. She was back in the cell near the stables, on the floor, with new bruises. The door closed; the bolt was rammed across. The hatch opened, and she heard a voice. Not Pavel. Someone with a deeper, darker tone. And now she heard the words. 'Don't forget. You have two chances to stop this punishment, provided you agree to the Ruler's request. Your guards will return to check on you twice during the daylight hours. If you change your mind, you have only to let them know. Otherwise, you will be summoned at dawn.'

Silence for a little, as she lay sobbing, barely understanding.

'Thirty lashes might be sustained,' the speaker continued, his tone level, 'though the recipient would be severely damaged. Fifty is a death sentence.'

23

ELISABETA

STANISLAV RETURNED AS she had requested, to report that the girl was in her cell again, and that he had explained clearly, and that the prisoner had said nothing that made any sense.

'Sit down, Stanislav. I have something to say to you.' Elisabeta motioned to the bench, but the tall guard looked at it as if he did not know what it was for.

'Thank you, I prefer to stand.'

'Very well. The episode with the woman, Stasya's companion, was… unfortunate. You might perhaps have carried out punishment of some kind without provoking her into such extreme action. You misjudged my instructions, Stanislav. You went too far.'

He cleared his throat. 'My apologies, my lady. I misunderstood, perhaps. She took us by surprise, with the knife. Remarkably quick and remarkably accurate.'

She refrained from comment, simply fixing him with her stare. As usual, it had little impact on the man. Well, she must not anger him; there was no doubt his services were useful. And he would make a dangerous enemy.

'I don't want this error repeated. It seems best that I explain the next step to you again. We go through the motions as if we are prepared to carry out this punishment. The girl stays in her cell; she is checked twice before nightfall, given the opportunity to call a halt, provided she agrees to give me what I need. We act as if the whole thing is real; I want the news of it to spread to the serving folk, the guards, anyone you encounter. I want her to believe we will carry out the penalty at dawn.' Surely that would soften her resolve.

'I understand, my lady.'

Elisabeta expected him to bow and wait for her formal dismissal. But he still stood there in his black garments, looking at her.

'My lady, what happens in the morning? If we go to her cell at dawn and she's still refusing to talk?'

That was the weak point in her plan. 'We'll face that difficulty if and when it happens,' she said, trying for a tone of complete confidence. 'Surely no young woman would hold out when she saw you with the whip, and your victim tied to the frame, not to speak of a crowd of gawking onlookers. Dismissed, Stanislav. If she gives in before nightfall, be sure to let me know immediately.'

'My lady.' Now he did execute the bow, turn on his heel and leave the chamber, closing the door behind him without a sound.

24

ALEKSIS

THE RAIN HAD abated. The last awkward meeting with Bishop Petras was over. Aleksis had suggested that a swift departure would allow him to present the troubling facts about the Birchlands to the Ruler without delay, meaning Lady Elisabeta should have a good plan in place by the time of the Grand Council. He'd emphasised that both he and she were fully aware of the need for any messages touching on delicate matters such as this – for instance, those that might be dispatched to the leaders of their neighbouring countries – to be handled with the highest degree of secrecy. He'd thanked the bishop for his hospitality. Petras had farewelled his visitors quite amiably. Whatever it was he'd been hoping to achieve, it seemed he believed he'd succeeded.

The ferryman got them across the choppy waters of the lake in good time, helped them unload the horses, and waved them off with a grin. The roads were slippery with mud. Aleksis knew he must restrain the urge to push the horses, or Karolis, too hard. The pace must be slower, but even with the required stops to rest the animals, they could be there by late evening.

Pavel had agreed to stay abreast of any developments at court during their absence and to brief them as soon as possible on their return. It had to be tonight. Aleksis needed to know how things stood before he saw the Ruler.

'Makes you wonder why Petras and his crew choose such out-of-the-way spots for their religious houses,' Matiss observed as they negotiated a slippery downhill stretch. One error here and a horse might fall and snap a leg or cause its rider some serious damage.

'They're not keen on visitors,' said Karolis. 'Or at least, uninvited ones. They like to keep their secrets as just that. Secret.'

Silence for a while. Then Aleksis said, 'You made a few friends there, from the looks of it.'

'Mmm. There are some good fellows among them, or they would be if they hadn't been drawn into a certain mode of thinking. It is what it is.'

No further discussion; even on an isolated track such as this, some matters were better not spoken of aloud. When it became safe – if they ever reached that point – there would be a whole world of things to say. He thought of Stasya, and the way sometimes she seemed to have so many words in her that she struggled to hold them all in, and sometimes locked herself into impenetrable silence. How much easier it was for her to tell a story than to answer questions or give an account of events. How she had her very own way of doing things, a way that was both powerful and, for her, perilous.

'Aleks?'

'Mmm?'

'Don't forget, there are plans in place.' And when Aleksis did not answer, Matiss added, 'And folk we can trust.'

He knew he should answer. But his thoughts were not under sufficient control.

'Having doubts? You look like you're carrying a heavy weight.'

'Some things you can't plan for. We saw that with Rihard's ludicrous activities in Heartwood. Achieved more or less the opposite result from what was wanted.'

A silence. The path levelled out; they rode beside a river fringed with willows. Birds called in their branches; the clouds had parted enough to let light fall on the rippling water.

'And yet,' Aleksis said, 'some would see our aim as no different from his. With the potential to cause significant harm.'

Matiss did not reply, and for some while they rode on in silence. The nearer they came to places of settlement, the more important it would be to speak only of immediate and practical matters.

'We might consider changing horses at the inn,' Karolis said, breaking the silence, 'rather than resting ours and taking them all the way. Could the host accommodate that, do you think?'

'They could, but it's an untidy arrangement. Someone's got to do the return trip, switch them over again. I'd prefer to be without that issue.'

'They'll need a fairly long break,' Matiss said. 'You as well, Karolis. Don't want to strain that leg any further than you need to.'

'I'll be fine,' Karolis said, but something in his posture told Aleksis he was starting to feel uncomfortable.

'We'll rest until we're ready to go on. The days are getting longer; we should have adequate light most of the way.'

'If it helps,' Matiss said, 'we know you're on edge, Aleks, and we understand. Chances are nothing will have changed at court; we've only been gone a few days.'

'Mmm.' In a few days, Aleksis thought, things could turn upside down. Under Elisabeta's increasingly unreliable leadership, the Northlands were vulnerable. The visit to Dragon's Keep had only underlined that. Petras might be considered an ally right now, but he was a man who followed his own visions and his own passions. The One and Only

God was not a deity of peace, friendship and goodwill. And Petras had what amounted to a substantial private army at his command. The Grand Council was drawing closer. If ever there was need for Elisabeta's senior adviser to provide her with a voice of common sense, it was now. Common sense. Support. Wise counsel. His father had been senior adviser before him, back in the days when court had felt almost like home. What would his father think at this moment, if he could look into his son's mind?

25

LUKAS

He was telling himself a story. In his mind, they were sitting on the grass, he and Stasya side by side, looking down toward the settlement. Late afternoon light; the goats enjoying their freedom but edging closer to the gate, knowing that soon he would return them to the safety of the home field. The story was of a hero on a quest, a man for whom a swooping dragon or a lurking mud monster was not a thing of terror, but an opportunity to use his skills, whether with the sword or with clever words. Everyone knew dragons loved riddles.

In this place he did not tell stories out loud, though he could imagine Stasya doing it and holding an audience of rough prisoners spellbound. For Lukas, storytelling was a private thing. Apart from Stasya, the only people to whom he told them were his younger sisters, who loved a thrilling tale before bedtime. Oh, where were they, those sweet girls? Was Heartwood still suffering under the iron fist of the Commander? Had his father survived, and how were his mother and Kristina coping? They needed him. He should be there, shouldering his share of the work. But… he had to be here. Had to. For Stasya.

'Hey, Goat Boy!' It was the man opposite him, incarcerated for being in the wrong place at the wrong time, according to his own account. The details were fuzzy, but Lukas suspected many of these men owed their imprisonment to quite minor offences. If they seemed half-mad, or foul-mouthed, or prone to inappropriate remarks, that was probably down to being locked up in this place and fed on the nameless grey substance that passed for food. It was enough to turn anyone a bit crazy.

'What?' he asked.

'Heard they've got something special lined up for you. Guards were whispering about it.'

Lukas did not ask the obvious question. This could not be anything good; he was not sure he wanted to know.

'Go on, then,' said someone else. 'What is it?'

'Fifty of the best, to be delivered at dawn tomorrow, that's what they said.'

Nobody said a word for some while. The profound silence spoke for them. Then one man said, 'Fifty? For Goat Boy? Great saints and sinners, what did he do to deserve that?' His voice was choked.

'Sounds like we won't be seeing you after tomorrow, lad.' That voice belonged to a man Lukas could not see. When the prisoners talked among themselves, which happened if there were no guards within earshot, that man was always the one to calm the storm, to quiet the often-turbulent waters. The one to settle the restless herd. 'Seems like your sweetheart wouldn't speak up to save your life. That's if the guards got it right. We'll say a prayer for you.'

'Speak for yourself,' someone muttered, but the others were quiet. The ready quips and insults that were part of their everyday conversation were absent now.

It felt as if he were in a dream: some dark tale where the hero was powerless to defeat the dragon or outwit the mud monster. They were saying he would die in the morning. They were talking about fifty lashes. *Your sweetheart*. Stasya, they meant. The authorities had told her they'd whip him to death, and she'd still refused to do what they wanted. It felt like his heart had been ripped out and stamped on. But what else could he have expected? She was never going to change her mind. For her, the forest came first, always. She was strong, brave, true to her beliefs. So why did this hurt so much?

'What did I do?' He spoke more to himself than to the others. 'I did what I thought was right.' A breath. 'I did my best.'

26

STASYA

SHE HUDDLED IN a corner of the cell with the horse blanket around her, knees up, head down, eyes shut. The darkness was complete. There was no keeping out the chill. There was no keeping out the spectre of the morning and what was to come. The truth was that when the sun rose she would die, horribly. Fifty lashes. Was that really what he had said? And two chances to stop it. But at what cost? To save her own life meant betraying everything she believed in, everything she lived by. It would mean the plundering of Heartwood, the deaths of ancient trees and the wild things that lived there. It would mean breaking her vow. Unthinkable.

Perhaps this was where her story had been heading all along. A sacrifice. Perhaps she had always been meant to die this way. Nobody would miss her much. Except for Lukas. But Lukas would be better off if she was gone. He'd be free to choose a wife and be happy without her getting in the way. Once she was dead, they'd set him free, wouldn't they? Once she was gone, once she couldn't do what the Ruler wanted, there would be no reason for them to keep him here.

Twice, over the long hours, the hatch opened and someone peered in, waiting long enough for Stasya to speak. Twice she sat silent, shivering, with her heart pounding and her stomach tying itself in knots, until the hatch closed again. She forced herself not to call on Flip. Best that Flip stay well away, much as Stasya longed for her comforting presence. She was safer out there, in whatever form she chose, and once this was over, she could fly home. That did not stop bitter tears from falling as Stasya remembered the good times: the forest walks, the cosy nights, the shared adventures.

She must have fallen briefly asleep, for she was startled awake when the bolt on her door shifted. It was a cautious sound, as if someone were sliding it across with infinite care. Was it dawn out there already? Oh, gods, let it not be so.

She got to her feet in the darkness, her back against the stone wall, her hands clutching the blanket. *Stand up tall*, she ordered herself. *You chose this path. Walk it bravely.*

Whoever was out there, they were moving very quietly. The hatch opened without a sound. The flickering light of a candle showed that it was still night out there. 'Stasya?' someone whispered. 'It's Matiss. Come quietly over to the door.'

Now she was wide awake. It could be a trap. But she knew his kind voice. She rose and moved to the door; the eyes looking in at her were indeed those of the big man. 'Keep very quiet,' he murmured. 'We're getting you out.'

The door opened, and there he was, wearing riding clothes. 'Got to be quick,' he said. 'Anything to bring? We won't be coming back.'

Stasya shook her head.

'Come, then. This way.' He did not drag her or push her along. Instead, he put an arm around her shoulders as a father might, and with the candle in his other hand guided her through the darkened stables. In a screened area at one end a small lantern burned, and by it a man stood utterly still. Aleksis. He watched them approach; the expression on his face was strange, unreadable.

'She'll need some fresh clothes before we go. And a wash.' Matiss was still keeping his voice to a whisper.

'Sort it out, then. Be quick.' Aleksis still had his eyes fixed on Stasya. 'What have they done to you?'

'I don't— I can't—' Her voice came out as a rough croak. She struggled to control it, to keep it soft. 'What about—'

'Hush now. Stay quiet. They're getting Lukas out, then we'll go.'

She wondered, later, how they managed to do it; wondered how many allies they must have had within Dragon's Keep to make things flow so swiftly and quietly. At the time it felt unreal, like a dream. Matiss took her to a little yard with a pump, filled a shallow basin, found her soap, a brush and a cloth to dry herself, stood with his back turned while she did her best to clean her filthy body and neglected hair. The water was icy cold, but she scrubbed and rinsed until her skin hurt. Picked out the splinters from her feet. Dried herself, shivering; got into the clothes Matiss had brought. They were garments like the ones she had been wearing when she left home – the practical trousers, shirt and over-tunic of a young working man. There was even a pair of boots, which fitted well enough. A warm cloak, a hat of felted wool which she pulled down over her damp, tangled hair. Everything in muted colours, as if to avoid attention.

'I'm ready,' she murmured to Matiss's back. 'Thank you.' And when he turned, 'Where are we going?'

'For now, to a place of safety some miles from here. A place where we won't be found. And we need to be gone swiftly.' He looked toward the darkened stable. 'Just waiting for your friend, then we're off.'

Stasya did not ask how long it was until dawn. 'We should tidy this up,' she said instead. 'Won't people wonder…?'

'I'll deal with it. Wait over there.' Matiss put away everything they had used. He emptied the basin into a drain. All was done with quick efficiency and almost no noise. He turned to regard her. 'Think you'll be able to ride?'

Stasya did not ask how far they were going, or how they could take horses from the stables without being heard or seen, or what would happen if Lady Elisabeta found out they were... What were they doing, exactly? Escaping? But Aleksis was the Ruler's personal adviser. Matiss was a court guard, and didn't a court guard always obey the Ruler's orders? 'I'll manage,' she said. 'Matiss— they were going to— they were—'

'I know. Hush now.'

They waited with Aleksis by the light of the lamp. The men did not talk. Stasya felt the tension in them, the need to be gone; she saw the looks they exchanged. It felt like an age before two men came into view, supporting another between them. One was Pavel, not wearing his uniform; another was a strapping fellow with auburn hair and beard. Between them was Lukas. Stasya would have rushed to him, spoken his name, wept against his shoulder, but she met Aleksis's eye and held still. Now Lukas was standing without support, lifting one foot then the other, bending his knees as if testing his strength. He looked shaky, pale, a hollow-eyed ghost of his old self. He did not so much as glance at her. Were they expecting him, too, to ride? They could hardly take a cart out without raising the alarm.

Nobody said a word. It was clear to Stasya that they were following a plan, and that someone – Aleksis, most likely – was making sure they did so as quickly and quietly as possible. They donned packs that lay ready, then headed along the stable block with Stasya and Matiss at the rear. From time to time, Matiss glanced over his shoulder. Stasya tried not to think what would happen if someone spotted them.

Matiss had halted; the others were heading on. There was a fine-looking grey horse in one of the stalls, a long-legged creature with gentle eyes. For a moment she caught what was in its mind as the big man stroked its face and whispered words she could not hear. Perhaps the two of them shared the same thoughts. *Goodbye. Be well, dear friend.* And, as the man briefly laid his brow against the horse's neck, *I will never forget you.*

They moved on. Out of the stables, not by the double door through which horses and riders might pass, but through a narrow opening to one side. Aleksis was carrying the lantern; its flame cast their shadows on the rough stone of the fortress wall, and on something else: a drainage channel that made its way beneath that wall, and an iron grating that kept wayward stock from coming to grief there. The red-bearded man went forward, picked up some kind of tool, and set to work on the grating. It looked as if that was their way out; had the tool been placed there in readiness? Wouldn't the sound of metal on metal alert every guard close at hand? But no. It seemed this, too, had been well prepared: the process was quick and efficient, almost as if the grating had already been cut, then set carefully back in place. Pavel lifted a section out, the other man stowed the tool in his pack, and in turn they crept through the opening. For Matiss it was a tight squeeze, not helped by the pack he was now wearing. Stasya came after him. The red-haired man was last. She heard him doing something with the loose grating, perhaps setting it back in place. Maybe it would pass a casual inspection.

The tunnel was cramped. There was no walking upright. Sometimes they moved at an awkward crouch; sometimes they went on hands and knees, moving through a trickle of water. Stasya heard Lukas grunting with effort; the others were helping him as best they could. What were they going to do at the other end? Where did this open up? Without horses, how could they possibly get far enough away before the sun rose? Foolishly, she found herself feeling sad that the good clothing she'd been given was getting damp. As if that mattered in the least.

At last, they emerged under a night sky scattered with stars. Stasya straightened up, back aching, and her heart lurched. Aleksis had held on to the lantern, how she could not imagine. They were outside the fortress, and before them a rocky hillside descended to a rough track beside the lake. They were no longer alone. On the track stood men and horses, how many she could not see. She opened her mouth to say something, to warn him, hadn't he noticed – but swallowed her words as Aleksis put a finger to his lips, signalling silence. He gestured for his companions to follow and set off down the precipitous slope.

It was impossible for Lukas; an awkward scramble even for the fittest of them. Matiss passed his pack to Pavel, squatted down, lifted Lukas onto his back, and commenced a careful descent. The others followed, the red-bearded man keeping close to Stasya, as if he thought she might fall.

'My name's Karolis,' he whispered, giving her a nod.

'I'm Stasya,' she murmured, surprised to find she wanted to smile. If ever there was a strange moment to be exchanging polite introductions, this was it. She'd tell the story one day, if they survived. A story whose terror and darkness were softened by such moments.

Few words were exchanged once they reached the track. It was soon clear this, too, was part of a well-prepared plan. The horses were handed over, fully harnessed up; words were exchanged in an undertone; and the two men who'd been waiting, both in dark clothing and hooded cloaks, vanished into the night. They might have been anyone.

Six horses. Five men and a woman. Stasya knew Lukas was an able rider, but tonight he would not be able to ride alone. It seemed Aleksis had expected this; one of the animals was a sturdy packhorse, with the appropriate harness and saddlebags. With remarkable speed, the men transferred the packs to this horse. Matiss mounted the biggest animal; Pavel and Karolis helped Lukas up behind him. Aleksis offered

Stasya a leg-up on her allocated horse, whose exact colour she could not tell in the lantern light. As she mounted, she reached out to the animal with her mind, offering trust. *Thank you, beautiful one. I will be kind to you, I promise.*

Aleksis was still standing beside her, one hand on the harness. The others were mounted and looked ready to go, with Karolis leading the pack horse. 'Stasya,' Aleksis said. 'What about your little dog?'

Before Stasya could decide how to answer, a small bird landed on her shoulder. Perhaps it had flown down from the castle wall; perhaps it had come from some hiding place known only to itself. It shifted its tiny feet, fluffing up its feathers against the cold. Stasya looked at Aleksis. Aleksis looked back steadily. He must have heard the whole story, or he would not have acted so quickly to get them out. He must know, or guess, the secret.

'As you see,' she said.

Something flashed across his hawkish features; it might almost have been a smile. He nodded, turned away, doused the lantern. Within moments, he was on his horse, and they were riding away from Dragon's Keep.

27

ALEKSIS

THEY WERE SAFE. But for how long? And how to deal with the problem of Lukas? They could hardly have left him behind. There'd been no time to consider. He'd had to put the emergency plan in place as soon as Pavel briefed them. He knew Stasya would have refused to leave without her friend. Besides, he knew Elisabeta. Once she realised Stasya was gone her fury would be immense, and if Lukas had still been at Dragon's Keep he might have borne the brunt of that.

Stasya hadn't asked him where they were going or why. On the ride she hadn't said much at all. It must have been truly shocking for her to have to wait the hours out, knowing what the Ruler had threatened. She'd faced an impossible choice, and he suspected it would weigh on her for the rest of her life. He should give her time to gather herself; time to talk to Lukas. But he owed her the uncomfortable truth. He had to tell her soon. On his own, but with Matiss on standby. There'd be only one night in this safe house, then they must move on, provided Lukas was up to it. They had to stay ahead of any pursuit. The Ruler would want her prize playing piece back.

She'd never give up the belief that she could bend Stasya to her will.

As for himself, Elisabeta would make him pay for what he had done. An act of treason, that was how she would see it. If she tracked them down, others, too, would face a grim penalty. Not only the three guards who rode with him, but also his other allies within Dragon's Keep, should the Ruler identify them. All those who had aided their escape would be at risk. He'd known that from the first, and he'd made sure anyone who became part of the plan did so in the understanding of what it might come to. Their agreement did not lessen the burden of responsibility; many lives depended on the venture succeeding, and it was a heavy weight to bear. But he must pursue his goal. The very future of the Northlands hung in the balance.

There'd been no way to send word ahead; their departure had been too rushed. Lukas's predicament had given them no choice but to leave on the same night they'd got back from Raven's Watch. Now they'd reached a certain farm cottage, at some distance from a small settlement, and Pavel had gone to find the owner, a man who was always ready with supplies and support when required. A man who would keep his mouth shut. He was also a breeder of horses, which meant he had good facilities for their animals. They unharnessed their mounts without waiting for him and settled them in a safe yard with water and shelter. The cottage was not locked up. It held basic supplies, as well as bedding, cook pots and the like. Matiss kindled a fire on the hearth; Stasya carried in wood from an outside pile without being asked. Karolis drew water from a well and brought a bucket in.

Lukas was plainly exhausted but refused to lie down and rest. Under different circumstances, Aleksis guessed, he would be the capable, competent one in the team. It wasn't hard to imagine how he felt now. Too weak to be useful. A burden. He was another victim of the Ruler's insistence on swift action. Aleksis had warned Elisabeta often enough, but when she was set on a goal, she could be blind to all else.

'Lukas,' he said, 'could you help Stasya stack that wood?'

A simple task, but a necessary one. He didn't want to insult the young man. Lukas went to work without a word. He wasn't even talking to Stasya. Indeed, he seemed to be avoiding her eye. His expression was grim as death.

It wasn't long before Pavel returned with the owner, Leon, and his son, bringing food supplies, more blankets, a warm mash for the horses. Conversation was minimal; the risk was well understood. They must keep ahead of the Ruler's men, cover their tracks where they could, and remember that what folk didn't know, they couldn't tell. Leon recommended a route to follow, with the need to evade pursuit taking precedence over speed. Aleksis did not mention their final destination, only the codename of the next safe house, which they should reach in less than a day's ride provided the weather stayed fair.

'The small bag has bandages, strapping, a salve for aches and pains.' Leon glanced at Lukas, who was laying wood on the stack with concentration, his jaw set firmly, his brow creased.

'That'll be useful,' Aleksis said. 'Karolis strained his leg not long ago, and we've had a long ride.'

'Stay an extra day if you want. The place is yours for as long as you need it.' Leon paused to consider something. 'You could go on by boat, if a trip along the lake will take you where you need to be. There's a fellow, trustworthy, who has a sound craft for loan. You could leave the horses with me, pick them up on— pick them up later.'

On the way back, Aleksis thought. That might never happen. If it did, it might be a disaster or, eventually, a triumph, depending on how this turned out. 'Thank you, you've been generous. It's more likely we'll take the horses on further, but we'll talk about it and make a plan.'

'I'll leave you to get settled, then. I'll come back before dark to check all's well.'

* * *

THEY WERE ALL weary. Tending to the horses, sorting out baggage, preparing and eating a meal happened in near-silence. The cottage had only one room, which served as both living and sleeping quarters, but an alcove-like area at the back allowed Stasya some privacy, and she arranged her share of the bedding there. There was nowhere private to talk. After the meal, Aleksis said he would take the platters outside to wash them and asked Stasya to help him. A few glances were exchanged, but nobody made comment.

'Ask your questions, then,' Aleksis said when the two of them were out by the well, washing and rinsing the items in a pair of buckets. 'You have many, I'm sure. But keep your voice down, even here.'

Stasya gave him a look that might have meant anything. The little bird was hopping about in the long grass, perhaps searching for insects. She'd offered no further explanation for that mystery, and he didn't plan to ask. 'There's only one question that matters,' she said now, continuing to scrub a cook pot as she spoke. 'Or maybe two. Where are we going, and why? I should have said thank you for rescuing us. For saving us. I do say it. But… this is a big thing for you, isn't it? Won't you get in terrible trouble?'

Aleksis drew a deep breath. This was hardly the best setting in which to tell her. But he had to get the truth out. Right now. 'Stasya… I can't take you back to the Heartwood settlement. Rihard – the Commander – and his men are still there. I suggested to the Ruler that she recall them, but she dismissed that idea. She did send a message requesting that they hold back on their advance into the forest until she'd had more time to consider the current situation. I wrote that for her. Whether Rihard has done so, I don't know. But with them still in place, it wouldn't be safe for you there. Or for Lukas.'

She crouched there very still, scrubbing brush in hand, saying not a word. Waiting. Knowing something was coming.

'We are going back to that general area. Not on main roads.

Not through any of the larger settlements. At a certain point we'll leave these horses in good care and continue on foot. That's if you agree to the plan.' *Say it,* he ordered himself. *Get the words out! What sort of man are you?*

'Plan,' Stasya echoed. 'What plan?'

'I'll tell you. I ask you to hear me out, please.' Silence.

'I need to get to the Hermit, Stasya.' He heard her indrawn breath. He could not meet her eyes. 'Or close to it. I'm asking you to guide me there, with my companions. Just this small group, no more. No cutting down of trees, no hacking out of paths now or in the future, I promise.' Her body had frozen up; he did not need to touch her to know it.

It was as if she were suddenly unable to move so much as a little finger. As if she'd stopped breathing. And then he made himself look and saw utter horror on her face. Worse than that, bitter disappointment. This was what he'd feared.

'Exactly what she wanted,' Stasya said. She kept her voice quiet, as requested, but her tone pierced him like a knife. 'The Ruler. The last time she questioned me. When you were away. She tried to coax me into it, said it would be a small party, no destruction, exactly this.' She was moving her fingers in some kind of pattern, perhaps to keep herself calm. He had thought she might shout at him, scream abuse, or perhaps shed tears. This was almost worse. 'You're a liar, Aleksis. You've been playing her game all along. Why did it have to come to this? They were going to whip me to death! I thought— I really thought—'

She was losing control of her voice. It was rising fast. He put a finger to his lips. 'You haven't let me answer the second part of your question.'

'How could that make any difference?' She got to her feet, hugging her arms around herself and turning her face away.

'It might, Stasya. First, I should make it clear that from the moment we left Dragon's Keep, I knew I was leaving my position of trust as Lady Elisabeta's adviser. It was my decision to act as I did, and mine alone. Those who helped me did so at my request, not the Ruler's; I gave them a choice. All of us will have lost our posts at court over this, and any return there would be perilous for us.'

'But— It doesn't make sense. You had a plan in place, horses ready to go. The way we got out through that grating… We did that in the middle of the night without anyone stopping us. Matiss and the others must have known about that plan even before you went away. It can't have been something you just decided that night. Last night,' she added, reflecting his own astonishment that so much could change in the space of a day.

'There was a plan in place, yes. It was waiting only for the right time. We had to act sooner than I'd intended because of the situation with you and Lukas. But yes, we were ready. It was sad that we had to leave our own horses behind; we couldn't expect them to go on straight after a very long day's ride.'

She turned back to face him, steadier now. The bird flew up to her shoulder; settled there. It, too, was watching him. Maybe, if he said the wrong thing, it might become a ravening wolf or ferocious bear at a snap of the fingers. Was that possible?

'If you wanted me to do this, why didn't you ask me when we were in Heartwood?' Stasya challenged. 'Why wait until so much went wrong and so many folk were hurt? Why take me and Lukas all the way to court, where she… I don't need to tell you what she did. You must know most of it.'

Aleksis sighed. 'I remind you that I was sent to Heartwood specifically to report back on Rihard's progress with his mission. Or so the Ruler believed; I had my own reasons for being there. The Commander's approach to the task he'd been given was, I knew, likely to be less than subtle. Rihard is not exactly known for his compassion. Once I saw the situation at Heartwood, I sent the note I mentioned before. Before there was any response from the Ruler, there came the fire. It was imperative to get the injured out, and I left Heartwood for that reason. Lukas was hurt. And you were in danger, having drawn yourself to the Commander's attention.'

'So I came with you, and so did Irina. Who was then imprisoned and tortured until she gave up hope and killed herself. And now you expect me to do precisely what I've refused to do every single time the Ruler pushed and threatened and badgered me to agree to it.'

Matiss had appeared in the doorway of the cottage, looking across the yard at the two of them. Aleksis gave him a nod that might have meant, *All's well*, and the big man retreated indoors. But all was far from well. 'Stasya… What happened to Irina was terrible. Every moment I regret agreeing to go to Raven's Watch. I regret staying as long as I did, though the delay was not of my making. I'm deeply sorry that I could not save your friend. She deserved none of this. But here we are, and I am doing my best to explain.'

Stasya put a hand to her face, perhaps wiping away tears. 'So explain. Why? Why do you want to get to the Hermit, if it's not to rip out the hidden treasure that's supposed to be there and enrich yourself? What is so important that you'd turn against the Ruler and risk not only your own life, but those of everyone who has helped you? Shouldn't you know better than that? Aren't royal advisers supposed to be wise? Haven't you been one for years?'

He grimaced. 'A few years, yes. For Lord Kasimir before Elisabeta. My father was senior adviser before me. I was more or less brought up at court.'

'Yet now you walk away from it.' There was a new note in Stasya's voice. Curiosity?

'It's time. I must walk away. I have my own mission. A story that began when I was young. A story that still isn't finished. But I can't tell you that tale now.'

'Why not, Aleksis?'

'Sometimes not knowing is safer. But a time will come when I can share it. I will tell you the tale then, I promise. Before we reach our destination.'

'I'm tired of secrets,' she said. 'And I don't trust promises, not now.' And although she did not add, *Especially not from you*, Aleksis heard those words as if she'd spoken them aloud.

'Then I will make promises only to myself. If you will come with us, you can help put an end to the time of secrets. We can make it a time of hope.'

Stasya had returned to rinsing out the cook pot, as if tired of his nonsense. It was only as he was collecting spoons, knives and platters to take them back inside that she said quietly, 'A time of hope. That sounds good. I wish I could believe you.' She bent to retrieve the other pot.

'Stasya.'

She looked up and met his eye.

'What you said before, about the whipping – what exactly did they tell you? Did they say the punishment was intended for you?'

After a moment, she said, 'That was what I heard. Thought I heard. Fifty lashes. At dawn. Two chances to stop it, if I agreed to do what she wanted. They came past twice, and I didn't speak.' A pause; she had gone ashen pale, and he regretted asking. 'What are you saying? Did I get it wrong? I thought that was why you…'

'The Ruler wouldn't have done that; she needed you alive. It was Lukas who was to be whipped. Pavel told us everyone at court was talking about it; the word had got around quickly. If you'd held out until morning, they would have made you watch, hoping you would change your mind before it was too late.' She made a sound that tore his heart; he crouched down next to her, putting his hand on her shoulder. 'You're safe now,' he said. 'You're both safe. And we'll do our best to keep it that way.'

'Oh gods,' Stasya said, her hands over her face. 'I was…

upset, angry. And tired, so tired. I think I was shouting, fighting… I can't remember, not properly. It's all a blur. Oh, poor Lukas, he must think…'

Would you have done as Elisabeta wished, if you had known? The question was in his mind, but he would not ask it. She'd been so strong, so steadfast. Clearly, she'd been prepared to die, painfully, rather than abandon her principles. Would she have held out if it had meant a hideous death for her friend? 'You'll want to talk to him,' he said. 'Explain what happened. He might need a bit of time.'

There was silence for a while.

'About the other thing,' Stasya said shakily. 'What you said. The forest. The Hermit. I'll need to talk to him about that too, find out what he wants to do. And I haven't said yes. It's hard for me to believe you're not asking me to do exactly what the Ruler wants. It's hard to believe this is not all a trick.'

'I understand why you wouldn't trust me, Stasya. All I can say is, we got you and Lukas out. And our reasons for wanting to reach the Hermit have nothing to do with amber or trading.'

'You wouldn't be able to go into the forest anywhere near our settlement,' she said. 'And I don't know any other ways in.'

'I do,' he said, lowering his voice further. 'I was there once before.' Even now, speaking of it hurt. He'd hoped he might not need to; not yet.

'Really? When?'

'When I was young. A child of ten. An adventure; an exploration. We were… we were with family. The place lay north of your settlement. Not right on the forest edge, but close. I think the way we took might also lead to that lake you mentioned.'

'The place where we found amber.' There was judgement in her tone.

'Yes. But we knew nothing of that.' *Don't ask me to tell the story. Not yet.*

Stasya made no comment. Still judging him. Still doubting him. He reminded himself that she had been alone and afraid not very long ago, thinking herself on the brink of death and no doubt wrestling with her conscience.

'Before we go in,' he said, 'I have something of yours to return.' He reached into a concealed pocket and brought out the amber owl, whose broken cord had been replaced by a fine silver chain. It was just as well Elisabeta had trusted him to lock it away somewhere safe and had not asked to see it recently. 'Here,' he said, putting it in Stasya's hand. The little bird that was Flip gave a chirrup; was he imagining the happiness in that sound?

'My owl,' Stasya whispered. 'I thought I'd lost it forever. You had it all this time?'

'It was locked away in a chest at court. I removed it before we left for Raven's Watch, thinking it would be safer in my keeping. May I help…?'

She was struggling with the clasp. At her nod, he stood behind her and fastened the chain around her neck. Briefly his fingers brushed her skin; briefly a curl of her hair fell across his hand, soft as a feather. The bird turned its head with a jerk, pointing its beak straight at his face, and he drew his hands away. It had stayed in that form throughout the journey. No sign of the little dog. It would take him a long time to get used to the oddity of that. 'We'd best go in,' he said. 'It's getting cold.'

Halfway back Stasya came to a sudden halt. 'What about Lukas?' she asked in a murmur. 'He's not looking well. He needs time to recover. A climb like that…'

'I thought we'd find somewhere for him to stay, at a safe distance from Heartwood. A place with folk who can look after him, nurse him back to good health.'

'Folk like Laima and Ivo? Could he go back there?'

'Sadly, no. That farm is too close to Dragon's Keep. There are other places, more out of the way. I don't expect him to undertake the climb to the Hermit. He's been through more than enough.'

Stasya considered for a moment. 'You need to tell him what you've told me. And make sure he knows I haven't said yes. He'll want to be treated like the man he is, courageous and kind. He'll want to make up his own mind.'

'You're the one he trusts, Stasya. You tell him.'

28

STASYA

'I DON'T WANT to talk,' Lukas said. 'There's nothing to say.'

He'd come outside with her, reluctantly. They could hardly talk about it in the barn, under the scrutiny of the others. But his tone was forbidding and he would not meet her eye.

'You need to hear this, Lukas. I got it wrong. I had no idea the Ruler intended to do that to you. I was expecting to be whipped myself. I was upset and I didn't hear them properly. You know how it is when sometimes I can't think straight and everything's just noise and I hardly even know where I am… I'm sorry, Lukas. I'm sorry you've been caught up in all this—'

'I said I don't want to talk.'

She could hear the unspoken message, clear as day. *How do I know you're not lying? Besides, would you have done what she wanted if you'd known it was me waiting to be whipped to death? You wouldn't have, would you?* And that wasn't fair. He knew quite well that she found lying impossible. He knew about those times when she felt overwhelmed and lost touch with what was right in front of her. 'You need to—' she began, but Lukas had already turned away and was heading back toward the cottage. He was moving awkwardly, as if in pain.

Stasya did not follow him straightaway. She lingered outside, sickened that her dear friend believed she would have let him die, and at the same time not sure what choice she would have made if she'd known the truth. Facing her own death to protect the forest had been truly terrifying, but she'd known she could not give in. To condemn Lukas to a hideous fate was different. It was unthinkably cruel; an impossible choice. What would Lukas have done if he'd been in her position? The answer to that was obvious. He would have saved her life. Lukas loved the forest. He understood her commitment to protect and preserve it. But for him, family and friends would always come first. Would she ever be able to make things right with him again?

It wasn't until the sudden sharp call of a passing bird startled her that Stasya realised she'd been biting her nails to the quick. She looked up to see that she was not alone. Matiss was by the cottage door, arms folded, leaning against the wall. While he was apparently deep in thought, gazing out over a stand of willows as the long day at last turned to dusk, she recognised that he was on watch, not only to deal with unwanted visitors but also to ensure she didn't try to run away, foolish as it would have been to attempt that under the circumstances. The idea had occurred to her. She and Lukas knew how to find a way through the forest, how to build a shelter, how to make fire, how to forage. Once well into Heartwood Forest, they could have snatched an opportunity to disappear, then gone to ground until Aleksis's party gave up looking for them. Though what the next step would have been after that, she had no idea. And one thing seemed certain now. The two of them would not be escaping together.

* * *

By the time she went back inside, Lukas was lying face down on a bench with his shirt and tunic off, and Karolis was dabbing something onto a raw-looking patch on his side. Could it be that the burns Lukas suffered when he rescued his father had never been properly tended to? How many people at court had been telling lies? Perhaps Aleksis was one of them. He said he'd tell a story to explain himself later. But maybe there was no story. On the other hand, if he was doing the Ruler's bidding, why the covert departure by night, straight after he and the others had returned from a long day's ride? That made no sense. Unless it was an elaborate trick to convince her the Ruler's senior adviser was friend, not foe. This was too hard. She was tired and cold. And worse, she could not forget that look on Lukas's face, the one that had said, *You are not my friend.*

'I'll brew some tea,' said Matiss. 'Not the answer to all problems, but generally welcome. Karolis, are you and Lukas nearly done?'

'I want to put a dressing on this; won't be long. After that, tea would be just the thing. And after that, I'll show you all some exercises that can be useful to ease the soreness after a long ride. We've got more of it ahead, and probably some rougher places to sleep in along the way. Ideally we'd all go through this routine every day, before we head out. Or in the evening. Just stretching, mainly.'

'Good idea,' Pavel said with a smile. 'But I warn you, this man's a hard taskmaster. I know from experience.'

'Adjusted to suit each person's ability. As always.'

An idea came to Stasya. She spoke quickly, before she could change her mind. 'About keeping fit enough to travel… I was thinking, if we could have one more night here, or possibly two, Lukas could ride on his own instead of going up behind someone else.' All eyes were on her now, save those of Lukas himself. She willed him not to challenge her. It felt uncomfortable to have the others' full attention, but it also felt right. Whether she ended up saying yes or no to Aleksis, there was no doubt she and Lukas would have to stay with the group at least as far as the forest edge. Better to make herself an equal partner in this, whatever it was, than feel like a person who couldn't think for herself. 'And it would give us longer to learn these exercises, whatever they are.'

'We'd be short of a horse,' Pavel said.

'That shouldn't be a problem,' Matiss said. 'Leon will let us take one of his, I'm sure, provided it comes back to him in good condition. But…' He glanced at Aleksis.

'It makes sense,' Stasya said. 'After what's happened, a full day's rest would be good for all of us and the horses. I'm not used to spending a whole day in the saddle. For some of you, it's been two days. I know it's important to move quickly. In the long run, this would help.'

29

ALEKSIS

Was it because she had her amber owl back? Could such a small thing make such a difference? Or was this the quality he'd seen in her on that first day, when she stepped out in front of a crowd to put all her focus on that terrified horse, work out what was wrong, and somehow fix it? Back at Heartwood people seemed to think she was odd, awkward. What he'd seen was a leader in the making. She could be an asset to his cause. But she still didn't trust him and might not do so even when she heard his story.

For a while that fine, courageous person had lost herself, and no wonder. What she'd been through was enough to shatter the strongest. But now he saw her again. Saw what the future might hold, with her on the team.

Foolish, to entertain such thoughts. Why would she ever want to help him? As soon as Heartwood was free of the Ruler's men she'd go back there, settle into her solitary life, be at peace. Marry Lukas, perhaps. Though now there was a rift between them that would be hard to mend. Lukas was doing everything he could to avoid speaking to her. He wasn't saying much to anyone. Aleksis had seen the expression on Karolis's face when he tended to those injuries, and knew they were bad. An inflamed burn. Bruises everywhere. The goatherd had good reason to be out of sorts. And although Stasya kept herself busy, she often looked as if she were holding back tears.

His mind was too much occupied with this. He had a plan, she was cooperating with it so far, and there was no point in trying to predict the future. He'd get his team to the forest, he'd make sure Elisabeta's men didn't track them down, they'd reach the lake and Stasya would guide them on from there. They'd reach a place that felt safe enough, and he would tell her the story. And then they would go on. To the Hermit, or as close to it as they needed to. If there was anything he believed from the old tales, it was that the place held secrets. A person might say it held magic. Maybe not the magic those ancient storytellers believed in, with spells and transformations. But there were other kinds of magic. The magic of the sun rising in the east every morning. The magic of the stars appearing in the night sky. The magic of finding something lost.

STASYA HAD BEEN right about waiting. After two nights Lukas was able to ride on his own, and they moved on. When they were riding, Flip accompanied them as a bird. By night she returned to dog form, keeping Stasya warm when they sheltered in their makeshift camps. Aleksis was never quite sure if the changing was something Flip did on her own or if Stasya was in control. Right now, it was convenient for everyone. The dog was too short-legged to keep pace with the group, and he could not imagine balancing Flip on a horse while riding.

He wondered if the creature thought like a dog, or a bird, or more like a human. He wondered if Flip was to be trusted. Might she be used as a messenger, able to fly ahead and bring back vital information? He couldn't ask Stasya about this. It would only increase her suspicion of his motives. *It doesn't matter what she thinks of you*, he told himself sharply. *Her approval is not required. Only her agreement.* And he reminded himself that although he was no longer the Ruler's senior adviser, he now had a far more important job to do. He must direct all his skills to achieving the goal. He could not afford to be distracted.

Not every night could be spent in the shelter of a safe house. The Ruler's men would be seeking them out. Some of those places presented too high a risk, not only to his team, but also to those ready to provide safe haven. This must not descend into a bloodbath.

His companions were practised at making camp quickly and efficiently, with minimal light and noise. They were good at finding concealed spots that suited the purpose: under the shallow overhang of a rock formation or in a hollow defended by thorn bushes. There came an evening when they reached what seemed a suitable spot, a derelict building by a burial ground, where oddly shifting shadows suggested the presence of ghosts, or would do if a person believed in such things. But Flip did not like that place. In dog form, with her ears laid back and her eyes wide, she stood rooted to the spot, whining. Stasya dismounted, picked her up, tucked the little one into the hood of her cloak, and scrambled back to the saddle unaided. So much for his doubts about transporting a dog on horseback. They rode on in silence and made camp later in a nearby woodland.

Everyone was edgy. To reach the point where Aleksis planned to enter the forest, they would need to skirt close to the village of Sweetwater, where folk might recognise Stasya or Lukas. With the Commander and his men still in the general area there was a possibility of running into someone who would alert him to their presence. If Rihard got word that Stasya was travelling with them, disaster might follow. Aleksis had a plan for that possibility, but he shrank from needing to use it. He would have to convince Rihard that they were in fact following instructions from the Ruler and hope the Commander would sanction their expedition without insisting they take some of his own men with them.

Ideally they'd be seen by nobody, but that was unlikely. Going by night might arouse particular suspicion, should someone happen to be outside after dark as they rode past. So, one cover story for Rihard's men and perhaps another for the local folk. But if Elisabeta had acted promptly, word might already have reached Rihard that they'd left Dragon's Keep and who was in their party. Rihard's men might have told the locals to keep a look out.

Silent. Quick. Invisible. But there were problems with that. They'd have to stop at the last safe house to get the horses settled and to catch some rest before they headed on into the forest. And they needed to know how things stood in Heartwood. What was the situation of the folk there? Had Rihard made further advances toward the Hermit, maybe as far as the lake they intended to pass? And, although Lukas was sunk in grim silence much of the time, Aleksis thought he might want to know if his people were safe and well, or as well as they could be under the circumstances. If the goatherd could be assured of that, he'd be less likely to take some unpredictable action and put them all at risk.

They talked about the options around their fire, a small one adequate for boiling water but insufficient to keep all of them warm enough. It came naturally now to speak in something just above a whisper, though it seemed they were alone save for an owl that contributed a sombre call now and then.

'We can't send anyone right into Heartwood,' Matiss said. 'We're all known to someone there, either the Commander's men or the locals. What we need is a general picture, how much damage has been done since we left, are folk going about their daily business as usual, and so on. We need to see without being seen. That's the challenge.'

Aleksis waited for Stasya to offer the services of Flip, but she did not speak. 'You're the giant among us, Matiss,' he said. 'Too easy to spot.'

'And you're the indispensable leader,' said Pavel with a smile. 'Not you either.'

'I could go—' Stasya began.

'No. You've got a job ahead that nobody else can do. Besides, think what might happen if you were seen.'

She gave Aleksis a look. 'The same sort of thing that would happen to any of us. If you're the leader, that's your choice. Whoever takes this on takes on the risk.'

Karolis and Pavel both spoke at once, then halted, looking at each other. Perhaps both had been intending to volunteer, but Stasya spoke next, surprising them.

'I have a suggestion. My cottage should be empty. I can't see anyone choosing to stay there in my absence; the local people are wary of the place. One of you could shelter there. From just a bit further along the hillside you can get a good view. You'd need to be careful to stay under the forest edge, out of sight, and not stay too long. And… if Pavel goes, he should wear a hat. His hair makes him easier to spot.'

They all looked at Pavel, whose head of honey-gold hair did indeed mark him out.

'I'll shave your head if you want,' suggested Karolis, lifting a brow.

'With that blunt thing of Matiss's? No, thank you. The hat will do. What do you say, Aleks? We'd need to arrange a meeting place, somewhere I can find you afterwards. And I'd have to go in on foot. Could be slow.'

'It's too high a risk for the small amount of information we'd get out of it, Pavel. And you'd be unlikely to spot anyone you recognised without being seen yourself.'

'I could get a general idea of how things stand there. Without that, we might head into the forest and walk straight into Rihard's men coming the other way. Some of those men are our friends; we've worked alongside them. Just imagine it. A pitched battle against our own. On those narrow pathways. It doesn't bear thinking about.'

Aleksis was reminded how young Pavel was: a year or two Lukas's senior, at most. He was reminded that being a leader brought the kind of challenges no man wants to face. 'We have to leave the horses at the safe house before any of us enters the forest. It's closer to Sweetwater than is ideal, but they can accommodate animals. We'd wait there for you. Their farmland borders the forest. I think you could make your way to the Heartwood settlement in a day and a half on foot, possibly less. But I'm far from sure it's worth the risk involved.' He'd have to ask her. 'Stasya, may I have a word with you in private?'

When they were camped out in the open, a private talk meant walking a certain distance from the fire and hoping the others couldn't overhear. They went to the spot where their horses, hobbled, stood quietly under the spreading limbs of a beech. Flip came with them, trotting along at Stasya's heels. At her approach, the horses shifted, suddenly restless.

'Don't answer this if you don't want to,' Aleksis said. 'Can Flip carry messages when she's in bird form? Can she pass on information to you in some way?' It was too dark for him to read Stasya's expression. He knew he was treading on perilous ground.

'You're asking if she could be sent to Heartwood instead of Pavel? Or are you trying to get me to admit to some kind of witchcraft?'

That felt like a slap in the face. 'Do you really need to ask me that? Don't we know each other well enough now for such a question to be plainly ridiculous?'

'What, the idea that I might be using magic, or the idea that you might accuse me of something punishable by death?'

'One moment you're acting as part of the team, and the next

you're speaking to me as if I were...' *As if I were Rihard. Or Elisabeta.* He ordered himself to stop talking; to draw breath. To remember why he was here and not at court doing his job. 'I'm not accusing you of anything. I mean you no harm, Stasya, I swear it. I'm asking because I think maybe Flip can help us, and all I want to know is whether that's possible, and whether you – and she – would be prepared to do it.'

She was silent for a little. 'You're asking me to talk about something nobody else knows. It's hard for me to trust anyone with this, Aleks.'

It was the first time she had used this form of his name. She had an almost uncanny ability to remind him that beneath the court adviser, the Ruler's trusted confidant, the leader, there was... just a man. An ordinary man, as prone to weakness and self-doubt as any other. A man who sometimes longed for everything to be as it had been when he was ten years old, before his world changed. 'I did say you need not answer.'

Stasya heaved a sigh. 'The answer is yes and no. She can be asked to bring back information, but... only the simplest, the kind of thing you could explain in pictures. And she can't take a message to someone else. Only to me. Not in words. It's more... thoughts and feelings. A dog can't speak human language, and a woman can't speak the tongue of dogs. Or birds.'

Although he could barely see her in the night, Aleksis knew her eyes were turned on him. He felt it all through his body. A gaze of such intensity could only be met by another of the same. He squared his shoulders and drew a deep breath. 'I promise I won't pass this information on to anyone else. So, you're saying she could be sent to do this particular job, but perhaps what we need to know is too complex? Or you have other reasons for not wanting to ask this of her?'

'It's more that she doesn't want to do it. I can feel that. She doesn't want to go back without me. She's afraid.'

'And that tells you… what? That none of us should go?'

Stasya did not answer straightaway. She bent to gather Flip up. 'She can't explain. It doesn't work that way. But her mind is full of things that could go wrong. Death. Loss. Disaster. She wants to stay with me. And I know I'm not the right person to go to Heartwood.'

A polite cough alerted them to the presence of Matiss, standing a discreet distance away, his tall form silhouetted by the fire. 'Tea's brewed. And then you should both get some sleep, whatever the decision is.'

'What do you think, Matiss?' Aleksis kept his voice down, wanting only his old friend's opinion. Matiss made safe choices, not reckless ones. He was a steady companion; a reliable adviser. And Stasya trusted him.

'We can't guess the situation with Rihard, but up till the time we left Dragon's Keep there was no mention of his being withdrawn by the Ruler. Pavel would have known if she'd set that in motion; word spreads quickly among the guards. In the morning, whatever we decide, we must move on to the farm and settle the horses in. We should leave early, at very first light. The fellow who lives there won't talk out of turn, I know that. Even so, he should be given as little information as possible. If Pavel's going to do this, we should part ways before we reach that place. We give him supplies and a good cover story; we take his horse to the farm along with ours. The farmer never sees him.'

'How do we explain the extra horse?' Stasya asked.

'We don't,' Aleksis said. 'The less explanation the better. The folk in our safe houses know, in a general way, what this endeavour is all about. They believe in our cause. They understand why we don't give them a lot of detail.'

'Tea,' said Matiss. 'It's late. And Lukas is sitting over there half asleep but trying to keep his eye on you two. If he's to ride again tomorrow, he needs rest. Aleks, I think you can trust Pavel with this. He's eager to help. He knows the risk.'

30

STASYA

TWO DAYS HAD passed since Pavel left on his solitary mission. Two days cooped up in this place, with far too much time for brooding. On this farm they were all accommodated in a barn, horses at one end in stalls, Aleksis's team at the other. The farmhouse was quite a distance away, and they'd seen little of its occupants, though fodder for their horses and supplies for themselves were left outside the barn door daily. Once or twice Aleksis had gone out to talk to someone, but he did not report back, and nobody asked.

Lukas still hadn't talked to her, not properly, and it hurt. They were on the very edge of the great forest, so close she could feel it, breathe it, smell it. She longed to walk up over the fields and in under the trees, to find a mossy rock and sit there for a while, on her own or with Lukas. The trees called to her. She needed to acknowledge them. And up there, her friend might have been prepared to talk. But Aleksis had made it clear nobody could leave the barn except to draw water from the well or to relieve themselves. The risk of being seen was too high.

Even Matiss was edgy. There was a shadow over them all, something new and troubling. Perhaps it was being uncomfortably close to Sweetwater. When Stasya finally managed to sleep on the second night, her dreams were full of bad memories. She saw the Ancestor toppling; she felt the fragile neck bones of that tiny, damaged creature snapping under her fingers. She heard the crackling of fire and the screams. She saw Irina plunging the knife into her own heart, and the whip laying raw the flesh of Lukas's back, as with stroke upon cruel stroke the punishment forced the life from him. She woke from that nightmare with a start, her heart pounding, her face wet with tears.

'All right, Stasya?' someone asked, and in the darkness of the barn, she could not tell who it was. Not Karolis. The men were taking turns at sentry duty in case of unwelcome night visitors, and Stasya could see him standing very still by the half door, a faint light turning his bearded features into those of some warrior from an ancient story. That was not cold moonlight, but the approach of dawn.

'Mmm,' she said. 'Sorry, did I wake you?' Perhaps she had been sobbing. Or screaming. Or saying something she wouldn't have wanted anyone to hear. Oh, for her own little house and her own hearth fire and the peace of being alone with Flip… Would she ever return there to pick up her old life? She thought of the picture on her wall, Mother and her creatures; imagined Pavel looking at that image right now, perhaps by flickering candlelight.

'I was awake already,' Aleksis said. 'Bad dreams?'

'Mmm.'

'Pavel may be back by the end of the day, if he's made good time. And we can move on.'

Stasya sat up, arms around her knees. Flip wriggled, then settled again on the straw pallet. Matiss rolled over heavily. 'Must be close to sun-up,' he said. 'Birds are starting a conversation out there.'

No sound from Lukas. Whether he, too, was awake, there was no telling.

Another day to get through, maybe more. Days when she couldn't walk up to the forest edge, so near but yet so far. Days when she couldn't be on her own for longer than it took to go out to the privy – a ramshackle shed over a pit – and come back in again. The dark things started to crowd in again, filling her mind, blotting out everything good. The verse, she had to say the verse. '*The oak's deep roots… I, too, will be strong…*' She whispered her way through it, taking her time, making herself breathe. '*… I, too, will dance.*' She pictured Mother again, this time walking barefoot on the shore of Clearwater, with a retinue of creatures following. They were not the same as those in the painted image. There was a kind-faced black bear, a handsome red fox, a young goat with proud horns. In the trees close by, a squirrel kept pace, leaping, climbing, scampering, so quick it seemed less creature than flash of light. A keen-eyed hawk flew above. Oh, there was a story to tell. The creatures walked with purpose. Where were they going, and why? Would they finish their journey? Who would fly and who would fall? Would there ever be a time for dancing?

She lay down again. Flip snuggled close, welcoming the warmth. Outside, more birds were joining in the dawn greeting, their voices chiming sweet and strong. *Awake! Awake!* The story teased at her, calling out to be told. If she had to be shut away in a barn even when the sun was shining and the birds were singing and the forest was just out there waiting, there had to be a way she could push back the storm of fears and troubles that was filling up her head. There had to be a way to get through the day. And there was, of course. What could be better than telling tales? Perhaps not that tale, though it had seized her imagination now. How could she invent an ending for it until Aleksis told the story he held so close? And even then, it was not for her to finish it. All of them would play a part.

* * *

SOME FOLK LOVED to tell stories. For some, like Lukas, it depended on who was listening. She knew he told stories to his young sisters at bedtime. Perhaps because of that, his tales tended to be of heroic adventures, and all of them had happy endings. It came to Stasya, looking across the barn at Lukas and Karolis working through the exercises together, that this might be a way to get her friend talking to her again. The bond between them had been as strong as the roots of an old oak. It couldn't be broken forever.

She waited until all of them were eating their breakfast, seated on benches near the little stove. 'I'm finding it hard to be cooped up inside with not much to do,' she said. 'Why don't we tell some stories, Lukas?'

Lukas mumbled something. She drew a deep breath and let it out slowly. Yes, he was angry with her. But there were other reasons for his dark mood. He longed to go home, he was desperate to check on his family, he was injured. She couldn't expect him to act as if nothing had

changed.

'Matiss, how about you?' she queried, hoping for better luck.

Matiss grinned. 'I need time to think something up. I'm a bit out of practice. Maybe later in the day?'

'Makes sense,' said Karolis. 'Lukas, I want to check those burns and bandage up what needs covering before we're on the move again. We'll need time for that this morning. When it's done, I'll be happy to tell a story. I'm seriously tempted to include a few warrior monks. Or would that be a bit close to the bone?'

'How about warrior toads?' suggested Matiss.

'It's all too easy to imagine a certain leader as a toad,' Karolis said with a crooked smile. 'I'll give it serious thought. How about you, Aleks?'

Aleksis glanced Stasya's way. 'My mind is too much on other matters. The rest of you do as you wish, later in the day. For now, make sure you're ready for travel. Provided Pavel gets back tonight, we'll be making an early start. The farmer will supply us with some rations.'

'And if you haven't run through your exercises yet, do it,' Karolis said. 'We have a very long walk ahead. Or more of a climb, from the sound of it. With surprises along the way. That's if there's truth in those old tales.'

Matiss had finished eating and was adding wood to the stove. 'I'll warm up more water. Last chance for a good wash. It'll be cold dips in a stream from now on, I imagine.'

'Clearwater's not bad for swimming,' said Stasya. 'But cold, yes.' An image came to her: Mother on the shore, her creatures with her, startling in their odd companionship. She wondered what surprises this journey would hold. What dangers. Maybe, what opportunities. If they climbed high enough, travelled far enough, they might find both wonder and terror. Both were present in the old stories. Then, of course, there was the undeniable fact that in none of those tales did human folk ever reach the Hermit and return home alive and well. Now was not the time to dwell on that.

The day unfolded. After the bath – a stand-up wash in a shallow pan of warm water, but still welcome – Karolis dealt with Lukas's burns once more while the others got to work feeding the horses, preparing food, hanging clothing by the stove to dry and packing things away. They worked through the exercises, each in their own time. Stasya noticed that Lukas was having what looked like a proper conversation with Karolis, though she was too far away to hear what they were saying. This was definitely an improvement on the brooding silences that were so unlike her old friend. When the salving and bandaging were done, Lukas lay down on his pallet and closed his eyes. Whether he was exhausted from the treatment or troubled about the coming journey or simply wanted to shut out the rest of them for a while, Stasya could not guess. It did not bode well for the long challenge ahead.

As if to recognise that challenge, the farmer brought over a pot full of hearty stew, rich in mutton and vegetables. He called quietly from outside the half door to let them know it was there, but by the time Matiss went to collect it, along with a package of provisions for the road, the man was gone. They ate in silence, each deep in their own thoughts. Flip accepted a share of Stasya's meal but was plainly unsettled. Every sudden move startled her; at every sound beyond a murmur she was sharply alert, checking the danger. Eventually Stasya carried the dog to her pallet and sat with Flip on her lap, sharing soothing images in silence. The men got on with clearing up after the meal; none of them looked in her direction. Whether Aleksis had spoken to any of the others about their earlier conversation, perhaps revealing what she had told him about her link with Flip, there was no knowing. She had not asked him to keep it secret, but Aleksis surely understood the peril of sharing such information even with… what? A friend? An ally? This group could hardly be called a team; she and Lukas were only here because they'd had no choice. She wished she could trust Aleksis. But how could she, when he still wouldn't explain why they were doing this?

If only she could ask Flip what was troubling her. But that would mean showing the little dog a series of possible disasters: falling down a cliff, losing the way in the mist and never finding it again, being confronted by uncanny beings intent on harm. Is it this? Or this? Or maybe this? Even gathering and eating the wrong sort of mushrooms was a deadly danger. Stasya simply stayed quiet and held the dog close. She turned her thoughts not to terror but to simple beauty. The peace of the great forest. The songs of many birds, blending into a great tapestry of sound. The delicate footprints of a hedgehog; the soothing sound of wavelets washing onto the shore as a family of swans passed by, ruffling the still water; the fragile, perfect wings of a butterfly. On her lap Flip settled, her eyes closed, her breathing slow and steady.

THEY GATHERED, LATER, by the stove. Matiss brewed tea; this orderly activity had become something of a ritual. Stasya passed the cups around. Story-telling time was here, and suddenly she was lost for words.

'Who's going first?' asked Karolis. 'Any volunteers?'

'Stasya should be first.'

Stasya nearly spilled her tea. Coming from Aleksis, this felt a little like an attack. Not a lethal sword thrust. It felt more like the opening move in a game of combat, in which the weapons were words. The only way to answer it was with a swift countermove.

'I'll start my story now,' she said. 'But I won't tell all of it, just the beginning. We have a long distance to travel, and we'll need to stop at night. Sometimes it'll be cold and uncomfortable. We may be tired or scared. And it's at times like those that people most need a good story. I'll tell you part of mine as we go, any time it feels right. And if any of you wants to do the same, you can.'

'That's some challenge,' observed Karolis. 'A test of the memory, among other things. You're right, though. It might help us stay sharp when we're feeling weighed down. Or worn down.'

'Not sure I'm up for an epic.' Matiss sounded amused. 'What say we add an easier option, tell a short tale if you're in the mood, or a longer one in instalments? That way we get a mix of the heroic saga with the sort of thing that gives you a good laugh.'

There was a murmur of agreement. They had kept their voices low all day, mindful of the risk of unwanted visitors. Stasya glanced Lukas's way and got a nod in return. A slight recognition, but it was enough to warm her heart. Somewhere, deep down, her kind friend was still there.

'Once upon a time,' she began, 'in a place that was either near or far, either in this world or in another, a strange set of companions set out on a journey. There was a far-seeing hawk, a brave red fox, a strong black bear with kind eyes, a nimble squirrel whose coat bore a sheen like gold. Where they were going, nobody knew; folk watched them pass with wonder in their eyes, for might not a fox or hawk catch and devour a squirrel? Might not a bear, in its turn, make a quick end of the fox? But the four moved on as one, in peace and purpose, the hawk flying above, the others following, each in his own fashion.

'There came a time for rest. The companions sheltered in the lee of a stone wall encrusted with moss. Hawk perched in the strong branches of a venerable oak; Squirrel found a convenient hollow in that same tree, and after checking that it was not already occupied, settled himself there. Bear and Fox dug out a shallow depression in the earth by the wall and curled up together for warmth. The night was long. The moon shone bright. Owls called their wise prophecies into the chill air, but whether anyone understood them, I cannot say. The companions slept; or half-slept, for Hawk never quite shut his eyes, and the others were restless, their thoughts on the long way ahead.

'Now it happened that nearby, a great ill had fallen on a peaceful place. The animals who lived there – goats, sheep, chickens – lived good enough lives, though a life can be short indeed if one's fate is to become food for humankind. They had learned to accept what they could not change. They were grateful for the safety of the walled field, the freedom to graze together in the sun, the fresh water in the trough and the kindness of their keepers, some of whom brought treats such as fresh carrots, and some of whom brushed them, and some of whom sang them sweet songs and held them with gentle hands, right up to the moment of death. Wild creatures, too, dwelt in that place, in the secret parts of the great forest. Those of the farm and those of the forest lived close, but separate. But now everything had changed. The orderly farms were no more, their work disrupted, their stock no longer cared for, their good folk set to ill work under threat of violence. The only choice, for those who could still move freely, was to flee that place and seek a new life elsewhere.'

Not a sound from her audience. Was Lukas wiping away a tear? He, at least, had recognised himself in this tale.

'So it was that when the sky began to lighten and the birds were heralding the approach of dawn, our small band of travellers awoke to find that they had company. Their strangely assorted crew had become still stranger, for nearby stood a sturdy long-horned goat, who looked ready to take on the most fearsome of them – that was Bear, without a doubt, despite his kind eyes – should it prove necessary to do so. And there was another with him, or maybe two others.

'Now, bears do not speak the same tongue as goats, any more than hawks and squirrels share a spoken language. But there are ways of understanding even between creatures so different in form and character. The gaze, the stance, the way the hackles rise or the wings lift or the head turns. The silent tongue can be more eloquent than the voice. The goat dipped his head, as if in recognition of the strangers. When the great horns rose again, the goat had his eyes on Hawk, seeing him immediately as the one to whom any sort of approach must be made. The bird had by this time flown down from his perch in the oak, and settled himself atop the drystone wall, just beside the bear. He put his head on one side as if to say, *Go on, then*.'

At this point Matiss put up a hand as if to indicate a question. Stasya gave him a nod of encouragement.

'What about the other one you mentioned? Or two? Did they show themselves?'

It was a good question. She'd have to include herself and Flip in this tale. The tale she'd had no intention of telling yet; the tale that had insisted on being told. The trouble was, she hadn't yet worked out what animal she would be. Nothing seemed quite right. An owl, perhaps; but that didn't work, since the group had to travel mostly by day. Ah! She had it.

'As the goat considered his reply, his two companions emerged from the woodland behind him. One was a little dog, the sort of creature you would expect to find sleeping on a mat in a cosy cottage. It was so small, a hawk could have seized it and ripped it apart in moments. It was not much more than a mouthful for a hungry bear. The look in its eyes as it cast its gaze around the strange company was not one of terror, as you might expect, but of careful examination. A person might translate that look as, *Are you worthy? Are you brave? Are you fit to travel with us?*

'As for the goat's other companion, nobody was quite sure what she was. A warrior? A human woman? A ghost? Or something else, perhaps from another world? She wore a grey cloak that seemed sometimes like mist, and sometimes like shadow, and sometimes like ordinary wool. Her hood shielded her features; all that could be seen was a pair of bright eyes, regarding them gravely. In one hand she bore a staff of oak, in the other a bag that made a sound as she moved, as if it might hold shells or pebbles or fragments of glass. Or indeed, something far stranger. Bones, maybe.

'Bear padded forward a few steps. He halted before the woman, if woman she was, and dipped his head in a gesture of respect. *Welcome here, stranger. We will not harm you.* It happened, by odd chance, that he had guessed who she was. Once, two winters ago, such a woman had taken a painful thorn from the foot of his mate and had spent time salving the hurt. And he knew *what* she was: a storyteller. The little dog was her heart-friend.

'Once Bear had made the first move, the others came up one by one to greet the newcomers, each in his own fashion. Hawk was last to do so. Like most of his kind, he was naturally wary. He knew humankind could not always be trusted. Hawk was leading his friends into danger, but it was a danger they understood, a quest they had agreed upon. The goat, the dog and the storyteller were an unknown quantity.'

Stasya paused, taking a sip of her tea. She made herself look at her companions, wondering if the manner of her tale might have offended them. She was about to call a halt when Matiss said, 'Go on, then. If you will.'

'I hope nobody gets eaten in this tale,' said Karolis.

Aleksis set his cup down. His gaze was intent, his dark eyes fixed on Stasya. 'This might almost be part of my own story,' he commented. 'But you cannot know how it unfolds. Or why.'

'None of us knows.' Lukas spoke at last, and Stasya knew instantly that her story had touched the right part of her old friend. The heart. The goodness he had somehow held onto through everything, though it had surely hung by a thread. 'That's the magic of stories,' he went on. 'Every time a tale gets told, it's different. You and Stasya might tell the same story, but one would be yours and the other hers. And both might change from day to day. And the ending… that can be anything you want it to be.'

Aleksis was gazing at him as if Lukas had suddenly grown wings or started dancing a jig. What had he expected, that a goatherd would have no insights into such a thing? Stasya reminded herself that he had hardly had an opportunity to see the old Lukas, the fine, brave one. That man had already been beaten down by the time the Ruler's senior adviser came to Heartwood.

'The story will go where it goes,' she said, working on sounding calm. 'And nobody will get eaten, I will make sure of that. I don't expect my adventurers to encounter any warrior toads or other beings of that nature. Though a person never knows.' And, when none of them made comment, she said, 'That's enough from me until some other time. And if I've— and if—' Her words deserted her all of a sudden. Why had she told this story, as if she knew these men well enough to put them in a tale, as if she had the least understanding of what they really thought of her or why they were travelling or anything at all? She'd been in the same space, stripping off to bathe and washing her most intimate garments and even sharing a joke or two, and perhaps she had made a complete fool of herself, a laughing stock, or maybe it was the same as at home, where folk tolerated her because she was useful, but behind her back talked about her as if she were some sort of freak. Maybe… She put her hands over her face.

She heard Lukas move; knew without seeing that he had squatted down by her side. 'Stasya. It's all right. Just take a breath. Take your time.'

'Great story,' observed Matiss quietly. 'And a good place to stop. Now we'll be thinking up a hundred ways it could go on, all of them different.'

'Fox might be called in to deal with the warrior toads. I'd like to see some heroics from him,' said Karolis.

'I think Bear might be a little afraid of toads,' said Matiss. 'Especially toads with weapons.'

Stasya was whispering Grandmother's verse, her hands still covering her eyes. *'The sun gleams on the still pool… I, too, will hold the light…'* When she managed to take away the shield, it was to meet Aleksis's gaze full on. There was something different in his expression now, as if her tale had woken up some part of him usually kept hidden. 'I didn't mean to offend you,' she made herself say. 'It's one of those stories that wants to be told.' Lukas shifted by her side, as if to remind her he was there.

'The story was remarkable,' Aleksis said. 'You have a gift, Stasya. But it takes a toll, I can see that.'

'I just thought… I thought…' *I thought maybe I had made a fool of myself. I thought I'd made a mistake…* Why were the words so hard to get out now? This was how she'd felt when she was six or seven and shrank away from the other children of Heartwood because she knew they would make fun of her. 'Sorry,' she muttered, looking down at her hands, now clutched together on her knee, knuckles white.

'More tea,' said Matiss. 'And don't tell me you're all awash with the stuff. You'll miss it soon enough; I doubt I have enough to supply our whole journey.' The sounds of clanking and clinking, the stove door opening and the poker stirring up the fire, told Stasya he was putting his words into action.

'There are always herbs to be found in the forest,' Lukas said. 'Plenty for a good brew at this time of year if you know where to look, and you can use them fresh or dried. We can show you.'

'Ah,' said Karolis, and Stasya could tell he was smiling. 'Every time someone speaks, I'll be imagining a new part of your story, Stasya. How the wild creatures wondered whether the goat would be a help or a hindrance, and how they discovered he knew things they'd never heard of. Not tea; I doubt any of them would have considered drinking that. But other things a goat would know that a bear or a fox or a squirrel might not.'

'A squirrel would know about herbs,' Lukas said. 'At least, which could be eaten safely by his own kind.' A pause. 'I'll tell a story while you're making the tea, if you like.'

At that, Stasya unclenched her fists and straightened her back. *I, too, will stretch high. I, too, will be strong.* 'I'd like that, Lukas,' she said.

He told a familiar tale, one of their favourites, about a farm dog that got in trouble by hiding a strange creature and stealing food to keep it alive. It was a story of courage and resilience, and also of the longing for home and hearth, and when it drew to a close, it was greeted by the few moments of complete silence it deserved. Then everyone spoke at once, telling him how much they'd enjoyed it, and in Karolis's case, applauding.

'Ssh!' hissed Aleksis, rising silently to his feet. His eyes were on the half door, beyond which the light was starting to fade. They'd been so caught up in the stories that they'd forgotten the need to stay alert, to maintain some kind of watch. Now, all was quiet. But by the door stood a figure, cloaked and hooded. Aleksis reached for the knife at his belt. Matiss and Karolis drew concealed weapons, while Stasya froze with Flip in her arms. Beside her, Lukas had gone deathly still.

'It's me, Aleks. Pavel.' The figure pushed back his hood, revealing a head of golden hair. 'May I enter without being skewered by one or other of you?'

Stasya released a breath she had not known she was holding, as Matiss went to open the half door and welcome Pavel in. Outside, the sky was fading to dark and the birds were singing their farewells to the day. Pavel's smile did not disguise the pallor of his face or the shadows around his eyes. He looked worn out. Aleksis threw his arms around the traveller in a hug, surprising Stasya, though the relief on Aleksis's face reflected her own feelings. The one-man venture had been risky indeed. Nobody plied the traveller with questions, though every face wore the same eagerness to know his story, Lukas perhaps more than the rest, for reasons that were plain to Stasya. Once Pavel was seated by the stove, with a bowl of food they had set aside in hope of his return, Aleksis asked him for a report.

'I didn't stay there long. At the settlement. Too many folk about. I didn't go inside Stasya's house, but you were right, Stasya, there was nobody living there as far as I could see. I got some quite good views from up in that area. The bad news is, the Commander and his troop are still there, in a new camp. I didn't see any work parties or the like, but there were guards around, and some activity up on the forest edge, near where they were cutting before.'

'Could you tell how far they've moved into the forest?' Aleksis asked. 'Signs of clearance, a track being made?'

'I couldn't get close enough to tell. The risk of being spotted was too high. But as I said, not much sign of work parties, no folk carrying tools up there. Not much movement in and out of the settlement by anyone. I'd say they've put the whole venture on hold. Our sudden departure from court might have something to do with that.' Pavel looked around the small circle of listeners, each of whom was hanging on every word. He caught Lukas's eye. 'I did catch a glimpse of your father at a distance, Lukas. Not hard to pick him out, since he's an older version of yourself. He was walking around, talking to other folk. Looked to be in good health.'

Lukas dashed away sudden tears. 'Thank you,' he said. 'You can't know how welcome that is to hear.'

'Pavel,' Aleksis said, 'on your way there and back, was there any sign of parties that might have been out looking for us? I'm assuming you stuck to the plan, avoided places where you might attract notice. But…?'

'One or two riders on the road, a long way off. I couldn't tell if they were the Ruler's men, or the Commander's, or simply some local fellows about their own business. Anyone tracking us covertly is not going to be wearing the Ruler's colours.'

'Good job, my friend,' Matiss said, putting a hand on Pavel's shoulder.

'Are you up for an early start tomorrow?' Aleksis asked. 'We need to get out of here as soon as we can. Every day we stay is another day's risk to the farmer. And another day closer for whoever Elisabeta's sent after us.'

'I'll manage.' Pavel shifted a little on the bench. 'A bit sore here and there, but a good night's sleep will help.'

'You, Lukas?' Aleksis queried.

'I'll be fine.' His tone forbade further discussion.

'Very well.' Aleksis spoke with calm confidence. 'We leave as early as we can. Before you sleep, check that all your things are packed and ready to go. Fill water skins. Don't leave anything behind. And may good fortune walk by our side.' He turned toward Stasya and Lukas. 'I think we all enjoyed the stories. They have an amazing capacity to lift the spirits. But once we're out there we must stay watchful. We must keep quiet.

In the forest there will not only be hungry animals, but most likely folk hunting us.'

Stasya could have pointed out that she probably knew more than he did about moving safely in the forest – wasn't that why she was here? – but she did not. Instead, she rose with Flip in her arms and headed off to her pallet. She fixed her mind on the good things. Lukas had told a story. His father was alive and well. Pavel was safe, and the news was not as bad as it might have been. And tomorrow, oh, tomorrow, she would be back in the welcoming arms of the forest.

31

ALEKSIS

How many years since he had last come this way? Sixteen, nearly seventeen? Long ago in another life, that was how it felt. The day two boys set off on an adventure and only one came back. The day everything changed.

Perhaps this was not exactly the same path. He knew it had been close to the farm they'd left this morning. And it had been close to Sweetwater, though they hadn't stayed there. A friend of his father's had lived nearby, a wealthy man who bred fine riding horses. They'd been accommodated in that household, which had many comforts. And they'd had watchful keepers. That was why they'd snatched the opportunity to go off exploring on their own at a time when they were supposed to be resting.

A fateful decision. It had haunted him ever since. He'd begged the gods he didn't believe in to turn back time so he could live that day again and make it all better. He'd endured the just fury of those betrayed, the hot tears of those bereaved. He would never forget the look on his father's face when he'd returned alone and confessed the truth. Under that look, he had felt his heart shrivel.

Later, being the man he was, his father had comforted him in his own sorrow, and explained that sometimes we make mistakes, and that some mistakes have very serious consequences, and that we must then find ways to carry on. Young Aleks had made his apologies, he had been quiet and dutiful, he had studied hard. His father was senior adviser to Lord Kasimir. In time Aleks, too, would become a court adviser.

But now, here on this forest track, part of him was that ten-year-old boy, running in dappled shade with his friend, laughing and joking, brimful with delight at escaping the confines of their highly supervised life. Not thinking ahead. Why would he? What could spoil such a perfect day?

He must put that out of his mind. He must stop brooding. It was past. It was gone.

Up ahead, Stasya had signalled a halt. She and Lukas were conferring in hushed voices. It seemed they had set aside their differences. The little dog nosed about in the undergrowth, while the others stretched their limbs and drank from their water skins, taking advantage of the pause.

'Problem?' Aleksis asked as he came up to them.

'A choice,' Stasya said. 'Up or around. Move along this way and take a look. It's much steeper than the track Lukas and I used to take from Heartwood.'

He came forward; eyed the rock face that was now in view, a towering thing across which ran a precarious ledge, too narrow to be called a pathway. In a few spots clung particularly tenacious bushes. His stomach churned. Familiar. All too familiar.

'Are you all right?' Stasya was regarding him closely. Gods only knew what his face was showing.

He ignored the question. 'You said a choice. What is the alternative?'

'One way or another we need to get to the top. Either we take the ledge across, or head back and take that branching downhill path we saw earlier. My guess is that would lead us around the foot of the bluff.' She pointed across the rock wall to an area where more trees grew. 'We could scramble up over that side, I think. There's some vegetation to hold onto. But the ledge would get us there quicker.'

The past crowded in again. He found himself without words.

Matiss broke the awkward silence. 'We'd be crazy to attempt the ledge. My vote's for the downhill path, even if it means a longer climb later.'

Stasya glanced at Lukas; he gave a nod. 'Agreed. We'll do that,' she said. 'Everyone ready?'

It proved a wise choice. The ascent through the steep forested area gave them branches to hold on to, small level areas where they could catch their breath, and also some cover, should pursuers draw near while they were still labouring their way upward. Aleksis kept an eye on his companions as they went; it helped to ward off the shadows that were invading his mind. Stasya's strength and balance were an example to them all. Matiss was strong and steady; for a solidly built man, he climbed well. Karolis probably could have done it in half the time of the others. And it was evident that Lukas knew how to climb, but he was tiring, perhaps in pain. As for Pavel, he looked weary now, his face waxen pale, his eyes shadowed. Coming straight after his solo walk to Heartwood, this had been too much to ask of him. An error. Another error.

He wanted to press straight on, to get to Clearwater and away before pursuit reached them. But a good leader does not push his team so hard they suffer for it; not unless there is an immediate risk to life and limb. *Balance, Aleks*, he imagined his father saying. *Balance is the key.*

'We'll take a brief rest as soon as we reach a sheltered spot,' he said when they stood at the top of the rise, catching their breath. During the ascent, Flip had transformed from small brown dog to small brown bird. They stopped to rest in a clearing shielded by whispering birch trees.

Here, great moss-covered stones lay like ancient, sleeping creatures. The day was warming; the air held a promise of summer. Flip was a dog again, lapping water from a puddle, checking scents, finding tiny wild strawberries bright with promise.

Stasya was sitting on the ground, leaning against a stone with her legs stretched out in front of her. Her head was tilted back and her eyes were closed.

Aleksis set his pack down and lowered himself to sit, not far from her. 'All right?'

Her eyes snapped open. 'Why wouldn't I be?'

'I just— Never mind. I thought you might be tired. That was a steep haul.'

'We're used to it. Lukas and me. But that was a tough stretch, yes.' After a moment she added, 'I think we can reach Clearwater before dark.' Aleksis cast his gaze around. Lukas was not far off, lying flat with his head pillowed on his pack. Flip had settled beside him on her belly, muzzle on paws, eyes closed to slits. Matiss and Pavel were sitting together, talking in low voices. Karolis was performing a series of stretching exercises that looked almost like dance; it went far beyond what he'd taught the others.

'It looks like we'll need to camp there tonight,' he said. 'Is there good cover?'

'Good enough. Above the lake the forest is mostly pine or larch, but there are smaller trees and bushes near the water. From there on it's pretty steep, I think. But I'm only going from the tales, and from rumour. We should get a better view ahead from higher up. Though the stories say the Hermit is shrouded in mist, even in fine weather. Another reason for those tales of the uncanny. Ghosts, spirits, fey folk.'

'How do you know which ones to believe and which are… fanciful?'

'You don't. Nobody does. Except, I suppose, whatever lives up there. That's if anything does, beyond wolves and hawks. It's easy enough to make up a story. Often they're sparked off by something real, and they grow from that, and it's up to the teller to add warrior toads or wee folk or uneasy spirits if they want to.' She went quiet for a little, thinking. 'Of course, even going up there might not give a person the answer. It's up to the Hermit what it shows us.'

'Stasya.'

She turned her head toward him, caught by something in his tone. 'Do you think there could be people living up there? I mean, ordinary people like you and me?'

Stasya's smile was more of a grimace. 'You think we're ordinary? Me, the outsider of my village? You, the Ruler's senior adviser at the age of… whatever it was?'

'I was a little shy of two-and-twenty when my father died. I stepped straight into his role at court, at the request of Lord Kasimir.' Aleksis drew a breath. 'I should have asked, might there be human folk living higher up the mountain?'

'I suppose there could be, though it's an out-of-the-way place to choose. The stories speak of caves. There could be a freshwater spring. Some folk would like the solitude.'

'Such as yourself?'

'It would depend. I like to be alone, yes. I like quiet. Space to think. It's good to hear the sounds of the forest. But… I wonder how it would be to live up there, perhaps with only a few other folk and not be able to get help if something went wrong because it's so far from everywhere.' She glanced at Lukas. 'Even if a person doesn't like too much company, it's good to have a friend you can trust.' Across the clearing, Karolis was balancing on his hands, his body perfectly straight and still. Matiss and Pavel were quiet now, watching him. 'Or friends. I think you are lucky.'

If only you knew, Aleksis thought. It seemed the right moment to change the subject. 'Do you have any family living, Stasya? Parents, brothers and sisters?'

She shook her head. 'My grandmother brought me up from when I was small. My parents are dead. I don't remember them, and I know almost nothing about them. Grandmother died when I was eleven. I'm used to looking after myself.'

'I can see that.'

'You?' she asked, surprising him. 'Any family?'

'Only distant connections. That's just as well; my work leaves no time for family.'

'Family comes in different forms,' Stasya said. 'And at different times. It can surprise you, I think. Irina…' Her composure faltered for the first time, and she dropped her gaze. 'Irina and Tomas – her son – were something close to family for me. She was always kind to me, even when I was a child. She didn't judge me the way some others did.'

He could not take time to consider his response. 'I'm deeply sorry we could not get your friend to safety. I regret very much that the boy lost his life. That was… it was part of what caused me to act when I did. To bring our venture forward so we could get you and Lukas out. But it was too late for Irina and her son, and for others who perished. I'll bear the weight of that all my life.' *Along with the old guilt. Along with the old burden.*

'The Ruler sent you away on purpose, didn't she? Sent you away so she could… so she could do whatever she wanted to try to make me talk.'

Her voice was shaky now. Aleksis saw her hands clench into fists and wished he had cut the conversation short earlier. 'Better that we do not speak of this further. I regret—'

Stasya stood up abruptly and moved a few steps away, her arms folded, her back to him. 'Regret doesn't help. Regret can't bring them back. It can't take away the pain.'

The silence that followed was broken eventually by a warbling comment from somewhere in the trees. The bird, clearly, had not caught the mood. When Aleksis spoke, it was in the merest murmur. 'It might stop me from making the same error twice. I will explain, I promise. At the right time. When we've put more distance between ourselves and...' He gestured in the general direction of Dragon's Keep. 'Because you and Lukas disappeared from court when we did, she'll make certain assumptions.'

'Why wouldn't she assume you're carrying out her mission as ordered? Taking me with you so I can guide you to the treasure but doing it in your own time and your own way? Why would I not think that? It's close to what she suggested to me herself.'

It was a fair point. Why, then, did it feel as if she had struck him? Why was it so hard to find the right answer, when as a royal adviser he had this skill down to a fine art? 'I was hoping,' he said, 'that by now there might be a small degree of trust between us.'

'Why should I trust you when you won't tell me the truth?'

'The truth can be dangerous, Stasya. You, of all people, should know that.' He had hinted, at least, that his venture might ensure a better future for the Northlands. But perhaps what he hoped for, what he so badly wanted to be true, really was only a dream. 'It's a story that could end in different ways,' he said, speaking more or less to himself. 'Good, bad or nothing much at all. But I don't need to tell you that. You know it better than anyone.'

32
STASYA

BEFORE THE LONG day turned to dusk, they reached the shining expanse of Clearwater. Thus far, finding the way had not been hard. The forest was dense, but she knew how to recognise where creatures large or small had passed. Voices reached her, too, from time to time; voices the others who travelled with her could not hear. *Welcome, friend. Ah! You're here!* And as they came closer to the lake, she began to see signs of a kind she had spotted before in this place. A forest animal was not likely to arrange pebbles in a small, neat heap beside a branching track, as if to indicate which was the safer way. A bear or marten or hedgehog did not twist grasses to form a kind of knot or lay leaves out in a pattern on a mossy rock. Flip saw them too but hurried on past. That was wise. Best not to draw such things to the attention of the others. But she wondered, now, what Aleksis would think if she showed him, after his talk of folk perhaps living on the mountain, higher up. What sort of folk would leave cryptic messages such as these? Would a climb to the Hermit become the kind of adventure undertaken by heroes in the old tales – heroes who inevitably came to grief in one way or another? Or had the patterns been no more than the result of children playing by the lake, part of an innocent game? If so, who were those children and how had they got here?

As the sky darkened, the air grew chill. A brief dispute in lowered voices was resolved when Stasya pointed out the folly of freezing to death when most likely there was nobody else around to spot the light from a campfire. She glanced at Matiss, whose bearded features wore a hint of a smile. 'Also, no fire means no tea.'

In the end they dug a small pit for their fire, on the shore but away from the water. The stretch of forest near the lake provided a good supply of fallen timber for fuel, and Matiss's sizeable pack proved to hold a folding contraption from which a small pot could be suspended over the flames for heating water.

Stasya found a private spot under the trees to relieve herself; by now, a simple gesture toward the others was enough to ensure she would not be disturbed. She washed her face and hands in the nearby stream. Maybe, in the morning, there might be time for a quick swim before they moved on. Though maybe not, in view of the need to keep her clothing dry. She'd have to hope for warmer weather higher up, and perhaps a chance to stay in one place for long enough to wash and dry things. And what about her moon-bleeding? If the Hermit was as far away as everyone seemed to believe, it would come again while they were on the way. Was that the reason the heroes of the tales were so often men rather than women? She resolved to tell a story, some time, where that particular issue proved to be the key to completing a quest. She contemplated this as she sat by the fire, watching as Matiss performed his tea-brewing routine with a skill indicating long practice. She wondered, not for the first time, where the big man's family was, and whether it included, or had included, a wife and children. If he had been a friend of Aleksis since they were boys, he must be younger than she had first thought: perhaps less than thirty. Stasya's thoughts turned to her own father, long gone, little known. Had he been a kind man like this one? If so, wouldn't her grandmother have told her stories about him, stories she could have kept as memories? Too late to find out now. Her people were all gone.

After a meal of dried meat and hard waybread, Karolis entertained them with a tale of how the warrior toads attempted to take over a certain forest pool, and how an odd alliance of newts, frogs and salamanders defeated them with clever tactics, no weapons required. Matiss contributed a strange tale of ghosts haunting a grain store. Then they organised a roster for night watch. Stasya thought it unlikely any pursuers would come up here in the dark, but Aleksis was adamant about the need for vigilance and took first watch himself. Stasya and Lukas were excused. If necessary, Aleksis said, they could be added to the roster another night, but he needed Stasya to be fully alert in the morning to guide them on, and Lukas looked asleep on his feet.

Flip had caught something for supper and eaten it a short distance away, crunching busily until nothing was left but a few scraps of hairy pelt and a heap of tiny bones that shone white under the rising moon. Now, as Aleksis found a spot to keep watch, shielded by trees but allowing a wide view, the others settled for the night beside the remnant of the fire. Stasya decided warmth was more important than privacy. She unrolled her bedding and set it down an arm's length from Lukas. They'd all be wishing for extra blankets once the fire went out. And the ground was hard. But she was in the forest; she was where she belonged.

Owls called in their mysterious language. There were other creatures not far away; Stasya caught snatches of their thoughts as they passed, some moving with stealth, waiting for the moment to dive, to snatch, to dart away with prey held fast in beak or jaws, some creeping low, shielded by the undergrowth, using all their skills to evade capture. There was no right and wrong in these small lives, no good and bad. The hunters killed to feed their young. The hunted might be carrying seeds or berries back to the den or nest for the same purpose. You lived your life and did your best to survive. Only human lives were more complicated, she thought as the others settled to rest, each in his own space. Or so it seemed now that she'd been taken away from the only life she'd known and plunged into the power struggles of court, and forced to endure situations she'd hardly dreamed might exist even in her worst nightmare. She wondered about the boy Aleksis, growing up at Dragon's Keep with all that going on. It was a wonder he hadn't gone completely crazy. But then, maybe court had been different back then. A kinder, more settled sort of place. When Aleksis spoke of the old Ruler, Lord Kasimir, it was in a gentle, almost reverent tone. Perhaps the cruelty, the harsh punishments, the strict rules were all down to Lady Elisabeta. But hadn't she only been Ruler for a short time? It didn't make sense. Unless she was the crazy one. Why hadn't they all stood up to her?

Stasya rolled over, trying to get comfortable. The hard surface was not helping the aches that came from a long day's climbing. She tried not to think of a soak in a warm bath or a bed with a soft mattress and a padded quilt. It felt like a very long time since she had experienced such pleasures. And it would be even longer before she enjoyed them again. Quite likely she'd never return to Heartwood. She would run off on her own rather than be taken back to court. Better to live wild in the forest than bend her will to that of the Ruler. She rolled over again, trying to pull the blanket more tightly around her.

'You all right?' someone asked. Not Lukas; she knew he would not try to talk to her with the others so close by. She raised herself on one elbow, glanced around. Pavel was sitting up, his golden hair touched by the firelight.

'I'm fine.' It was a lie; she wished she could banish the

longing for warmth and comfort, which felt almost shameful when she considered what might have happened if Aleksis had not decided to get her and Lukas out of Dragon's Keep. 'A bit cold, that's all.'

On the far side of the fire, Matiss rose without a word. He stirred up the embers and added a sizeable log.

'Aren't we supposed to let it die down now?' Stasya asked. 'Oh. Thank you,' as Karolis passed her his cloak. 'But now you'll be cold.'

'I'm tough. And I still have my blanket.'

'At least it's not raining,' put in Pavel.

'Don't tempt fate,' Matiss said. 'As for the fire, that's my decision. If our fearless leader disapproves, I'll bear the consequences.'

It was, in fact, unlikely that Aleksis had heard any of this interchange, standing where he was, well away from the group. It occurred to Stasya that renewing the fire might give her an opportunity; a risky one, perhaps, but worth taking. She'd need to wait until they were all asleep. Would that log burn for long enough?

SOME TIME LATER, with the others still and silent under their blankets, she decided to try it. The fire would soon be down to embers again, but for now there was enough flame left there. She could have added more wood, but that might have woken someone or attracted the attention of Aleksis, who still stood watch. Stasya judged he might have another hour or so before it was time for one of the others to take his place. A long, lonely vigil.

She crept over to the fireside and settled cross-legged there. Flip had been curled up beside her, deeply asleep, but there had been no need to wake the little dog. In the space of a breath, she had flown to Stasya's shoulder and now perched there waiting, an owl no bigger than a child's fist.

Tonight she could not lay out objects representing the elements or pace a circle lest she wake the sleeping men. Stasya reached into her tunic and drew out the tiny form of the amber owl. Its wise gaze would strengthen the ritual.

She went through the pattern of breathing, slow and slower. She calmed her body, cleared her mind. It took some doing, for her thoughts were a tangle of dark memories and fears of what the future might hold. Then there was the distraction of Aleksis, not so very far away and still wide awake, unless he had mastered the art of falling asleep while standing bolt upright. If he did happen to look her way and guess what she was doing, she hoped he'd have the common sense not to disturb her. *Breathe, Stasya. Banish those thoughts.* She looked out over the lake. The moon was reflected there, mysterious and powerful. Some night creature was chirping. *Hear me! Hear me! Listen!* Another answered, further down the lake. *I hear! I hear!*

Stasya gazed into the fire, watching the changing patterns of the flames. She thought of the painting on the wall in her cottage; pictured the woman beside the water with the creatures from the tale she herself had told: hawk, squirrel, fox, bear. In a whisper, she asked her question. Not, *Can I trust Aleksis?* Not, *Will my life ever be as it was before?* She wanted answers to both. But the most important thing now was this: 'What lies ahead of us, up on the mountain? How can I find the strength and courage to meet it?'

She waited, her back straight, her hands open and relaxed on her lap. Against her cheek she felt the gentle ruffling of the owl's feathers and sensed Flip's silent message: *I'm here. All will be well.* Out in the forest a creature cried out, and for a moment Stasya felt a searing pain in her belly, so strong that she sank her teeth into her lip to hold back a cry of her own. The sound was cut short; the pain faded. Out there, a life had been lost. While she prepared for the ritual, it was harder to maintain a protective shield over that part of her mind; in a way it felt wrong to do so, for if she could help an animal in trouble, surely she should. But not this time. Every night, owls would be hunting in the forest; every night, small creatures would be killed so bigger ones could eat. It was not for her to intervene in that. She was no goddess.

She raised one hand to touch the amber owl and quieted her thoughts again. For a while the flames showed nothing but their own dancing pattern, and she began to wonder if it was nearly time for the watch to change. Better if the men did not see her doing this. It was not witchcraft. Not exactly. She did not work spells. Knew nothing of them, save for a few rhymes Grandmother had taught her, a few blends of herbs that might reduce pain or help keep a person calm. If that was magic, and some folk might say it was, then many women in villages like Heartwood could be called witches. But if a person worked on the land and lived in a settlement like theirs, some things were tolerated because they were useful. A herbal mix to dull pain; a rhyme that would help the most restless child fall asleep. Small things. Small, important things that helped keep folk and their animals healthy and content. If it was magic, it was the magic of the hearth, simple and good. It took a person like the Commander, or that priest from the Church of the Godly who had once visited Heartwood, to sow the seeds of doubt about such practices.

Now there was something new in the flames: a pair of hands, reaching out. It was the old woman Stasya had seen before, with her long white hair and her steady gaze. Beckoning. *Come. Come closer.* The rock wall behind her, and the entry to what might be a cave. Then, swift as a blow, a sequence of images that made Stasya's gut clench tight. Mist and confusion. A narrow way with a formidable drop to either side, the sort of place where a single misstep spelled death. Then, suddenly, weapons drawn, blood spilled, screams and shouts and confusion. Who was that falling? Who held that knife? A momentary glimpse of Aleksis, his face sheet-white, his eyes blazing with a fury that jolted her heart. Then, as quickly, the chaotic scene was gone and the old woman was there again, a wry smile on her lips. *What is it you truly want?* she seemed to say. *Who would you be? What would you do with your life?* Without waiting for an answer, the crone pulled her hood up over her hair and turned away. The vision faded and was gone.

Stasya closed her eyes as the fire died down to embers and ash. Was that what lay ahead: fighting, confusion, disaster? Should they turn back? But that might see them all at the Ruler's mercy. Might the old woman's questions be answers to her own question about being brave? Perhaps she need not share this with anyone. But if the vision came true, and some of them lost their lives…

'Keeping vigil, Stasya?' Aleksis spoke softly, but still she started in fright, her eyes snapping open to see him standing quite close, across the fire. How had she not heard him approach? Matiss was getting up, ready to take the next watch. Those images would not leave her mind: Aleksis white, shocked, furious. Someone falling, falling. Tears pricked her eyes; she scrubbed them away.

'Just trying to warm up,' she mumbled, getting to her feet. But that was a lie, and although she did not fully trust the man, she owed him better. 'And… seeking some kind of wisdom. Sometimes it comes this way. In the flames.' Flip chose that moment to flutter down from her shoulder and become a dog again, contributing to the awkwardness of the situation. Both men stared; neither had seen the transformation at quite such close quarters before.

'Did you see anything useful?' Aleksis reached down to warm his hands at the fire, though there was little heat now. 'Or shouldn't I ask?'

'I need to think about it for a while. It was… confusing. If I can work out what it meant, I'll tell you. Now I need to sleep. And so do you, Aleks. I think you've done more than your share of the night watch.'

The shadow of a smile crossed his features, gone almost before she saw it. 'True,' he said. 'Matiss, don't extend your watch; wake Karolis when it feels like the right time. We may not need Pavel tonight. He has more reason than the rest of us to be tired.'

Stasya had thought it might be hard to go back to sleep, with the dark images chasing one another around her mind. But it seemed she, too, was tired, for when she woke the dawn chorus in the trees was beginning, and she found she was almost as warm as if she were tucked up in her bed back home. She remembered Karolis giving her his cloak. But now, as she sat up, she realised Lukas was right beside her; they'd been sleeping back to back, with Flip squeezed in between them, and they had two blankets over them as well as the cloak. No wonder she'd been warm. Just how that had come about, she had no idea. They were in the same spot where she had fallen asleep, so it must have been Lukas who moved. Comfortable as the arrangement was, she couldn't stay like this. The others would get the wrong idea entirely.

Awkward. Or it would have been, had Matiss not appeared at that moment with an armful of fallen branches and started rebuilding the fire. The sun had yet some time before rising; the birds were early with their greetings to the light. She got up, laid the blankets back over Lukas and Flip, and felt around for her boots.

'Tea,' murmured Matiss. 'After you do your business, maybe you could fetch me some water.' He handed her the empty pot.

'Of course. I hope you slept well.'

'I did, thank you. No alarms during the night. We should be good for an early start.'

They were all waking now, some quickly, some more gradually. Stasya made her way to a spot where she was well out of view, relieved herself, then went down to the lake's edge for water. Boots off, trousers rolled up, she dipped the pot to fill it, then stood ankle deep, simply breathing while the birdsong swelled and rose and danced across the water and through the trees and high into the air. From here, she could not see the others. *Who would you be?* said the voice in her mind. *What would you do with your life?* There was no easy answer to that. It was a question about hopes, dreams, possibilities. What was the point of that when right now every step was governed by other people's decisions, their rules, their choices? Unless she ran off to be a hermit in the woods, answerable only to herself. A life lived entirely alone, save for the forest creatures. Once, she might have convinced herself that such a life would be perfect. That it would be enough.

Ah, well. She was certainly not alone now. And if she had to be among other folk more or less all the time, she could have done much worse than her current companions. But the vision had thrown a shadow over the way ahead. On the one hand, it had shown someone wise, a possible friend, a mentor; but it had also shown pain, fear and loss. Should she tell Aleksis? Or should she wait? Often the true wisdom in a vision came clear only after time for thought. Right now, she had no idea what those disturbing images meant; only the voice of the crone rang true. A call to move on; to be brave; to live her life in the spirit of Grandmother's verse. The water. The tea. She'd best go back. But… what was that, under the foliage at the forest edge? Something out of place, something half-hidden there? Her spine prickled; she remembered the day she had first found Flip, a prisoner in the thorns. There was no voice in her mind now, no silent plea for help. She crouched down to look, and there in the undergrowth was a sign, woven into the prickly lower branches of a red-berried bush. Not made by human hand, surely, unless a person could do such intricate work while wearing thick protective gloves, for the thing was studded with vicious thorns. She would not touch it. But as she looked, wondering what the complex swirling pattern of it meant, the noise came, so deep and booming that she shielded her head with her arms and curled in on herself like a frightened child, thinking of lightning, thunder. But this was no storm. The monstrous sound rang out all around her, like the voice of some huge angry god, and there were words in it. 'Go back! Leave this place!' And a drumbeat, deep, insistent, ominous. Yet not a drum, for this, too, had words in it, words in some tongue she could not understand.

Quick. Grandmother. The verse. Stasya forced herself to stand, to stretch her arms out before her, palms up. To open her eyes, with the great noise still surging over her, around her, through her. Where were the others? Wouldn't someone come running to find her? She did not look down at the thorny sign, but up toward the tall pines of Heartwood Forest.

'The oak's deep roots hold fast to the earth.' A pity her voice was so shaky. 'I, too, will be strong.' Stasya thought of the Ancestor; thought of young trees growing, keeping the ancient story alive. Her ears were aching from the sound; she thought of Grandmother's soft voice, singing young Stasya a lullaby.

'The graceful willow moves with the wind. I, too, will dance.' Out on the water, a pair of swans moved, reflecting each other's pose, their snowy plumage touched to gold by the early light. Clearwater was as beautiful today as on that long-ago, glorious day when she and Lukas had first discovered the place. Stasya thought of Kristina's embroidery, flowers and petals captured in linen and wool; a magical dance. She remembered Kristina's words of courage in that place of horror and sadness. If the world came to rights, there would be dancing in that woman's future.

Was the booming sound dying down, just a little? Her head still throbbed with it. She would not look at the sign.

'The mighty ash towers to the heavens. I, too, will stretch high.' She looked skyward, raising her arms in greeting. *There is always hope*. This thought came in her grandmother's voice. *Always. Find what is good and true within yourself. Look for it in every living soul.*

A bird flew over, graceful, lovely. A lark, singing of freedom. Oh gods, what a gift! Tears rolled down her cheeks. She let them fall.

'The sun gleams on the still pool. I, too, will hold the light.' She laid both hands over her own heart. *I will*, she thought. *No matter what happens, I will.* A promise to Grandmother, to the old woman in the vision, to the Mother of the painting. And to herself.

There was Lukas, walking barefoot along the shore toward her. He seemed in no hurry. At last the sound was fading away. It dwindled from a great roar to a growl to a murmur. Now she could hear the wavelets lapping on the lake shore, and the breeze in the birch leaves. The frantic drumbeat of her heart calmed and slowed. She looked down at the woven sign. Wondered how the thorn bush had felt about being twisted and contorted and made into something evil, something it was surely never meant to be. Had the tight weaving loosened up a little now? Lost some of the malign force that had been worked into it?

She squatted down again. 'Sorry,' she whispered, without touching. 'So sorry someone did this to you. Uncurl if you can. Slowly, slowly. Your berries are beautiful, so red and shiny. Maybe you could feed a bird? Maybe you could stretch up toward the sun? You chose a lovely place to grow. I'm sorry you were hurt, and I wish you well.' She rose and turned, and there was Lukas, only three strides away, watching and listening.

She spoke before he could. 'Did you hear it? The sound, the roaring voice?'

He looked at her as if she were mad. 'What voice?'

'A huge noise, as loud as a thunderstorm…' Stasya stepped away from the thornbush, down onto the shore. 'I can't be the only one who heard it.'

'We didn't hear a thing,' Lukas said. 'What were you doing just now? Who were you talking to?' He motioned toward the thornbush, but when she glanced back, the woven sign was all but gone; only a few crooked stems, a few broken twigs showed that it had ever been there.

'It doesn't matter. I was supposed to be fetching water; where's the pot, I'd better—'

'I'll do it.' Lukas had the pot in his hand. 'Are you all right, Stasya? You look a bit...'

'I'm fine.' She would be fine at some point, thanks to Grandmother's verse. But what had that sound been, that terrible voice? Why would she be the one to hear it and not her companions? Because, without her, they might not reach the Hermit?

Lukas had waded into the lake and filled the pot. He was waiting for her. She wouldn't talk to anyone about what had just happened. But this might be her only opportunity to talk to him about something else.

'Lukas, there's something I need to ask you before we go back. I saw something last night, in the fire, after I'd asked what might lie ahead. It was... terrifying. A fight, knives and blood, someone falling. Aleksis was in it. And the rest of us, I think, though that wasn't clear. I don't know if I should tell them about it.' And when he simply stood there, not quite looking at her, she said, 'What do you think?'

He met her eye, just for a moment, and the morning light showed Stasya how weary he was, even after a good night's sleep. And angry, still. She'd thought the rift between them was mended, but Lukas turned and headed back toward the camp without a word.

33
LUKAS

So far they'd been lucky with the weather. But he knew that particular luck was about to run out. A man didn't spend season after season on the land without learning the signs. First the wind would get up, a tricky gust here, a sudden chill there, the grasses in uneasy motion. Then gradually it would build, until the trees were shuddering and debris was blowing about and the animals were unsettled. And if a person didn't act soon enough, both he and his stock would be caught in the rain and he'd be bringing them to the sheltered yards in a downpour, his boots thick with mud. In the worst storms, branches would drop without warning, and too bad for man or beast caught underneath. The rain would come in sudden bursts, as if determined to fall when folk were least ready for it. And then the sheeting, relentless wet, and soil being washed away, and rivers breaking their banks, and not much to be done but huddle in whatever shelter could be found and wait for it to be over.

A farmer learned how to handle it. How to keep the stock safe and dry, or dryish; how to tell when a big storm was on the way and make preparations. Not that you could ever be quite sure a shed roof was not going to take flight or a bridge collapse under the flood, but in Heartwood they were good at protecting their property, animals included. They helped one another. They shared space in barns and outbuildings, made sure workers were fed, built barriers or cleared debris as needed.

Storms could do a lot of damage, cause a lot of heartbreak. But they brought everyone together. Stasya had always preferred to be on her own, to live in her own little house – the old folk called it the Storyteller's Cottage – and to take charge of her own life. To be silent or to speak at a time of her own choosing. But when storms came, she'd be out there with the rest of them, working to keep folk safe.

The coming of the Commander and his troop was, Lukas thought, a bit like a storm. Not a spring storm, though. It was more like the kind that came when autumn was turning toward winter: hard, chill, fierce. A man could make up a story about that. It might contain an evil dragon, not the fiery kind, but a creature whose breath could freeze a hapless goat, or man, in his tracks. Not that he was in any mood to tell such a tale, or indeed any tale at all. The climb was beginning to feel endless. Many days had passed since they entered the forest. Nobody really knew how far away the Hermit was; there was nobody alive who had made that journey and come back to tell of it. Growing up, Lukas had heard the stories, not only those Stasya told, but others that were full of monsters and malign spirits, tales in which folk set out to discover the secrets of the mountain and were never seen again, or returned with their wits so scrambled that they could never take up their old lives again. He had to hope those were pure fancy. But hadn't Stasya once said that every old story had some truth in it? That even the strangest had begun, long ago, with some real happening? On this journey, with Flip turning from dog to bird and back again when it suited her, and Stasya hearing imaginary noises and talking to plants as if they were people, that was not at all difficult to believe.

Exactly why Aleksis was so determined to reach the Hermit, the man had refused to explain. It was beyond belief that the rest of them were prepared to follow his lead. Even Stasya was going along with it.

What if the Ruler's adviser was leading them into some kind of trap? Aleksis's three men were all fighters, strong, able and well-armed. There'd be no escaping them if things turned ugly. Once there might have been a slim chance, if luck had been on their side. At least he and Stasya knew how to disappear into the forest and, up to a point, how to survive there. But not now. Lukas was weary to the core, his body aching, his heart sick. Over and over, his mind showed him images of home and his loved ones suffering under the Commander's rule. He was finding the climb hard going. After Stasya had told Aleksis what she'd seen at Clearwater, the man had really been pushing the pace. Lukas had tried to hide how much everything hurt. He'd done his best to keep up and to help with the business of setting up and striking camp each day. He thought Stasya could see through his pretence, and he suspected Karolis did too. He'd made checking Lukas's burns a nightly routine, along with making the rest of them do stretching exercises and confirming that everyone was all right to go on. A few times Karolis had gathered herbs, then prepared a makeshift poultice for the burn that was proving the slowest to heal, the one on Lukas's side. The man spoke light-heartedly, making a joke of things. But the look on his face told a different story. Lukas did not ask him for an opinion. Out in the forest, miles from any sort of help, he thought he would rather not know if the wound was failing to heal as it should. There was little anyone could do about it anyway, and his mind was already burdened. His father, his mother, his sisters… At least Pavel's brave trip back to the settlement had lightened that load. It had warmed his heart to learn that his father was alive and doing well. He'd made sure to thank Pavel for the welcome news, scant though it had been. Pavel had responded with a quick smile. He was growing quieter as the journey went on. Perhaps he shared Lukas's doubts about the venture.

There was bad weather coming now. All the signs were there. Aleksis called a halt as the clouds thickened and the air cooled. They were emerging from a tract of dense pine forest onto open rocky ground. From here, it was possible to see a fair way ahead.

'There could be caves up there,' Stasya said. She stood perfectly relaxed, arms folded, gazing ahead to the next forested area and beyond. The ground continued to rise, but the slope was gentler than before, the way perhaps less challenging. And yes, she was right as usual. He thought he could see, if not a cave, at least a place where a rocky outcrop might provide a more sheltered camping spot. But it was only midday.

Lukas made himself speak out. 'Bad storm on the way. We should get up there and find shelter.' He glanced up at the sky. 'Might be wiser to hunker down until the worst of it's over.' Indeed, it would be selfish, stupid and risky if Aleksis made them go on, but he did not say that. 'Good opportunity to tell a few stories.'

There was a sudden silence. All of them looked at him as if he'd come out with something remarkable. Maybe they were surprised that he'd spoken at all.

'He's right,' said Stasya. 'We've made good time this morning. It would be wise to get under cover and wait until the storm has passed.' She glanced at Aleksis. 'That would probably mean not going on until tomorrow.'

'Mmm.' Aleksis was narrowing his eyes, looking up beyond the next band of pines. 'The terrain may not be so steep over there. But the forest is just as dense, if not more so; it'll still be slow going. We'll investigate that area, see if there are caves.'

'Go carefully over this next bit,' Stasya said. 'It may look easier, but it's tricky. We don't want any twisted ankles or broken wrists.'

Speaking as if she, too, were a leader, Lukas thought. As if she and Aleksis were a team. The man wanted something from her, he was sure of it. And she… she was different now. Changed. Aleksis was changing her. Or maybe, he considered as the group moved on over the rocks, it was being taken away from home, from her safe place, that was making her different. The old Stasya would never have been comfortable in the constant company of relative strangers, living at close quarters, expected to make conversation. The old Stasya had done her work and helped whoever needed help with scant need for words to be spoken. She had talked with her trusted few; she had found Flip sufficient company most of the time; she had retreated to her cottage or into the forest as often as she could, as if the outside world simply did not suit her. And he had been her friend; the one friend whose company she'd always welcomed. His feelings on the matter confused and troubled him. It would be different if Aleksis had made it clear why they were on this mad venture and what he hoped to gain from it, he thought as he picked his way over the rocky ground. The fact that the man was keeping his motives secret suggested all was not right. Why the pressing need to keep going, to cover more ground, to exhaust everyone in the group? Didn't that suggest that Aleksis was simply carrying out the Ruler's orders independent of the Commander and his men? All that talk about being followed might be lies told to reassure them that Aleksis was *not* still the Ruler's loyal man. He was taking Stasya because she could find the way, and as for Lukas himself, he was no more than excess baggage, dragged along because Stasya had probably refused to leave without him. Refused to cooperate if he was hurt any further. He remembered, sharply, that he had been less than a day away from being flogged to death. The uncomfortable fact was, he owed Aleksis his life.

He stumbled; nearly fell. Matiss, who was close by, reached out to help him balance. 'Careful,' the big man said quietly. 'All right now?'

'Fine.' It sounded curt. Unmannerly. 'Thanks.'

'I think we could all do with a rest,' Matiss said. 'I'd give a lot for a good night's sleep, not to speak of a chance to wash my smelly clothing. But with rain coming there's no hope of getting things dry.'

'Might set some traps,' said Karolis, coming up behind. 'Rations won't last forever. Not sure what might be out and about in this sort of terrain.'

'Bears,' suggested Matiss.

'Not quite what I had in mind, my friend. A marten or two would be more like it. Not that there's much meat on them, but it'd still be welcome.'

Karolis had a fishing line as well as the wherewithal for traps. In one or two of the lakes they'd passed, he'd had some luck and they had enjoyed a sustaining meal. But they'd need to hunt and trap more as they went; the supplies they'd carried were already running low. Lukas wondered how Stasya would cope with the killing. She'd never really explained how it was for her, but he knew she could feel the suffering of creatures nearby, almost as if she herself were being hurt. She wouldn't be wanting to tell Aleksis about that. Their fledgling friendship surely wasn't strong enough.

34

STASYA

IT WAS MORE overhang than cave, but deep enough to provide shelter for all of them. By the time they reached it the rain was bucketing down, though the tall pines surrounding the outcrop provided an added shield against the deluge. Aleksis had no choice but to agree to a halt. Still, he made sure the time was not wasted. After helping set up camp, Karolis and Matiss went off hunting, or possibly fishing, depending on what they found upstream. A narrow watercourse emerged from the forest not far from their place of shelter. They'd need to keep an eye on that if the rain persisted. But if there was a pond or small lake further up, there might be fish or eels to be had. Matiss had brought a supply of salt, which was being carefully rationed. A good catch might be preserved for a leaner day.

Aleksis had insisted the two men stay together. Nobody was to wander off alone, except on the short walk required to relieve themselves in relative privacy. Stasya and Lukas collected wood for the fire, stacking it well under the overhang. There was a depression in the ground, below the outer rim of the cave roof; flat stones had been laid around it. It seemed this had been used as a camping place by others in the past, though from the look of it, not for some time. Which raised questions nobody was asking right now.

By nightfall the storm was raging, with bright flashes of lightning punctuated by furious thunderclaps and heavy rain. The wind added its howling voice, and around the cave the stately pines shivered and moaned under the onslaught. Once or twice Stasya heard a cracking sound, as if somewhere out there a forest giant had dropped a limb. Flip had retreated into the darkest recesses of the cave, where she'd snuggled into someone's cloak.

They'd had a fine meal, thanks to the fish the men had caught. Their fire had stayed alight so far. Before the worst of the storm, Stasya had found some wild mushrooms and a handful of herbs, and Matiss had cooked everything into a kind of soup. They still had a small supply of the hard wayfarers' bread. Each took a chunk which, dipped in the warm brew, softened enough to be eaten without endangering a person's teeth. It seemed unlikely they'd be able to go on in the morning. The storm was relentless, scourging the land all around them. The gentle trickle of the stream had become a wild gushing, but so far the water was spilling out onto the open ground rather than coming sideways into their place of shelter.

Now, as they sat around the fire with their bellies comfortably full, it was time for stories. She was glad Lukas had suggested it, though surprised as well. He was uneasy about their situation. She only had to look at him to know that. Up till now he'd been reluctant to add his voice to the planning. Which was silly. He was a farmer, a practical man, a solver of problems. Who better to help this strange expedition reach its destination safely? Whatever the true destination was.

'Who's first tonight?' Karolis asked. 'Stasya? Matiss?'

'We're waiting for Aleksis's story, aren't we?'

Stasya could have told Lukas this was not the way to get Aleksis talking. But she did want to hear that story. She looked across at their leader. They were all losing weight on the journey, conserving the rations and working their bodies hard. Aleksis looked almost gaunt. The name Hawk Man was more apt than ever. The look in his eye was forbidding. 'It does feel like time,' she said quietly.

A silence. Seemed nobody else was going to back her up. But then, the rest of them probably knew all about Aleksis's plan. It was only herself and Lukas, the outsiders, who had been kept in the dark.

'It's not safe.' Aleksis's voice was barely audible above the wild noise of the storm. He was looking in her direction, but she thought he was seeing something far, far away. Perhaps far away and long ago. 'Not yet.'

'Who's going to overhear you, Aleks?' It was Matiss who spoke, his deep voice calm and reassuring. 'Who's going to be out here on a night like this? Except crazy folk like us, that is.'

Aleksis shook his head. Made some kind of gesture Stasya didn't understand.

'You could tell part of it,' said Karolis. 'Save the end until you're ready to go on. Like Stasya's tale of the strange companions on their journey.'

A silence. Matiss reached to stir up the fire. Stasya wished she could talk to Aleksis the way she did to Flip, or indeed to any animal needing reassurance. *If it's so hard, why not get it done now, when you're among friends? Be brave. Just say it.* Because this wasn't solely about being followed by the Ruler's men, or by any kind of enemy, including those whose weaponry was eldritch voices. Looking at Aleksis, she saw the shadow of the boy he had once been, and knew without needing to be told that there was some hurt deep inside him, a burden he had carried for years, growing up at court, learning the strange ways of folk there, becoming indispensable to the Ruler, and then…

'Tell us what you can, Aleks,' she said softly, not sure if she was speaking to the man sitting opposite her, or to that long-ago boy, or only to herself. 'Take all the time you need.'

Aleksis drew a deep breath. Squared his shoulders, as if preparing for a physical challenge. Out in the forest, above the noise of the storm, something let out a howl that brought sudden tears to Stasya's eyes. A cry of sorrow; a song of loss. The others sat silent, waiting.

'I'm no storyteller,' Aleksis said. 'I have no gift for that. But I'll do the best I can.' The firelight was on his face, the stormy dark behind him. 'As I told you, Stasya, I was in these parts once before, as a child of ten. Staying for a short while on a holding near Sweetwater with a friend close to my own age, and our parents.' He drew a deep breath. Whatever it was, it hurt him still. 'My friend had a grand future ahead of him, and because of that there were many folk to watch over him. Servants, tutors, guards. A privileged sort of life, but lacking freedom. Even his friends were carefully chosen for him.'

This was not what Stasya had expected. There was such pain in his eyes. They should not have pushed him into this. But she wanted to hear more. 'What was your friend's name?' she asked.

Aleks glanced at Matiss, then at Karolis, almost as if seeking permission. Both were listening with quiet attention. 'Markus.' Aleks's voice cracked as he spoke the name. 'We slipped away one afternoon to go exploring in the forest. An expedition. Running, climbing, finding small treasures. Playing games. Then the light began to fade. It was later than we'd thought, and people would be looking for us. So we headed back, or tried to. But we'd lost our way.'

Whatever was coming, it couldn't be good. Aleksis had fallen silent, bowing his head. Stasya became aware of Flip beside her, pressing up against her legs. She gathered the dog onto her knee, welcoming her warmth. It seemed Aleks needed to tell this, reluctant as he had been. But it was hurting him, anyone could tell that. Stasya felt that hurt in her own heart. Almost as if… No, that could not be so. She would not believe it.

'We tried to find the way. It was dusk, and we knew we'd be in trouble. No sign of the house, only branching paths that might have led anywhere. And…' Suddenly, it seemed Aleksis could not find the words. He was somewhere else, Stasya could tell. Lost in the past, seeing it before his eyes.

'Here,' said Matiss, offering his friend a water skin. 'Take a drink. I'll make tea later; still got some of the chamomile mix left.'

'Stop if you want, Aleks,' Stasya said. 'The rest can wait.' Though she hoped he would go on. She hated the thought of those two children out in the forest with the dark coming. Wouldn't they have heard the voices of folk looking for them? Calling their names?

He drank; wiped his hand over his mouth. 'We split up. My idea. Went down separate paths, arranged to call out if we spotted the house. We said we'd count to fifty as we walked, then come back if neither of us found it.'

Stasya wondered if she really did want to know what came next. Pavel had moved in closer; he looked like a big-eyed ghost. Something in this had disturbed him badly. Lukas was grim-faced. But Aleks went on, led now, she thought, by a force he could not stop.

'I saw it before I got to fifty. The high slate roof, the light from a window. I called out. No answer. I could have gone straight there and fetched help. But I headed back instead, shouting his name. I couldn't run; the dusk was closing in and it was hard to see the way. I got to the place where he should have been waiting. But he wasn't there.'

In the silence, Stasya saw that every listener was caught by the tale; each waited with bated breath, as she did. Even if they knew the story, even if they knew the outcome, perhaps they had not heard it told this way, raw, cruel, straight from the heart. Lukas looked as if he might cry. Pavel's face was a story in itself. Perhaps this had awakened some fearsome memory for him.

'I went along the path Markus had taken,' Aleksis said, 'and it led to that place we saw on our way up, with the rock wall and the ledge. I called his name one last time. Then I turned back, and after a while I heard other voices. My father. Markus's father. A search party. But they were too late. It was too dark for searching. They went out at first light next morning, with tracking dogs. But Markus was never found.'

This time the silence was longer. Aleks sat staring into the fire. Stasya had no doubt that this story was true. He had borne this burden since the day the terrible thing happened. Perhaps it had governed many of his choices as a man. How would a family ever recover from such a blow? How could they ever forgive young Aleksis? But then, these were only children. She imagined Tomas in that situation, a boy of around the same age, and how a child might not make the same choices as a man or woman.

Matiss broke the silence by rising and filling the pot from a water skin. He hung it over the fire. 'Not that tea is the answer to everything,' he murmured, more to himself than to the others, 'but it always helps.'

Stasya was still watching Aleksis. Her heart broke for him, leader and royal confidant though he was. They were all tiptoeing around him, as if afraid to recognise that the child was still there. Matiss was the wisest. But now, seeing the haunted look on Aleks's face, the defeat in his posture, she knew something more was needed. *Don't think too much, just do it,* she told herself, rising and walking over to him. 'You were a child,' she said softly and, sitting down beside him, she put an arm around his shoulders. 'Whatever happened, it was not your fault. You did your best.' She thought of that boy running, running and calling, keeping going as night fell and the silence drew out. In that child was the seed of this driven man, a man who tried to do everything perfectly. A man who continued to judge himself, every moment of every day.

He did not flinch or pull away from her, but she felt the tension in his body, a tight trembling that suggested he might give way to tears if he were not that man. A pity he did not let himself weep. It might have helped.

'She's right, you know,' said Karolis quietly. 'We all make mistakes; we all make wrong choices sometimes. None of us is perfect. If you let those errors eat you up you can't move on, live your life. I nearly made a very bad one; nearly said yes to joining the warrior monks. Loved the fighting, the training, the discipline. Never could get my mind around the prayers and chanting and rituals. Other things too, which I won't speak of here in case I give you all nightmares. It was a hard choice. I made some friends there. But looking back, I thank whatever gods might be inclined to listen for the decision I did make.'

'Besides,' Matiss said, glancing over at Aleksis, who still had his head bowed, 'your story is unfinished. Don't forget that. Don't give up before every path has been exhausted.' He busied himself with the tea preparations. 'Lukas, will you pass me those cups? I think we all need a hot drink after that. And maybe a plan for tomorrow. Though it's looking as if the foul weather may be with us for a while. Might be another day of enforced rest.'

THE RAIN DID not abate. As for the wind, if anything it grew stronger as time passed. Aleksis agreed that keeping watch at night would be pointless, and they all settled to sleep, glad that the very back of the shelter was still dry. The firewood they'd stacked there would do for the morning. They'd never keep a fire alight overnight unless someone stayed up to tend it, and nobody was volunteering.

Stasya's mind was whirring with Aleksis's story, the possibilities, the link with what he was doing now, if there was one. He must have had opportunities over the years to conduct a new search for Markus's body. Couldn't he have used the resources of court, if the Ruler approved? As a senior adviser he was probably wealthy in his own right. Not that finding a small, sad set of bones somewhere in this vast landscape would have been an easy task. But… perhaps it was something else that had sparked this journey. He'd asked her, earlier, whether she thought there might be people living up near the Hermit. Could he really believe his childhood friend might have survived all these years, rescued by some unknown person who, instead of returning him to his family, had chosen to keep him up there? Surely any right-thinking person, any kindly person, would take the child straight home to his family. He'd been old enough to explain who he was and where he'd come from. But… how could a child of that age have made his way from down there, close to Sweetwater, to the distant mountaintop? The answer was, he couldn't, not on his own. Did Aleks think someone had snatched him and kept him? Taken him away? She shuddered to think of that. If Markus had survived, he would be terribly changed by his experience. Might Aleks find him and regret making the attempt? If he did find his friend, what was his plan? To take him home to his family for a happy reunion? That kind of thing happened in stories sometimes. But she could not see it in this one.

She rolled over, cursing under her breath. At this rate she was never going to get to sleep. The others were all quiet now, motionless under their blankets. The only one awake, apart from herself, was Flip, who was watching her, big-eyed, as if waiting for something. Stasya reached to stroke the little dog's back and scratch behind her ears, the way she liked. The temptation to send Flip ahead was always there; as a bird she'd be able to fly quickly up the mountain, armed with a question such as, *Is there anyone up there?* But Stasya wouldn't send her. She hadn't forgotten that warning down by Clearwater, the twisted thorns, the powerful, threatening voice that only she could hear. Someone, or some*thing*, did not want her to be on this journey. There was danger out there. Flip had been unusually clingy for quite some time, reluctant to leave Stasya's side for long. She, too, was feeling the peril, the risk, the possibility that they were unwelcome. Besides, the weather was appalling. What bird would fly out in that unless it was a life-or-death choice?

She made herself calm; went through her pattern of breathing. Whispered the words of Grandmother's verse to herself, knowing that in some way Flip would understand. 'The oak's deep roots hold fast to the earth. I, too, will be strong.' She imagined Grandmother saying, *Breathe, Stasya. Make your body still. Listen to what is around you. Hear the voices.* The howl of the wind; the ceaseless drumming of the rain; someone snoring gently. 'The graceful willow moves with the wind. I, too, will dance.' When the storm was over. When they reached home, wherever home was now. When they found what they were looking for. 'The mighty ash towers to the heavens. I, too, will stretch high.' She was trying. Doing her best. Sometimes it was hard. Sometimes it felt as if she had stretched herself to breaking point. But it was always possible to do more. Always. To reach out a hand in kindness. To help a person in trouble. To keep going even if you were weary to the bone and full of doubts.

Flip sent her a mind-picture: Stasya turning into a bird, not a lark this time but something much bigger, perhaps a wild goose. Spreading her wings, rising to the sky, her snowy feathers touched to gold by the sunlight. Beautiful. Powerful. The bird flew across a cloudless sky, away, away, leaving behind all that was familiar. A moment of sheer magic. 'Thank you,' Stasya whispered. The little one was wise. Stretching high could mean being prepared to leave the past behind. Growing, moving on, learning new things, making new journeys. Taking new risks. 'The sun gleams on the still pool. I, too, will hold the light.' The light was the love of all creatures, wayward humankind included. It was understanding. It was knowing how to make wise choices, how to keep going when things got overwhelming and all you really wanted was to curl up and stop thinking for a while. It was keeping on walking. Being a true friend. Offering comfort when you knew someone was suffering. Because it wasn't only holding the light; it was sharing the light. Perhaps the light showed the way forward. Or the way out. 'Hold the light,' she whispered to Flip. '*Be* the light. All of us can do that, if only we can find it in ourselves.'

35

ALEKSIS

He woke to the sound of troubled voices. Matiss. Karolis. And the voice of the rain, still pelting down. Although they were in shelter, everything felt damp. He struggled up, wrapping his cloak around him. 'What is it? What's happened?' The two of them were standing at the cave mouth, looking out. Lukas was there too, with a blanket around his shoulders.

'We can't find Pavel,' Matiss said. 'I've checked as far as the stream. We've called out, but I doubt he could hear us over the rain. None of us has seen him since last night; if he went out to take a piss in the woods, he did it before we woke, and he hasn't come back.'

A chill ran through Aleksis's veins. Terror rose in him, a monster from long ago. He forced it down. He was leader. He must take control, stay calm, put a plan in place quickly. 'How long? Why didn't you wake me earlier?' Then, at the look on Matiss's face, 'Forget that. Lukas, will you make up the fire? He'll be cold when he gets back. We need to search straightaway. He can't be far off, surely.'

'Aleks.' Karolis spoke in the voice a parent might use to a panicking child. 'We can't search in this weather. We'll do nothing but wear ourselves out. We should warm up, prepare as best we can, and head out looking as soon as the rain eases off. Not all of us at once. Two at a time. Or maybe two pairs, with someone staying here in case he comes back on his own. He may have found a bolthole somewhere in the forest and be waiting for the same thing, a break in the weather.'

'Why would he have gone so far away that he couldn't get back?' Lukas asked. 'A piss in the woods, Matiss said. But that can be done a stone's throw from here.' As he spoke, he was building the fire again.

Aleksis found himself unable to respond. In his mind, he was running through the forest in the pouring rain, shouting until his throat felt raw. *Markus! Markus, where are you?* He ordered himself to take control. Make a plan. Get a grip. But he couldn't move.

'Aleks.' Stasya's voice, steady as a rock. 'Get dressed. Warm up. One step at a time.'

He drew breath. Came back to the here and now. If Karolis was the strong father at this moment, he thought, Stasya was the wise mother, bidding the frightened child be calm. He did as he was told; it made perfect sense. Besides, what other choice was there?

'Aleks.' Something in Karolis's tone drew all eyes in his direction. He was standing by the inner wall of the shelter. 'Pavel's things are gone. Clothes, weapons, pack, even the blanket.'

A deathly silence. Then, 'Are you sure?' Aleksis asked. 'He hasn't just moved them? What possible reason could he have for heading off on his own?'

'Without saying a word.' Matiss was sombre, even as he began the familiar routine of tea preparation. 'Did anyone hear anything?'

Shaking of heads; murmurs of *no*.

'Some of the tales have travellers going missing,' Stasya said. 'But they also have Forest Folk living in the woods, and all kinds of uncanny beings on the mountain.' She paused to think. 'If such folk do exist, they might be friends or enemies. It depends which story you hear.'

'You're saying they might actually help us? If they're real?' Matiss was staring at her, brows up.

'In some stories they do. But you'd need to know how to call them. And there are right and wrong ways to ask beings like that for a favour.' Aleksis wanted to believe it was that easy. Say the right word, and a horde of magical folk would appear and find Pavel and then conveniently vanish so they could get on with the journey. But he could not. 'And you don't know the magic word?' He addressed this to Stasya, who quickly turned her attention to helping Lukas with the fire, but not before he glimpsed the look on her face. He'd upset her. He'd sounded mocking, unkind. And now he had no words to apologise.

'I think they leave signs sometimes,' Stasya said, still not looking at him. 'They mark pathways, showing which way to go, or which way is safest. But who or what they are, exactly, I don't know. Believe me, Aleksis, if I knew the magic word I would say so. It's not a good time for a man to be out there on his own.' After a bit she added, 'Pavel's been looking worried, don't you think? And unusually quiet, as if something was troubling him.'

'Something on his mind, yes,' said Matiss, hanging the pot over the new-kindled fire. 'Should have asked him if he wanted to talk it out. But I thought he was just tired. Like all of us. Missing his family, most likely. What in the name of the gods would make him head out on his own? Has he taken any supplies?'

'Hardly worth checking,' Aleksis said. 'There's not much we can do about it either way.'

'Makes sense to know what we've got left,' Lukas said. 'I'll check, if nobody has any objections.'

'None at all.' Aleksis watched him as he went through the packs, wanting to tell Lukas he was a trusted part of the team now, but not quite prepared to say it. The truth was, the two of them, Lukas and Stasya, would be assets to any team. They were strong, capable, practical. It was all too easy to forget that Lukas still had a wound that was troubling him. And that the two of them had been through a nightmare before he brought them on this journey. If he'd been delayed by a mere few hours in getting back from Raven's Watch, Lukas would have been brutally killed, and Stasya would have been forced to watch it happen. How could the Ruler set such an act in motion? Gods, now his mind was circling again, showing him vile images of what might have been, and terrifying ones of Pavel being attacked by a bear or falling down a cliff or simply getting lost in the forest, wandering and wandering and never finding his way home…

'I'd say he's taken a few days' rations for himself, no more,' Lukas said, breaking into the whirl of his thoughts. 'If he's headed home, he'll need to trap or fish.'

Silence again. It was Karolis who carried the trapping equipment and the fishing line.

'What would make him do this now?' Stasya mused. 'If he changed his mind about coming, why leave it so long? And why not say anything?' Matiss was shredding herbs into the pot. The smell was comforting, a reminder of better times. 'The story of Markus,' the big man said. 'The missing boy. Made me think again about this place and its mysteries. Maybe Pavel saw something or thought of something that was a clue of some kind. Something he thought he'd go and investigate on his own, in case he'd got it wrong and wasted everyone's time. Maybe it isn't far off. Could be he'll walk back in here with answers. You never know.'

'The story of Markus troubled him.' Stasya was lining up cups for Matiss to fill. 'He looked as if he'd seen a ghost. Or remembered something so terrible he couldn't speak of it.'

The story. The wretched story that never left him for one single moment of one single day. The story that kept him awake at night and, when he finally slept, haunted his dreams. If only the answer were so simple. 'Possible,' Aleksis said, 'but not likely. He already knew the gist of it.'

'He was tired,' Karolis said. 'It would have been hard making that trip to Heartwood and then heading straight off again, more or less. And upsetting, no doubt. He had friends among the men Rihard took there. Friends who may well still be in that settlement.'

'Drink, everyone,' said Matiss. 'It'll warm you up. And we'd best have something to eat. This storm can't go on forever. As soon as it dies down, the search begins.'

'This can't wait,' Aleksis said, working hard for a steady tone. 'He could be lying out there injured in this chill. The man doesn't have days, he may only have an hour, or even less. We eat, we wrap up, we head out, no matter what the weather. We find him today and bring him back to safety.'

36

STASYA

'ALEKS?'

'What?' He had his back to her and was shrugging on his cloak. Even a wet garment could stand between a body and the chill wind.

'Before you go. Something I didn't tell you about at the time, because… because it would have sounded odd. Crazy.'

'Whatever it is, just say it, Stasya. We need to move.' He pushed his feet into his boots, not turning. Around them the others were doing their own preparations. Nobody had tried to argue with Aleksis, though their faces told a different story. Stasya had been given first shift at camp, keeping the fire going, waiting in case Pavel made his own way back.

'Down by Clearwater I got a strong message that somebody doesn't want us here on the mountain,' she said. 'Not a person, a… a power. I saw a sign woven into thorns and I heard… I heard a massive voice, like thunder, warning me to go back.'

He was suddenly very still. 'And you chose not to tell me?'

'Lukas said none of you had heard anything. I was quite close by, just along the shore. I wondered if that sound was only in my mind. But…' How could she tell him her whispers of kindness and peace had unwound the thorny token, released the plant from the curse or spell or whatever it was? She didn't understand that herself. It had been all too close to magic. 'I've seen other signs, all the way up. Patterns in leaves and grasses, stones placed in piles, markings on bark, like ancient letters. Those are different. They help me find the way; whoever left them was a friend. But now Pavel's disappeared, I wonder if… well, if he might have been led astray. Or taken away.' Oh gods, she shouldn't have said that, even though she knew it was possible. Because Markus, too, might have been taken by some malign force. Taken and killed. Or taken and twisted into something he should never have become. 'Sorry,' she said. 'But… we all need to be alert. And careful. Not just of rain and mud and cold, but of strange things. Unexpected things.'

Aleksis turned his head and gave an abrupt nod. 'Make sure the others know,' he said. Which meant, at least, that he was prepared to believe the threat was real. 'Everyone ready?'

Stasya felt the cold deep in her bones as she searched for more fallen branches, doing her best to stay within sight of the shelter. There'd been a good stack of firewood before the rain came, but it was running low now, and anything she collected would take a long while to dry out. Ah, there was a fallen limb that looked somewhat like a strange creature with many limbs and a grinning face. She dragged it out, broke it up as well as she could, holding it down with her foot as she snapped off the smaller branches. Whispered thanks to the tree for its gift. Enough for now; her hands were growing numb.

Back at the shelter she laid the wood down in the dryish area at the back. Flip was snuggled under a blanket with only the tip of her nose showing. 'Maybe you could change into a fire-breathing dragon,' Stasya murmured. 'That might come in useful. But not right now,' she added hastily as the little dog started to wriggle out of her cosy spot. If there were malign forces out looking for them, a dramatic transformation of that kind would only bring them closer. And Flip, Stasya imagined, would not be well-practised at aiming her fiery blast, even supposing she could execute such a change. Flip had once become a larger dog, yes. But there must be limits to her ability. 'Some other time.' Gods, it was cold! She'd rather be out there searching than waiting here, imagining all sorts of disasters, reliving all the things she'd got wrong, hearing herself making some stupid remark and upsetting people…

Flip sent her a mind-picture: Karolis standing on his hands, then going through his personal stretching routine, which was far more challenging than the one he had taught the rest of them. Stasya could not help smiling. 'Good idea,' she said. 'It will warm me up. And what will *you* do?'

A NIGHTMARE DAY. On the second shift, Stasya went out with Matiss; they found no trace of Pavel. Unsurprising – though a person could always hope for miracles. On the next shift, she went out with Karolis. The rain kept falling, the wind kept blowing and the paths were a nightmare of dropped branches and slippery mud. Under the pines there was some shelter, but the ill weather made it a place of heavy shadow, and it would be all too easy to lose the way. Or to lose a companion. They had made a point of remembering landmarks to be sure they could find their way back. Their search to the south-west provided no clues, no sign a man had passed that way. They'd have had to find the man himself, dead or alive. The bad weather would have wiped out any other trace.

'Time to head back!' Karolis yelled through the storm.

'Good!' Stasya's voice was hoarse. This couldn't continue. None of them should try to do it again. But who was going to tell Aleks that?

They slogged their way through the mud; waded across a stream whose water had been ankle-deep before and was now almost waist high. So much for even pretending their clothing was dry. They helped each other as best they could. One last haul now, up a steep but navigable path to a spot where a particularly tall tree grew, and then down toward the shelter. *Let the fire be still alight*, Stasya prayed. *Let everyone be all right. Let Pavel be safe.* Karolis had told her Pavel had a wife and a baby son back at Dragon's Keep. Would they pay the price for his disappearance from the Ruler's household? It didn't bear thinking about.

Karolis was ahead of her. At the top of the rise, he stopped dead. 'What in the name of—?'

Stasya stepped up beside him. This was the way they'd come, she was absolutely sure of it. From here, there should be a stony slope down, a few young trees and the camp site not far off.

Instead, they stood on a cliff edge. Below them stretched a vast lake, its dark waters turned to a seething cauldron by the storm. As they stood unbelieving, lightning flashed, thunder rolled and a wayward wind clutched at their clothing, threatening to hurl them to their deaths.

Karolis let out an oath. 'What in the name of the gods is this?' He took a step back.

'Something doesn't want us here,' Stasya said, with her heart thudding. *Breathe*, she reminded herself. This could not be fixed with a few words of kindness. This was the dark heart of the old tales, the curse that had likely driven travellers mad enough to leap from clifftops or run off into the forest heedless of their own safety. Had Pavel fallen victim to the same malign power? If so, gods help him.

'What do we do?' Karolis shouted above the voice of the wind. 'Turn back?'

Stasya imagined turning to find another alien landscape laid out before them. 'Stay where you are. Take my hand.

Trust me!' Karolis took her hand in his; he stood strong against the storm. As the wind lashed the trees and the cold clawed at heart and mind, she called: 'Powers of goodness and light, powers of the old forest, help!' Then she whispered the familiar words of the verse, imagining three women standing around her and Karolis: Mother from the painting, her own grandmother Helvi, and the old woman from the vision, together weaving a spell of protection. Sharing their wisdom, sharing their courage. *It's not real*, she told herself. *What's real is the two of us and our comrades, doing our best to help a friend in trouble.* And she thought, *We're still in Heartwood Forest, and Heartwood Forest is ancient and good and wise. What we see is not the true tale. What we see is a falsehood, a lie, a trap. And what we need to do is...* Oh, gods. 'Don't look behind you!' she warned, even as a low growling came from that direction. 'We're in the right place, we just can't see it. Remember it's a slope down, with stones, so we need to go slowly, step by step. Keep hold of my hand, shut your eyes and keep them shut. On a count of three, we both move forward.' She squared her shoulders and closed her own eyes as the wind howled around them and something in the sky above screamed a warning.

Stasya pictured the three women; felt their power, deep as the oak's roots, strong as the ancient earth, wise and true. 'One... two... three.' Hand in hand, they stepped forward into nothingness.

'Strangest experience of my life,' said Karolis, as, wearing little more than a blanket apiece, they tried to dry their garments by the fire. 'And there've been a few. How did you know what to do, Stasya?'

She couldn't stop shivering. 'Just... did what felt right. I knew it couldn't be real. Sorry I couldn't take time to explain...'

Karolis's smile lit up his whole face. 'Sorry for saving my life? What you did was remarkable. Let's hope whatever-it-is doesn't try that again. Getting down that hill with my eyes shut was an experience I've no wish to repeat. Are you hurt?'

'I have my share of bruises. Just as well neither of us broke anything. What do I tell Aleks?'

'Tell him the truth. Or I will, if you prefer. He's got to see sense at some point. Searching in this weather puts all of us at risk. Even without the landscape rearranging itself.'

Lukas had been the one keeping watch at camp. Now he was peering out into the rain. 'They're late,' he observed. He'd had nothing much to say when they told him what had happened, though he'd been quick to offer them the dryest of the blankets.

Stasya's heart sank. Neither Matiss nor Aleks would have much defence against an uncanny threat such as she and Karolis had just encountered. Expertise with weaponry went only so far. Pure courage on its own was not enough. Not in this place. In her bones she knew they were moving into a different realm.

'We should brew tea,' Karolis said. 'That'll bring Matiss back for sure.' As a joke it was less than hilarious, but under the circumstances any light touch was welcome. Stasya did her best to cover herself with the blanket while she got into her spare tunic and trousers, which were marginally less soaked than the ones she'd taken off. She busied herself with the water skin, the pot, the fire.

'You know the whole story, don't you?' There was a harsh note in Lukas's voice as he addressed Karolis. 'About why Aleksis is doing this, why he's trying to get to the Hermit. The lost friend can't be all of it; it's crazy to think we'd find any trace now.'

Stasya focused her attention on what she was doing, though her whole body was tense. Flip chose this moment to patter out from the back of the shelter and settle by the fire.

'We know, yes.' Karolis sounded perfectly calm. 'But it's not for me to tell. What he's shared with you so far is the truth; Matiss and I can vouch for that. The rest of it has to wait. What you don't know, you can't be forced to divulge. What we don't talk about can't be overheard and carried to the wrong ears.'

Silence, save for the heavy voice of the rain. Then Lukas said, 'We're in danger here. Pavel's gone, perhaps taken. If Stasya hadn't known what to do just now, you and she would both be dead. He needs to tell us the truth. And he needs to stop making ridiculous demands. We're tired, we're cold, we're wet through. We all know there's next to no chance of finding any trace of Pavel in these conditions. If he keeps this up, we'll soon be in no fit state to do anything. I don't understand why you obey his orders, when it's…'

'Foolish? Stupid?' Karolis sounded remarkably calm. 'I can't give you an explanation, Lukas, not without revealing what I'm bound not to speak of. All I can say is that Aleks has good reason for what he's doing. A lot more depends on this than finding answers to what happened when he was a boy. As for the search… none of us wants to leave Pavel out there on his own. But I agree that we can't keep this up all day. Especially after our near miss. That was truly terrifying. I still can't quite believe it happened.'

'One last try for today,' Aleksis said. They were all back now, a motley crew standing around the fire in whatever garments, or blankets, were the least sodden. Beyond the shelter, the rain still fell, but perhaps the worst was over. That didn't mean any less mud or debris, Stasya knew. The streams would be swollen, the paths perilous to follow. Not to speak of the oddities of the place. It was as if Aleksis had barely taken in the horror of what they'd told him. But it was Karolis who'd related that story; surely Aleks believed the word of his trusted friend. 'We'll rest a while, then head out again.'

Better speak up now rather than risk another dispute. 'Lukas and I should work together this time,' she said. 'I want to go the other way, uphill. I know Pavel's more likely to have headed back down, but we should get a wider view from up there, and maybe we'll spot some sign. Also, if you want me to find the best way on from here, I need to go higher, get a better idea of the terrain ahead.' A pause. Aleks was frowning. 'I suppose you've been splitting us up because we're both wayfinders. But this needs the two of us.'

Lukas wasn't saying anything. Which meant, at least, that he was prepared to go along with the suggestion.

'Good idea,' said Matiss. 'If Karolis is up to it after that alarming experience, he and I will make up the other team, and perhaps take the fishing line with us. And you can keep watch here, Aleks. Make plans for the next step in the journey.'

'Mmm,' was all Aleksis said. Stasya chose to take that as a yes. And perhaps an indication that he, too, was exhausted. Not invincible. Human, like the rest of them.

37

STASYA

THEY MOVED UPHILL on a narrow track. Here the trees stood among great mossy stones, and the high canopy had shielded the ground beneath from the worst of the deluge. The storm was dying down. The cold wind still clutched at them, but here and there the clouds were giving way to patches of cool blue, and the drenching rain had dwindled to an intermittent pattering. With luck, once they climbed high enough, the view might provide some wisdom.

Flip had chosen to come with them as a tiny wren, but she did not lead, simply fluttered along nearby. She did not share her thoughts. Something was amiss with her, and it troubled Stasya. Did her small friend believe the whole venture was misguided? Was it stupid to put any trust at all in Aleksis? It was clear Lukas felt that way.

'You're quiet,' Lukas said, jolting her out of her musings.

'Mmm. Going uphill, it helps not to talk.'

'We could rest for a bit. No rule against it.'

'All right. Up there, where the— Oh.' Stasya came to a sudden halt. Beside the narrow track they were following through the forest a great stone loomed, clad in a mossy cloak. On the ground directly before it stood a miniature cairn, the piled-up stones uniformly round and grey. Not toppled by the storm. Not washed away, though the ground was muddy and streamlets tumbled down between the trees. This tiny construction was neat and perfect.

'Is someone trying to tell us something?' Lukas asked.

She could have hugged him at that moment. Clearly, she had underestimated her friend. 'I think so. There were signs like this further down. You probably saw them.'

'You could have told me,' he said after a silence.

Stasya heard the words he wasn't saying. *Don't you trust me? Your oldest friend?* 'It's hard with other people around all the time. Always someone listening.'

'You've been talking too much to Aleksis.' Lukas spoke without judgement, as if he were simply stating fact. 'The man who's afraid to speak up in case the wrong person hears the truth. The story whose ending never gets told. I'm happier if folk say whatever it is they want to say, even if it hurts to hear it.'

The shadow of what had happened at court, the pain of that misunderstanding, still lay between them, not far below the surface. He hadn't spoken out then. But who was she to judge him? Stasya slipped her hand into his. 'I'm sorry,' she said. 'You know what people think about this kind of thing – the pattern, the stones. It's too easy for someone to say *witchcraft*, and for other voices to join in, and then everything turns to hate and violence. Grandmother taught me to avoid that at all costs. It's bad enough that Aleks and the others have seen Flip change. And what happened before, when Karolis and I... If I'd done something like that back in the settlement I'd have been judged harshly.' She watched as the wren darted up to a low branch, gave one hard peck, then came down again with a wriggling morsel in her beak. 'They seem like good men, but...' It was too hard to finish that sentence. They *were* good men; deep down she knew it. 'Only, under enough pressure even a good man or woman can give away secrets,' she added. 'And the Ruler knows how to apply pressure.' She shivered, releasing his hand to wrap her arms around herself.

'Up,' said Lukas, pointing ahead to the point where forest once more gave way to steep rocky rise. 'Let's get to the top of that and then take a break.'

Again, she understood the unspoken message. *And for now, we'll stop talking about the whole messy situation.*

It was a steep climb. No question of talking; all their effort went into hauling their bodies up the rock face, finding the next safe hand- or foothold, sucking in another breath. Not a race; that was something they might have tried in the past, on a safer climb, in the time before. Before the Commander came to the settlement; before their world turned upside down. They reached the top more or less together and found a secure spot to stand, not too near the edge. Flip had perched not far off, in a little tree that clung to the rock, its roots in a crack that seemed too narrow to sustain any life at all. But there it was, a strange thing with heart-shaped leaves that were almost silver in colour, and branches that curved curiously, as if not quite sure which way to grow.

'It does feel as if we've moved into somewhere… different,' Stasya said.

Lukas was gazing back down the mountain. 'We wouldn't see Pavel from here,' he said, as if he had not heard her. 'Even if he was wearing something bright, something that would stand out. The trees block out almost everything.'

'Maybe from higher up? We need an idea of the best way on.' *Higher up* would mean further into the part of the mountain that was different, Stasya thought. The place might change again, and they'd walk off a cliff or fall down a ravine or find themselves at the bottom of a lake. Some signs meant, *Yes, this is the way*. Some meant, *Flee or perish*. In the tales, travellers in Heartwood Forest tended to die at the hand of monsters, be driven mad by ghosts, vanish without a trace. Or return home changed beyond recognition, unfit for the world as they'd known it. What did the Hermit hold for them: the wise woman stretching out her hands in welcome, or the knives and the blood, the terror and the fury?

'Perhaps a bit higher,' Lukas said, and for a moment she couldn't remember what they'd been talking about. He sounded less than enthusiastic. 'Take too long and we'll have Aleksis thinking he's lost us too. I think if we go that way,' he pointed north-eastward, 'there might be a spot where it flattens out for a bit. We might get a clearer idea of the lie of the land up ahead. That would help you decide on a route when we all move on. Don't you think?'

'Sounds good. Let's just sit here awhile first and enjoy the quiet.'

They settled as comfortably as they could. Flip stayed in bird form, hopping from stone to stone, perhaps seeking out insects.

'Stasya?'

'Mmm?'

'Why didn't you choose to go out with one of the others this time? Why me?'

'We're the best team for this. Especially after what happened before, with Karolis.'

'What, because we know how to move safely through the forest? What happened was something completely different. I'd have had no idea what to do. There's something strange and evil here, just like in the tales.'

'I can't explain what it is, Lukas, nor why I did what I did. It was risky. I couldn't know what would happen. But… I think there's a power here that wants us to find the right way. And another that wants to stop us. You and I know the forest. We respect it and understand it, as much as a man or woman can. And the forest knows us. The others may be well-meaning, but they're strangers in this place, and… because of that, they don't have the full trust of that good power.'

'What about Aleksis? He's been here before. If you believe the story.'

'As a child. Not far into the forest, and not for long. And he made a bad choice.'

'And now all of us are paying for that bad choice.' Lukas's tone was bitter. 'What chance is there, really, of finding any trace of this lost boy? The man's lost sight of what is reasonable.'

'He drove all of us too hard today, yes. And I agree the chances of tracking down Markus are slim. I was surprised the reason for being here wasn't something grander. He spoke to me once about making the Northlands a better place.'

'Stasya?'

'Mmm?'

'Say we go up there, all the way to the Hermit, and Markus isn't there, and nor is anyone else. Just the five of us, with hardly any supplies left. Say that against the odds we make it safely back down, all the way to Sweetwater. What happens then?'

'I can't answer that,' Stasya said. 'If he's been telling us the truth, then doing this will mean he's lost his trusted position at court. And the Ruler will be angry. He defied her orders, he took us away, meaning she couldn't use me for her own purposes. And… the Commander will still be in Heartwood, as far as we know.'

'I should be there,' Lukas said. There was an unsettling edge to his voice now, like the first hint of a storm. 'They need me. Even though Pavel said Father is well, even if things have settled down a bit, that man has done terrible damage. He's evil. He's a curse on the place. I should be there.'

'I understand. But be sensible, Lukas. If he's still in the settlement, the moment he learned you'd come back he'd target you. Pump you for information. Hurt you, as he did before. And…' She hesitated, seeing the grim look on his face.

'And what?'

'If you go back, you put your family at risk. The Commander might use them to force the truth out of you. Your loved ones could be hurt. And you'd put all of us at risk too. If you refused to speak, you'd probably end up dead. That's the way the man does things.'

Lukas picked up a pebble and threw it with some violence over the drop. 'You can't understand,' he said. 'You have no family. You can't know how it feels.'

Stasya blinked back sudden tears. She rose to her feet. 'Let's move on,' she said. 'We'll try this way you suggested.' And she thought, *We can't afford to spend time making each other feel bad*. But she did not say it. To keep going required faith in the mission. It required heart. Perhaps, for that, a person only needed to believe in their companions. If men like Matiss and Karolis had faith in Aleksis and his quest, that had to be worth something. If Pavel, to start with at least, had been prepared to put his loved ones at risk in order to support Aleks, that meant a great deal. Pavel was gone now, and they might never know what had happened to him. That made it all the more important to see this through.

The two of them went on. The silence was full of things unspoken. Full of what had been between them and what might have been. Higher up there was open ground and a track that might have been used by wild goats, weaving between rocky outcrops and a scattering of hardy trees. Here and there a tall larch stood, majestic against the sky, as if guarding the land around it. Flip kept pace, flying from tree to tree, coming down occasionally to drink from puddles left by the recent storm. Stasya tried to banish the troublesome thoughts. She would have liked to say, *You are my family*. But that would have been neither accurate nor fair. Lukas *felt* like family; he had from early times. Like a brother, only not quite. But he wasn't blood kin, and she would never have a place in his family. Both of them knew it, though they never talked about it. And even if things changed at Heartwood and she went back to her cottage and her old life, Lukas was sure to marry soon. She doubted his wife would approve of a close friendship between her new husband and the village outsider.

Maybe the only answer was to retreat into the forest, build herself some sort of shelter, become a hermit. She imagined herself clad in garments woven from leaves and grasses with her hair a wild nest, walking barefoot under the trees, seeking wisdom in still pools or the smoke of a tiny campfire, and when humankind came close, hiding away like a wild creature. It had a certain appeal. But in practical terms, it was unlikely. In the settlement she had an understanding with ordinary folk. Work hard, make yourself useful, earn your keep in food and other necessities. Be treated fairly, if somewhat warily. And in the case of certain people like Farmer Vidas, receive some respect, because those folk saw that what made her different also made her valuable. She hoped Vidas was safe, and Kiril. She hoped everyone was safe. If by some miracle the Commander withdrew his men from Heartwood, maybe the folk who were left would not be too damaged to set things to rights. Maybe they would be stronger than before. But they'd need leaders. People who could set an example; people others would be glad to follow. Irina was gone. But Jurgis could be one of these leaders. Lukas, in time, would be another. If the Commander left. If things changed. If, if, if…

'There,' Lukas said, coming to a halt. 'What do you think?'

The rain had ceased. From this point they could see a fair way ahead, though not once had there been even a faraway glimpse of the mountaintop and its crowning rock formation. But a route forward suggested itself, at least as far as what looked like a broad flat area perhaps housing a mountain tarn, for a stream flowed down from there, bouncing over the rocks in a series of miniature waterfalls. Many birds flew above that place, dipping down, rising up, winging off and away. A flock of swallows. Higher up, Stasya thought she saw a hawk hovering. 'Fresh water,' she said. 'Fish, I expect. And…' It was another sign. Unless she was imagining things.

Flip left her shoulder, flying upward. Too late to say *danger*. Too late to do anything but hold her breath and hope. The flock turned and turned in the sky, a marvellous skein of feather and bone and beating heart. Flip was lost somewhere within it, but Stasya could feel the rhythm and swirl of this dance in her own body. Flip was full of joy, bursting with the thrill of freedom, and at the same time safe within the unity of her tribe. No longer closed off, no longer timid or fearful or uneasy, Flip was home.

'Stasya?'

Lukas had said something, and she'd been so wrapped up in those sensations that she'd missed it. He was looking at her strangely.

'What?' The elation drained quickly from her body. In the sky above them the flock was no longer making patterns, but dispersing, some flying this way, some that. She wondered if Flip might not come back. If, like Pavel, she would disappear without trace. If she lost Flip, she would lose part of herself.

'You looked as if you were somewhere else,' Lukas said. 'Are you all right?'

Before she needed to answer, there was a small whoosh of wings, and Flip was on her shoulder. Stasya felt again that wondrous sense of being both free and safe. Had she ever truly felt that way before? Perhaps; but only long ago, when she'd been too young to know what a precious gift it was. 'Thank you,' she whispered to the bird, who responded by pecking her gently on the ear, as if to say, *You're welcome, silly.*

Lukas was waiting for an answer.

'I'm fine,' she said, thinking how pale he looked. Was he standing a little crooked, as if in pain? 'Getting tired, that's all. Maybe we should head back.' She wouldn't ask him about that troublesome burn; better to have a discreet word with Karolis when they returned to camp.

Lukas was frowning. 'We should go up as far as the lake, if that's what it is,' he said. 'Get a feel for the track. Then report back and hope Aleksis agrees to go this way. Come on, Stasya. It's not like you to be so cautious.'

She shut her mouth over the words, *Are we arguing again?* 'That's a fair climb,' she said instead. 'Aleks will take our advice on this, surely.'

'Mmm.' His face gave nothing away. 'What if he wants more from us? From you? What if being here is stopping us from doing the things we should be doing?'

Like going back to Heartwood and getting ourselves killed. She didn't say it. 'I'm heading back down now, Lukas. I'm too tired to climb any further. And there's no point in trying to guess what Aleks wants, apart from finding out what happened to his lost friend.' As she spoke, she turned and headed back. She didn't like the way he was moving. And she didn't much care for the way he was talking. He sounded almost angry. What it meant she had no idea, but getting him back to camp seemed important.

It took them longer than it should have to get down. The steepest parts were a trial. Stasya insisted on going first, though if Lukas lost his grip, there'd be no way she could stop him from falling. She thought of the climbs they'd done back at Heartwood, in old times: the two of them joking, laughing even as they put themselves to tests whose peril they scarcely thought of. They'd been so full of delight and confidence. They'd been lucky in each other. Perfect friends. She tried not to think of that vision: someone falling, falling.

By the time they reached the foot of the steepest pitch, Lukas couldn't hide his weariness, an exhaustion that was out of proportion to the effort they'd made. They stood there a few moments, not speaking. Lukas had a hand out against the rock wall, as if he could not stand upright without support.

'Sit. Breathe.' Stasya got out her water skin. That Lukas obeyed her without question was another sign all was not well. She drank, handed him the skin, waited without saying more. Flip found a perch nearby.

'Dizzy. Sorry.' Lukas put his head down on his knees. His voice sounded odd, distant, as if he might be close to losing consciousness.

'Just sit quietly for a while.' And then what? She'd seen that look on someone before, an older man from the village who'd been stricken with chest pains while unloading sacks of grain from a cart. So pale his face looked almost grey. Unable to stand straight; his voice like that of a ghost. The next thing had been a complete collapse. The man had died later that day. She wouldn't let that happen to Lukas. So what to do? Leave him here, get quickly down to the others and fetch help? No. Two would be out searching, only one on watch in the shelter. She couldn't leave Lukas on his own. If only she could send Flip with a message. Not possible. But…

'Can you hear me, Lukas?'

'Mmm.'

He was still conscious, at least. Stasya reached out to Flip, sending her a mind-picture of Lukas in pain, unable to walk; then an image of him at the shelter, with Karolis applying a poultice to the troublesome burn, and Matiss offering a cup of tea. *What do I do, Flip? I need to get him there safely.*

She might have known what Flip's answer would be. Stasya had carried Lukas before, across her shoulders, when they were testing their strength on a long-ago walk in the forest. Each could carry the other's weight. Lukas was strong from handling the goats, and Stasya from a myriad of tasks on folk's farms. In Flip's mind-picture Stasya heaved Lukas up across her shoulders without any apparent effort and strode with confidence down the track. It was an image from an old, heroic story, not reality. Still, she could do it, if not with quite the same grace and ease. Flip let out a chirp, then sent another image: the little bird winging her way down toward the shelter, a messenger travelling ahead as Stasya bore her friend to safety.

'Good,' Stasya whispered. For Flip would need neither words nor mind-pictures to pass on a message asking for help or suggesting urgency. Her bird-voice, her fluttering wings would speak for her. At the very least, it would warn Aleksis that something was amiss.

Lukas was reluctant at first, mumbling that he was too heavy, that she should just leave him. But he did not fight her when she got into position to manoeuvre him up. 'No talking from now on,' she said. 'I'll need all my breath for the job.' Just as well they'd carried little apart from the water skin, which she could hang from her belt. She was about to lift him when the tale of the boy called Amber and his healing talisman came to her: the tale she had told Lady Elisabeta in what now felt like a different life, though it had not been so very long ago. 'Here,' she said, and reached to unclip the chain that held the amber owl. She fastened it around Lukas's neck, her hands brushing against his curly hair, which was now almost down to his shoulders and more than a little wild.

'But—'

'Ssh. I'll take it back when we're safe. Now give me a bit of help if you can. Arm around my shoulder and one… two… three.'

It was a long way. She was close to giving up a few times, her back fiery with pain, her steps less steady than she'd have liked. Maybe she'd misread the signs: the little cairn, the joyous dance of birds that had so captured Flip's heart. Perhaps they'd been messages of warning. *You are entering another realm. Be prepared for everything to change.* It was easy to believe. Since the Commander came to Heartwood, their lives had been all change. *Don't die, Lukas,* she willed him, pausing to shift her stance a little, to balance his weight more evenly. *Heartwood needs you.* She gritted her teeth and walked on. No sign of Flip; no knowing if she had delivered any kind of message.

As she drew near the last steep descent, with her strength ebbing fast, there was a cry of birds above her, and she saw the flock winging across, circling, dipping, rising. She stopped in her tracks, with Lukas still balanced on her shoulders. Then, as gently as she could, she squatted down and eased him onto the ground. He murmured something. It made no sense, but that didn't matter. For now, coming up toward them, she saw a sturdy figure, and then another. Matiss. Karolis. Stasya found herself smiling through exhausted tears. Never mind that the two of them, and Lukas, resembled hairy monsters from a tale, for all the men now wore unkempt beards, and they would no doubt look even shaggier by the time they reached the Hermit. *If* they reached the Hermit…

Karolis was examining Lukas, speaking to him in a low voice, looking into his eyes. Matiss crouched down beside Stasya, who was sitting on the ground now. 'Well done,' he said quietly. 'We'll need Aleks, too, if we're to get him down to the shelter. One of us will go back.'

'No, wait,' she said. 'Just give me a bit of time.' Perhaps it was risky, but common sense said the risk was worth taking. The day was passing, Lukas was ashen and barely conscious, and she judged herself to be almost too tired to climb safely down the rest of the way. Almost. She could do it. But… She reached out to Flip with her thoughts, and saw one bird detach itself from the flock, flying down to perch nearby, not so close as to draw attention. She showed Flip an image of Aleks alone in the shelter, gazing up toward them, though he would not be able to see them. She showed Flip flying down there and returning with Aleks; then the three men manoeuvring Lukas down the drop and carrying him to the shelter in a makeshift sling made from blankets, with herself walking along behind, the bird on her shoulder. It was only when Flip arose from the stunted tree where she was perched and flew off that Stasya blinked and became suddenly aware that both Matiss and Karolis were staring at her with some fascination. 'She'll bring

Aleks,' she said. 'I think.'

Matiss grinned with apparent appreciation. Karolis gave a solemn nod. 'Good. The three of us should be able to get him down safely. And you.'

'I'm all right to do it.'

'No doubt you are,' Matiss said. 'But allow us a little concern, will you? You've just done a mighty walk carrying a man's full weight. That takes a toll even on the fittest of bodies.'

Stasya found herself smiling back, tired and sore though she was. 'Sometimes you simply have to keep going,' she said.

WHILE THE OTHER two tended to Lukas in the shelter, Stasya told Aleksis about the terrain they'd seen, the lake higher up, the clearer ground. A suitable path forward. He listened without much comment, busying himself with building up the fire and warming water. Karolis washed and dried the burned area on Lukas's side, then surprised Stasya by asking her to come and offer an opinion.

She was no expert on such things. But she'd seen plenty of injuries while working on the farms, burns included. She'd seen already the toll his time at Dragon's Keep had taken on Lukas's body, on top of the damage done when he rescued his father from the fire. Living at such close quarters, it had been hard not to see. He'd be scarred for life. A man could live with scars. But this burn, which had been the slowest to heal, was now inflamed to the point of looking raw, with red streaks spreading out beyond the original wound. There were ill humours in it, without a doubt.

'It's impossible to keep up a supply of clean dry bandages,' Karolis said, his voice held carefully calm. 'Pity there are no spare shirts to tear up.'

'Mmm.' Lukas was still conscious, if barely. He'd probably hear whatever they said; she must match Karolis's control.

'Perhaps something different for the poultice? Coltsfoot, if it grows somewhere nearby? Blackberry leaves?'

The questions hung in silence. They must all know Lukas would not be able to go on for several days at least. He was lying with his head on a folded cloak and his eyes closed. Karolis was unrolling a length of linen, perhaps the last clean supply. Matiss gathered the old bandage and the shirt Lukas had been wearing, adding them to a heap of items to be rinsed out and hung by the fire to dry. Aleksis wasn't saying a thing. As for Flip, she was back in dog form, and looking as if she intended to curl up by Lukas's side for a nap.

'No, Flip,' Stasya said aloud, and sent her a mind-picture of Lukas sleeping alone, while Flip herself lay on someone else's bedding. But her mind soon moved to a different matter. All the men were here; it was quiet. And she had something to say.

'I think we have to give up searching for Pavel. We're exhausting ourselves when the chance of finding him is slight. We need to let Lukas rest and recover for however long it takes, and then move on. What happened earlier tells me there's truth in those old tales about the forest and the Hermit. There could be more nasty surprises, tricks that couldn't happen out in the world we're used to. I see things in visions sometimes, in the fire or in the water, and not all of them are good. There have been signs on the way up, some of them telling us we're on the right track, and some warning us off. I know it sounds crazy. That's why I didn't say anything for a while. But we can't ignore those signs.'

'Real life can be crazy,' observed Matiss, looking around at the others. 'Crazy and wild. A surprise at every turn, and not all of them good ones. Stasya, how do you tell the difference between good signs and bad ones?'

'I can't, not really. It's more a… a feeling. What happened to Karolis and me… there's no doubt at all that was a warning. We could have died. I used to see the good signs back at Clearwater sometimes, before all this began. I took those to mean that someone recognised Lukas and me as friends of the forest.'

Nobody said a word.

'We need to be careful. Not only of the Ruler's people coming after us. Careful of the mountain and its secrets. Watchful. Respectful.'

Aleksis spoke at last. 'If the mountain is going to welcome anyone, surely it will be you, Stasya.'

His simple words, spoken with unusual feeling, robbed her of the ability to say a thing. Her face felt hot, and her heart was performing a strange little dance.

'He's right,' said Matiss. 'The land knows you as a friend, I think, despite what happened earlier. Whether that carries over to the rest of us, as your companions, remains to be seen. I see Lukas is wearing your amber owl, Stasya. That was generous of you.'

Not generous, Stasya thought. Only common sense. If there was a chance an amber token could help folk heal, it made sense for Lukas to wear hers now. She missed it; she would rather have kept it close, its small presence warmed by her body. 'Mmm,' she said, avoiding further discussion.

After another silence, Matiss asked, 'Tea, everyone? And then I'll wash these things. Might be the last chance for a while.'

38

ALEKSIS

THEY WERE SEATED by the fire again, with the long day turning to night. Matiss had made a familiar soup, using wild mushrooms and herbs gathered by Karolis and Stasya and flavoured with a few slivers of the salt fish. Considering their circumstances, it was a good meal.

Aleksis had relaxed the requirement that there always be someone awake at night. The lack of sleep was taking a toll. Not that he slept much himself; each day must bring the pursuit closer. When they did get moving, they'd be slower. Lukas would be weakened by this illness. Chances were this tale that they were living would be, not a heroic saga, but a story of bitter failure. But no; he must not think that way. Stasya would say that a tale could end in all sorts of ways. That the teller could steer it according to their own wishes. He must move on and make the next part happen.

Balance, Aleks, his father had said long ago. *You need to hold the balance.* People had forgotten that when Elisabeta became Ruler. Perhaps she had never really understood it. Bishop Petras, he suspected, had never grasped what it meant. And now the Northlands was teetering on the brink, a once strong and peaceful realm falling under the control of individuals governed by their hunger for power, their need for control outweighing their understanding of those for whom they had responsibility. Some, like Rihard, were not true leaders. That was a man trying to do a job he'd never been fitted for. A man desperate to make up for past errors, a man clinging to his last threads of authority and doing appalling damage as a result.

Oh, Lord Kasimir, Aleksis thought, *you would weep to see how quickly your peaceable realm turned to the dark once you were gone.* He wanted to say, *I will make it right. I will restore the balance.* But he could not. Not yet. It was not for one man or woman to make such a promise. He studied his companions on the journey: stalwart, dark-bearded Matiss, a friend since they were young; Karolis, a quick-witted man with the hands of a physician and the strength of an elite fighter; Lukas, who might yet prove asset or burden; and Stasya. The irreplaceable Stasya, whom he lacked the words to describe. Without Pavel, they were only five. But great works often started small. Given the time they needed, this could grow and grow and become something great. With the death of Lord Kasimir, the heart had been ripped out of the Northlands. But it was not entirely broken. It could be restored, if the people kept faith, stayed strong, held their nerve.

Sometimes the thought of what lay ahead filled him with terror. To lead such a movement was to risk all, not only for himself, but for those who put their faith in him and his cause. He bore their suffering as his own burden; he grieved their loss invisibly, as another wound to the heart. Hold the balance. Gains and losses. A step forward; a fall backward. Maintaining the pretence where he needed to; speaking the truth when it was the time.

'Aleks?'

Stasya's voice jolted him back to the here and now. He met her gaze, lifted his brows in question.

'I'll tell the next part of my story tonight. Maybe you can tell us the rest of yours. It feels like time you trusted us with that.'

She meant *tell us the whole truth*. The dangerous truth. He hadn't expected that so soon. But he couldn't make any assumptions about Stasya. She was full of contradictions and surprises. Those oddities added up to a person of formidable strength. A person who understood what *hold the balance* meant.

'Go ahead, then,' he said. She had given them several instalments of her animal tale as they made their way up the mountain. Hawk and his companions had progressed through some dramatic adventures and had formed an iron-strong bond despite their differences. Their strange company had become smaller; Squirrel had been snatched away by ghosts, never to be seen again. Somehow, the way Stasya told it, the whole thing was entirely believable.

Tonight, she had Hawk and his expedition surprised in the forest by a pack of wolves, who circled, growling deep in their throats, making Fox's hackles rise. Goat swung his head to and fro, displaying his fearsome horns; Hawk dived and rose, demonstrating his own mode of attack. But the wolves only moved in closer. Bear, Stasya explained, had been delayed after picking up an interesting scent, and was quite a distance behind the rest. When the wolves were close enough to be plainly visible, the human character, Storyteller, intervened.

'Now, the thing about storytellers,' Stasya said, 'is that they sometimes jump the barrier of language. Sometimes what they say, or rather what they see in their mind, can reach creatures who lack the gift of human speech. Thus it happened this time, and just as well, or Hawk's friends might have been dinner for the wolf pack. None of them heard Storyteller speak. But she stood very still and lifted her hands, and they knew she was sending some kind of message, for her eyes were distant, and her face was curiously blank, as if she had stepped into another realm entirely. As for the little dog who was her constant companion, the creature startled them all by sprouting miniature wings and flying to the woman's shoulder, where it settled with a soft hoot. It had become a tiny owl. For a storyteller can turn things any way that suits her; she can conjure magic from nothing, provided folk are willing to listen.

'So, she held out her hands, and stood quiet, and after a time the growling in the shadowy depths of the wood diminished, then faded right away. A creature with excellent hearing, such as a fox in fear of attack, would have detected the soft pad of the wolves' feet as they retreated into the forest. *They are gone*, Storyteller said aloud. *I promised them peace. We must keep that promise*. She turned her gaze on Bear, who had caught up now, and was perhaps the only one who might have considered a wolf as a possible supper. And Bear gave something close to a nod, showing he understood.' Stasya looked around the group and smiled. 'That's all for now. I'm too tired to go on.'

The silence drew out. Who could have thought a man who had been senior adviser to two Rulers of the Northlands might find it so hard to get a single word out? *Tell the story. Tell the truth,* he willed himself, but still he sat mute.

Matiss got up and started a fresh round of tea preparations, with somewhat more clinking and clanking than was strictly necessary. 'Don't mind me,' he said, managing to sound completely natural. 'Start whenever you like.' Which was nonsense, of course, since Matiss and Karolis both knew the whole story already. But it helped Aleksis to take the first step.

'Very well, then.' He gathered himself. 'Long years after young Markus went missing in the forest, later to be assumed dead, I heard a rumour. It sounded far-fetched, a pure invention. I don't usually give credence to such tales. But I had never forgotten my lost friend, and this story touched me. It made me hope.' He paused, looking directly at Stasya. The firelight on her face; the keen attention in her eyes. 'I'd grown up at court. When my father died, I took his place as senior adviser to the Ruler, first to Lord Kasimir, and then to Lady Elisabeta. Dragon's Keep under her rule is no place for imagination or wonder or anything beyond the known world. And this was only a fragment of a tale, passed on third- or fourth-hand. Unreliable. Barely believable. But… it was a tale of a lost child found, and protected, and raised far from home. The details were vague. Nothing as to how, or precisely where, or by exactly whom. It might have been a story from ancient times. But it could have been a tale of my own time. I was already concerned about the future of the Northlands; I was aware certain leaders were erring in their decisions. I thought of Markus; of what kind of man he might have grown to be. And of what he might achieve if I could find him and bring him home.'

Matiss chose that moment to put a steaming cup in his hands, and then to set his own large hand reassuringly on Aleksis's shoulder.

'What are you saying?' Stasya's eyes were wide.

'Markus was the only child of Lord Kasimir. He would have become Ruler on Lord Kasimir's death. He was raised in peaceful ways. If he had grown to be a man, he would have learned to keep the balance as his father did. He would have governed his realm wisely. But everyone believed him dead. When Lord Kasimir died of a malady the best physicians in the Northlands could not banish, Elisabeta was the next in line. A capable, competent woman, so folk believed, though she had been raised far from court and had seldom visited Dragon's Keep. Lord Kasimir's death was a shock. The way things played out afterward was… None of us was ready for it.'

They sat quiet for a while, thinking. It was Lukas who finally spoke up, his voice a shadow of what it had been. 'Say he did survive and was raised by someone who lived up there on the mountain. Why wouldn't they bring him home? It's cruel to keep a child from his family. And… he'd be changed by this, no matter what. Twisted, warped, taken off his true course. Yes, he'd be a man by now. But not the same man he would have been if he'd grown up with his family and his friends and the familiar places of his childhood. He might be…' His voice tailed off, as if whatever came next was too terrible to speak aloud.

'Unsuited to rule?' Aleksis could not keep the bite from his voice.

'Not ready to rule,' said Stasya. 'Perhaps even less ready than Lady Elisabeta was. You might find him, and he might not want to come back.'

How to answer that question, which he'd pondered over for hour on hour? 'I'm not a fool,' he said. 'There are plans in place; there have been for some time. How do you think we managed to get away from Dragon's Keep that night undetected? Only with help from folk who live and work there, folk who support this cause but keep their allegiance secret for obvious reasons. Not many have the full story; it's too dangerous to share. But they know we are working for a better future.'

'And that explains why there were safe places to stay. Those farms, those households so ready to take us in without question, to take the horses…'

'It's been a long while in the planning,' said Matiss. 'The support is widespread. But everything needs to be covert. You'll understand why.'

'And all because of a tale.' Stasya's gaze was warm now; something about it felt almost… healing. 'Who'd have thought you had it in you, Aleks? The stern court adviser.' Her mouth quirked into a crooked smile.

He found himself smiling back, despite the weight of the whole situation. 'If we manage to find him, and if he's willing to come with us, we most certainly don't plan to head straight back to court and present him publicly as the true heir,' he said. 'Many folk are loyal to Elisabeta, and others are too fearful to risk speaking out against her. His return will need careful managing. But… I have faith in him. Even at ten years old, he had qualities that shone bright as a beacon of hope. Another like his father. But we must prepare him, and we ourselves must be prepared. That will take time.'

'And first we have to get there,' Karolis said, 'whether that means all the way to the Hermit, or to some point where the truth becomes plain.'

'All the way, I think.' Stasya might have been speaking to herself. 'The place in my visions looks like the Hermit, as I imagine it. A rock wall, a cave. And the old woman. If she's real, if those are visions of now, maybe she's the one who rescued him all those years ago.'

39

STASYA

THE DAYS PASSED, the weather warmed and the new poultices worked their own kind of magic. Maybe the amber owl played a part. Though not entirely his old self, Lukas recovered well enough to go on, though he still tired quickly, slowing their progress. The increasingly steep terrain was an added challenge.

It grew harder to find adequate shelter, and there were some uncomfortable nights. Flip was restless again, changing her form when there seemed no real need for it, or flying one way then the other as if unable to decide which would be safer or quicker. Stasya could get nothing useful from her. By night, in her dog form, she pressed close against Stasya under the blanket, sometimes waking with a start, sometimes whimpering in her sleep.

As they climbed higher, Stasya saw more and more signs. Stones balanced in ways that seemed unnatural. Long, spindly grasses whose leaves were woven into patterns even as their roots held fast to the hard ground. A flat leaf holding a tiny harvest of berries that must have come from lower down, for the terrain they were crossing now was a place of bald stone, treacherous gravel and a few spiky bushes. She did not eat the berries, tempting as they were; they were clearly set out as an offering to some god or spirit.

Here and there were hollows, places where a creature might snatch a rest or hide from birds of prey. And there were mountain goats, strong and nimble. Lukas proved his worth the first time they encountered the creatures. Aleksis was in the lead with Lukas behind him. Their path wound through a defile with steep rock walls on either side, and as they rounded a bend, there in front of them was an animal so formidable they stopped dead. The goat lowered his head as he saw them, as if to charge forward and skewer Aleksis on his horns. Backing up was not an option; Stasya was right behind Lukas, the others behind her, and the look in the goat's eyes was not one of retreat.

'Duck.' Lukas spoke in an urgent undertone. 'Now.' As Aleksis did so, Lukas drew a deep breath and raised his voice in a call that took Stasya right back to past times, when he was working the goats through the gate. A long, strong note sliding up to a higher-pitched cry: 'Ooooo-up! Ooooo-up!'

A goatherd has his own magic, even if the goats in question live wild and free on a mountain. Stasya understood that, but she still watched in wonder as Lukas gestured, holding both hands up in the air, palms forward, then making a pushing motion above the crouching Aleks's head. This held the goat briefly still. Lukas seized the moment to edge past the other man and stand directly facing the animal. He gave the cry again, this time in a more insistent tone. '*Ooooo-up!*'

The goat tried the lowered head once more, showing this upstart man how splendid and sharp his horns were, but Lukas held his ground, feet slightly apart, head high, back straight, hands making the order clear: *That* way. Stasya found herself counting silently. *One, two, three…*

The goat backed up, demonstrating the considerable skill

such animals have on mountain tracks. As the creature ceded ground, taking its time, Lukas moved forward step by careful step, with the others following: Aleksis, Stasya, Karolis, and Matiss as rear guard. By the time they had emerged from the defile the creature was nowhere to be seen.

Stasya did not pause to think but threw her arms around Lukas in a hug. 'Well done!' she said. Then, suddenly aware that all eyes were on them, she stepped back, releasing him. His cheeks were flushed. She must have embarrassed him. For a moment, she had forgotten that the easy trust between them no longer existed.

'Thank you, Lukas,' Aleksis said. 'I think you just saved my life.'

'Or at least your pretty face,' put in Matiss. 'That was a fine set of horns.'

Lukas made no comment, save for a nod of acknowledgement.

'Goat magic,' said Karolis. 'Remarkable. How did you know the creature wouldn't flip you over its head and leave you in a mangled heap?'

That got a smile from Lukas. 'I didn't,' he said. 'But it works with the goats at home, so I thought I might as well try it.'

'Well done, friend.' Karolis gave him a comradely slap on the shoulder.

'I would answer, *Any time, friend*. But I'm hoping there won't be another time. With luck, he'll spread the word that we're not to be meddled with.'

They moved on with Stasya in the lead, picking out a route in an area of broken rocks, sudden dips and rises, and increasingly narrow pathways. One foot placed wrong, and a person might fall so far there would be no coming back. After some time, a solitary larch came into sight, a towering giant of a tree standing atop a rise. Stasya halted, gazing up at it without speaking. A sentinel. A marker. Provided it was not like that place where she and Karolis had found themselves facing a different world.

'Up there,' she said. 'There should be a useful view ahead.'

Flip responded instantly, becoming a bird and flying away to alight high in the larch. Oh, for a pair of wings. They could have completed this weary journey in a single day.

At the top of the rise they halted under the great tree, silenced by the sight before them. Ahead – miles ahead – was a still higher peak, crowned with a rock formation that could only be the Hermit. It was of remarkable size and steepness, and it wore a robe of green. There were pines up there, and summer-leafed trees as well, though Stasya was not sure what kind they were.

The end was in sight at last. But a formidable challenge lay ahead. The terrain dipped again, narrowing to a ridgeway barely broad enough for one person to walk along. To one side the land dropped away to bare rock, fissured and cracked; a fall onto this would be certain death. To the other side the slope held here and there a tenacious bush or small clinging tree. Around these was a nightmare of small stones on which even a sure-footed mountain goat would be hard put to find a purchase. A fall to that side might not instantly kill a traveller, but climbing back up would be near-impossible. The ridgeway ran for some thirty paces before it broadened. On the other side there would be room for their whole group. And from that point it was not far to the next tract of forest.

Thirty paces. It might as well be thirty miles.

Matiss muttered an oath. Karolis scratched his beard, a sure sign that even he, the fittest of them all, was uneasy. Lukas stood quiet, arms folded, his face revealing nothing. Stasya glanced at Aleksis, saw that he had gone sheet-white, and looked quickly away. *He's scared of heights,* she thought, remembering his account of the day Markus went missing and the impossible ledge.

There was something on the ground by her feet. She crouched down to examine it. Twigs. Feathers. Stones. This was no random scattering of bits and pieces. It was a pattern.

'It's a warning,' she said, rising to her feet. 'Something like, *proceed at your own peril.* I hate to say this, but it looks almost too risky.' Gods, what if this had to be done with one's eyes closed? How could she possibly ask that of them?

'It's doable. Keep moving steadily. Look ahead, not down.' Lukas sounded remarkably calm.

'Arms out to the sides for balance. Don't forget to breathe.' Karolis was already adjusting his pack to sit more securely.

Matiss looked doubtful. 'Would it be worth backtracking, Aleks? Stasya? This surely can't be the only way in and out from the Hermit. I don't like the look of it at all.'

'I'm sure there are other ways,' Stasya said. 'But finding them might well mean going all the way back and starting again.' She glanced at Aleks. 'That would be inviting a different kind of trouble, yes?'

'We can't go back,' he said. 'Not now.' Something in his tone clutched at Stasya's heart, but there was nothing she could say.

Matiss cleared his throat. 'There's a mist coming in,' he observed. 'If we're going on, we should move now. We should cross this thing at least, then if we can't see far enough ahead, there's room on the other side to bunker down and wait for it to clear.'

'Who's for trying this?' Aleksis asked.

One by one, slowly, they all put their hands up. Karolis; Lukas; Matiss; Stasya. No backing out now. 'Right. Have a drink and check your gear is secure. Karolis, you should take the lead.'

She had to speak. 'Aleks. I should go first. And you need to follow my instructions, all of you, no matter what I say. This may be a… a different sort of place.'

Silence from the men. Nobody challenged her. Stasya looked up into the tree but saw no sign of Flip. She made a mind-picture of the little bird flying straight across the ridgeway, finding a secure perch, and waiting until they were all safely over. There was no response. Was that a bad sign? Wouldn't

Flip warn her if she was walking into danger? Or had she flown on elsewhere while nobody was looking? No time to ponder.

'All ready?' She tried to keep her voice calm and confident.

'Ready.'

Karolis had taken the position behind her; then came Aleksis, Matiss and Lukas at the rear. *Look straight ahead*, she told herself. *It's not so far.* She stepped out onto the narrow path.

They were halfway over when the mist came down around them, blanketing the land below and ahead, swirling as if with a mind of its own. Matiss cursed; Karolis made some sort of reply, his tone calm. *Just keep walking*, she told herself. *It shouldn't be hard.*

A voice came from the mist, making her wobble. Then a hand, brushing her face, chill as the depths of winter. Another voice, another touch, words in a language unknown to her, but the meaning was clear: *Help us! Traveller, help us in our trouble! Save us from despair! Or die as we did, broken and bloody on the mountain!* The fingers again, pulling at her clothing, poking at her face. An illusion, it had to be, it was all in her mind. She mustn't think of falling—

A sharp clap of hands behind her, as one of her comrades tried to scare something off. The sound echoed strangely. Matiss cursed again. And now, within the swirls and waves of thickening mist she saw them: men, or the shadows of men, for they were surely no longer living. Their eyes were hollow, empty. Their limbs were spindly, their hands long-fingered, like claws reaching for her.

'Halt!' she shouted, struggling to stay upright. The beings were all around her. *Help us!* they wailed. As they plucked at her garments, threatening her balance, their shrill pleas made her heart ache. *We can never leave this place! Endless sorrow is ours. Help us or fall and shed your lifeblood as we did!* Through shifting shreds of mist, she glimpsed them far below in the ravine, their once-strong bodies now no more than shattered bones and staring skulls: the dreadful aftermath of some long-ago conflict. Yet at the same time they were here beside her, sobbing, screaming, a cacophony of woeful voices. They called for their wives, their mothers, their sweethearts, and there was nobody to answer them. *What use your hearth magic now? You cannot even save yourself!* A bony arm reached around her waist. This was no dead warrior, but something old and dark and sinister.

'Don't touch me!' she gasped out as her gut churned with terror. She squeezed her eyes shut, clapped her hands over her ears, felt her legs turn to jelly… Why couldn't she be strong?

A shout went through her like a blow. Matiss, falling. Lukas crying out, the sound cut off abruptly. She forced her eyes open. Made herself turn, just in time to see Aleks toppling over the edge, enveloped by a figure all mist and shadows.

'No!' she yelled. 'Stop!' Her heart was racing, her throat tight with horror. 'Karolis! Lukas! Are you there?'

Nothing but the mist. She was all alone. Alone, save for… *Jump,* something said, deep in her mind. *Go on, jump.* A rock-hard hand touched her back, as if preparing to push. *Get it over quickly, hearth witch. Your kind is not welcome here.*

Even as she fought for balance, even as shock and grief tore at her, something flared to life inside her, burning bright. *Help us*, they'd pleaded. And she could, despite everything. Even though she could no longer see them, hear them. They were here. She could reach them. And… even in the darkest place, there had to be hope. Flowers blooming after a winter storm. Young oaks growing up around the fallen Ancestor. Aleks, oh gods, Aleks, holding onto the fragile thread of hope because of a story… Lukas following her into this place of peril…

She stretched out her arms again, ignoring the touch of the malign hand. Fought to slow her breathing, imagined the Mother watching over her, and opened her mind fully to the lost ones. 'I hear you!' she called aloud, making mind-pictures for them as she spoke. 'I honour your loss! In the world of the living, your loved ones remember you! They weep for your passing, they tell tales of your brave life and your sacrifice! Your children tell your story. Your community celebrates your courage! You were kind fathers, loyal brothers, faithful sweethearts, loving sons. Be at peace now!' One last mind-picture, a mother's arms around her son, a tear shed in acknowledgement of his pain… 'They love and honour you, brave hearts. You will never be forgotten.'

Her own tears were coming fast now, threatening to blind her even as the mist thinned to wisps and the ground was once more visible beneath her feet. Above her a solitary bird flew, but the ridgeway was empty. They had fallen, all of them. A great sob burst from her. Gone, lost, her friends, her comrades… *Let yourself fall,* came the voice from behind her. *Make it quick, why suffer? Join your foolish companions. Pay your fee.*

'I will pay you no fee! I am a friend of the forest, sworn to protect and preserve it!' She hardly recognised her own voice; it had become iron-strong. She would not give up. Not even after this. If she was the last one left, it was for her to complete the mission. And… if she could speak to those things, those departed souls, if in this strange realm the landscape could change in the blink of an eye, maybe, just maybe, hope could work a magic of its own.

One step at a time. That being was still present, vile, threatening. She could feel it behind her. With all her fading strength, she reached out to Flip again. *Help!*

Sunlight struck down through the last shreds of mist, golden bright, and across the sky flew a great bird, crow-like in shape. This was no creature of flesh and feathers, but a thing of bones and air. Its eyes carried the light; it opened its beak to release, not a cawing sound, but a strange kind of music, a song whose message was clear: *Come! Come with me!* A swirling mass of spectral beings arose from the depths and followed the crow as it flew over the ridgeway as if in a farewell display, then away across the great forest of Heartwood. Stasya heard something collapse behind her, as if into fragments of bone. She watched the flying dance of ghosts until she could no longer see them, then made herself walk, one shaky step at a time, to the other side of the ridgeway. She took off her pack; turned and made herself look back, hoping for a miracle. Sunlight still illuminated the narrow pathway, but nobody was there.

40
LUKAS

HE CAME TO with a start to find Karolis bending over him. 'Lukas, are you still with us? I need your help!' Where in the name of heaven were they? A sharp rise to one side, a ravine to the other… 'Don't try to move yet,' Karolis said. 'We've fallen onto a sort of shelf, a thing that wasn't here before, and Matiss is stuck. Sit up slowly, let me help you.'

He could sit; that was a good thing. But they were… He looked about. They were in an impossible spot. He must have been knocked out. What had happened? He couldn't remember falling, let alone all of them falling, though it felt as if he had new bruises. Matiss was groaning in pain; he was wedged between the branches of a small, spiky bush that looked barely strong enough to support his weight. Aleksis was trying to cut him free, while standing on the same unlikely shelf not far off. Lukas looked up. A long way to the top. Long and steep. And… His heart lurched. He forced the words out. 'Where's Stasya?'

The pause before Karolis spoke told its own tale, as did the way he kept his voice to a murmur. 'We don't know. Right now, we need to free Matiss, then try to get him up to the top. I think he's dislocated his shoulder. It'll be almost impossible for him to climb. But I can't deal with the injury down here.'

Stasya. Fallen to her death. It couldn't be true. She couldn't be gone forever. Lukas made himself stand, though his body hurt all over. Made himself speak. 'I'll carry Matiss's pack up, then climb back down. It'll take all three of us to get him to the top.'

'Good. See if you can get the pack over to the safe side. Take care on the way, we need you.' Briefly, Karolis put a hand on Lukas's shoulder; it was the recognition of a bond between brothers. 'Aleks, what can I do to help?'

Lukas was halfway up when a tawny butterfly appeared, fluttering in to land on his arm as he attempted a particularly tough haul between the awkward purchases this cliff allowed. He swallowed another curse. The butterfly flew upward, just far enough to show him there was a good handhold he hadn't spotted before. He stretched for the projecting stone, positioned his right foot, dragged himself up. The butterfly moved again, hovering over a crack where he might possibly wedge the toes of his left foot to support the next effort. It moved its wings as if to say, *Come on, then*, and he did so. Any help was welcome, though the thought of trying to get Matiss up here appalled him.

Now the butterfly fluttered away from him, up to the top, then came down again. Was it trying to make him fall now?

A voice from up above. 'Lukas? There's a good handhold about an arm's length above you to your left. Take your time.' Stasya sounded as if she was crying. Crying, but being a leader. Doing her job. His own tears had begun the moment he heard her voice. She was alive. By all that was wonderful, she was alive.

'Pass the pack to me,' she said as he reached the top.

Somehow, he managed to get the thing off his back without dropping it. Could that butterfly have been Flip? There was no sign of dog or bird now, but he was in no doubt that something had helped him. But there'd been those shadow-men in the mist, pulling them down, wanting them to die. Crazy. The whole thing was crazy. It made no sense at all. But never mind that. Stasya was here. She was safe. Right now, that was all that mattered.

'I'm going back down,' he said, allowing himself one long look at her face, seeing the tears, knowing that however hard this had been for the rest of them, it was doubly so for her. 'Matiss is injured. Stay here, we'll need you to help get him up.' And he would have said something more, but he heard Matiss groaning and headed back down instead. This was too big for words.

THERE WAS NO time to speak of what might or might not have happened, or how it was they had all survived. Matiss was in terrible pain. The awkward climb to safety had been a nightmare, his screams fit to curdle the blood. It would have made sense to get right away from this cursed spot, to walk to that nearest tract of forest and find a place of shelter before doing anything else. But the big man's face was a mask of suffering. What had to be done must be done here, now, at the end of the ridgeway where there was enough level ground for them to spread out some bedding and take off their packs. All of them were exhausted and shocked. But there would be no resting for a while yet.

'His shoulder joint's out of place,' Karolis explained, fishing items from his pack while Lukas and Aleks settled Matiss on the bedding, doing their best to keep him calm. 'We need to get it back in position quickly. Ever helped with something like this before, Stasya?'

'Broken limbs, yes; but not this. Tell me what to do and I'll help as best I can.'

Karolis gave her an assessing glance, then spoke in a murmur, with his back to the injured man. 'I want you kneeling beside him, on his good side, and keeping him as still as you can. This is going to hurt him a lot, and he'll probably fight against it. Stay strong and steady. Once I get the joint back in place the acute pain will die down, perhaps quite quickly.'

Stasya moved into position without a word.

'One hand on his left shoulder, and a strong hold on the left arm. I'll be exerting a lot of force on the right arm while I manipulate the joint back into place. Keep hold no matter what. We don't want to have to repeat this.' Somehow, Karolis was managing to sound steady, calm, confident. He crouched down beside the injured man, who was moaning in pain. 'Matiss, I won't lie to you. This is going to hurt like the devil, but it has to be done. I'll be as quick as I can, and it'll help if you can stay still. Lukas, we may need you to help hold him. Keep alert, everyone, and do as I say. We all work together, yes?' He bent to take off his boots, surprising Lukas.

No words could truly capture what followed. Later, Lukas remembered how quiet they had been coming up the mountain; what care they had taken to avoid raising their voices above a murmur, lest pursuers should hear them. Stasya knelt by Matiss, holding him firmly and murmuring words of comfort. Karolis, standing on Matiss's other side, took hold of the injured arm, stuck his bare foot, toes first, into Matiss's armpit, and pulled hard. The big man let out a shout that rang far, far across Heartwood Forest. Birds rose from the trees nearby, screaming in response. Still pulling on the arm, Karolis performed a twisting, turning manoeuvre, waited a moment, then relaxed his hold. Matiss released a great sigh. It was as if the tension left his body almost instantly. A kind of magic, Lukas thought. Or as close to it as you could get.

'It's done,' Karolis said. 'Just lie there a while, friend. You'll need that arm in a sling before you move. Lukas, you might see if there's something we can use. Anyone want to give up a shirt? He'll need some strapping around the chest, too, to keep the arm safe as it heals. I'll prepare a draught for him. Painful experience, that.'

Matiss put his good hand over his eyes and muttered, 'Great heavens, man. That felt... like being... ripped apart. Thought I might... pass out...'

Karolis was carefully measuring something from a small bottle into a cup, then topping it up from a water skin. 'Lukas, help him hold that arm across his chest, bent like this. Go gently. Now help him sit up. Slowly does it. Yes, good. Just sit awhile, Matiss. Breathe. And when you're ready, drink this. One sip at a time. Try to keep still while I get the sling organised.'

'First... torture... then... poison,' Matiss said, with the ghost of a smile.

'No poison, just good herbs. I don't think we're ready to talk about what just happened. But we can't move on for a while. Stasya, could you manage a story? Then, when Matiss is ready, we'll find a safer spot to camp.' Karolis glanced at Aleksis, now crouched by Matiss's side. 'We can't go far. Certainly not before everyone's had a night's sleep.'

'Karolis?' Matiss croaked. 'Thank you. Thank... all of you.'

'No need for thanks. Just recover soon, will you? Nobody makes tea the way you do.'

41

STASYA

IF SHE EVER had to make a mind-picture of exhaustion, this would be it. Aleks had a faraway look in his eyes, as if, like her, he was gazing into a series of dark possibilities. Even Karolis, who often seemed strong enough to go on forever, was lying on the ground now, with his head resting on a rolled-up blanket. What with the unkempt hair, the scruffy beards and the clinging dirt of the journey, the men resembled a pack of sad vagrants, and no doubt she looked just as dishevelled. But those things only helped make them what they were: comrades in adversity. True brothers. And one sister. Two sisters, if you counted Flip. A story… She was so tired. Tired and sore and sad, even though by some miracle they had survived this.

As for what had just happened, she might not be ready to tell that story for a long time. She still couldn't quite get her head around it. This story, now, should be about gratitude. They had survived, all of them. And it was not only human endeavour that had seen them through this. The mountain had challenged them, yes. It had shown a dark and evil face. But it had allowed them to move forward. Someone, or some*thing*, had shown them the way.

'Are you brave enough?' she began. 'That was the question the strange group of travellers faced when they reached the perilous slopes and hidden traps of the faraway mountain. Are you strong enough? Even a tiny beetle can be brave; even the smallest hatchling can find its courage in a moment of challenge. How brave would the travellers need to be? What might they face on the mountain? As for being strong, there was more than one kind of strength. Yes, there was the strength that allowed an ox to pull a heavy cart, or a man to chop wood, or a woman to give birth to a child. There was also the strength that allowed a community to stand up for what was right, or a court official to question orders that seemed unjust, or men and women to leave their homes and all that was familiar in order to serve a higher cause. For the animals, the quest was not quite as grand as that, but it was done in the same spirit. Hawk was searching for a lost friend. Bear and Fox had joined him out of comradeship and loyalty. Goat had been drawn into it somewhat against his better judgement, but as the strange adventure unfolded, he'd found a certain satisfaction in being part of a team; in knowing he was useful. As for the Storyteller and her little dog, nobody was quite sure why they had joined the group, but they had their uses, if only to keep the others entertained.'

Stasya went on a while, presenting the group of travellers with challenges they met with courage, strength or quick thinking. She had not planned the story when she started, but knew she needed to keep it brief. They needed to move on as soon as Matiss was ready. Maybe that dark presence had collapsed into bones, and maybe it was still out there in some form. They were too exposed here.

'With that disaster averted,' she said, 'the adventurers stopped for a while to rest. And it is when one stops to rest that the doubts and fears often flood back in. So it was with Hawk, leader of the expedition.' Sometimes a story takes its course almost despite the teller. This was one of those times. 'One of them was gone, perhaps forever. One had been so sick that for a while he could barely walk. One had been terribly injured and was still in pain. All had almost fallen to oblivion. As for the little dog, she had been key to their survival, but now she was gone. Where, nobody knew. Hawk felt the weight of those losses, those sorrows; he carried them deep in his spirit. He waited for his companions to ask, *Is your quest truly worth this? Is the cost simply too high? What if it proves to be in vain?* But they did not speak.'

Nobody looked at her. Nobody moved. It was Karolis who broke the silence.

'You can't end it there.'

'It's not for me to answer those questions,' Stasya said. Aleks wasn't looking at her. His unease was written all over him. Perhaps he blamed her for what had just happened. Perhaps he thought she'd led them astray. But she had followed the signs, and the signs had been a clear invitation to take a certain path. Perhaps everything that had happened was part of a test. *Are you worthy?*

Aleksis spoke at last. 'I don't know what you want from me.'

A silence, in which the sound of Matiss's breathing, quieter now but still laboured, was a reminder of the horror they had escaped. Stasya stayed silent. Aleks was the leader. He must work this out for himself.

It was Lukas who eventually spoke. 'We have no choice but to go on. Turning back now would be foolish. And… what happened before… it feels as if the mountain is helping us to move on.'

'The mountain is listening to Stasya,' said Karolis.

'If you're worried… about… right path,' Matiss put in, 'Stasya might do what she does… with the fire…'

Aleks moved, sitting up straighter, turning to face his companions. 'Hawk was not prepared to accept defeat,' he said, and a nameless feeling rushed through Stasya, warming every part of her. 'Not even when he'd come close to losing all of his comrades. Not even when exhaustion had driven them to the brink of despair. The place they sought was in sight now, mist-shrouded and strange, but entirely real. He would not turn back. His companions were worn down, sad, hurt. But they were also a team. They had helped one another, they had shown courage, kindness, strength even in such adversity as this. What should he do? How should he speak to them?'

The silence that followed was one of sharp attention. Matiss sipped the draught Karolis had given him, his eyes fixed on Aleks. Stasya had no idea what was coming next. He had already astonished her.

'He wondered if now was the time for a rallying cry, a stirring call to duty. An invitation to the building of a better future. For although he would rejoice if his lost friend was found, he knew that would be the start of a far greater quest. But Hawk was no legendary hero. He was as flawed and broken and mixed-up as anyone else. It came to him that something different was needed now. So, he said to them, *I'm sorry. You are my friends. You've shown strength beyond what I could ever have expected. I'm sorry I have let you be hurt, scared, unsettled. I'm sorry I have led you close to death. From my heart, I'm sorry, and I thank you for your loyalty.*'

There were tears in Stasya's eyes now. She was not the only one. Matiss set down his cup to dab at his cheek, and both Karolis and Lukas gave nods of understanding.

'And now we move on,' Aleks said. 'We move on to the end together. I hope you can forgive me for my errors.'

'First, forgive yourself.' The words were out before Stasya could stop them. 'Then you can move on.' She felt her face flush. Aleks was the Ruler's senior adviser, and she was... whatever she was. A farm worker, a labourer, a woman who sometimes let her words come out when she should have held them back. She was about to mumble an apology when Aleks rose to his feet.

'Not easy,' he said, looking at the ground.

'Not easy for any of us,' said Karolis quietly. 'We all have regrets. We all have things we wish we'd done better. We've all made decisions that later proved to be less than perfect. Yes, it's hard to acknowledge your errors and set them behind you. But that's the only way forward. Lay aside the burdens of the past. Learn from your mistakes. Recognise your own strengths. And move on.'

There was something stirring in this speech, softly though it was delivered. And Aleks had listened; she saw that on his face. 'When you're ready, Matiss,' he said now, 'we'll set out and find that safe camping spot. I will take time to think on what you said, Stasya. And if you're willing, perhaps you will look in the flames for us tonight and ask for insights.' There was a brightness in his eyes now, the fledgling spark of something new and good. But there were long, weary miles ahead. 'We'll talk again later,' Aleks added. 'Thank you for your honesty. For saying what had to be said.'

She nodded, not daring to speak again lest the tears become unstoppable.

SCRYING WAS BEST done alone. An audience was a distraction, even when those watching stayed silent and kept their distance. But there was only one fire in this new camp, the fire that was keeping them all warm, the one on which they'd heated a makeshift soup made more palatable by the inclusion of small fish caught in a nearby pond. Lukas had strained this through a piece of cloth, so the meal provided flavour without tiny, sharp bones. The food did little to satisfy Stasya's hunger, and she imagined it was the same for all of them, but nobody complained. It was what it was. Perhaps the onward journey would provide better opportunities.

And now here she was, with the rest of them around her at a discreet distance, waiting. The fire had died down, but smoke still rose in lazy swirls, and the embers glowed in the half-dark of late evening.

'Stasya.' Lukas moved on soft feet, coming up beside her. 'You'll be needing this.' The amber owl dangled from its chain, catching the fire's light as he passed it to her. Stasya took it, smiling, and cupped it in her hand; its small presence was steadying. Lukas retreated to sit with the others, and she began the ritual.

She'd done this often enough. The steps came without conscious thought, despite the awkwardness of being watched. Because she had an audience, she made the ritual simpler. First, slow breathing. Then Grandmother's verse, spoken in a murmur. The mind clear; the body upright but relaxed. Eyes on the fire. And… between one breath and the next, the tiny owl came from nowhere to alight on her shoulder. Stasya heard the gasps of surprise, the soft sounds of recognition from the men as Flip settled in her rightful spot. She was back. She was safe. Now Stasya's tears fell, not in the outburst of emotion she had choked back after Aleks at last spoke from the heart, but in a steady, silent stream. She did not wipe them away. They were tears of relief, delight, joy; without a doubt, they were part of the ritual.

There were so many questions that could be asked. Too many. And sometimes it was safer, and better, not to know the answers. Stasya took her time, keeping her mind open, hearing only the whisper of leaves, the steady breathing of her companions, the distant calls of birds. What rose to the surface was this: *At the end of this journey, will we find answers?* She spoke the words in a murmur, then waited.

What came in the smoke was a familiar scene: the old woman smiling, beckoning, as if to say, *Come, daughter. Seek your answers here*. Another was there too, a tall figure in a hooded cloak, the same she had seen in a much earlier vision. This could be man or woman or something else entirely. Again, the two stood in front of a rock wall. This time shadows danced on the expanse of stone, forms moving with grace. Then, all too soon, the vision dissipated, leaving only trailing wisps of smoke. She sat utterly still, wanting more, needing more. But there was no more. Eventually she drew a deep breath, let it out slowly, and looked over toward the men.

'I didn't see much,' she said. 'Only what I'd seen before. An old woman, most likely at the Hermit. Someone else with her. A cloaked figure. And the sense that she would welcome me and perhaps share knowledge with me, if I went to her.'

A silence. Then Karolis asked the question Aleks would not. 'Anything about Markus?'

'Nothing. And I'm not sure asking that question would have helped. There's so much we don't know. What I saw did seem… hopeful. I'm sorry I can't tell you more. Visions don't show you exactly what will happen in the future. They can't. Our choices shape the way things turn out.'

'The cloaked figure… could that have been him?' Matiss asked. 'Markus?'

'It could have been him or anyone else the height of a grown man. I saw no clues. Except that it was someone who chose not to show me their face. Someone hidden. You could interpret that in different ways.'

'It does sound hopeful,' Karolis said. 'I would take it that this old woman exists, that she is well disposed toward you, and that she is not alone at the Hermit. That much is surely sufficient to keep us moving on, once we're all ready to do so. As for the hooded figure, it's not hard to guess why Markus might wish to keep his presence there secret, at least until the right time came to reveal himself. If others are living in those wild parts of the Northlands, perhaps they have their own reasons for secrecy.'

'The old woman has shown herself to me several times now. Every time, it's looked as if she wanted me to go forward.

Toward her.' It felt odd to be talking openly about this; Grandmother had taught her that the substance of visions was deeply secret, to be shared only by the seer and whoever sought answers. Though, in a sense, their team of five was made up of seer and truth-seekers. And if that was so, now was the time to tell all she had seen. Not to do so would feel like a betrayal. 'In earlier visions of that old woman, I've seen bad things from the past. From when the Commander came to Heartwood.' Gods, it was in front of her eyes now, in all its horror. But she must get the truth out now she'd started. All of it. 'In one of those I saw the ridgeway, the mist, the ghosts. Someone falling. But when it really happened, just now, I didn't recognise it until it was too late. And… in that earlier vision, there was a fight. A terrible, violent hand-to-hand fight. Maybe, because of some choice we've made along the way, that never happened.' She glanced around the circle: Karolis, calm and capable; Matiss, his arm in a sling, his shoulder bandaged, the look on his face showing the draught had not entirely eased the pain; Lukas sitting cross-legged by the fire, frowning as if his thoughts hurt him. And Aleks, watching her like the hawk he was. Waiting because he suspected she was holding something back. He would just have to wait. She was not going to say *You were there, with fury in your eyes.* 'Maybe I should have warned you when those images were first shown to me,' she said instead. 'I was still learning to trust, and I've been taught to keep what I see to myself. Visions are not easy to interpret. A warning might itself end up causing disaster.'

A silence. Then Matiss said, 'Nobody's judging you, Stasya. Your wisdom is essential to the team. I understand what a burden that must place on you, and I thank you for using your gift to help us.' He shifted awkwardly in place, trying to get comfortable. It seemed cruel to expect him to go on with the journey.

'You speak for all of us, Matiss,' said Karolis.

Stasya stared into the dying fire. She'd told them; that was good. But something felt wrong still. Aleks was too quiet. And the task of reaching the Hermit loomed larger than before, even though the place itself was now in sight. Matiss would be slow, and Lukas still wasn't his old strong self. Tonight there was a pinched look about his features. Perhaps, in helping haul Matiss back from near-death, he had done himself new damage. As a storyteller, it was part of her job to bring hope. But hope was hard to reach right now. She imagined her old life in Heartwood, wondering if she would go back to it if there were such a choice. A quiet, orderly life. In that life, she'd been looked on as odd. Strong and reliable, yes, but never part of the community. Now the future held danger, challenge, uncomfortable change. But she was among friends. Here, she was… equal.

Aleks spoke at last. 'What are you thinking, Stasya?'

'Asking myself if I would go back to my old life, if I still could.'

'And what was the answer?'

'I don't think I'd fit into that life anymore. None of us can go back to exactly what we were.' Into the silence that followed this, she said, 'I hope we'll be the better for the way this tests us. But there are times when that's hard to believe.'

A silence, broken eventually by Karolis. 'If we achieve our mission, the whole of the Northlands may change for the better. It's worth reminding ourselves of that when we feel low.'

'Well said, my friend.' Matiss added his voice.

'A change of Ruler can't undo the damage already done,' said Lukas. 'The folk who suffered, the folk who died in Heartwood.' He glanced at Stasya. 'The work of destruction.'

Stasya waited for Aleksis to respond to this, but he did not. Eventually she said, 'If the new Ruler was a peace-loving man, if he could be relied upon to make good choices, and if folk followed him because they believed in him, not because they were afraid of him, then such horrors would not happen under his rule. He couldn't undo the ills of the past; nobody can bring the dead back to life.' The Ancestor; Irina; poor Tomas. And so many others. 'Markus is the son of Lord Kasimir. And it sounds as if Lord Kasimir was that kind of leader.'

Aleks looked up; met her gaze. His smile was like the first cautious touch of sunshine on a frozen landscape. It warmed her heart. 'Thank you, Stasya. You did not know Markus or his father, but Lord Kasimir was indeed a wise and peaceable leader, and although Markus was only a boy when I knew him, he showed every sign of growing into the same kind of man.'

'Or would have done, if he'd grown up in his father's household.' That was Lukas.

Stasya held back words she knew she would regret. She reminded herself that Lukas was probably in pain; that he was missing his family desperately. 'True,' she said. 'And he may still have done, growing up elsewhere. Perhaps learning more than he ever could have learned if he had not set out on that adventure long ago. We're learning on our own journey, aren't we? Everything from how to make a great cup of tea to how a strangely assorted group of animals can end up helping one another, supporting one another, sharing understanding. They can become friends. And maybe achieve what none of them, alone, could ever have done.'

42

ALEKSIS

STASYA'S WORDS HAD given him new hope. Despite the injuries that slowed them they were making progress. The Hermit was not always in view, for they were working their way through dense tracts of forest now. But whenever they caught a glimpse of the towering rock formation in its cloak of mist, it seemed a little nearer. And Stasya was still finding signs. He'd started seeing them too: patterns on bark, almost like writing, but in a script indecipherable by humankind, its swirling shapes almost dance-like. Small stones in piles, sometimes balanced in ways that looked impossible. He noticed how Stasya picked up feathers, touching them almost as if they were sacred and whispering words he could not hear. She tucked them into her pack; they were some sort of gift, an understanding between her and the forest.

There was no pushing the pace. They were all worn out. Matiss could not carry a pack and needed help to climb. Lukas was clearly still in pain, though refusing to admit anything was wrong. They'd given up keeping watch at night. Rest was imperative and likely safe enough now. There'd been no more uncanny occurrences since they got across the ridgeway, and surely even the most dedicated of the Ruler's followers would not – could not – pursue them so far.

And then, as they prepared for sleep in fading light, they heard it. An outburst of shouting. A scream. Those sounds were not made by wolves or bears or night birds. They were the voices of men.

For a few moments, all of them froze, silent. Then Matiss cursed under his breath. Stasya and Karolis jumped to their feet and began to throw on various items of clothing. Flip started a high-pitched barking; Stasya quickly hushed her. Aleksis's heart was pounding like a war drum. He felt chill all through. After all this time. After everything.

'Pack up quietly,' he murmured, struggling to sound calm. *Keep the balance.* The shouting had ceased. The only sounds now were the sleepy calls of birds in the forest around them. But that cry had been unmistakable, and surely not so very far away. 'Stasya, what's your estimate of where they are?'

She was busy rolling up her bedding and did not look at him. 'Sounded close. But everything's tricky up here. They might be at the ridgeway, though they'd be crazy to try it at night. We need to move on right now. Find a hiding place and hope they pass us by.'

'Make sure you have a weapon at hand,' Karolis said, keeping to an undertone. 'And pack up everything. Leave no clues behind. Quick as you can.'

They doused the remnant of the fire and did their best to erase other evidence of the camp. The moon was waning; with luck, the pursuers would miss the signs. Why were they out there at night? Who were they?

'Stasya?' Aleksis asked.

'What?'

'Couldn't Flip fly back? To find out who it is?'

No reply.

'I know what you said. But…'

'She's scared, Aleks. It's getting dark. And we have to move on anyway. She might find us somewhere to hide. But I won't ask for more than that.' A silence, then she added, 'There are wolves nearby.'

Wolves. That was all they needed. 'Will you lead us?' he asked. He wished he could keep her safe instead. Karolis was giving her one of his big knives, helping her attach it to her belt. Aleksis did not want Stasya fighting; he did not want her under attack.

Without replying yes or no, she hitched up her pack and said, 'All set to go? Don't talk unless you must. If we can hear them, they can probably hear us.' Sounding unafraid. Sounding like a leader. She walked away down a near-invisible forest track, with Flip in dog form by her side, and the others followed without a word. But Aleksis saw the look Lukas gave him, even in the dim light of the waning moon. That look said: *If she is hurt, I will lay the blame on you. If she is killed, I will make you pay.* Aleksis understood all too well. In Lukas's place, he would have felt the same. But he knew, deep down, that Stasya was her own woman and would make her own decisions. Then there was the undeniable fact that of the five of them, Karolis and Stasya were currently the fittest and strongest. He felt deep gratitude for the covert tutoring in close combat that both Matiss and Karolis had given him in the months leading up to their departure from court. He was a scholar, a negotiator. His early training in the wielding of weapons had been limited, unlike that of Markus who, as a future Ruler, had been provided with a far broader education. *Oh, Markus. Please be there, and please remember me. We need you.* All very well, but first they had to get there. Scant hours ago, the remaining distance to the Hermit had looked achievable. Not so now.

Stasya stayed in the lead, with Flip pattering along at her heels. Matiss came behind her, then himself, with Lukas next and Karolis as rear guard. Not a whisper; the loudest sound he could hear was Matiss's breathing, which held a rasp of effort the big man could not suppress. Gods, what if this killed them all? His loyal friends who had set aside their own lives for the sake of his cause, and the two innocents from the Heartwood settlement, caught up in a disaster of his making? *Stop it, Aleks,* he ordered himself. *Be the leader you should be and bear the consequences.*

43

STASYA

If they kept on going, they'd soon be overtaken. Hiding somewhere and letting whoever it was pass seemed the best option. But what if they had a tracking dog, or more than one? How else could they possibly have worked out the way, when the paths she'd followed were unlikely to have been trodden by humankind before? But how would a dog have managed to get across the ridgeway? She sent Flip a mind-picture of a large hound stepping nimbly along the narrow path, and Flip responded with an image of the creature turning into an eagle and soaring up to fly to the nearest tall tree. *An ordinary dog, Flip. Not like you.* There was no reply. She tried a different picture: Flip as a bird, finding a hidden cavern shielded by thick undergrowth and leading them in. All of them crouched deep in shadow as pursuers headed on past, oblivious. The reply came swiftly: a pack of wolves, moving with purpose through a tract of forest that bore a close resemblance to the place they were in right now.

Stasya motioned to the others to halt. Cupped her ear to signal *Listen.* She did not expect to hear wolves, but if men were following their voices, their footfalls might betray them. All was quiet save for the hoot of an owl, a sorrowful echo through the trees. She took a moment to judge the position of the moon, which was shielded by the canopy. Losing the way would be disastrous.

A choice lay ahead, one she did not want to make. The sound of the Ruler's men killing those rats would be forever with her. Yes, wolves were dangerous; yes, they might launch an attack on an unwary party of travellers. She could, perhaps, ask the wolves to stay back, to let them pass. But there was always a risk in using her gift that way. And she would not say, *Let us pass, but do not let* them *pass.* That was to assume the role of a god. How could she order a fellow creature to kill? She did not yet know who was following them. It might be someone with no ill intent. She couldn't do it. Wouldn't do it.

Aleks came close. 'What is it?' he whispered.

'Wolves. We must get under cover somewhere, hide away. It's either that or stay alert until whoever it is catches up and…' And fight. She couldn't say it.

'Sounds travel oddly here.' Karolis had moved up to them, and whispered as the others did. 'If they were on the ridgeway when we heard them, that puts them a couple of days behind us – too far, you'd think, for us to catch the sound. But we know already that the usual rules of time and space may not apply here. Provided we're under good cover before first light, we could wait them out.'

'Stasya.' There was a note in Aleksis's voice that made her heart shrink. 'Could the wolves… help us? Would you use them in that way, if it were a life-or-death choice?'

The question hit her like a punch to the gut. How could he ask that? Didn't he realise what it meant? How much it would hurt? Couldn't he understand that it would lie like a shadow over her forever?

'It's all right.' His tone had changed. 'I shouldn't have asked.'

The words burst out, unstoppable. 'It's not all right, it's never all right, there's always hurt, there's always a price to pay—'

Karolis's arm went around her, holding her still; his other hand came over her mouth. Aleks hissed, 'Shh!' Oh gods, she'd been almost shouting, so loud, too loud…

Karolis released his hold. Stasya put her own hands up to cover her face. 'Sorry,' she whispered. 'I'm so sorry…'

'We move on.' Aleks spoke in a murmur. 'Stay alert, be ready for whatever comes.'

Stasya felt the small weight of a bird settle on her shoulder. Flip had changed again. Why now, there was no knowing, but it was a good thing. They'd be quicker this way. She drew a deep breath, scrubbed her cheeks with a hand, straightened her back. *I, too, will be strong. I, too, will hold the light*. The trees seemed to whisper a response; the moon looked down through a break in the canopy as if to remind her that the light still shone, even if she had made a foolish mistake. She nodded in Aleks's direction without really looking at him. What she saw was the face of Lukas, who stood behind him. For just a moment, a deep yearning to go back to old times flooded her heart. To have the old Lukas back, the one whose quiet company helped her cope with the confusion of dealing with the world; the one whose kindness was a gift beyond measure. The brave, true Lukas. She managed a smile, though no doubt it looked as wobbly as it felt, and Lukas smiled back at her. She gave him a nod: *We'll cope. We always do*. He returned it. Then she hitched up her pack and led the team onward.

THEY WALKED ON in the moonlight, pausing only when sheer exhaustion overtook one or other of them. They kept going until the sky lightened with the first hint of dawn and it was plain they could go no further without rest. They had heard no more shouting, no human voices save their own, but Stasya felt in her bones that the pursuit was drawing closer. There were signs. A flock of small birds, what kind she could not tell, rising from the forest lower down as if startled, then winging overhead in rapid flight toward the Hermit. A curious wind that shivered through the trees, stirring the leaves to a troubled whisper. And something more: the silent voices of small creatures, martens, mice, hedgehogs, animals she would not have expected to be here so high on the mountain. All of them were giving her one message: *Beware. Danger. Hide.* Or was that message only for their own kind? Perhaps *she* was the danger. Perhaps, now that she had come so far with Aleks's team, the forest no longer saw her as a friend.

The endless ranks of pine and larch gave way to more open ground again. For some miles ahead Stasya could see no caves or crannies, no thickets in which they might hide and rest. Matiss's breathing was painful to hear. Lukas was struggling despite his efforts to keep up. And her own head felt fuzzy. They had to stop.

'Aleks?'

'Mmm.' He halted; so did the others.

No need to say a thing. They made their way back under the pines, eventually finding a patch where they could set down their packs and stretch out on the needled ground. No undergrowth beyond a few scrubby bushes. No large stones to shield them. No rock faces with handy concealed caves. But it was clear they could not go on. Stasya's mind showed her the five of them lying down and falling immediately into exhausted sleep. Then pursuers moving in and slaughtering every one of them, with almost no resistance. A victory for the Ruler. A triumph for cruelty and injustice. That couldn't be allowed to happen. It was all wrong. The Hermit… Markus… the Ruler… Oh gods, she couldn't keep her eyes open…

A peck on the ear from Flip. *Wake up!* Then a sequence of images: the little bird flying away, swooping over another group of travellers – their number and character were not clear – then returning to this place, where Stasya and her companions were waiting, alert, with weapons in their hands.

'Yes,' Stasya said aloud. 'Go.' And did her best to send Flip a triumphant mind-picture in return – the bird in soaring flight, a rescuer, a champion. A moment later, Flip was gone. No explanations were necessary.

'We set a watch,' said Karolis. 'Short shifts. I'll go first. Keep your weapon to hand and be ready to act the moment you wake.'

'Drink before you rest.' Stasya lowered herself to the ground. Every bit of her was aching. How much worse must it be for Matiss? She watched as Aleks helped the big man find a comfortable position; as Karolis handed Lukas a water skin. If she let herself fall asleep, she might wake to find the others all dead. That terrible moment on the ridgeway would be with her forever. 'Flip will bring back information if she can.' As for why Flip had done this now when she been so unwilling earlier, Stasya was too tired to think about it.

'Wake me as soon as you need to, Karolis.' Aleks looked grim. 'No longer than an hour.'

'I'll take third watch,' Stasya said, wondering if there was any possibility they would have that long. As she lay down, her bones heavy with weariness, she sensed the wolves again. Not as close as the last time, but close enough. Moving cautiously. Alert to trouble. One among them was a leader; he was watchful, as Karolis would be. Should she reach out to him now? At least let him know she was a friend and meant them no harm? That much was true; but she could not promise harm would not befall them at the hand of humankind. Not with two parties on the mountain, one hunting the other. She would wait until Flip came back and she knew more. As for sleep, it was doing its best to blot out her troubles, to steal away her ability to think. But sleep felt perilous.

'Stasya?'

Aleks's voice, a murmur. He must be closer than she'd thought.

'Mmm?'

'Try to sleep. And… thank you.'

'For what?'

'For all you've done. For being brave. For… for holding the light.'

Oh gods, now the tears were coming again. What was that but a final farewell? *Pull yourself together, Stasya*. 'We'll win through, Aleks,' she whispered. 'We'll find him. We'll give the story the best ending we can.'

FLIP WAS BACK before the first watch ended, waking Stasya from deep sleep with an urgent peck. Stasya sat up, rubbing her eyes. Around her the others, too, were waking. Stasya struggled to open her mind to Flip's; her thoughts were still half-caught in sleep. But the gnawing fear in her belly overcame the weariness, and she managed to focus. *Show me, Flip.*

Only one image, and she knew the place. Gods help them, it was not long since they had walked through it. The men were clustered around her now, holding back their own words, waiting for the news. She made herself speak. 'They're almost here. At least six men, armed. And there's a dog.' She swallowed, wondering if she might be sick. *Tell them*. 'I think one of them is the Commander. And… one of them looked like Pavel.'

Shocking as that glimpse had been, she could imagine how it might have happened. An unspeakable threat to his wife and baby son if he did not cooperate. An impossible choice. But when? Had his solitary expedition to the settlement seen him apprehended and hauled before the Commander? That could hardly be right; pursuit would have been almost immediate if he'd told the authorities the truth then. Perhaps the person Flip saw wasn't him. Perhaps it was some other young man with hair that shone golden in the dawn light, some other poor soul forced to act out the Commander's will.

'We can't stay ahead of them,' Aleks said. 'We'll have to stand and fight.'

'No choice,' said Karolis, nodding. 'We have a little warning, at least. Matiss, what can you manage one-handed?'

'Throwing knives. Once they're gone, I'll need to resort to kicking.'

'Keep the sling on, don't even think of trying to use that arm. How about an axe?'

'One-handed? No. Best give that to someone else.'

'Maybe this.' Lukas had found a sturdy fallen branch and was using his knife to strip it into a makeshift staff. 'Keep it close by, grab it when you need it.'

'Good,' said Karolis. 'Stasya, you're the one they'll be after. Not to kill; to take back to Dragon's Keep. Be ready to fight. But let us protect you if we can.' As the sky brightened above the high limbs of pine and larch, he gestured, guiding the team into position. Lukas to one side; Matiss to the other. Himself in the centre with Aleksis and Stasya just behind him. All too soon came the sound of stealthy footsteps.

Stasya stood with feet planted firm and knife in hand, wondering if she could bring herself to use it against a man, even one so vile as the Commander. Her heart was hammering, but she held her body strong. Flip had flown up into a tree and could no longer be seen. That was one blessing, at least. For now, padding with steady purpose and nose to the ground, came a large dog.

'Don't—' she began, knowing the creature was only doing the work it had been trained to do.

There was a sharp whistle, and the dog dropped immediately to its belly, while out from the tree cover came the pursuers, their own weapons at the ready. Not charging in to kill; they, too, were waiting for an order.

'*Master* Aleksis!' The Commander came to a halt, standing with legs apart. His voice dripped with disdain. 'And you, Witch! Why is that no surprise?'

The look in his eyes made Stasya's gorge rise. His belt was hung about with knives, and in his right hand he gripped a wooden bar from which hung a chain with a studded metal ball at the end. That thing would crush a man's skull like an eggshell. And… that fair-haired man behind him *was* Pavel. He looked as sick as she felt. The whole band of them – seven? eight? – was armed to the teeth. How could they possibly… unless… Oh gods, she didn't want to do it. She might have to do it…

'Well met, Rihard.' Aleksis spoke like the seasoned negotiator he was, with perfect confidence and calm. As if he were not looking death in the face. 'Perhaps you were not aware that we came here on the Ruler's orders. A mission to unlock the secrets of the mountain without destroying half of the place in the process. What exactly is *your* purpose in this out-of-the-way spot?'

'You're lying,' the Commander said. 'Ruler's orders? Bollocks! She's got folk out hunting for you all over the Northlands. Abandoned your post, took your unsavoury friends with you, not to speak of the girl there, and left court in the middle of the night without telling a soul. Fortunately, this young fellow'—he gestured toward Pavel—'saw the utter idiocy of your venture. Told us the whole story after a bit of persuasion. Could have done with that information earlier, but he's making up for it now, aren't you, lad? Now what's it to be, Master Aleksis? Do you admit your folly and hand over the girl, or does this end in blood? Give her to me, take yourself and your cronies quietly off across the border, and you may yet avoid the penalty for treason.'

Aleksis didn't say a word, but his rage was in every inch of his body. It was Lukas who responded, his voice harsh with fury. 'Lay so much as a finger on her and you're dead!'

Rihard threw back his head and laughed. 'Oh, dear. The goat boy. The village troublemaker. Got a fondness for the witch, have we? But then, the girl's been travelling with you men, sleeping rough, living wild… How did that work? Did you share her among you? A different one each night? She must have learned a thing or two by now. And on the way home my team will indulge in the same pleasure, if you could call it that.' He glanced Stasya's way, an expression of disgust on his face. 'On second thoughts, maybe not. A fellow might find himself turned into a toad or a weevil.'

'You always did talk too much, Rihard.' Somehow, Aleks was still managing to sound calm. A glance passed between him and Karolis, who gave the smallest of nods. The quiet woodland was suddenly filled with shouts of challenge and clashing weapons and bodies hurling themselves one way or another. No shield; no protective clothing. Rihard was coming Stasya's way, whirling his hideous weapon, but suddenly Matiss was there, reaching out left-handed with his makeshift staff, catching the chain with its spiked ball and hauling the whole thing bodily away from its wielder. Rihard roared with fury. One of his men crashed into Matiss's right side and sent the big man sprawling. The only thing in Stasya's mind was, *Save him.* She leaped forward, sliced upward – her knife met resistance – then pulled the weapon out. The man clapped two hands to his belly. Blood welled between his fingers. Oh gods, the sound he made... *Stasya, focus.* Another man was close, fighting Aleks, their arms locked, both knives within inches of their marks... She kicked out, her boot striking the man's shin, making him stagger, and Aleks's weapon delivered the death cut. Her head was whirling, her heart was pounding, she could hardly breathe. Matiss. Still on the ground. Struggling to rise. And there was... there was Pavel, reaching out a hand to help him up. Or was he about to strike? In the chaos, it was hard to see clearly. The thud of blows, the cries of agony, the curses and gasps for breath... Karolis was fighting like a legendary warrior, all speed and skill, and Aleks was beside him now. She couldn't spot Lukas. Three of the enemy were on the ground, dead, dying, there was no knowing. But they kept on coming; there were surely more than seven.

'Aleks!' she shouted. 'Get down!'

He ducked as a sword slashed through the air at neck height, then threw himself at his attacker, knocking the weapon from his hand. Stasya saw the look on his face, the same she had glimpsed in the flames: pure fury, sheer intent. He would die rather than surrender. They might all die. Matiss was struggling, limping as he wielded the staff. There was Lukas, backed up against a tree, fending off two attackers. New men. Men who'd been waiting at a distance until they were needed. And Rihard, now, was simply watching the whole thing unfold with a smug smile of satisfaction on his face. He turned to look at her, and the smile turned to an expression that froze her heart. He pointed toward Aleks, whose tunic wore splashes of blood, and addressed his men. 'Take him! The royal adviser! Eliminate him and they'll all give up. I'll deal with the witch!' He strode toward her.

Now. It was time. *Quick, Stasya.* She backed up, ducked into the shadows under the pines, and sent an urgent message to Flip, a mind-picture of her comrades falling, and then of wolves. As the Commander came closer, cursing as he tripped on a tree root, she opened her mind to the wolf leader. He and his pack were not far off; she had sensed them circling, disturbed by the noise, the smell of blood, the possible threat to their safety. She made herself breathe; getting this wrong would be disastrous. *We need your help, right now! This man is a danger to the forest and all its creatures. My comrades and I seek only to reach a wise friend*. Her image was of the old woman from the vision, beckoning, smiling. *But these men would kill us all. Please help! I am a friend of the forest.* Rihard was right on the other side of this tree. She could hear his breathing. And now, from out there, came a cry of pain in a voice she would know anywhere. Lukas. She couldn't wait. She couldn't let him die. *Come now! Please!*

One deep breath. Knife at the ready. The blade was stained red. There was blood on her hands; blood spattered on her clothing. Wrong. So wrong it made her want to scream. But Rihard was there, just waiting for her to move so he could grab her. *The oak's deep roots hold fast to the earth. I, too, will be strong.* She stepped out from cover and moved swift as a deer, darting past the Commander and forward. One of the enemy had Lukas pinned against a tree trunk; the man had his forearm across Lukas's neck and was pressing hard. No time to think, except that she risked hurting both of them if she aimed wrong. She dived forward and slashed low with her knife, cutting into the assailant's inner thigh. He gasped, staggered, fell. Blood spurted. She had known where to strike.

Lukas put his hand on her shoulder. Not to comfort, but to keep himself upright. He was saying something, but it made little sense. 'Back… can't… Stasya, run…'

The gurgling, dying man at her feet had lost control of his bowels. She had done that. She had killed, once, twice, maybe more. Lukas was wobbling, close to collapse. 'Just go,' he croaked. 'Save yourself.'

The numbers were thinning. Karolis accounted for another man, apparently with his bare hands; Aleks was under attack again, two against one, and Karolis moved in to support him. She caught a glimpse of Pavel. He and Matiss were fending off attackers together. And Rihard… Rihard was coming toward her again. He had taken his time. Changed his mind, perhaps, about what he wanted. Stasya stepped in front of Lukas, shielding him with her knife at the ready and the body of his attacker at her feet. *Now! Please!*

The forest came alive with wolves. They streamed across the scene of battle, and with them flew a bird. It was a plain little thing, brown in colour, easy to overlook. But this bird darted about, always clear of the thrust of knives or the blow of staves, working with the creatures, showing them where to attack and where to hold back, guiding them between friend and enemy even in the confusion and carnage. The Commander's surviving men fell, screaming as sharp teeth bit into arm or leg or neck, writhing and bleeding on the carpet of pine needles, crying for their mothers. Stasya watched in horror. She had called the wolves in; she had known how it might be. And how it might have been, had Flip not thought to direct the attack. The wolves had spared her friends. Still, it was hell. It was horror. It was unthinkable. But here it was before her eyes, and she should never use her gift this way again, because nobody should have so much power, nobody… She dropped her knife and squeezed her eyes shut. *I can't look, I can't see this…*

A howl of pain. A blow to her heart, hard and final as death… Her eyes sprang open. The wolf leader was on the ground, writhing, screaming. A great cut had sliced open his belly. Over him stood the Commander, long knife bloodied, grin triumphant, even as his men lay dead or dying all around him. The hurt was in every part of her body, her heart, her gut, her limbs, her head… She had never felt such agony. It froze her where she stood. In that moment Rihard moved, and she found herself pinned back against him with a knife at her throat.

'Drop your weapons or she dies right now!'

One by one they obeyed. Even Aleks. Lukas's face was a mask of horror. Were none of the Commander's men left alive? Not one? Oh gods, the wolf… The wolf still lived, but its life was draining away with each moment that passed. And somewhere in the clearing a man was dying. She dared not move her head to see who it was, lest the Commander make good his threat. She dared not make so much as a gasp. But she felt that man's anguish, his regret, his confusion…

'Let her go, Rihard.' Aleks had found his senior adviser voice, though it was not quite steady. 'What's your plan, to walk all the way home on your own?'

'Shut your mouth, *Master* Aleksis! She'll do what I want, or she'll die. And you'll go along with it if you put any value on your own future. Look what you've done. See the carnage your ridiculous plan has caused. I lost five good men on that wretched ridgeway, and I've lost more here, thanks to you and your foolish quest. What in the name of the gods did you imagine you were doing?' His grip tightened; Stasya felt the cold bite of the knife against her skin. Through tears, she saw a subtle glance between Aleks and Karolis, and knew what it meant. '*Don't—*' she breathed.

Something flew across the open area with a wild screech. It came within inches of Stasya's face, making her blink. The Commander started in shock. His fingers lost their hold on the knife and his grip on Stasya slackened. She twisted, freeing herself, and delivered a swift kick to his groin. He grunted in pain, cursed, bent to retrieve the weapon. As he rose to stand, something whirred across the clearing and struck him on the temple, felling him.

'Do with him what you will. Do what justice demands.'

A figure had appeared from under the trees, holding what appeared to be a slingshot. A warrior. A woman. But not a human woman, for there was a subtle difference about her features. She was tall, fair, clad all in green, and she wore vine leaves in her hair. Stasya and her companions stood mute as others came out to join her, both men and women, encircling them. Their beauty and composure suggested ancient times, ancient tales. Some were fair, some dark. Some carried bows and quivers; some had shining knives at their belts. Some carried woven baskets. The Forest Folk. Or if not the folk of the tales, exactly, then something very like them.

For a few shocked moments everyone stood still and silent. It was Lukas who moved first, stepping forward and bending to retrieve the knife the Commander had dropped. He knelt by Rihard. The man's chest was moving; he still lived. And now, his lids fluttered and he opened his eyes to stare up at Lukas. Stasya's teeth were clenched. Her face was wet with tears. The pain still throbbed in her chest.

'May you find forgiveness in the Afterlife,' Lukas said quietly, and with one steady stroke he drew the blade across the Commander's throat. He'd always been good with knives.

Oh, gods. The pain was unbearable. It was calling her to action, for she too had a farewell to make. She would not beg for forgiveness. Too late, with that handsome creature lying on the forest floor with his belly cut open and the last light fading from his eyes. None of the other wolves was in sight, but she could feel their presence, feel their anguish. And… closer at hand, there was a dog. A good dog who had just witnessed hell. A dog who had crept in now that things were quiet; a dog whose master was probably lying here among the dead. Perhaps she had killed that man.

Aleks had moved under the trees. He was crouched down beside a figure whose clothing was soaked in blood, whose struggle for breath could be heard even from here. A man with hair the colour of sunshine on ripe barley. Pavel. He was saying something to Aleks, even as he gasped for air. Aleks was supporting him, helping him into a half-sitting position; she knew he was speaking words of comfort and forgiveness. Stasya had her own work to do, and it must be now.

She knelt by the fallen wolf, laid a gentle hand on his side, struggled to make herself calm through the pain. If she felt like this, how much worse must it be for this beautiful creature who had sacrificed himself today? She opened her mind fully to his; knew his regret, his sorrow to leave his mate, his pack, his life in the great forest. There was only one way to farewell him, only one thing to do. She sang a song she remembered from long ago, a lullaby Grandmother had sung to her at bedtime, much of which was wordless. It was a song of the forest: the wind in the trees, the splashing of frogs in the pond, the footfalls of deer, the many calls of birds. The voices of wolves and of owls. The sun, the moon, the starry night. She sang, and under her hand the wolf calmed, and his heartbeat slowed, and in her own heart the pain began to ease. She sang until he released his last breath. Around her the clearing was silent as the men sat watching, and the tall folk stood under the trees listening. 'Sleep, my dear one,' Stasya whispered. 'Sleep, my brave one. Fly high; dive deep; dance with the wind; run fleet in the forest. You will never be forgotten. Sleep, sweet soul.'

She sat there a while after the wolf was gone. When she opened her eyes, it was to see Aleks closing the eyes of Pavel, who lay limp in his arms. Karolis bowed his head; Matiss did the same. Lukas was standing beside the fallen Commander, the knife in his hand. He dropped the weapon now and dashed away tears, leaving a bloody mark on his cheek.

'Come!' he said, clicking his fingers, and the tracking dog padded over to him and sat obediently at his feet, though it was shivering hard. 'Good boy.' Lukas crouched to stroke the dog's head, and when he got up to walk away, the dog walked by his side.

44

ALEKSIS

UNDER THE TREES all was still. A strange kind of peace had fallen over the place. The Forest Folk waited, not advancing, simply holding respectful silence and biding their time. Karolis eased the limp form of Pavel from Aleks's arms to lay him on the ground, and Aleks rose to his feet, facing the woman who had used the slingshot to such precise purpose. Never mind that his heart was breaking. It was time to be a leader.

'Greetings to you. My name is Aleksis, son of Feliks. My father was senior adviser to the late Lord Kasimir, Ruler of the Northlands. I have held that position since my father's death, first with Lord Kasimir and then with the current Ruler. Events have caused me to take a different path; I am not here as a representative of Lady Elisabeta. With me are my friends and comrades on this journey.' Why was it so hard to hold onto his composure? He would not look at Stasya, whose song had made him weep. He would not look down at the young father who had lost his life because of others' evil scheming. He cleared his throat. 'I had hoped to find your people under less desperate circumstances, but I thank you for turning the tide of this… this confrontation. I offer my deep regret for the blood shed on your land. And… I hope you may be willing to assist us further.'

'We know who you are.' The tall woman's voice was both soft and authoritative. 'One among us has followed your journey. Your loss saddens us.' She glanced at Pavel; at the fallen wolf; at the bodies strewn around the clearing. 'We will assist you to reach our home, the place you call the Hermit. Practical matters first. You are hungry, thirsty, weary, sad. And…'

'With your permission,' Aleks said, 'we should lay the dead to rest. Our own, and those who have been drawn into this because their orders demanded it. And one other.' Rihard was gone. He should have lived long enough to answer for his crimes. He should have suffered more… No, it was wrong to think that way. Lukas had spoken with wisdom and balance. He had astonished Aleks with the precision of his act and the power of his quiet words. The goat boy was far more of a man than he had ever realised. *Worthy of Stasya*, his treacherous thoughts whispered.

The Forest Folk moved then, to walk among the still forms of the dead and to murmur soft words over each. They did not gather them up. The woman spoke again. 'This must be done, yes, or the place will forever bear the shadow of what happened here. But not yet. There are wounded among you; you are exhausted and full of sorrow. Come a little way with us. We will provide refreshment and attend to your hurts.' And when Aleks glanced around him, troubled at the thought of leaving the scene of death unguarded, one of the forest men said, 'We will set a watch on the place. Nothing will be touched until you are ready.'

HE COULD NOT bring himself to ask the question, not even when they had been escorted to a grassy bank beside a stream, assisted to settle themselves, and offered food and drink from baskets carried by the uncanny folk. He remembered old stories about the dangers of accepting such food, such as the possibility of being trapped in another realm forever or somehow irrevocably changed. But if they were now to walk on to the Hermit, he and his comrades must be prepared to trust.

He wanted to ask, *Is there a human man among your number? A man who was lost in these parts as a child years ago? Is the true heir to the Rulership with you at the Hermit?* But it was not yet time for that. Pavel had died because of him. Matiss was hurt, Lukas was hurt, Stasya looked utterly drained. He wanted to sit down with her, just the two of them, and try to offer some comfort. To let her talk, to be a listening ear. But not here, with all these folk around, quiet as they were. Besides, Flip had reappeared and was now in dog form again, sitting beside Stasya, apparently quite calm. He guessed she'd been the one who'd startled Rihard and allowed Stasya to escape. As for this peaceful spot, so unlike the terrain they had passed through, he wondered if it had been conjured from nowhere for the purpose of giving weary travellers respite.

The tall woman came to seat herself by him on the grass, while others of her folk tended quietly to his comrades' injuries, both old and new. He realised there were questions he could ask, safer ones. Best start with the formalities. 'Might I know your name?'

'I am known as Kadri. I am a leader among my people.'

'Mistress Kadri, you mentioned that one among you had followed our journey,' he said. In his mind was the crone of Stasya's visions, a person she believed to be at the Hermit. Could visions go both ways? 'You knew we were coming here, and who we were? You rescued us just in time, and I will be forever grateful for that.' He would not ask why, if they had been somehow watching his team's progress, these folk had not intervened earlier, when some lives might still have been saved. 'Did you know the purpose of our venture?'

The woman smiled. Her eyes were most certainly not human, for they seemed full of light. 'Do not the tales tell of a quest for treasure?'

'Treasure can mean many different things,' Aleksis said carefully. 'To some, gold and jewels. To others, the ancient trees of the forest. It might be amber. And amber may be valued for different reasons. Or… the treasure might be a man or woman.'

The woman nodded. 'Indeed, Master Aleksis. I see you have learned much on this journey. More, perhaps, than you would have learned had you stayed at court.'

Karolis was coaxing Stasya to eat some of the fruit the folk had provided; to drink from a cup carved of wood. Her hair was damp and flowed loose across her shoulders, for one of the women had taken her to the stream to wash away the blood and grime, and the thick braid of the journey had been unfastened. Now she wore borrowed clothing of the same green as the garments of the Forest Folk. She managed a smile; it was a wan memory of the way she had looked when she told a story by the fire.

'We still have quite a way to walk, I think. Two of my companions carry serious injuries,' Aleksis said. 'All of us sustained hurts when we were attacked. And… Stasya is distressed. It is not her way to wield a weapon in combat. And the wolf…'

'You may find the long way shorter under our guidance, Master Aleksis. As for your companions, they all need time to heal. Time to recover. You also. When we reach the Hermit, we can provide that. And learning.'

She left him then, going off to join a group of her own people. And Matiss came over, his old sling replaced by a neat new one. He lowered himself awkwardly to sit beside Aleksis. 'Poor Pavel,' he said. 'I saw him talking to you, at the end. Did he tell you how he came to be there?'

'Mmm.' He'd remember those faltering words forever. 'The

Ruler had come to doubt my loyalty. She ordered Pavel to watch my movements closely and report back. The night when we left Dragon's Keep he could have alerted her, but he came with us instead, intending to tell me everything. He meant to come all the way with us. But when we sent him to Heartwood on his own, he met two men he knew among Rihard's guards, not far from the settlement. He had a cover story, and it seemed they believed it. But they also shared some terrible accounts of what Rihard had been doing to men who disobeyed his orders. Acts of cruelty toward their loved ones in particular. Pavel came on with us. But fear for his wife and son eventually overwhelmed him, and he headed back on his own, hoping to get them out of Dragon's Keep and disappear somewhere. He was apprehended by Rihard's men near Clearwater and taken to the settlement to explain himself. Again, his family was threatened if he refused to lead the Commander up the mountain. Perhaps they were luckier with the weather than we were. They must have made remarkably good time.'

'The mountain may have played a part in that. Maybe these folk will have some answers.'

They sat in silence a while, then Aleks said, 'Pavel asked me to get his wife and son to safety. But…'

'Elisabeta has no cause to harm them while we're still away from court. She knows nothing of what has happened here. Rihard wouldn't have advised her of what he was intending. He always did like to go his own way. He'd have wanted to find the treasure first, then report triumphantly back to her.'

'Mmm.' A request from a dying comrade could not be ignored. But so much was unknown. Solutions suggested themselves, but all seemed fraught with peril.

'Leja might be able to do something about Pavel's family,' Matiss said. 'That's if I can get a message to her.'

Matiss seldom spoke his wife's name in company, and only ever in a secure place, among trusted friends. 'We must wait and see what unfolds here first,' Aleks said. 'Leja shouldn't visit Dragon's Keep in person. But she might be able to send someone unobtrusive. Someone who can get Pavel's wife and child out on a pretext.' He did not add, *If they are still alive.*

'Master Aleksis?' A man of the Forest Folk, clad in a nut-brown robe and wearing a friendly smile, had come over to address them. 'My name is Juho. We have clean garments to offer you.'

Aleks glanced over at Stasya. Her shoulders were tense; her arms were tight around her drawn-up knees. He could imagine what havoc the fight must have created in her mind. He wanted to keep her in sight; to watch over her. But the next task would be laying the dead to rest, and to do so while filthy, bloodstained and unkempt would be deeply disrespectful. 'Thank you, I will.'

The cold embrace of the stream was welcome. With Juho's assistance he scrubbed away the worst of the dirt, shaved off his unruly beard, and accepted the garments offered him – plain, comfortable items in the green and brown of the Forest Folk. He kept his belt but surrendered his weapons, which he was assured would be cleaned and returned to him, as would his travel-worn clothing. The Forest Folk had made no attempt to inspect the contents of the travellers' packs. Whatever it was they had known of this expedition, it had apparently resulted in a significant degree of trust. Or had their ability to fight won them that? He made sure to thank Juho for his assistance, and the man acknowledged this with a grave smile.

'You'll want time to talk with your companions,' Juho said. 'Then we will do what must be done, with due respect. We are hoping to reach the Hermit before nightfall.'

'Surely it's too far away to be reached so quickly.'

'Perhaps. Let us see how things unfold, Master Aleksis. In this realm, distances can be deceptive. We will not push you too hard; you have already endured much.'

'Juho… the wolf, too, should be laid to rest. I am not sure how that should best be done.'

Juho nodded understanding. 'She who called the wolves will have the answer.'

'Give her a little longer. Then ask her.'

By the time he got back to Stasya, Lukas was sitting beside her. He had a hand on her shoulder, as if for comfort. Stasya was talking and gesturing while he listened with grave attention. Aleks could see she had been crying. It was clear his own presence was not required. He walked past them, dipping his head in acknowledgement but saying nothing. He squashed down the feelings that rose in him; they were inappropriate, unworthy of someone who was supposed to be a leader. What mattered was the Hermit and the story of Markus, whatever it was. If Juho was right about how soon they could reach the place, he might have his answer this very day.

45

STASYA

AT THE TIME it seemed fragmented, dreamlike, though the feelings that coursed through her were entirely real and painful. The Forest Folk moved with the quiet of wild creatures and the grace of dancers, even when digging graves and carrying the bloodstained corpses of the fallen to their resting places. For Rihard's guards, the words to be spoken were simple enough. All were known by name to one or other of the team, and the men took turns to speak, each offering a brief but compassionate statement about the one being laid in the earth. These had not been evil men, simply folk doing the job they were required to do. It was their misfortune to find themselves under the Commander's leadership. She found herself shedding tears for each and sending a silent message to the wives and sweethearts, the children, the bereaved parents, the brothers and sisters who might never know what had befallen their loved one. And she asked the forest to receive them kindly; to let their bodies become part of the rich soil that sustained life here. Through that magic, these men would live on in a place of peace and beauty. Their stories would be woven into the long tale of Heartwood; they would witness the passing years as the ancient trees did.

They laid Pavel to rest with prayer and song. Matiss spoke. 'He was a friend; a brother; a comrade in arms. He was a husband and father. His little son is named Tarvo, and his wife is Hanna. As he took his last breath, he thought of them. May he walk in the light now; may he find peace.'

It was Aleksis who stood by the Commander's grave. There was a look on his face that Stasya had never seen before; whether it was fury or grief or sheer exhaustion, she could not tell. He stood there in silence for a while, as if lost for words. But this was the Ruler's senior adviser, someone whose duties included finding the right words for any occasion. She wanted to go and stand beside him; to take his hand as one might to reassure a frightened child. But she held back, and eventually he spoke.

'This was a man whose past errors haunted him; whose failures governed his decisions. I will not dwell on his faults. He is gone now. The words Lukas spoke at this man's death were wise and compassionate. *May you find forgiveness in the Afterlife*. And I will add, May the embrace of the forest, the songs of birds, the sound of rippling water, the passage of sun and moon across the sky grant you peace.'

Stasya had not believed him capable of such a speech. This was a man of power games and intrigues, of planning and calculation. And yet… and yet… She would be a fool to think the journey had not changed him profoundly. Just how much, she had not realised until now.

ALEKS HAD ASKED her about burying the wolf – how should it be done, and where. She had spoken to Mistress Kadri again, wanting her agreement. And she had asked Flip, showing her different pictures of how it might be. In the end, they carried the corpse some distance from the spot where the creature had fallen, and only a few of them came to bear witness: Stasya and Lukas, Aleksis and representatives of the Forest Folk: Kadri, the man named Juho and two others. And Flip, who had become an unusually small raven.

They laid out the body beside the grave, with a green cloth covering the wound that had killed him.

'Ready?' Stasya asked, and the others nodded or murmured *yes*.

The wolves were not far away. She could feel their presence. A risk, certainly. She opened her mind to them; tried to convey that this was a ritual of farewell, of gratitude, of sorrow and recognition. And after a long time, or so it felt, there came a mind-picture in return: the pack moving close under the trees, but not too close. Waiting in the shadows. Watching. Her eyes were shut, but she knew from the small sounds made by her companions that the wolves were present, not only in her mind, but also in physical form. She opened her eyes, looked down at their fallen leader and began her story.

'Once upon a time, a tribe of wolves lived in Heartwood Forest, up in the higher reaches where few human folk walked. It was the realm of the Forest Folk and of many kinds of creatures. On a spring night when the woods were alive with the calls of owls, a wolf cub awoke in the den and sent his tiny howl up toward the moon, feeling deep in his bones that his life would be one of courage and service. His mother woke and licked his fur, settling him back to sleep before he could disturb his littermates. He dreamed of being big and bold. He dreamed of leading the pack, one day when he was grown.'

As she told of the young wolf growing up and watching his father and learning about keeping the balance for the pack, Aleks and Lukas lifted the body of the slain wolf into the grave. The Forest Folk sang a soft wordless melody, their music reflecting the course of the tale as the little wolf experienced fear and loss, love and opportunity. In time he found his mate; he became leader; he fathered his own small ones. He was a protector, a wise elder. His wisdom and that of his beloved mate helped the pack through bitter winters; through times of storm; through the loss of a cub taken by a great eagle. She spoke, in the end, of his untimely passing.

'I am sorry,' she said, fighting back tears. 'So deeply sorry. And I will be forever grateful to your kind. You saved our lives today. And more. From this act of courage may rise new hope. Your leader's sacrifice may help us to save the forest and all who dwell in it.'

The music came to an end. Kadri and Juho moved forward to fill in the grave. He had a wooden spade; she knelt and used her hands.

'Rest well, brave spirit,' Stasya said. 'And to your pack, deepest respect. May you raise strong young; may you live your lives as he did, with courage and honour.'

The job was almost done. Kadri and Juho stepped back from the grave and Flip, once more a dog, crept forward to hunker down at the edge of the disturbed soil and lay her muzzle on the ground, as if in mourning. The wolves howled their lament, their voices ringing out through the forest. Their song was of both sadness and celebration, for this was not only a ritual of loss, but the recognition of a life lived well and to the full. Flip added a howl of her own; perhaps only Stasya heard it.

They retreated, then, human and Forest Folk together. Perhaps the wolves moved in once they were gone, to keep their own vigil at the grave site. Perhaps they slipped away into the depths of the forest. Stasya never knew.

IT WAS CURIOUS indeed how short the path to the Hermit seemed that day, proving again that the rules of the outer world did not apply in this realm of the Forest Folk. Nobody talked much along the way, and Stasya guessed that Aleks had not yet told these people about the boy who had gone missing all those years ago or asked whether a man of human lineage lived among them still.

Those who had come to the rescue along with Kadri and Juho seemed to Stasya varied in appearance. Some, like Kadri, had features that marked them out clearly as something other than human: those unusual eyes, or the strong bones of the face, or an indefinable difference in bearing. But some so closely resembled human men or women that it was only the green and brown of their loose tunics and trousers, and the use of leaves, vines or flowers to hold back their flowing hair or to wear as decoration, that indicated a difference. Now that her companions were clad in their borrowed clothes, she thought Karolis might easily pass for one of the Forest Folk. Perhaps she, too, could have passed for one of them. Matiss was bigger than any of their men. Lukas, with the tracking dog by his side, still seemed to her entirely of the human world, a man who belonged there with his own tribe. As for Aleks, she could not imagine him as anyone but himself. A man with a purpose. A driven man yet plagued by self-doubt. Why had he not yet asked that question? As they passed along forest tracks and walked by lonely lakes and climbed a precipitous, winding path up a rocky escarpment, she thought about the old tales in which so many travellers went missing in these parts, never to be seen again. Might not some of those missing folk have encountered these apparently peaceable people or their antecedents, and chosen to live with them rather than return to the human world?

Among the Forest Folk, might there not be some whose blood blended the human with the uncanny? That would be a tale full of possibilities.

THEY REACHED THE Hermit before nightfall. Nobody commented on the oddities of distance. Wounded and exhausted as they were, relief outweighed all else. Matiss badly needed rest, proper rest in a comfortable bed. Lukas was in pain again. Stasya saw through his efforts to hide it. The tracking dog had walked by his side all the way. Lukas had given him a new name: Shadow. Flip had spent most of the journey on Stasya's shoulder in the form of a wren.

'Nearly there,' Juho said as they hauled themselves up the last stretch. The stark rocky heights of the Hermit towered above them, but the place was softened by the trees that grew around its base, not pine and larch here but gentler birch and willow, in which birds exchanged quiet observations. The path ended in a broad open area, clearly a gathering place. Under the trees that bordered it Stasya glimpsed signs of a settlement: dwellings made from branches and woven foliage; a spot where there must be a freshwater spring, for there was a pool, and stones placed for seating, and various scoops and jugs standing nearby.

For a while she was too breathless to speak. Aleksis touched her gently on the shoulder. 'Look!' he murmured, pointing. His voice was full of wonder.

There it was: the cave mouth of her visions, just as she had described it to her companions. And there was the old woman, clad in a robe the hue of birch leaves in springtime. Her white hair was in long plaits and she wore a circlet of twigs and leaves. Her face was a map of age and wisdom; her grey eyes were bright.

'Come,' Kadri murmured, gesturing for Stasya and Aleksis to move forward. 'Mother Rowan, here are the travellers. We made good time. There have been losses. Some are injured, and all are weary.'

As Stasya approached with Aleksis by her side, the crone had eyes only for her. She stretched out her arms in greeting. 'Welcome, my dear.' The warmth in her gaze and in her voice filled up Stasya's heart. 'We have seen glimpses of your journey. A long way. A path of many challenges. You have been stalwart.' She turned her head to look at Aleksis. 'And you, the seeker for truth. At last you are here. Welcome to you and to your companions.'

Stasya had seldom seen Aleks lost for words. But now he seemed rooted to the spot, struck dumb, his gaze on Mother Rowan. 'You… you know me? You know…?' His voice was so unsteady that Stasya feared he might collapse. She reached out to lay a reassuring hand on his arm. *It's all right. It's all right, Aleks.*

'We know of you, yes. And there is one among us who knows you, Aleksis son of Feliks.'

A figure appeared behind the old woman. Stasya sucked in a breath. Again, the vision had become reality. A tall person in a hooded cloak. As she stared, and as Aleks tensed beside her, the figure pushed back his hood. His was a face of great charm, handsome, open. A human face.

'Aleks!' he exclaimed, and a joyful smile lit up his features. 'You're the image of your father!'

'And you,' Aleksis breathed. 'Lord Kasimir reborn… And yet, still truly yourself, my friend.' Tears flooded his cheeks. The two moved forward and threw their arms around each other, and Stasya found that she, too, was weeping. Good tears. The tears a person sheds at the end of a wonderful tale of losing and finding, heartbreak and heart-mending, sorrow and joy. This was a story beyond her skill to tell.

Mother Rowan's smile was gentle. 'There are many tales to be told here,' she said, and Stasya wondered if the wise woman – for such Mother Rowan surely was – had the ability to read her thoughts, or was simply very good at seeing the truth in a situation. 'Time enough for that later. Let us leave these two friends to renew their acquaintance in private. Travellers, you need rest.'

Juho stepped forward to usher Matiss, Lukas and Karolis away under the trees, with the dog at Lukas's heel. Markus put his arm around Aleks's shoulders and the two of them followed. None of them looked back, and Stasya found herself feeling just a little sad. *They don't need me anymore.* Which was foolish. After the exhaustion, the fear, the deaths, the bloodshed, she should be feeling nothing but delight that the quest was over, the lost one found.

'You and I,' Mother Rowan said, taking Stasya's arm, 'have much to discuss. The past, the present, the future. Weighty matters. And I have wonders to show you. But for now, let us spend some time in quiet reflection, just the two of us. Then you'll want to rest. You are weary in body and spirit, I think.'

A chirping comment from Flip, who still occupied Stasya's shoulder, made the wise woman chuckle. 'How could I forget you? The three of us, of course,' she said with a wry smile, giving a nod in the bird's direction. 'You, too, have acquitted yourself well, young one.'

Was it possible that Flip belonged here, among the Forest Folk? That she had been sent to Stasya on some kind of mission? Surely not. Years had passed since the day she'd discovered the little dog trapped in the forest and rescued her. It didn't make sense. Perhaps the wise woman was referring only to what she'd seen in visions: Flip changing her form, Flip saving lives. Flip comforting Stasya. She had most certainly acquitted herself well. Those times of hesitation and reluctance were no more than anyone might have felt on such a confronting journey.

'You'd rather be outdoors, I imagine, on your own,' Mother Rowan said. 'Travelling with a bunch of men, you'll have missed your quiet time under the trees. But this is the hour for biting insects, so we'd best retreat inside. Most of our folk live out in the forest, but my dwelling is within the caves. I have room for you there. And the little one, of course. A private corner. Come, I'll show you.'

THERE WERE so many questions to ask. Stasya did not know where to start, or what might perhaps cause offence. The private corner proved to be quite a spacious cavern with a hearth on which a small fire burned. The smoke did not fill the chamber but rose through what looked like a natural chimney within the rock ceiling. There were two shelf beds, each with a straw mattress and neatly folded blankets; an oak dresser holding pots, cups, bowls and other useful items; garments hanging from pegs attached to the stone wall. Bunches of dried herbs dangled from a natural protrusion high above them – surely too high to be reached by anyone who could not fly. Two cushioned chairs stood by a small oak table. It was a home. It felt almost like her own home, back on the fringe of Heartwood. It lacked only the picture of Mother and her creatures… but in a sense, Mother was here. That was how it felt.

Flip, a little dog again, leaped onto one of the beds and curled up, making herself comfortable. Mother Rowan had busied herself filling cups from a flask; she handed one to Stasya. 'This is a very fine mead. Not made by me; there's a skilful brewer among the folk here, Ilona is her name, and she makes excellent use of what the seasons offer us. Sip slowly. It's quite strong, and you are tired.'

'Thank you.' It was indeed strong. One sip, and Stasya's mind filled with the warmth of summer, and bees working around a hive, and fruit ripening on trees. 'It is so good to be here, Mother Rowan. I feel… I feel as if you are an old friend, or even family, but I've never met you before.' Stasya felt her cheeks grow hot. Why had she blurted that out, when this was someone important, a wise woman among the Forest Folk, and she was… 'Sorry,' she mumbled. 'I don't mean to be…'

'Honest?' Mother Rowan was smiling again. 'You have met me before, Stasya. In your visions. Unless I am wrong in thinking you saw me there. I only wish my own visions had revealed a little more. In time, perhaps you will tell me your story. You have remarkable gifts, my dear. More powerful than you realise, I think. Who taught you to conjure visions in the fire and water?'

'My grandmother. If she had lived longer, I might have learned better control over the other thing. The link with creatures. I… Maybe you saw. When I call on creatures for help – I only do that when things are desperate – they can end up suffering, even dying because they came to my aid.' Oh gods, now she was crying again. 'Sorry.' She dashed away the tears. 'We were followed and there was a fight on the way here. A terrible, fierce fight. I called on wolves to help us, and one of them was brutally killed. My fault. It's not the first time my gift has caused terrible harm.' In her mind was the sound of boots kicking and trampling as the Ruler's men crushed those rats to death. 'Grandmother died when I was eleven. I was on my own after that. And I haven't always got things right.'

There was a silence. Stasya sipped her mead. From outside, faintly, came the sound of someone singing.

'What was your grandmother's name, Stasya?' The question was gently put.

'Helvi. She was a storyteller; I learned that from her, too. I was sent to live with her in Heartwood when I was four years old. I don't remember my parents.'

'Mmm. So there is an untold story there. Have you wished to know more about them? Tried to find out?'

Stasya shook her head. 'They're gone. Dead. Grandmother never spoke of them; whatever their story was, I think it made her sad. And there was nobody else to ask.' She met the wise woman's gaze. 'Maybe we both have questions,' she said, and felt herself smiling.

'Maybe we do. And since you and your fellow travellers are not only worn out, but also injured, it will be necessary for you to stay with us some while, until all are mended well enough to attempt the journey back. You and I have time to talk. I might, if you wish, teach you some further controls over your gift. More than that, if you wish. For now, I have something to show you. But first, perhaps one question each? What is most pressing, my dear?'

Where to start? Flip, Aleks, the forest, the Ruler, the whole woeful situation at court… Impossible to choose from those. 'It's a personal question,' she said. 'Don't answer if you prefer not. But… are you one of the Forest Folk yourself? Or are you fully human? It's just… in some ways, you remind me of my grandmother. I feel safe here, with you. I haven't felt truly safe for a long while.'

'That is hard to answer. I have lived many years among the Forest Folk. My heart lies here; my true calling lies here. I grew up among human folk. Like you, I chose to come here. Perhaps as a newborn babe I was human. As an old woman I am more than that, I believe.'

That was another story: a mysterious, almost magical one. Stasya was not sure she understood it, not fully. Perhaps that would take time.

'And so could you be, Stasya,' said Mother Rowan. 'You have the makings of a wise woman already. Should you choose to stay here among us, I would guide you along the path of learning. The folk of this community would introduce you to wonders you would never encounter in the outside world. Deep wisdom. Understanding beyond words.'

How wonderful. How blissful to live here in the heart of the forest, among these calm and understanding folk, with a kind friend and wise teacher. But… 'Would there be a… a purpose… beyond gaining wisdom and skills? Would I then go back to the human world?' She imagined returning to Heartwood after ten years, twenty years, for surely this path of learning would be long. If folk had suspected her of witchcraft before, how much more likely would that be after living among uncanny folk? It would be as if she had suddenly stepped out from one of those old tales. They'd drown her, burn her, destroy her.

'I have a purpose here,' said Mother Rowan. 'I'm known as the Forest Guardian. My work is to watch over Heartwood Forest; to guide folk in understanding its special nature and how best to learn from it and look after it. And to share the wisdom of storytelling. We can speak more of this later, and there are some among the Forest Folk who will be happy to give you their understanding. About what I do; about what they do. We play a part in the outer world, the human world, as well. But I do not go beyond the borders of this land these days; I'm growing older.'

It was almost too much to take in. 'So… the Forest Folk do cross those borders sometimes? Go out among human folk?' Stasya could only imagine the risks that would bring, when there was such distrust out there. But then, there were some among the Forest Folk who might pass as human men and women. She imagined them at Dragon's Keep, and what terrible things Lady Elisabeta might do if she discovered their true nature.

Mother Rowan smiled. 'Your one question became several, Stasya. I think it's my turn now.'

'Oh. Sorry.'

'My question is this,' said Mother Rowan. 'Who made your amber owl?'

A simple, easy question was not at all what Stasya had expected. She reached to touch the owl, which hung outside her borrowed tunic. 'Lukas. My friend from home, who came with us here. He and I found the amber in a lake we call Clearwater, and he carved the owl from it.' She noticed, then, that Mother Rowan also wore an amber token around her neck. It was a bird in flight, perhaps a swallow, delicately crafted.

'But Lukas did not provide that silver chain, I imagine.'

'It's a long story. After the Ruler's men came to our village my owl was taken. First by the man they called the Commander, and later by Lady Elisabeta, the Ruler. Aleks – Master Aleksis – got it back for me, before we left court. When he returned it, he provided the chain; the original cord was broken when the Commander… when he…'

'You need not tell that part. I know the man was brutal. The ill work he did in your settlement will take some mending.'

'There are good folk there,' Stasya said. 'But they lost so much. So many people dead or injured; terrible damage from the fire. And the trees… He made the men cut down the Ancestor. He killed her. She'd stood watch over our village for longer than anyone could remember. She'd provided a home for more creatures than anyone could count. I don't know how that can ever be made good again, Mother Rowan.'

'We will speak more of this. And of your friend Lukas, for I think he is one of those who might make a difference in the village, and perhaps in that part of the forest. A true friend; one who has listened to you and learned from you. A good man.'

'He was brave. On the journey. But he's hurt, though he doesn't like to admit it.' Stasya would always remember Lukas drawing the knife across the Commander's throat, and the strange calm in his voice as he spoke those words. She would always remember the hideous moment when she'd realised he was the one the Ruler had threatened to whip to death. Sometimes it was hard to recall the peaceful times in the field, the goats quietly grazing, the stories shared. 'Lukas would never have chosen to come here, even though he loves the old tales of uncanny things. He wanted to go home; to be with his family. But if Aleks and his friends hadn't got us out of Dragon's Keep, Lukas would have been killed. Cruelly killed. It wasn't safe for him to go back to the settlement then, with the Commander still there, so he came on with us.'

'Thinking to protect you, perhaps?'

'Perhaps. Even though there were three court guards with us. He didn't trust Aleks. Master Aleksis. I don't think he does even now.'

'And you? Do you trust him?'

Stasya wondered what Aleks and Markus were talking about now. Such a long time; so many years apart. They'd only been children. What if Markus didn't want to leave this peaceful haven? What if he had no interest in becoming Ruler of the Northlands? Even if he did say yes, what lay ahead would be hard. Lady Elisabeta was formidable.

'Aleks kept the most important parts of his story secret from Lukas and me,' she said. 'He wouldn't explain his reasons for wanting to come to the Hermit while he thought someone might overhear and take information back to the Ruler. So I doubted him, even though he'd saved our lives. I suspected he wanted me on the journey only to guide him safely through the forest so he could claim the treasure the old tales speak of. After a long time, he told the full story about losing his friend as a child, and about who Markus really is. By then I'd learned to trust him anyway. I can see he's a good person. He's driven by his mission, but he also cares about his friends. He cares about the Northlands and making it a better place. I'm happy he found Markus here, among your people. But… I don't know what will come next, except that it will be dangerous and difficult. For all of them.'

Silence, then. Mother Rowan was looking at her as if she expected something more, but there was no more to say. Eventually the wise woman said, 'Come, then. Before you rest, let me show you what lies within and beyond this dwelling place. The tales do indeed tell of treasure hidden here, guarded by unknown forces. We have neither sleeping dragons nor fearsome fey warriors, though our folk can take on that role if required. The secret nature of our realm has been protection enough. Human folk seldom step past the barrier unless we choose to let them in. Thus it was with young Markus, a human child found deep in Heartwood all alone. He had spent many days wandering, drinking from forest pools, eating what little he could find. One of the Forest Folk, out on a mission far beyond our border, came upon the boy in a place frequented by bears and brought him back here. The child was too exhausted, too frightened, to tell us who he was and where he had come from. While he recovered within our community, I sought answers in the water and in the fire. What I saw convinced me that he should stay with us, learn what the young people of the Forest Folk learn, discover ways of wisdom and paths of peace. I saw that he was destined to be a leader among human folk. But only if we strengthened him, taught him to hear the voices of the trees, the rocks, the creatures of forest and lake, would he grow strong and wise and courageous enough to be, not only a good leader, but a great one. Great in justice and wisdom; great in forbearance, in tolerance, in his embrace of all living things.'

It was hard to know what to say, so Stasya held her tongue. Lord Kasimir had lived the rest of his life believing his only son dead. People had searched long and hard for Markus. Aleks had borne the burdens of guilt and sorrow all these years. The decision to keep the child, a boy even younger than poor Tomas, seemed cruel, though the intentions had been good. If Aleks were here, he would ask the hard question. He would not hesitate. Perhaps he had already asked Markus. She wished she could hear that conversation.

'Come,' Mother Rowan said, rising to her feet and gesturing toward an opening in the wall, where a passageway seemed to lead directly into the mountain. 'Will you bring the lantern? It's quite dark on the way in. Leave the little one to her sleep.'

Flip twitched an ear, then curled herself still tighter on the bed. Stasya took up the lantern and followed the old woman along the curving tunnel through the rock. The roof was high. Even Matiss would be able to pass through without stooping. Had this place been laboriously carved out by hand? Made by magic? Or perhaps it had formed naturally over the course of more years than anyone could count.

'There were trees here once, in another age,' Mother Rowan said. 'Great, wonderful trees something like the one you called the Ancestor. Such things they witnessed in their long lives: the fall of kings, the deeds of heroes, the passing away of tribes and the grief of survivors. Courage and cowardice; justice and tyranny; love and hate. No wonder old trees are so full of wisdom. This way, now. Watch your step.'

The rock floor was uneven here. Mother Rowan was walking ahead of her while Stasya held the light, but the old woman seemed to have no trouble finding her way or staying steady. Well, she had said she was something other than human now; perhaps finding her way in the semi-dark was a skill she had come by during her long life among the Forest Folk.

The passageway opened up and they were in a larger cavern, where there was natural light. Something whirred past overhead, making Stasya start. Bats, she thought, smiling as she gazed upward. There they were, hanging neatly in groups, their dark forms like shadows in corners of the cavern roof. The one that had taken flight settled again. Stasya opened her thoughts to them; sent a message in mind-pictures. *We come in friendship. We mean you no harm. Rest well, small ones.* And felt the faintest response, like a contented sigh: *Rest. Sleep.*

The light came from a narrow gap where the stone opened to the outside world. Through that opening came a faint sound of birdsong, a twilight conversation. Closer at hand, Stasya could hear a trickle of water.

'Set the lantern down over there.' Mother Rowan gestured, and Stasya saw there was a pool in the cavern, small and round, the water touched by the light from above. She put the lantern down where she was shown, by the wall, and came to stand beside the wise woman, looking into the water.

'A place of visions,' she said. 'Is this where you...?'

'One of the places, yes. We will try together, but not now. You are weary. It can be hard to find the right question at such times. I have something else to show you. Look up, above the lantern. What do you see?'

How had she not noticed it before? Her mouth dropped open; she blinked and looked again. The cave wall, illuminated from below by the soft light, was golden, glowing, rich as fine clover honey. Stasya stepped closer. She held back from touching; to do so would seem almost like sacrilege. 'Amber,' she breathed. Gods, if Lady Elisabeta ever found out about this, she would wreak absolute havoc on the mountain. Fire-breathing dragons would not be enough to hold her back.

'Indeed. And not only in this cave, Stasya. Amber is found in many places within the Hermit. The rocks hold a honeycomb of chambers and passageways. Guarding them is part of our people's ancient trust. If we take from the store of amber, it is always with the forest's permission, and with due ritual of thanks. And never for selfish reasons. This amber heals; it protects; it guards. But only if it is both taken and worn in the right spirit.'

Stasya's hand went around her amber owl, gently, in recognition and thanks. She could find no words.

'We will sleep now,' Mother Rowan said. 'I'll show you where we go to relieve ourselves and where we wash; that's close by and entirely private. Then rest until morning. We might seek answers in the water then. Later in the day there will be a gathering to celebrate the arrival of your party. A feast, singing, an exchange of stories. But only when all of you are well rested and able to join in. Don't look so worried, my dear; it will be a joyful gathering. You might be invited to contribute a story. Nothing more would be asked of you. The folk here know you walk under my special protection now.'

'Really?' The idea seemed at the same time unbelievable and entirely right. Mother Rowan saw in her the next Forest Guardian. An apprentice. A student on a very long path of learning, if she chose that way.

'Yes, really. Now, come, I'll show you where to wash. You look half-asleep on your feet.'

'I expect the bats are waiting for us to retire before they fly out on the hunt,' Stasya said as they returned to the dwelling place. She could sense it; the air was alive with their need to be on the wing.

Mother Rowan glanced back at her. 'I expect so,' she said with a grin. 'They are a little late to leave.'

46

ALEKSIS

'THIS MUST HAVE taken years of preparation,' Markus said. 'And a great deal of caution, when a single error might have drawn the whole plan to my cousin's attention.'

They were under the trees in the half-light of evening, Markus with the three of them, enjoying some very good mead while Aleksis attempted to explain the situation concisely and clearly. Why was it so hard to summon that voice now, the measured voice of the royal adviser? Markus would think him incompetent. He might say no to coming back. Matiss kept glancing his way; the big man knew him well. And now Matiss spoke in his stead.

'We have many loyal folk within the Ruler's household, Markus. Among the guards; in the kitchens, the gardens, the stables. One or two key folk in senior, trusted positions. And many more out in the community, though that network is harder to maintain safely. We can't – couldn't – keep travelling out to talk to folk, to exchange information. And we didn't want to risk messages by pigeon, though we do have birds in certain households, and we use them when we must. We have a network of safe houses. If not for that, our flight from court would have been far more difficult. And we've placed some of our folk in strategic locations. Places where they may gain information not available elsewhere. A broad reach. It has taken time, yes. But not years; Lady Elisabeta has not been Ruler so long.'

'A pity we were never able to place a spy with Bishop Petras at Raven's Watch,' put in Karolis. 'Or in one of the other houses of his Order. We judged that simply too perilous. The Church of the Godly wields significant power. Second only to that of the Ruler. And since Petras became bishop, its power is still greater. He's a man of enormous ambition.'

'I don't remember much about the warrior monks.' Markus's voice was low, warm. 'They did visit court once, long ago. I recall the tricks they did with their swords and the combat displays they put on. As a child I found them dazzling.' A pause. 'Strange, the things I quickly remembered, while barely understanding what they were, and the things that came back much later, aided by visions that were not my own. To know you were coming to find me, Aleks, and wondering why now? The news of my father's passing came from the outside world; a message reached us. I knew there was unrest. But I had not expected to be… called upon. I'm ill-prepared for it. I know little of the wider picture. Borders, leaders, what the people truly want. The warrior monks must be a formidable fighting force. I fear that this bishop might challenge my claim to the rulership, valid though it would seem to be. It would be deeply wrong to achieve this at the cost of more lives; perhaps to face an armed conflict within the Northlands. That would defeat the purpose. My father's wish was to lead in peace; to open his ears to the voices of the people; to serve them rather than to rule them. And, I imagine, to maintain friendly relations with our neighbouring territories. If our venture began with bloodshed, my time as Ruler would be forever tainted.'

'Your father knew how to deal with Petras.' Aleks had

got his voice under control again. 'Lady Elisabeta lacks the required subtlety. I don't think she reads him well. And he, of course, does not believe women have what it takes to hold positions of leadership.'

'We can't charge straight into this,' said Karolis. 'If you agree to come back with us, Markus, we'll need to keep you under cover, hidden, for some while. We thought you might stay with someone who can help prepare you. There's a trusted scholar of our acquaintance, a man with an extensive personal library and an immense knowledge of the Northlands, our neighbouring territories, and history both recent and ancient. You'd be safe there; he's an ally. His dwelling is nowhere near court, and it can be kept secure. As for the rest of us, we cannot reappear at Dragon's Keep, or anywhere Elisabeta might track us down, until everything is in readiness. But we will continue to work toward that day. All of us. That includes those of our team who are at present out in the community playing their own parts.'

'What of the others who came here with you?' Markus asked. 'The young man, Lukas, and the woman? What part do they play in your grand plan?'

Matiss was about to speak, then clearly thought better of it. All eyes were on Aleksis.

'That's for each of them to say.' Why did this feel like an admission of defeat? Why did it make his heart shrink? 'Lukas has made it clear he wants to go back to Heartwood. He has family there. But he's carrying an injury. Karolis has been helping him as we travelled. I understand your healers here will provide further treatment; they said he would spend tonight in their house. He needs to be completely well before he can attempt the journey home, and he shouldn't go to Heartwood until the Ruler's men have been withdrawn. Elisabeta will very likely want to keep a force there even with the Commander gone. Who knows what story will be attached to his disappearance along with a number of his men? One thing is certain. I can play no part in that situation. Whatever authority I held was gone the moment we left court.'

'A few misleading messages might help,' Matiss suggested. 'There would be ways of doing it. But you're right, we should make sure Lukas doesn't go back until it's safe for him to be there. He may have been a reluctant member of our team, but he's acquitted himself bravely. We owe him for that.'

'He'll want Stasya to go with him.' Karolis stated the blunt truth. 'He'll expect it.'

Silence. Then Aleksis drew a deep breath and said, 'That's her decision to make. Whatever their choices, we must ensure their safety on the journey, and perhaps maintain some protection until the two of them… settle. I am hoping that…' He looked at Markus, who was regarding him with a half-smile, as if both puzzled and amused.

'You will travel under the protection of the Forest Folk,' his friend said, 'at least while you are in Heartwood Forest. All of you. As for the future, its pathways are numerous and changeable. How soon had you hoped to make news of my return public, Aleks? When would I step up and identify myself to my cousin?'

'I had hoped we might do it at the Grand Council, when the leaders of our neighbouring territories will be gathered at Dragon's Keep, along with Bishop Petras. The time of the Harvest Festival. That gives us the summer to prepare.'

Markus lifted his brows. 'The longer the preparation, the more likely it is that information will leak to the wrong ears, and the greater the possibility that one of you – of us – will be recognised, my friend. A disguise goes only so far. Could it not be sooner?'

'We must get it right,' Aleksis said. 'Part of that is to spread the message among ordinary people, the people whose lives will be changed if they have a wise Ruler, someone who will lead in the same spirit of justice and tolerance your father lived by. No secrets exposed; no grand plans announced until the Council. Instead, something much simpler and more palatable. We have an idea about that, too. Or rather, Karolis does. But we'll talk about that tomorrow. I see Juho hovering; it must be past time for sleep.'

He was tired beyond exhaustion, worn out in body and mind. But sleep eluded him. The three of them had been housed in one of the leafy dwellings within the forest, and now lay under a roof of branches and greenery, on pallets that were sheer luxury after so many nights spent on rocks or bare ground. He was clean, he was warm, he'd been well fed. He should be lost in dreamless slumber, as it seemed his companions were, Matiss gently snoring, Karolis motionless and silent. But Aleksis's mind was restless, swirling with questions to which there were no answers. He felt like getting up and hurling something out into the night. What did that make him, an angry child thwarted in some selfish desire? A fool who'd lost the capacity to find his own answers?

He rolled over for the hundredth time, covering his eyes with his forearm. The moonlight was dim through the woven lattice of the roof. Somewhere out there an owl hooted, as if to remind him that it was night-time and all sensible human folk were asleep. Then Karolis spoke softly, startling him.

'Talk to her, you fool.'

'What?'

'You're worried about her. Stasya. You wonder where will she go, what will she do now this part of the story is over. That's muddling up your thoughts. So talk to her. Ask her.'

'She had no choice but to come with us. To save her friend. To save herself. Now we're here, we've found Markus, and these folk will see us safely back down the mountain. So we don't need her to find the way anymore. She's free to go.'

Silence.

'They'll escort her and Lukas home when the place is rid of the Ruler's men. And they can pick up their lives again.'

'Mm-hm. Didn't you say not long ago that it's Stasya's decision? Sounds as if you're making the decision for her.'

Matiss stirred. 'Storyteller,' he mumbled. 'You really think we don't need one in the team?'

'Vital role,' said Karolis. 'If you're reluctant to ask her, Aleks, then I will. And if she says no to an escort home, then you may need to consider why she might not want to go back to the settlement.'

'Do what the royal adviser would do,' added Matiss, struggling up to a sitting position. 'Put all the facts in front of her and give her time to think it over. Answer her questions honestly.'

'The royal adviser does not always answer questions honestly. Even when he isn't plotting the overthrow of his Ruler,' Aleksis said. 'He answers them… cautiously.'

They were both staring at him in the semi-dark. It was curiously unsettling. He wondered for a moment whether the mission had turned him crazy. *Be honest, Aleks. These are your trusted friends.*

'Stasya is one of us,' Matiss said. 'Part of our team. A wayfinder, yes; but so much more. What she does, none of the rest of us can.'

'But—'

'You want to protect her. To keep her safe from harm. But would she want that? So far, she's done a pretty good job of protecting herself. And us, on occasion. You don't want her wielding a weapon, doing harm to folk when it's so alien to her nature. We feel the same, and we'd try to stop that from happening again. But Stasya may be prepared to risk it in order to help the team. In order to achieve the greater goal.' Karolis paused. 'Could be you're letting your personal feelings get in the way, Aleks. That's not like you.' Now he sounded mildly amused.

The temptation to throw something was becoming harder to resist. 'She could have been killed today. Did you happen not to notice Rihard with his knife to her throat?'

Matiss sighed. 'How often do you think I imagine Leja in trouble, Leja under threat, Leja scared or trapped or hurt? But do I try to stop her from playing a part in our work because of that? Do I ask her to set that work aside and wait on her own at home while I put myself at risk for the same reason? Of course not. Why? Because she's doing a job none of the rest of us can do. A job she's good at. She's playing her part, as all of us are. Do I worry about her, do I often wish I could protect her, keep her safe? Of course I do. She's my wife and I love her. It's only natural to feel that way. But I don't act on it. We're all part of this, Aleks. We trust one another. We work as a team. Stasya belongs to our team; at least give her the chance to say yes or no to going on with us.'

'She's a grown woman, not a fragile child, Aleks. I should point out that she got herself out of Rihard's clutches pretty efficiently, taking advantage of a moment's opportunity. And made herself remarkably useful in that fight, considering she has no combat training at all. I could remedy that. Indeed, if we take up the plan I suggested, I should do so. That might help allay your fears.' Karolis sounded perfectly calm. Aleksis began to wonder if the two of them had planned this assault on his feelings. If that was what this was. He did feel… attacked.

'Maybe you should lead the team from now on, Karolis,' he said with some bitterness.

'Bollocks. You're the leader; you were from the first, and you will be to the end. We trust you, Aleks. We hope you trust us enough to listen, even when what we say is unpalatable to you. Just talk to Stasya, will you? Allow her the freedom to make her own choices. You can't deny that she's earned it.'

47

STASYA

SHE WOKE EARLY after a night of blissful, dreamless sleep. Mother Rowan was already up, tending to the fledgling fire. It was light outside; not the first light of dawn, but the warmer glow of a fine day in the making and a bright summer to come. As Stasya rose from the bed, Flip edged over into the warm space she had left.

'May I help?' Stasya asked.

'Have a wash first, get dressed, take what time you need. I'll brew some tea.' The wise woman added more wood to the fire, then rose to her feet. 'Did you sleep well, my dear?'

'The best sleep I've had in a long time, thank you. It's so peaceful here.'

Some time later, they were by the pool in the inner cavern, side by side. The bats had settled to sleep long since, though an occasional whisper of movement passed through the shadowy mass of them. Enough light was entering to show Stasya her own reflection, and she was shocked by how gaunt she looked, how worn out. This was surely a far older, sadder person than the Stasya of Heartwood. Yet here she was, with a wise friend, in the safest of places and among peaceable folk. The forest was all around her. Her companions of the journey were here too, all but one. Why was that face in the water so weary, so full of doubt?

'I'm not sure I'm ready for this,' she admitted. To seek wisdom in the fire or the water, a person needed to clear their mind, to open it to possibilities. To find the right question, a person needed to be calm and peaceful.

'What is your usual practice, Stasya?' Mother Rowan asked. 'We are within the earth, with the water before us. This, perhaps, to represent fire.' She fished a twig from her pocket and laid it by the pool. One end was charred, perhaps from the hearth fire.

Stasya reached into her own pocket and withdrew a feather that had lain in her path as she approached the Hermit. Soft, grey, with a touch of vivid blue: a thing of wonder and beauty. She placed it gently alongside the twig. 'There's a verse my grandmother taught me. After I slow my breathing, I say that, one line at a time.'

'Good. Shall we begin? Take my hand, if you will. It is for you to ask the question when you are ready.'

The two breathed together, a gradual slowing. In her mind, Stasya thanked each of the elements in turn for the blessings it bestowed. Then, when it felt like time, she spoke the familiar words. '*The oak's deep roots hold fast to the earth. I, too, will be strong.*' Standing up to an attacker. Keeping on going, even when she was worn out and sad. Ending the pain of a small creature beyond saving. Challenging the Ruler. '*The graceful willow moves with the wind. I, too, will dance.*' Not yet. But soon, perhaps, in this realm if not her own. The lost boy was found. Despite the challenge ahead, this was a time of joy. '*The mighty ash towers to the heavens. I, too, will stretch high.*' To climb a rock face. To reach out a hand to the Ruler's senior adviser when he lost his way. Perhaps, in time, to become a wise woman. '*The sun gleams on the still pool. I, too, will hold the light.*' She had held the lantern for Mother Rowan; she had seen the wonder of the caves. But there was a greater light to hold: the light within. Not only to keep it burning, but to share it. Mother Rowan might teach her about that, if she chose to stay.

She asked the question in a murmur. 'I seek guidance for the pathway forward. Choices lie ahead for me. Which is best, wisest, most true?'

They waited, hand in hand. From beyond the cavern came the morning voices of birds, a rising chorus. A flutter of wings closer at hand, and Flip landed on Stasya's shoulder, a tiny owl. It was not long before their reflections on the water broke up and reformed as something new. A scene of fields and trees and modest houses; a village hall, a bakery… And there was Lukas, older but unmistakable, striding across the square. Two curly-haired children were running around him, playing chase. Lukas looked out of the water and raised a hand in greeting. His smile was radiant; he was a picture of contentment. Beside him walked an old and somewhat familiar dog.

The vision faded, and slowly, slowly another formed in the water. Stasya's breath caught. The scene was the Ruler's council chamber, and it made her gut churn, almost jolting her out of the trance. Mother Rowan squeezed her hand gently and she gained control of her breathing once more.

People at the long table. Familiar people. Markus, with Aleksis by his side. And more folk, their manner and dress telling her this was a council of elders or leaders, people of power. Aleks was talking, intense, passionate, troubled. Gesturing. Matiss stood behind him on watchful guard. No sign of Karolis. A man stood up and interrupted Aleks, a man whose expression chilled her heart. Aleks's jaw tightened; his hands became white-knuckled fists. He sprang to his feet, eyes furious, and the image faded away. What sort of answer was that?

Mother Rowan squeezed her hand again, as if to say *Wait*, and now a different image appeared. Great trees above; a forest clearing below. Two women sat there among moss-cloaked stones, while a little dog busied herself investigating something in the undergrowth. Through the high canopy, sunlight filtered down on the women. One was of middle years, her chestnut hair threaded with grey. The other was a wizened ancient, but Stasya knew her as Mother Rowan. The two looked relaxed, content; they were deep in conversation. Each wore the robe of a wise woman. Each bore around her neck an amber talisman; one was a swallow in flight, the other an owl. Stasya reached up, now, to touch her own amber owl, and felt the brush of Flip's feathers against her cheek. The image faded and was gone. Only the water, and the two women reflected there, one getting on in years, the other young. For a moment, they looked like two of a kind.

Stasya found herself unable to move. Mother Rowan released her hand, then put an arm around her shoulders and ushered her back to the other room, and to the table. 'Sit, my dear. Take some time.'

'That was... it was...' *It was no help at all.* She couldn't say that. There was always something to be learned from visions. But right now, she couldn't think what it might be. Not long ago she had been filled with delight that the wise woman would consider taking her on as a sort of apprentice; deeply happy that she might make the Hermit her home. But shouldn't the vision have shown her following the other pathways? There had been nothing of her in them. Unless the Lukas of the future had indeed turned that joyful smile on her. Unless the Aleks of the future had been looking in her direction for reassurance. She did not think she could believe in either of those. Herself as a village wife, a mother of children, with Lukas's disapproving parents part of her everyday existence, and scarcely a moment of the day free to be alone under the trees? Herself seated at a council table with the leaders of the Northlands and beyond, where someone like her would surely never be taken seriously, even if she could manage to get her words out? She had loved the image of herself with the wise woman, quiet under the trees, working together. It was the kind of life she had always longed for. Had something changed in her, that it no longer felt like enough?

Mother Rowan set a fresh cup of tea in front of her, along with a small platter of cheese and dried fruit. 'Remember,' she said, 'these visions do not show you what will be, only what might be. Perhaps the answer lies elsewhere entirely. Or perhaps the possibilities are more flexible than you believe. Maybe they can be stretched to fit.' She sat down opposite Stasya, lifting her own cup to take a sip. 'This morning, before the gathering, you might go to visit your friend in the healers' house. I think he would welcome that. And you might have a word with Master Aleksis, in private. Ask him about his plans.'

'The possibilities may… stretch? Are you saying there might be a place for me in more than one of these?' How could that be?

'The future is yours to make, Stasya. Don't rush to a decision. There is time.' Mother Rowan's voice was gentle. 'I find it helps to turn your dilemma into a story. Think on that. I should make it clear that wherever your choices take you, you will always be welcome here. Have no fear that you will ever be barred from this realm. You belong here, just as I did. But perhaps you also have a place in the human world, and work to do there.'

48

LUKAS

AT LAST HE was free from pain. At last he could stop pretending all was well, ignoring the deep aching, forcing his body to keep going even when he could hardly bear it. Now he could move, breathe, rest. But for all that, he was not comfortable in this place with its strange folk and the feeling that magic, if not right before his eyes, was all around him. He'd felt it in the touch of the quiet man who'd applied a pungent-smelling poultice to his side while Lukas lay very still on the bed. He'd tasted it in the draught the healers had given him, which was an unlikely shade of green. To be fair, it had tasted far better than it looked. After that he'd slept, not waking until dawn light entered the airy dwelling that housed the Hermit's healers. At present he was the sole occupant except for the dog, which had refused to leave his side and which now lay quiet alongside his pallet. He was glad the healers had allowed Shadow to stay. They had checked Matiss's shoulder, supplied him with a fresh sling, given him, too, a draught to take. But Matiss had then left the healers' house. He had not returned here to sleep.

Lukas hadn't seen Stasya since the old woman took her away. Perhaps she had slept in the crone's quarters, or with some women of the Forest Folk. Now that there were choices, she surely wouldn't be sharing quarters with Aleksis and the others. He would have gone to find her, but the healer had given him instructions to stay where he was, at least until someone came to check on him this morning. He could hardly argue with that after all they had done for him. He wondered what was in that odd-looking draught. There were too many disturbing tales about what might happen if human folk ate or drank in the Otherworld.

There was to be a great gathering later in the day. The whole community. Before that happened, before Stasya could talk to Aleksis again, he wanted to see her. He needed to find out how she was really feeling and what she wanted to do. Or was it too soon for that discussion? He might only upset her. They weren't going to let him go home until the settlement was safe, and who knew how long that would take? So he was stuck here for a good while. Each day of delay was another day of endurance for his parents, his sisters, his community. Another day of backbreaking labour, of constant fear. Who was looking after the goats? Were there even any goats left?

At least the Commander was gone. Perhaps the others would be withdrawn. A man could only wish. Even so, there was a huge task ahead. Putting things to rights. Mending what was broken. Rebuilding the community again, piece by piece. He needed to be there.

His heart was racing now; the healers would not approve. He closed his eyes, imagining what Stasya might say. *Breathe slowly, Lukas. Make it a pattern.* And she'd repeat some sort of rhyme or charm to calm him. *It's hard to be patient*, she would say. *It's hard to take things slowly. Think of trees; how long they stand there, looking out over the world, watching as the years pass and humankind does all sorts of stupid things. As those years pass, their roots go deeper and deeper, and their branches stretch wider, and they make room for all sorts of creatures to live in them. They give us shade in summer; they give us their berries and nuts; when they drop branches, they give us wood for building or fuel for our fires in winter. They gladden our hearts with their beauty and their mystery. Breathe like a tree.*

'Lukas?'

His eyes snapped open; he'd been lying there in a daze. He sat up too quickly, wincing.

'Careful,' Stasya said, reaching out an arm to steady him. 'Don't undo the healers' good work.'

'I'm fine. Much better.' He heard how sharp that sounded and drew a couple of long breaths. 'Sorry. You startled me. You came in so quietly.'

'I thought you were asleep.' Stasya sat down on the stool beside his bed. 'I wanted to come and see you yesterday. But Mother Rowan – she's the wise woman here – had other things for me to do. Including a bath and a sleep. I stayed in her home. It's in the caves, within the Hermit. And there really is amber here; the stories don't lie.'

He didn't want to think about amber. Even though that was what had started all this. Was it possible, *still*, that Aleksis was lying about all of it, and that he would carry the news of amber straight back to the Ruler? He didn't want to believe that. It couldn't be so, could it? After finding his old friend, and the joyful reunion, and the way they had fought the Commander's men? Risked their lives? Even poor Pavel had changed sides again in that terrible fight. He thought of Stasya with a bloody knife in her hands; Stasya with the Commander's blade against her neck. He never wanted her to be in such a position again. It was wrong. So wrong.

'What?' she asked, making him start. 'What's troubling you? I thought you said you were fine. If something's wrong, tell me.'

'It's nothing. It's just… This feels odd, us here, safe, and the lost boy found, and everything suddenly to rights, when…'

He faltered, unable to go on. The thing was too big to put into words.

'When yesterday we were killing people? Almost getting killed ourselves? Not to speak of what happened at the ridgeway. It's odd, all right. Hard to talk about. Hard to believe it's real and we're not sitting down there on the edge of the forest, watching over the goats. When I first woke this morning with Flip tucked in next to me, for a moment I thought the whole thing had been some mad dream. Then I looked up and saw the cave roof and heard Mother Rowan poking the fire. Not a dream. It's our lives, Lukas. This is where we are right now.' She paused, looking down at her hands. 'Where we go next is another question.'

'You know I'll go back home. These folk have said they'll take me there when it's safe. Though how long that'll be I have no idea.'

'Lukas.'

Something was coming; something he didn't want to hear. He stayed quiet. Waited.

'She – Mother Rowan – she said I could stay here if I wanted to. She said she'd teach me to use my gift wisely. I think she meant I would live here and work with her for a long while, and maybe take over her work when she's too old to manage it. They call her the Forest Guardian. She watches over Heartwood and teaches folk to treat it with love and respect. She tells stories.'

Stasya was gazing at him, her eyes so bright it made him want to weep. Stupid fool of a man. Of course she loved that idea. Wasn't that exactly what she tried to do every single day of her life? It was only wretched Aleksis who had led her on this path of fear and blood. This was a good thing, a wonderful thing. Best for her. Of course. 'You would really do that? Say goodbye to the human world? To your own kind?'

Stasya smiled. 'Mother Rowan is my own kind. Born to a human family. But raised by the Forest Folk, and rich in wisdom. Not all of the folk who live here are of that other race. And not all of them stay within this realm all the time. There are some links with the outside world. Those are necessary. But this place is... protected.'

What to say? This was perfect for her. It was what she wanted. And she was his dearest friend, the companion of his childhood, the one who could tell a story just for him, turning his mood from dark to light with the magic of her words. She was... herself, whole and true. How could he suggest anything else? He thought of her little cottage on the edge of the forest, with its welcome hearth and its well-tended garden; he imagined it empty, desolate, the door half-off its hinges and banging loose in a chill wind. He thought maybe his heart was breaking. What else could cause such terrible pain?

'You'll wed a fine girl, Lukas.' Stasya spoke so softly he could hardly hear the words. 'There's someone waiting for you, I'm sure of it. You'll make a wonderful husband, a great father, a leader loved by your whole community. It's the truth.' She released his hand and rose to her feet. 'I'd better go. I'll see you later at the gathering. Surely they'll let you out for that.' And she was gone.

49

ALEKSIS

He rose early and went out walking, leaving the others either fast asleep or making a convincing pretence of it. Too early to look for Stasya. But he would not lie abed wakeful while his mind teemed with unanswerable questions. Were they doing the right thing by taking Markus back as soon as he felt ready to go? Should they leave him here, safe, until they'd done more preparation out in the community? Perhaps until they had garnered more support among the powerful? More pressing, even, than those weighty matters was the issue of Stasya. What right had he to disrupt her life still further by asking her to come with him, to continue risking life and limb and perhaps her sanity by walking his pathway and not her own? She'd almost been killed. More than once. That was his fault. Yes, he'd rescued her and Lukas from a terrible fate at Dragon's Keep. But they'd only been there because of his decision to load them on a cart and take them out of Heartwood.

A small, contrary part of his mind pointed out that both Lukas and Stasya had attracted Rihard's attention at the settlement, not in a good way, and that back then, removing them had been the only way to protect them. But, but... surely there had been some other alternative. What he'd done to Stasya had been wrong. He remembered her calming the frenzied horse; he thought of her curled up with the little dog sleeping beside her. He imagined her telling a story of courage and friendship and hope. As he walked under spreading beech trees, he pictured her by his side, perhaps finding treasures he would have missed: a stone with a hole in it, a feather of many colours, a tiny, perfect flower half-hidden in the undergrowth. That woman had no place in a game of strategy, with the leadership of the Northlands at stake and players who would stop at nothing to win.

He did not walk far. He'd seen for himself how distances seemed to change of themselves in this realm, and he had no wish to embarrass himself by getting lost on his first morning here. He'd go back, see if the others were awake yet, have a word with them. But he had to talk to Stasya. Soon, before this gathering at which Markus would speak to the Forest Folk about the situation. He wanted to talk to her. He could tell her about Karolis's idea and how there would be work for her if they went ahead with it. But what if she said no, as she quite reasonably might? What if she said yes and later came to grief as a result? One thing was certain. He did not want to say goodbye.

He lingered on the way back, watching a bird of some kind as it flew from branch to branch above him in what looked like a mysterious dance. Hunting insects? Seeking a more comfortable perch? Checking out the territory before announcing to its friends that all was safe, except for one wandering human who didn't seem to know where he was going? Stasya would know what that fluttering dance meant. A remarkable skill; one that sometimes made her life difficult, and sometimes helped her keep out of trouble. She'd been devastated by that wolf's death. He'd ached to put his arms around her in comfort. But that had been neither the time nor the place. *There is no time or place, you fool,* he told himself.

'Aleks?'

And there she was, coming down the path as if she'd been looking for him. The loose-fitting garments of the Forest Folk suited her; she looked like a part of the forest, leaf-green, earth-brown.

'Stasya. You're up and out early. I wanted to talk to you.'

'And I wanted to talk to you, before this gathering. Not back at the settlement; somewhere private.'

Some rocks nearby provided a comfortable enough seat. 'Did you sleep well?' he asked.

'Like a log. Perhaps because of a draught Mother Rowan gave me. Perhaps only because I know we're safe at last. How did you sleep, Aleks?'

He opened his mouth to say, *Fine*, but closed it with the word unspoken. *Time to tell the truth, Aleks. About everything.* 'Not well, despite the comfortable bed and the kind hospitality. My mind is too full. There's too much ahead. It's another mountain to climb. Not a physical journey, but… an equally taxing one. And despite Markus being willing to accept the challenge, despite all the planning, I don't feel ready for it.'

'You'll be ready,' Stasya said, her tone quietly confident. 'You have good friends, good allies. You know how to lead. How to plan. If it weren't for that, we wouldn't be here. You found Markus. A real achievement. There's been sorrow. There have been losses. You must have known there would be. This was never going to be easy. But you've done it so far, and you can do what lies ahead too. Why doubt yourself now?'

'May I ask you something?'

Her smile was a little crooked; she looked amused. 'Go ahead. I may not answer, of course.'

'You know Lukas can't go back to the settlement until it's safe; until the Ruler's men are withdrawn from there. That might take a long while. It may have to wait until we establish Markus as Ruler. I'm assuming you'll want to go back with your friend.'

Stasya was looking out into the forest; for a few moments he wondered if she had not heard him. Then she said, 'I've just seen Lukas. I told him I'm not going back to Heartwood. There's nothing for me there. I was never really part of that community, and if I went back now it would be even worse. Accusations of witchcraft, because of what's happened. People have always thought me odd. I never had plans to become a village wife. I'm not right for that life. Lukas will be happy in time. He'll be a husband and father and a leader in the settlement. I told him that.'

Delight filled Aleksis's heart; he struggled to conceal it, knowing how easily Stasya could read his moods. 'Are you sure?' he made himself ask.

'Mother Rowan and I looked in the water together; we performed a ritual. I saw it. Lukas in the settlement, busy and content. And not with me. He is a dear friend; we've been close since we were children. But we wouldn't be happy as husband and wife. I've known that for a long time, and I thought Lukas knew it too. But it seems not. I upset him.'

Aleksis told himself to move slowly. Not to leap in with suggestions about what else she might do with her life. At least, not all at once. But he did need to say it.

'There's more,' Stasya said before he could speak. 'What I saw in the water... there were different possibilities. Though those visions don't actually show the future, only what might happen. I saw myself and Mother Rowan, both much older, working together. She told me afterwards that I can stay here if I want. Stay and learn; in time become a wise woman like her. And eventually I might take over her work of guiding both uncanny folk and human folk in understanding the ways of the forest, what we can learn from it, how we can best care for the land and the trees and the creatures. Aleks, if Markus becomes Ruler, he will surely forbid the thoughtless felling of trees, the search for amber as if it were just another thing to be ripped out and sold for profit. Since he was brought up here among the Forest Folk, he must understand that.'

'He does,' Aleks said. His heart had turned to lead; he felt sick. For a few moments there, he had been full of hope. And now... 'Living at the Hermit. Becoming a wise woman. That seems... entirely right for you. You must be happy. As if the journey, with all its ills, was... worthwhile.'

Stasya took her time to reply. 'In the vision, in the... possibilities, this was the only one where I saw myself. My future self, complete with grey hair.'

Aleks thought she was going to say more, but she fell silent. Into the quiet came the songs of birds, and in the distance, faint sounds of folk starting to go about their daily business. His companions would be stirring; he should go back. What he wanted to say, he could not say. This was good for Stasya; it was surely the sort of life she had longed for. And at least he would know she was safe. Right now, that was little comfort. 'I should go.' His voice sounded strange, almost choked, and Stasya turned a searching gaze on him. He was on his feet and walking away when something stopped him and he said without turning, 'Talk to Karolis before the gathering, if you can. Ask him about his plan for spreading the word out in the community.'

If she answered, he did not hear. Perhaps she only whispered a reply. Perhaps the voices of the birds swallowed her words. He could only hope.

50

STASYA

THEY WERE IN an open, grassy space shaped like a shallow bowl. It seemed the entire community of Forest Folk had gathered to meet the travellers, to greet them with some formality, and to share a meal afterwards. A crowd. She'd never been comfortable in crowds, though this, at least, was a quiet, orderly one, and those who were setting out food and drink, or greeting friends, or helping others find a spot to sit, were doing so without any fuss. Flip had taken bird form and was up in the trees somewhere. Right now, Stasya would have liked the little dog by her side to remind her that she could be strong even with so many folk around. Failing that, she would use her breathing and the reassuring presence of Mother Rowan to keep her calm. That awkward conversation with Aleks had hardly helped. Just as well she'd spoken to Matiss and Karolis afterwards, while Aleks conferred with Markus in private. That had helped her make sense of things. *I, too, will hold the light,* she told herself. *I, too, will be strong.* Nobody was leaving right now, or even soon. There was time for thinking, for planning. There was time for all of them to make up their minds. Or to change their minds.

She was seated beside Mother Rowan. That placed her more prominently than she really liked, since the wise woman's age meant she was provided with a low bench and she'd invited Stasya to share it. Everyone else sat on the grass or perched on the mossy stones that dotted the clearing. Lukas was there with Shadow by his side. He looked as if he was trying to be invisible, not easy for a man of his height, especially one with such a head of curls. Dear Lukas. She'd hurt him badly. But once he'd really thought about it, surely he'd realise she couldn't go back. The settlement had been home for a long while, but it would never be again.

A few latecomers settled into the crowd, and suddenly the place was full of anticipation. Not a hush, exactly, for it was always quiet here. Kadri stepped forward, a fresh circlet of flowers on her head, and addressed the assembled folk.

'Greetings, all, and welcome,' Kadri said. 'In particular, we welcome our visitors from the world beyond our border and congratulate them on a gruelling quest bravely achieved. We greet them with both joy and sorrow, since their coming means we will be bidding farewell to a beloved member of our own community.' She inclined her head, smiling, toward Markus. 'Our son. Our boy, now become a man, and with a destiny before him. Markus, will you speak to our people?'

He rose to his feet and moved forward. A fine-looking man, a strong man, a man whom others would follow. In an old tale he would be the handsome prince, the leader of men, the hero who saved the day. But he had his own story, and that was of a lost boy found, and found again.

'My people,' Markus said. 'My family. I owe you my life, my sanity, my health. You will always be dear to my heart. I could go on all day, but I'll spare you that, friends.' He gave a rueful smile; a soft ripple of laughter passed through his audience. 'In time I will be leaving you; I need not explain why, for by now everyone must know. Whatever comes of my journey back to the place of my birth, I make you a solemn promise. Whether or not I am elevated to leadership of the Northlands, I swear to live by the values you taught me as I grew up, as well as those I learned early from my father. I will do everything in my power to protect this realm as well as the human lands I may be entrusted to rule. I will honour the forest and all it holds; I will never allow it to be exploited for gain.' Murmurs of approval from the crowd. The whisper of the trees, the songs of the birds, the movements of creatures large and small came to Stasya as an echo of that feeling. All were content; this was a true son of both realms, a treasure indeed. 'Although I will be leaving you for now, I will not leave you forever. I pledge that as Ruler of the Northlands, once a year I will come back to visit you. You know well the ways that can be done without attracting undue attention. And Master Aleksis and his comrades are expert at handling such matters in their own world.' His gaze moved to the three men sitting at the front of the crowd. He glanced across at Stasya, giving a little nod. 'They faced challenges on their way here; they endured loss, sorrow, hurt. It is never easy for outsiders to make their way to the Hermit. Some obstacles, I know, exist for precisely that purpose: to keep human folk out. Some owe their presence to darker elements of this realm. Some, this time, came from those who followed Master Aleksis's team with ill intent.' Markus looked direct at Mother Rowan. 'And some were designed as tests, to determine the courage, the fortitude, the worthiness of the man who never gave up his dream of finding me. Tests, also, to prove the qualities of his chosen companions. It was known they were coming; it was known what they sought. I am sorry for the ill you suffered on this journey, my friends.' His voice was suddenly uneven, as if tears were close. 'A brave leader; a stalwart team. Our deep thanks to you.' He cleared his throat. 'And now, I think, it is time for a story. After that, we will eat and drink. We will sing and dance. We will celebrate what has been achieved and what is to come. Mother Rowan, will you tell a tale?'

The wise woman did not get up, though her smile as she looked at Markus was that of a proud parent who sees in her child all that she has hoped he might one day be. 'Stasya, perhaps you should tell a story,' she said, putting a gentle hand on Stasya's shoulder. 'Will you do that for us?'

For just a moment, the old fears came back. Who did she think she was, standing up to speak in front of such a crowd? Had she forgotten how much she hated to have everyone's eyes on her, expectant? But she had to do it. What Karolis and Matiss had told her had changed everything.

She rose to her feet. Lukas was watching her from a distance; he gave her a smile that said, *You can do it*. Aleks was watching her. He acknowledged her with a grave nod. Time to step forward. *I can be brave. I am the Storyteller.* This was a kind of test. Whatever she decided to do in the future, she would keep on telling tales. That was part of her very existence.

She stood before her audience, taking time to breathe. Flip flew down, alighting on her shoulder to appreciative murmuring from the crowd. A dove, messenger of peace.

The words came. 'On the way here, around one campfire or another, we told a lot of stories. Old ones, new ones, funny ones, sad ones. Now and then I told the tale of our own journey in one form or another. Perhaps, now, my companions of that journey might help me with the telling.'

She told the beginning, but gave the odd group of travellers new names: the Leader, the Protector, the Acrobat and, for poor Pavel, the Quiet One. She was the Storyteller, Lukas the Farmer. Flip, she called the Small Companion. The Leader was seeking a lost friend; the others were his comrades. The story flowed well, and there was no need to ask for help until the characters had reached their destination after a gruelling journey during which they lost the Quiet One, whom they would always remember, and came close to losing more. She told how his steadiness and care for others made the Protector beloved of all; she told how the Acrobat was strong in both body and spirit, generous with his knowledge and as apt with healing as he was with wielding a weapon. The Quiet One's story was sad; in time, his friends would make sure his family learned how he had stood up for the good cause in the end. He would never be forgotten. The Farmer was a brave man who'd been drawn into the adventure despite himself; along the way, all had come to admire his strength and courage.

'At last, they had reached their destination, and there was the lost boy, now a fine man well equipped to take his true place as Ruler of the realm. With only a few words, the Heir made it plain he would rule with justice and forbearance. He would guard the forest and its creatures as carefully as he would the human folk of his territory. He knew and understood the uncanny folk whose secret realm bordered his own, for it was they who had raised him in tolerance and understanding of all things. He would be a Ruler for the powerful and the wealthy, for there was no escaping that, but he would also be a Ruler for the folk who farmed the land and the folk who baked the bread.' An image of Irina flashed through her mind, bringing sudden tears to her eyes. She blinked them back. 'But how could the Leader and his companions get the Heir safely to the court? How could they ensure he was treated with justice and fairness when he declared himself? Some would resent this claim and try to prove it wrong. They might seek to do the Heir or his followers harm. The Leader pondered this; it kept him awake at night. His mind was burdened with dark possibilities, despite the careful work his team had done in advance to smooth the way. He wondered how they could get the word out to the people without putting the Heir at risk.' She glanced over at Karolis with a smile.

'The Acrobat came up with a daring plan,' Karolis said, rising to his feet. His stance suggested he was preparing to fight, or perhaps to dance: perfectly poised, with the light touching his auburn hair to flame. 'He and the Storyteller would join up with a team of travelling entertainers – musicians, dancers, folk of many talents – as they moved around the Northlands from settlement to settlement. They would not tell the Heir's story openly; that was far too risky. But they would tell tales of a peaceful realm where all folk were treated justly, and the natural world was honoured, and disputes were settled not by blood and violence, but by discussion, negotiation, regular meetings from the smallest village to the largest township. A place where leaders were not distant, but present to hear the voices of their people with respect and to take action when it was needed. Those tales would not be dreary pronouncements of how things should be. They would be full of delight and fun!' A gasp from the crowd as Karolis performed a backflip, landing on his feet with a grin on his face. 'Fortunately, there were two among the Leader's small group of comrades who were perfect for this job.' Karolis nodded to Matiss, and the two changed places. Aleks was speaking to someone sitting behind him; she wished she could see his expression. He knew about this general idea. Karolis had put it to him some while back, but likely not in such terms.

'Now you might think,' Matiss said, his voice deep and soft, 'that with so few in the Leader's team, this might be a risky choice. The Farmer would be going home; this was not his quest, and he had pressing matters to attend to. That left the Leader with three companions. If two joined the travelling players, he would be left with only one. Just as well that one was the Protector.' He looked at Stasya, smiling. 'I like that name well,' he said. 'But, of course, those who came on the journey were not the Leader's only supporters. They were scattered across the Northlands, from within the Ruler's court itself to the far borders, from isolated farms to fishing villages to every corner of the land. Men and women who, as well as their ordinary lives, handled the secret business of preparation for the Heir's arrival. Yes, even though the Leader and his companions had journeyed without knowing if the man they sought was alive or dead, the support for their cause was gradually growing. Through the travelling players, more folk would be awakened to the possibility of change. They would learn that the realm could be a better place.' Matiss paused, taking time to look around his audience. His expression, now, was utterly serious. 'It was fortunate indeed, then, that within his team the Leader happened to have, not only an Acrobat who could sing, dance and play tricks, but also a skilled Storyteller.'

Time for Stasya to speak again and bring this to a conclusion. 'While those two were out working their magic among the ordinary people, the Heir would live in a safe place, well guarded, and study those things he would need to know to take up his new role. The Leader and his Protector would move with subtlety and caution among the powerful, the wealthy, the folk with influence. The folk who might be valuable allies or dangerous enemies. They would journey beyond the borders of the Northlands and talk to people in the neighbouring lands. Only when all was prepared would the team gather once more and bring the Heir home.' She looked out at the assembled Forest Folk, all of whom were silent, their full attention on her. Mother Rowan's expression spoke for her. *Well done, my dear.* 'The Heir would always have two homes: the one where he was born and lived as a child and where his destiny lay, and this one among the Forest Folk, the home where he was raised to be a fine man, fit to lead with justice and compassion.' Stasya looked directly at Markus. 'I know he will honour both in his future life.' Gods, she was actually finished. She'd got through it. 'And that's all from me,' she said, as Flip arose from her shoulder and flew in a circle over the crowd as if in recognition of a deed well done.

Folk rose then and moved about, while some began to set out food and drink. There was a low buzz of conversation. For a little, Stasya lost sight of the others. Suddenly she did not want to be here, with so many people milling about. She made her way through the crowd until she found a spot under a tree whose name she did not know, something small and compact with a friendly look to it. She sat down with her arms around her knees and bowed her head. For a moment, just a moment, she longed for her little house on the edge of the forest, and the old days with Flip and Lukas. Things had been so much simpler then. But… she'd never have met Aleks or Matiss or Karolis. She'd never have come to the Hermit and met the Forest Folk. She'd never have encountered Mother Rowan, who had opened a magical door on the future. How could she even think of wishing that away? It was her life now, and although it was often confusing and sometimes terrifying, she wanted it with her whole heart.

'Stasya?'

There he was, looking down at her. His sharp features were softened by a smile such as she had never seen on his face before.

'Thank you,' he said.

Stasya patted the ground beside her in invitation, and Aleks lowered himself to sit.

'You really want to come with us,' he said. 'After being offered an opportunity to stay here.'

'When our work is done, when Markus is established as Ruler, I'll come back here. The Forest Folk will make sure I reach the Hermit safely.'

'You set that up, the three of you. When?'

'Not long ago, while you were talking to Markus. The others had a few honest words with me. They may have explained a little about why you seemed so reluctant for me to stay with you.'

'I was wrong, and I'm sorry.' He took her hand in his. 'It troubles me to see you hurt. I will worry about you every moment you're gone with these travelling players, even though you'll be with Karolis, and if anyone can protect you, he can.

You are one of us, Stasya, an essential member of the team. I insulted you by treating you as anything less.'

Finding the right words was easy now. 'And I'm sorry. For using your story that way when it's so personal. But it was the only way to make you understand.'

'A striking demonstration of your storytelling skills.' His smile was crooked now. He lifted her hand to his lips, just for an instant, and Stasya felt the touch right through her body. Then he released his hold with a sigh. 'A long road ahead,' he said. 'With its own kind of trouble. Sometimes I think it's better for folk who take on such tasks to be quite alone. Sufficient unto themselves. I've always wondered how Matiss and his wife do it, both of them working for our cause, hardly ever seeing each other.'

'There's a bond, I suppose. Strong enough to survive even a long parting. And perhaps the end of this trouble is in sight. You found the lost boy. You rekindled hope, Aleks.'

In the silence that followed, what lay unspoken between them seemed vast and terrifying and wonderful all at the same time. *One day,* Stasya thought. *One day maybe I'll tell him what I feel. Maybe one day I'll understand it. Maybe I'll tell him straight out, not in a story. If I'm brave enough.* 'We should go back,' she said, looking over to the clearing where folk were eating and drinking, and there was music: a harp, a whistle, a little drum. Was that Karolis dancing with a woman of the Forest Folk?

'I suppose we should.' Aleks got to his feet, reached out a hand to help her up. Quickly, before she could change her mind, Stasya touched her lips to his cheek and made him smile again. *One day*, she thought, *we too will dance.*

THE END

ACKNOWLEDGEMENTS

I'M IMMENSELY GRATEFUL to my publisher, Dylan Ingram, for believing in my project of the heart, and for supporting the venture all the way from the spark of an idea to publication. It's been great to work with the New Dawn team. Thanks to my editor, Eleanor Narey, for a thorough and expert job and for her tactful feedback. Copyeditor Chelsea Wilcox was understanding about my rather entrenched position on punctuation – those inverted commas are a story in themselves.

The gorgeous cover for The Amber Owl was created by the very talented Micaela Alcaino. A huge thank you to Micaela – this cover truly captures the spirit of the story. Deep thanks also to Virginia Allyn, whose delicate map of the Northlands is a wonderful addition to the novel.

Fiona Leonard, writer and one-time critique partner, provided challenging but immensely useful editorial advice along the way. Thoraiya Dyer, writer and veterinarian, gave me expert guidance on stressed-out horses.

Last but not least, I send love and thanks to the Rainbow Bridge, where a little dog called Pip is waiting (probably not very patiently) for me. She does have plenty of company up there. Pip was a big personality in the tiny body of a miniature pinscher. She was the inspiration for a certain character in this story.

AUTHOR'S NOTE

THE SETTING OF *The Amber Owl* is imaginary. However, the world of the books is very loosely based on the Baltic region, where amber can be found. The character names are from that region, with some flexibility applied since this is a work of fiction. I am grateful for the inspiration sparked by a visit to the Baltic states a few years ago, where the joyful singing and dancing, along with the lovely landscape, made an indelible impression on me. The events of this story have nothing to do with real history. Except, possibly, the activities of the warrior monks.

ABOUT THE AUTHOR

JULIET MARILLIER WAS born and raised in Aotearoa New Zealand. She is a graduate of the University of Otago and has had a varied career that included music teaching and performing. She now lives in a historic cottage in Western Australia.

Juliet's historical fantasy novels and short stories are published internationally and have won numerous awards, including five Aurealis Awards, four Sir Julius Vogel Awards, the American Library Association's Alex Award, and the Sara Douglass Book Series Award. She is the author of twenty-four novels, including the *Blackthorn & Grim* series, the *Sevenwaters* series, and most recently the *Warrior Bards* series, well as two collections of short fiction. Juliet loves mythology, folklore and strong, complex characters.

Juliet is a member of the druid order OBOD (the Order of Bards, Ovates and Druids.) When not writing, she is kept busy by a small crew of rescue dogs.

FIND US ONLINE!

www.rebellionpublishing.com

/solarisbooks

/solarisbks

/solarisbooks

SIGN UP TO OUR NEWSLETTER!

rebellionpublishing.com/newsletter

YOUR REVIEWS MATTER!

Enjoy this book? Got something to say?

Leave a review on Amazon, GoodReads or with your favourite bookseller and let the world know!